"Christina Lauren's done it again! *Sweet Filthy Boy* has the perfect dose of romance that sexy comedy fans of the *Beautiful Bastard* series have come to expect and adore. But with leading lovebirds Mia and Ansel's sexy story unfolding from Sin City to the City of Light, this twisting, turning tale of gambling with your heart has both pure *joie de vivre* and *très* dirty fun galore."

—*The Stir*

"*Sweet Filthy Boy* had my heart pounding from cover to cover and reminded me of first loves and being young. A must-read!"

—*Fangirlish*

"I didn't know if anything could be as deliciously filthy as *Beautiful Bastard*, but Christina Lauren has done it again! *Sweet Filthy Boy* is a deliciously filthy romp that you're going to love!"

—*Martini Times Romance*

"The writing team of Christina Lauren is at the top of my auto buy list. These ladies write the best stories, full of heart, sass, and heat. They have the unique ability to capture the way real women talk to each other. And seriously, they own the angry sex market. *Sweet Filthy Boy* is a story about facing your fears, moving away from your past, embracing your future, and being true to yourself."

—*Scandalicious Book Reviews*

"Christina Lauren have taken me back to being young, in lust, and brave enough for a new adventure. I challenge you not to fall in love with Ansel's charm, looks, and that breathtaking accent."

—*HenryCavill.org*

"*Sweet Filthy Boy* lives up to every yummy bit of its title. Each word, each thought, each touch from Ansel is pure, unadulterated SEX. Christina Lauren's assured writing and their ability to create a scorching and witty love story makes them an *automatic* 1-Click for us."

—*The Rock Stars of Romance*

"Christina Lauren fans rejoice and prepare to get hooked. If you're looking for a smokin'-hot read, look no further than *Sweet Filthy Boy*."

—*Harlequin Junkie*

"No one is doing hot contemporary romance like Christina Lauren. *Sweet Filthy Boy* is beyond swoon worthy. Just give me Book Two right now."

—*Bookalicious*

"It's official: I'd read Christina Lauren's grocery list if they'd let me. The girls wrote the French-boy fantasy I didn't know I had. Just when I thought I didn't have time for yet another book boyfriend, I made time for Ansel. . . ."

—*That's Normal*

"A whirlwind of hot lust and wild nights in seductive cities— but with the inescapable desire to love and be loved—bursts through the *Sweet Filthy Boy*."

—*Robsessed*

"*Sweet Filthy Boy* is a sexy love story that reminds us that the path we sometimes build for ourselves isn't always the one that makes us truly happy. Five sexy, sizzling stars."

—*The Subclub Books*

"The prefect combination of a flirty and dirty love story! Entertaining, romantic, and full of sexy hotness. Christina Lauren are my go-to gals for when I'm in the mood for a laugh-out-loud, sizzling sexy romance."

—*Flirty and Dirty Book Blog*

"Thank you, Christina Lauren, for bringing back to books the guy who motivates and nurtures who he loves without taking away from her independence while still bringing sexy and molten-lava HOT to the pages!"

—*Once Upon a Twilight*

"Ansel is damn near perfection. He is what those swoony YA boys grow up to be. And he speaks French. . . . Do you even need more? And I don't know if the sweet or the filthy killed me more, but damn, what a way to go."

—*Too Fond of Books*

"A refreshing and brilliant modern new twist on a fairy-tale love story. The story was fun, exciting, steamy with great sex and the right amount of heart to have the reader cheering on these great characters, Mia and Ansel, right to the end."

—*Love, Words and Books*

"Fun. Sexy. Captivating. *Sweet Filthy Boy* was everything I've come to expect from this dynamic duo!"

—*The Autumn Review*

Books by CHRISTINA LAUREN

Beautiful Bastard

Beautiful Stranger

Beautiful Bitch

Beautiful Bombshell

Beautiful Player

Beautiful Beginning

Sweet FILTHY BOY

BOOK ONE OF WILD SEASONS

CHRISTINA LAUREN

G
GALLERY BOOKS
NEW YORK   LONDON   TORONTO   SYDNEY   NEW DELHI

G

Gallery Books
A Division of Simon & Schuster, Inc.
1230 Avenue of the Americas
New York, NY 10020

First Gallery Books trade paperback edition May 2014

GALLERY BOOKS and colophon are registered trademarks
of Simon & Schuster, Inc.

For information about special discounts for bulk purchases,
please contact Simon & Schuster Special Sales at 1-866-506-1949
or business@simonandschuster.com.

The Simon & Schuster Speakers Bureau can bring authors to your live
event. For more information or to book an event, contact the Simon
& Schuster Speakers Bureau at 1-866-248-3049 or visit our website at
www.simonspeakers.com.

Interior design by Davina Mock-Maniscalco

Manufactured in the United States of America

10   9   8   7   6   5   4   3   2   1

Library of Congress Cataloging-in-Publication Data

Lauren, Christina.
  Sweet filthy boy / Christina Lauren.—First Gallery Books trade
paperback edition.
      pages cm—(Wild seasons; Book 1)
  1. Women college graduates—Fiction. 2. Americans—France—Fiction.
I. Title.
  PS3612.A9442273S94 2014
  813'.6—dc23

                                                        2014010800

ISBN 978-1-4767-5180-1
ISBN 978-1-4767-5181-8 (ebook)

To K and R,
for coming with us to Paris and letting us bring it home

Sweet
FILTHY
BOY

Chapter ONE

Mia

THE DAY WE officially graduate from college is nothing like how it's depicted in movies. I throw my cap in the air and it comes down and cracks someone in the forehead. The keynote speaker loses his notes in a gust of wind and decides to wing it, delivering a thoroughly uninspired commencement address on turning mistakes into the building blocks for a brighter tomorrow, complete with awkward stories about his recent divorce. No one on film ever looks like they're going to die of heatstroke in their polyester gown . . . I'd pay someone a lot of money to burn all the pictures that were taken of me today.

But it still manages to be perfect.

Because holy shit, we're *done*.

Outside the restaurant after lunch, Lorelei—or Lola for the rare few who make it to her inner circle—pulls her keys from her purse and shakes them at me with a celebratory shimmy. Her dad kisses her forehead and tries to pretend he's not a little misty-eyed. Harlow's entire family forms a circle around her, hugging and talking over each other, reliving the Top Ten Moments of When Harlow Walked Across the Stage and Graduated from College before pulling me close and doing the same rehash of my own fifteen seconds of fame. When they release me, I smile, watching them finish their sweet, familiar rituals.

Call me as soon as you get there safely.

Use the credit card, Harlow. No, the American Express. It's fine, honey, this is your graduation present.

I love you, Lola. Drive safe.

We shed our sweltering gowns, tumble into Lola's old beater Chevy, and escape San Diego in a plume of exhaust and giddy catcalls for the music and booze and madness that await us this weekend. Harlow pulls up the playlist she made for the trip—Britney Spears from our first concert when we were eight. The completely inappropriate 50 Cent song our class somehow negotiated to be the theme for our junior homecoming. The bass-heavy hair metal anthem Lola swears is the best sex song ever, and about fifty others that somehow build our collective story. Harlow cranks the stereo loud enough for us all to scream-sing above the hot, dusty air blasting in through all four windows.

Lola pulls her long dark hair off her neck and hands me a rubber band, begging me to tie it back for her.

"God, why is it so damn hot?" she yells from the driver's seat.

"Because we're hurtling through the desert at sixty-five miles an hour in a late-eighties Chevy with no air-conditioning," Harlow answers, fanning herself with a program from the ceremony. "Remind me why we didn't take my car again?"

"Because it smells like Coppertone and dubious

choices?" I reply and shriek when she lunges for me from the front seat.

"We're taking my car," Lola reminds her as she turns down the volume on Eminem, "because you nearly wrapped yours around a telephone pole trying to get away from a bug on your seat. I don't trust your judgment behind the wheel."

"It was a spider," Harlow argues. "And huge. With pincers."

"A spider with pincers?"

"I could have died, Lola."

"Yes, you could have. In a fiery car wreck."

Once I've finished with Lola's hair, I sit back again and feel like I'm able to exhale for the first time in weeks, laughing with my two favorite people in the world. The heat has sapped every bit of energy from my body, but it feels good to just let go, close my eyes, and melt into the seat as the wind whips through my hair, too loud for me to even think. Three blissful weeks of summer lie ahead before I move across the country, and for the first time in forever, I have absolutely *nothing* I need to do.

"Nice of your family to stay for lunch," Lola says in her steady, cautious tone, meeting my eyes in the rearview mirror.

"Eh." I shrug, bending to dig in my purse for a piece of gum or candy, or whatever will keep me busy long enough not to have to try and justify my parents' early exit today.

Harlow turns her head to look at me. "I thought they were going to lunch with everyone?"

"I guess not," I say simply.

She swivels fully in her seat, facing me as much as she can without taking off her seat belt. "Well, what did *David* say before they left?"

I blink away, looking out at the passing, flat scenery. Harlow would never dream of calling her father—or even Lola's—by his first name. But ever since I can remember, to her my father is simply David—said with as much disdain as she can muster. "He said he was proud of me and he loves me. That he was sorry he didn't say it enough."

I can feel her surprise in the answering silence. Harlow is only ever quiet when she's surprised or pissed.

"And," I add, though I know this is the point where I should shut up, "now I can pursue a real career and contribute meaningfully to society."

Don't poke the bear, Mia, I think.

"Jesus," she says. "It's like he loves to hit you right where it hurts. That man lettered in being an asshole."

This makes us all laugh, and we seem to agree to move on because, really, what else can we say? My dad *is* kind of an ass, and even getting his way when it comes to my life decisions doesn't seem to change that.

The traffic is light and the city rises up out of the flat earth, a tangled cluster of lights glaringly bright in the fading sunset. With each mile the air grows cooler, and I sense a rebound of energy in the car when Harlow sits up straighter and puts on a new playlist for our final stretch. In the backseat, I wiggle, dancing, singing along to the catchy, bass-heavy pop song.

"Are my girls ready to get a little wild?" she asks, pulling the passenger sun visor down to apply lip gloss in the tiny, cracked mirror.

"Nope." Lola merges onto East Flamingo Road. Just beyond, the Strip spreads brightly, a carpet of lights and blasting horns rolling out before us. "But for you? I'll do gross shots and dance with questionably sober men."

I nod, wrapping my arms around Harlow from behind and squeezing. She pretends to choke, but puts her hand over mine so I can't get away. No one rejects cuddles less convincingly than Harlow.

"I love you psychos," I say, and even though with anyone else, the words would get lost in the wind and street dust blowing into the car, Harlow bends to kiss my hand and Lola glances over to smile at me. It's like they're programmed to ignore my long pauses and pluck my voice out of chaos.

"You have to make me a promise, Mia," Lola says. "Are you listening?"

"This doesn't involve me running off and becoming a showgirl, does it?"

"Sadly no."

We've been planning this trip for months—one last rush before grown-up life and responsibility catch up with us. I'm ready for whatever she's got for me. I stretch my neck, take a deep breath, pretend to crack my knuckles. "Too bad. I could work a pole like you don't even know. But okay, hit me."

"Leave everything else back in San Diego tonight," she

says. "Don't worry about your dad or which fangirl Luke is banging this weekend."

My stomach tilts slightly at this mention of my ex, even though we parted on good terms nearly two years ago. It's just that Luke was my first, I was his, and we learned everything together. I feel like I should be earning royalties on his current parade of conquests.

Lola continues. "Don't think about packing for Boston. Don't think about anything but the fact that we're done with college—*college*, Mia! We did it. Just put the rest of it in a proverbial box and shove it under the proverbial bed."

"I like this talk of shoving and beds," Harlow says.

Under any other circumstance, this would have made me laugh. But as unintentional as it may have been, Lola's mention of Boston has just obliterated the tiny window of anxiety-free space I'd somehow managed to find. It immediately dwarfs any discomfort I felt over the subject of my dad's early departure from the biggest ceremony of my life or Luke and his newfound slutty side. I have a rising tide of panic about the future, and now that we've graduated, it's impossible to ignore it anymore. Every time I think about what comes next, my stomach turns inside out, ignites, chars. The feeling happens so much these days I feel like I should give it a name.

In three weeks I'm leaving for Boston, to business school of all places, and about as far from my childhood dreams as I could have imagined. I'll have plenty of time to find an apartment and a job that will pay my bills and accommodate a full schedule of classes in the fall when I finally do what my father has always wanted and join the river of business-types doing business things. He's even paying for my apartment, happily. "Two bedrooms," he'd insisted, magnanimously, "so your mother and I and the boys can visit."

"Mia?" Lola prompts.

"Okay," I say and nod, wondering when, out of the three of us, I became the person with so much baggage. Lola's dad is a war veteran. Harlow's parents are Hollywood. I'm just the girl from La Jolla who used to dance. "I'm shoving it under the proverbial bed." Saying the words out loud seems to put more weight behind them. "I'll put it into the box with Harlow's scary sex toys."

Harlow throws me a sassy kiss and Lola nods, resolute. Lola knows better than any of us about stress and responsibility, but if she can put it away for the weekend, I can, too.

———

WE PULL UP to the hotel and Lola and I tumble from the car, holding our simple duffel bags and looking like we just emerged from a dust storm. I feel gross and filthy. Only Harlow looks like she belongs here, climbing from the old Chevy as if she's exiting a shiny black town car, somehow still presentable and wheeling a glossy suitcase behind her.

Once we get upstairs, we're all speechless, even Harlow—clearly this is the *surprised* form of her silence. There are only a couple of other rooms on the floor and our Sky Suite is enormous.

Harlow's father, a big-shot cinematographer, booked it for us as a graduation present. We thought we were getting a standard Vegas hotel room, some complimentary shampoo, maybe we'd even go crazy and raid the minibar, charging it to his card. Snickers and tiny vodkas for everyone!

We were not expecting this. In the entryway (there's an *entryway*), and tucked next to a decadent fruit basket and a complimentary bottle of champagne, there's a note. It says we have a butler on speed dial, a masseuse to come to the room when we need it, and Harlow's dad is more than happy to provide unlimited room service. If Alexander Vega wasn't the father of my best friend and happily married, I might offer sex acts to thank him.

Remind me not to tell Harlow that.

———————

I GREW UP wearing barely anything onstage in front of hundreds of people where I could pretend to be someone else. So even with a long, jagged scar on my leg, I'm decidedly more comfortable in one of the dresses Harlow chose for us than Lola is. She won't even put hers on.

"It's your graduation present," Harlow says. "How would you have felt if I turned down the journal you got me?"

Lola laughs, throwing a pillow at her from across the room. "If I'd asked you to tear out the pages and make them into a dress that barely covers your ass, yes, you would have been free to turn down the gift."

I tug at the hem of my dress, silently siding with Lola and

wishing it was just a touch longer. I rarely show so much thigh anymore.

"Mia's wearing hers," Harlow points out and I groan.

"Mia grew up in *leotards*; she's pocket-sized and built like a gazelle," Lola reasons. "Also? I'm sure if I looked hard enough, I could see her vagina. If I'm five inches taller than she is, you'll practically be able to see my birth canal in this dress."

"You're so stubborn."

"You're so slutty."

I listen to them argue from where I stand near the window, content, watching pedestrians walk along the Strip, and forming what looks like a trail of colorful round dots from our view on the forty-fifth floor. I'm not sure why Lola continues to fight this. We all know it's just a matter of time before she gives in, because Harlow is a giant pain in the ass and she always gets her way. It sounds strange to say I've always loved this about her, but she knows what she wants and goes after it. Lola is the same in many ways, but a bit subtler than Harlow's in-your-face technique.

Lola groans, but as expected, eventually admits defeat. She's smart enough to know she's fighting a losing battle, and it takes only a few minutes for her to slip into her dress and shoes before we head downstairs.

———

IT'S BEEN A long day. We're finished with college, have washed the dust and real life worries from our bodies, and Harlow loves ordering shots. More than that? She loves watching everyone else drink the shots she's ordered. By the time nine thirty rolls around, I decide our level of drunk is sufficient: we're slurring some words, but at least we can walk. I can't remember the last time I saw Lola and Harlow laugh like this. Lola's cheek is resting on her crossed arms and her shoulders shake with laughter. Harlow's head is thrown back and the sound of her giggles rises above the thumping music and clear across the bar.

And it's when her head is back like this that I meet the eyes of a man across the crowded room. I can't make out every feature in the dark bar, but he's a few years older than we are and tall, with light brown hair and dark brows over bright, mischievous eyes. He's watching us and smiling as if he has no need to participate in our fun; he simply wants to appreciate it. Two other guys stand beside him, talking and pointing to something in the far corner, but he doesn't look away when our eyes meet. If anything, his smile gets bigger.

I can't look away, either, and the feeling is disorienting because normally when it comes to strangers I'm very good at looking away. My heart trips around inside my chest, reminding me I'm supposed to be more awkward than this, maybe suggesting I focus on my drink instead. I don't do eye contact well. I don't usually do conversation well, either. In fact, the only muscles I never seemed to really master were the ones required for easy speech.

But for some reason—let's blame the alcohol—and without looking away from the hot man across the bar, my lips readily form the word "Hi."

He says it back, before pulling the corner of his lip between his teeth, and *wow*, he should do that every day and to every person he meets for the rest of his life. He has a dimple and I reassure myself that it's just the lighting and shadows playing it up because there's no way in hell something so simple could possibly be this adorable.

I feel something strange happen to my insides and I wonder if this is what people mean when they say they melt, because I am most definitely feeling less than solid. There's a distinct flutter of interest from the vicinity below my waist, and *good God*, if his smile alone managed to do that, imagine what his—

Harlow grabs my arm before I can finish that thought, jerking me from my careful study of his face and into a crowd of bodies rocking and snaking to the rhythm of sex blasting from the speakers. A boy like that is way *way* out of my comfort zone, and so I shove the urge to go find him into the proverbial box, under the proverbial bed along with everything else.

WE MUST BE easing into Vegas, because after dancing and drinks, we're in our room by midnight, all three of us worn-out from the commencement ceremony in the sun, the hot drive, and the alcohol we rushed into our systems without enough food.

Even though our suite has more space than we need, and

even though there are two bedrooms, we're all piled into the one. Lola and Harlow are out within minutes, and the familiar string of Harlow's sleep-mumble starts. Lola is almost shockingly silent and still. She buries herself so completely in her bedding, I remember wondering when we were younger if she somehow disappeared into the mattress during sleepovers. There are times I actually consider checking for a pulse.

But across the hall, a party rages.

The heavy bass of music rattles the light fixture hanging above me. Male voices rumble across the empty space separating the rooms; they shout and laugh, have their own little cacophony of whoops and man-sounds going on. A ball hits a wall somewhere in the distance, and although I can only identify a few unique voices in the mix, they're making enough noise that I can't believe the entire suite isn't full of drunk boys tearing up a weekend in Vegas.

Two a.m. passes the same: I'm staring at the ceiling, growing somehow both more awake and more asleep. When three hits, I'm so irritated, I'm ready to be the Vegas buzzkill just so I can get a few hours of sleep before our early spa appointments.

I slip out of bed, being quiet so I don't wake my friends, before laughing at the absurdity of my caution. If they've slept through the ruckus across the hall, they'll sleep through me padding quietly across a carpeted floor, grabbing a room key, and slipping out of our suite.

I pound my fist on the door and wait, chest heaving with

irritation. The noise barely dips, and I'm not sure if I can pound hard enough for them to even hear me. Raising both fists, I try again. I don't want to be that person—in *Vegas* complaining about people being joyful—but my next stop is calling hotel security.

This time the music dies down and footsteps slap on the tile just in front of the door.

Maybe I expect some older, sun-bleached trust fund douche to answer, a bunch of middle-aged investment bankers visiting for a weekend of debauchery, or a roomful of fratty guys drinking shots out of a stripper's belly button. But I don't expect it to be *him,* the guy from across the bar.

I don't expect him to be shirtless, wearing black boxers that hang so low on his tanned stomach that I can see the soft trail of hair, lower.

I don't expect him to smile when he sees me. And I most definitely don't expect the accent when he says, "I know you."

"You don't," I say, completely steady, if a little on the breathless side. I never stutter in front of friends or family anymore and only rarely in front of strangers I'm comfortable with. But right now my face feels hot, my arms and legs prickling with goose bumps, so I have no idea what to make of my completely stutterless words.

If possible, his smile grows, blush deepening, dimple taking center stage, and he opens the door wider, stepping out toward me. He's even better looking than he seemed from across the room, and the reality of him immediately fills the doorway. His presence is so huge I step back as if I've been pushed. He's all easy posture, eye contact, and beaming smile as he leans close, and playfully studies me.

Being a performer, I've seen magic like his before. He may look like any other human, but he has that elusive quality that would force every pair of eyes to track him onstage, no matter how small his role. It's more than charisma—it's a magnetism that can't be taught or practiced. I'm only two feet away from him . . . I don't stand a chance.

"I *do* know you," he says with a little tilt of his head. "We met earlier. We just haven't exchanged names yet." My mind searches to place his accent before I trip into understanding: he's French. The asshole is French. It's diluted, though. His accent is soft, mild. Instead of curling all of the words together he spreads them out, carefully offering each one.

I narrow my eyes, forcing them up to his face. It's not easy. His chest is smooth and tan and he has the most perfect nipples I've ever seen, small and flat. He's ripped, and tall enough to ride like a horse. I can feel the warmth coming off his skin. On top of all of that, he's wearing nothing but his underwear and seems completely unfazed by it.

"You guys are being insanely loud," I say, remembering the hours of noise that brought me out here in the first place. "I think I liked you a lot better across a crowded room than across this hall."

"But face-to-face is the best, no?" His voice causes goose bumps to spread across my arms. When I don't answer, he turns and looks over his shoulder and then back to me. "I'm sorry we're so loud. I'm going to blame Finn. He's Canadian, so I'm sure you understand he's a savage. And Oliver is an Aussie. Also horribly uncivilized."

"A Canadian, an Australian, and a Frenchman throw a rager in a hotel room?" I ask, fighting a smile despite my better judgment. I'm trying to remember the rule about whether or not you're supposed to struggle when you fall into quicksand, because that's exactly what this feels like. Sinking, being swallowed up by something bigger than I am.

"Like the beginning of a joke," he agrees, nodding. His green eyes twinkle and he's right: face-to-face is endlessly better than through a wall, or even across a dark, crowded room. "Come join us."

Nothing has ever sounded so dangerous and so tempting all at once. His eyes drop to my mouth, where they linger before scanning my body. Despite what he's just offered, he steps fully out into the hallway and the door falls closed behind him. Now it's just me and him and his naked chest and . . . *wow*, strong legs and the potential for mind-blowing spontaneous hallway sex.

Wait. What?

And now I also remember I'm only in my tiny sleep shorts and matching tank top with little pigs all over them. I'm suddenly aware of the bright light in the hallway and feel my fingers move down, instinctively tugging the material lower to cover my scar. I'm normally fine with my body—I'm a woman so naturally there are always little things I'd change—but my scar is different. It's not entirely about how it looks—though let's be honest, Harlow still does the full-body sympathy shudder whenever she sees it—but what it represents: the loss of my scholarship to the Joffrey Ballet School, the death of my dream.

But the way he looks at me makes me feel naked—*good* naked—and beneath the cotton of my top, my nipples tighten.

He notices and takes another step closer, bringing with him warmth and the scent of soap, and I'm suddenly sure he's most definitely *not* looking at my leg. It doesn't even seem like he *sees* it, or if he does, he likes how I come together enough to ignore what this scar says. It says *trauma*, it says *pain*. But his eyes only say *yes,* and *please,* and *mischief.* And that he'd like to see more.

The shy girl inside me crosses her arms over her chest, tries to pull me back to the safety of my own room. But his eyes pin me in place.

"I wasn't sure I would see you again." His voice has gone gravelly, hinting of the filthy things I want to hear him growl into my neck. My pulse is a frantic, pounding drum. I wonder if he can see it. "I looked for you."

He looked for me.

I'm surprised my voice comes out so clear when I say, "We left pretty soon after I saw you."

His tongue slips out, and he watches my mouth. "Why don't you come . . . inside?" There are so many unspoken promises tucked in those five words. It feels like he's a stranger offering me the most delicious candy on the planet.

"I'm going to sleep," I manage finally, holding up my hand to keep him from moving any closer. "And you guys are going to be quieter or I'll send Harlow over. And if that fails, I'm waking up Lola and you'll find yourself thanking her for leaving you beat up and bloody."

He laughs. "I really like you."

"Good night." I turn to walk back to our door on less than steady legs.

"I'm Ansel."

I ignore him as I slide my key into the lock.

"Wait! I just want your name."

I look back over my shoulder. He's still smiling. Seriously, a kid in my third-grade class had a dimple and it did not make me feel like this. *This* boy should come with a warning label. "Shut the hell up and I'll tell it to you tomorrow."

He takes another step forward, feet bare on the carpet and eyes following me down the hall, and says, "Does that mean we have a date?"

"No."

"And you really won't tell me your name? Please?"

"Tomorrow."

"I'll just call you *Cerise,* then."

I call out, "Fine with me," as I walk into my room. For all I know, he's just called me uptight, or prude, or pig jammies.

But somehow, the way he purred the two syllables makes me think it was something else entirely.

As I climb back into bed, I look it up on my phone. *Cerise* means "cherry." Of course it does. I'm not sure how I feel about that because something tells me he wasn't referring to the color of my nail polish.

The girls are both asleep, but I'm not. Even though the noise across the hall has stopped and everything grows still and calm in our suite, I'm hot and flushed and wishing I'd had the guts to stay out in the hallway just a little longer.

Chapter TWO

*H*ARLOW ORDERS FRIES before dropping her shot into her beer and downing it.

She pulls her forearm across her mouth and looks over at me. I must be gaping because she asks, "What? Should I be classier?"

I shrug, drawing the straw through the ice in my glass. After a morning massage and facial, an afternoon spent at the pool, followed by a few cocktails, we're all more than a little tipsy. Besides, even after chugging a beer with a shot in it, Harlow *looks* classy. She could jump into a bin full of plastic balls at McDonald's Playland and come out looking fresh.

"Why bother?" I ask. "We have the rest of our lives to be sophisticates, but only the one weekend in Vegas."

She listens to what I say, considers it before nodding firmly and motioning to the bartender. "I'll have two more shots and whatever that monstrosity is that she's drinking." She points to Lola, who's licking the whipped cream from the rim of a hideous, LED-flashing cup.

He frowns before shaking his head and says, "Two shots of whiskey and one Slut on a Trampoline, coming up."

Harlow gives me her best shocked face but I barely have time to register it before I feel someone press up behind me at the crowded bar. Large hands grip my hips only a split second before "There you are" is whispered hotly—and directly—into my ear.

I startle, turning and jumping away with a gasp.

Ansel.

My ear feels damp and warm, but when I look at him, I see the same playful light in his eyes he had last night. He's the guy who'll do a ridiculous robot dance to make you laugh, who'll lick the tip of your nose, make a fool out of himself for a smile. I'm sure if I tried to wrestle him to the ground, he'd let me win. And enjoy every minute.

"Too close?" he asks. "I was going for seductive, yet subtle."

"I'm not sure you could have been any closer," I admit, fighting a smile as I rub my ear. "You were practically inside my head."

"He'd make a horrible ninja," says one of the guys with him.

"Oliver, Finn," Ansel says, first pointing to a tall friend with messy brown hair, stubble, bright blue eyes behind thick-rimmed glasses, and then to the one who spoke, with short-cropped brown hair, dark backlit eyes, and what I can only imagine is a permanently cocky smirk. Ansel looks back at me. "And gentlemen, this is *Cerise*. I'm still waiting for her real name." He leans in a little, saying, "She'll have to give it up sometime."

"I'm Mia," I tell him, ignoring his innuendo. His eyes

trip down my face and stall at my lips. It's precisely the look he would give me if we were about to kiss but he's too far away. He leans forward, and it feels like watching an airplane fly ten feet from the ground for miles, never getting closer.

"It's nice to put a face with all the man shouts," I say to break the thick sexual tension, looking around him to Oliver and Finn, then point to my wide-eyed friends beside me. "This is Lorelei, and Harlow."

They exchange handshakes, but remain suspiciously quiet. I'm not usually the one meeting guys in situations like this. I'm usually the one pulling Harlow back from hooking up on a table within minutes of meeting someone, while Lola considers beating up any guy who dares speak to us. They may be too stunned to know how to respond.

"Have you been looking for us?" I ask.

Ansel shrugs. "We may have gone to a couple of different places, just to peek."

Behind him, Oliver—the one in glasses—holds up seven fingers and I laugh. "A couple?"

"No more than three," Ansel says, winking.

I spot movement just behind him, and before I have a chance to say anything, Finn steps up, attempting to yank Ansel's pants down. Ansel doesn't even blink, but instead asks me, "What are you drinking?" and simply grips his waistband without looking even a little surprised or annoyed.

As if I can't see a considerable amount of gray boxers.

As if I'm not staring directly at where the distinct bulge in the cotton would be.

Is this what boys do?

"It's nice to see you in your underwear again," I say, struggling to restrain my grin.

"Almost," he clarifies. "At least my pants stayed up this time."

I glance down, wishing I could get another eyeful of his toned thighs. "That's debatable."

"Last time Finn did that, they didn't. I beat his road time this week and he's been trying to get me back ever since." He stops, brows lifting and seeming to only now hear what I said. He leans in a little bit, asking in a soft, low voice, "Are you hitting on me?"

"No." I swallow under the pressure of his unwavering attention. "Maybe?"

"Maybe if my pants go down, your dress should go up," he whispers, and no sentence *anywhere* has ever sounded so dirty. "To level the playing field."

"She's way too hot for you," Finn says from behind him. Ansel reaches back, putting a hand on Finn's face and moving him farther away. He nods to my drink, wordlessly asking what was in my now-empty glass.

I stare back at him, feeling the strange warmth of familiarity spread through me. So *this* is what chemistry feels like. I've felt it with other performers, but that kind of connection is different from this. Usually chemistry between dancers diffuses offstage, or we force real life back in. Here with Ansel, I think we could charge large appliances with the energy moving between us.

He takes my glass and says, "Be right back," before glancing at Lola as she steps away from the others. She's watching Ansel like a hawk, with her arms crossed over her chest and stern mom-face on full display. "With a drink," he tells her good-naturedly. "Overpriced, watered-down alcohol, probably with some questionable fruit. Nothing funny, I promise. Would you like to come with me?"

"No, but I'm watching you," she says.

He gives her his most charming smile before turning to me. "Anything in particular you desire?"

"Surprise me," I tell him.

After he walks a few feet away to get the bartender's attention, the girls give me exaggerated *what the hell* stares and I shrug back—because, really, what can I say? The story is laid out right in front of them. A hot guy and his hot friends have located us in a club, and said hot guy is buying me a drink.

Lola, Harlow, and Ansel's friends make polite conversation but I can barely hear them, thanks to the booming music and my heartbeat pounding in my ears. I try not to stare down the bar to where Ansel has wedged himself between a few bodies, but in my peripheral vision I can see his head above most others, and his long, lean body leaning forward to call out his order to the bartender.

He returns a few minutes later with a new tumbler, full of ice and limes and clear liquid, offering it to me with a sweet smile. "Gin and tonic, right?"

"I was expecting you to get me something adventurous. Something in a pineapple or with sparklers."

"I smelled your glass," he says, shrugging. "I wanted to keep you on the same drink. Plus"—he gestures down my body—"you have this whole flapper girl thing going on with the short dress and the"—he draws a circle in the air with his index finger near my head—"the shiny black hair and straight bangs. And those red lips. I look at you and I think 'gin.'" He stops, scratching his chin, and adds, "Actually I look at you and think—"

Laughing, I hold up my hand to stop him there. "I have no idea what to do with you."

"I have some suggestions."

"I'm sure you do."

"Would you like to hear them?" he says, grin firmly in place.

I take a deep, steadying breath, pretty sure I'm in *way* over my head with this one. "How about you tell me a little about you guys first. Do you all live in the States?"

"No. We met a few years ago doing a volunteer program here where you bike from one city to another, building low-income housing as you go. We did it after university a few years back and worked from Florida to Arizona."

I look at him more closely now. I hadn't given much thought to who he is or what he does, but this is far more interesting than a group of asshole foreign guys blowing money on a Vegas suite. And biking from state to state definitely explains the muscular thighs. "That's not at all what I expected you to say."

"There were four of us who became very close. Finn, Oliver, me, and Perry. This year we did a reunion ride, but only from Austin to here. We're old men now."

I look around for the fourth one and then raise my eyebrows at him meaningfully. "Where is he?"

But Ansel only shrugs. "Just us three this time."

"It sounds amazing."

Sipping his drink, he nods. "It *was* amazing. I dread going home on Tuesday."

"Where exactly is home? France?"

He grins. "Yes."

"Home to France. What a drag," I say dryly.

"You should come to Paris with me."

"*Ha*. Okay."

He studies me for a long beat. "I'm serious."

"Oh, I'm sure you are."

He sips his drink again, eyebrows raised. "You may be the most beautiful woman I've ever seen. I suspect you're also the most clever." He leans in a little, whispering, "Can you juggle?"

Laughing, I say, "No."

"Pity." He hums, smiling at my mouth. "Well, I need to stay in France for another six months or so. You'll need to live there with me for a bit before we can buy a house Stateside. I can teach you then."

"I don't even know your last name," I say, laughing harder now. "We can't be discussing juggling lessons and cohabitation quite yet."

"My last name is Guillaume. My father is French. My mother is American."

"Gee what?" I repeat, floundering with the accent. "I wouldn't even know how to spell that." I frown, rolling the word around in my head a few times. "In fact, I'm not even sure what letter it begins with."

"You'll need to learn to spell it," he says, dimple flashing. "You'll have to sign your new name on your bank checks, after all."

Finally, I have to look away. I need to take a break from his grin and this DEFCON-1 level of flirtation. I need oxygen. But when I blink to my right, I'm met with the renewed wide-eyed stares of my friends standing nearby.

I clear my throat, determined not to be self-conscious about how much fun I'm having and how easy this all feels. "What?" I ask, giving Lola the *don't overreact* face.

She turns her attention to Ansel. "You got her talking."

I can feel her shock, and I don't want it to consume me. If I think too much about how easy I feel around him, it'll rebound and I'll panic.

"This one?" he asks, pointing at me with his thumb. "She doesn't shut up, does she?"

Harlow and Lola laugh, but it's a *yeah, you're insane* laugh and Lola pulls me slightly to the side, putting a hand on my shoulder. "You."

"Me what?"

"You're having an instalove moment," she hisses. "It's

freaking me out. Are your panties still on under there?" She bends dramatically as if to check.

"We met last night," I whisper, pulling her back up and trying to get her to lower her voice because even though we stepped away, we didn't move that far. All three men are listening in on our exchange.

"You met him and didn't tell us?"

"God, Mother. We were busy this morning and I forgot, okay? Last night they were partying across the hall. You would have heard them, too, if you hadn't had enough vodka to kill a horse. I walked over and asked them to quiet down."

"No, that wasn't the first time we met," Ansel interjects over my shoulder. "We met earlier."

"We did *not*," I insist, telling him with my expression to shut it. He doesn't know Lola's protective side but I do.

"But it was the first time she saw Ansel in his underwear," Finn adds, helpfully. "He invited her in."

Her eyebrows disappear beneath her hairline. "Oh my God. Am I drunk? What's in this thing?" she asks, peering into her obnoxiously flashing cup.

"Oh stop," I tell her, irritation rising. "I didn't go into his room. I didn't take the gorgeous stranger's candy even though I really wanted to because hello, look at him," I add, just daring her to freak out even more. "You should see him with his shirt off."

Ansel rocks on his heels, sipping his drink. "Please continue as if I'm not here. This is fantastic."

Finally—mercifully—Lola seems to decide to move on. We all step back into the small semicircle the guys have made, and drink our cocktails in stilted silence.

Either ignoring or oblivious to the awkward, Ansel pipes up. "So what are you all celebrating this weekend?" he asks.

He doesn't just speak the words, he pouts them, pushing each out in a little kiss. Never before have I had such an urge to touch someone's mouth with my fingers. As Harlow explains why we're in Vegas, drinking terrible shots and wearing the world's sluttiest dresses, my eyes move down his chin, over his cheeks. Up close I can see he has perfect skin. Not just clear, but smooth and even. Only his cheeks are slightly ruddy, a constant boy-blush. It makes him look younger than I think he is. Onstage, he would remain untouched. No pancake, no lipstick. His nose is sharp, eyes perfectly spaced and an almost intimidating green. I imagine I'd be able to see the color from the back of a theater. There is no way he can possibly be as perfect as he seems.

"What do you do when you're not riding bikes or juggling?" I ask, and everyone turns to me in unison. I feel my pulse explode in my throat, but force my eyes to hold on to Ansel's, waiting for his answer.

He plants his elbows on the bar beside him and anchors me with his attention. "I'm an attorney."

My fantasy wilts immediately. My dad would be thrilled to know I'm chatting up a lawyer. "Oh."

His laugh is raspy. "Sorry to disappoint."

"I've never known an attorney before who wasn't old and

lecherous," I admit, ignoring the looks Harlow and Lola have trained on the side of my face. At this point, I know they're counting how many words I've said in the last ten minutes. I'm breaking a personal record now.

"Would it help if I said I work for a nonprofit?"

"Not really."

"Good. In that case I'll tell you the truth: I work for the biggest, most ruthless corporate firm in Paris. I have a horrible schedule, really. This is why you should come to Paris. I'd like a reason to come home early from work."

I attempt to look unaffected by this, but he's watching me. I can practically feel his smile. It starts as a tiny tug in the corner of his mouth and grows the longer I pretend. "So I told you about me, what about you? Where are you from, *Cerise*?"

"I told you my name; you don't have to keep calling me that."

"What if I want to?"

It's really hard to concentrate when he's smiling like that. "I'm not sure I should tell you where I'm from. Stranger danger and all."

"I can give you my passport. Will that help?"

"Maybe."

"We can call my mom," he says, and reaches into his back pocket for his phone. "She's American, you'd get on fantastically. She tells me all the time what a sweet boy I am. I hear that a lot, actually."

"I'm sure you do," I say, and honestly, I think he really would let me call his mother. "I'm from California."

"Just California? I'm not an American but I hear that's a pretty big state."

I watch him through narrowed eyes before finally adding, "San Diego."

He grins as if he's won something, like I've just wrapped this tiny piece of information up all shiny and bright and dropped it into his lap. "Ahh. And what do you do there in San Diego? Your friend said you're here celebrating graduation. What's next?"

"Uh . . . business school. Boston University," I say, and wonder if that answer will ever stop sounding stiff and rusty to my own ears, like I'm reading from a script.

Apparently it sounds that way to him, too, because for the first time, his smile slips. "I wouldn't have guessed that."

I glance to the bar and, without thinking, down the rest of my drink. The alcohol burns but I feel the heat seep into my limbs. The words I want to say bubble up in the back of my throat. "I used to dance. Ballet." It's the first time I've ever said those words to anyone.

His brows lift, his eyes moving first over my face, then trailing down my body. "Now that I can see."

Harlow squints at me, and then looks at Ansel. "You two are so fucking *nice*."

"It's disgusting," Finn agrees under his breath.

Their eyes meet from either side of me and hold. There's some sort of silent acknowledgment there, like they're on the same team—them against us—each trying to see which one can mortify their friend the most. And this is when I know we're only about an hour and a half from Harlow riding Finn reverse-cowgirl on the floor somewhere. Lola catches my eye and I know we're thinking the exact same thing.

As predicted, Harlow lifts her shot glass in Finn's direction. In the process, much of it slops over the side and onto her skin. Like the classy woman she is, she bends, dragging her tongue across the back of her hand before saying to no one in particular, "I'm probably gonna fuck him tonight."

Finn smiles, leaning closer to her and whispering something in her ear. I have no idea what he's just said but I'm sure I've never seen Harlow blush like this. She reaches up, toying with her earring. Beside me, Lorelei groans.

If Harlow looks you in the eye while she takes her earrings off, you're either going to be fucked or killed. When Finn smiles, I realize he's already figured out this rule and knows he's coming out on top.

"Harlow," I warn.

Clearly, Lola can't take any more, because she grabs Harlow's hand to haul her up and out of her chair. "Meeting of the minds in the ladies' room."

"WHY IS HE calling me 'Cherry'?" I blink up to my reflection in the mirror. "Does he think I'm a virgin?"

"I'm pretty sure he's talking about your blowjob mouth," Harlow says, winking. "And if I may, I'd like to suggest that you hit that French boy like a hammer tonight. Is his accent not the hottest thing you've ever heard?"

Lorelei is already shaking her head. "I'm not sure Mia is the best one to be talked into a one-night stand."

I finish dragging the wand of my lip gloss across my mouth, press both lips together. "What does that mean?" I hadn't planned on having a one-night stand with Ansel. I'd planned on staring at him all night and then going to bed alone, where I'd fantasized that I was someone else and he would in fact teach me the ins and outs of hallway sex. But as soon as Lola says this I feel a rebellious pull in my ribs.

Harlow studies me for a beat. "I think she's right. You're a little hard to please," she explains.

"Seriously, Harlow?" I ask. "You can say that with a straight face?"

Lola's eyes are similarly wide in disbelief as she turns to me. "That's *not* what I meant."

"Oh, I'm definitely impossible to please," Harlow admits. "I just love watching men try. But Mia takes about two weeks before she converses without a thick sheet of awkward."

"Not tonight, she doesn't," Lola mumbles.

I shove my lip gloss back in my clutch and give Harlow a look. "Maybe I like going slow and getting past that weird need people have for nonstop conversation. You're the one who likes to bang off the bat, and that's fine. I don't judge."

"Well," Harlow continues as if I haven't spoken. "Ansel is adorable and I'm pretty sure from the way he stares at you, he won't need you to do much talking."

Lorelei sighs. "He seems really sweet and they're obviously both into each other, and what's going to happen?" She shoves everything back in her clutch and turns to lean against the bay of sinks and face us. "He lives in France, she's moving to Boston, which is only marginally closer to France than San Diego. If you have sex with Ansel," she says to me, "it will be solid missionary with tons of talking and soft-focus eye contact. That's not one-night-stand sex."

"You guys are freaking me out right now," I tell them.

"Then she can just insist on doggy, what's the problem?" Harlow asks, bewildered.

Since I'm clearly not needed for this conversation, I push my way out of the bathroom and back to the bar, leaving them to decide the rest of my night, without me.

———————

AT FIRST, IT'S as if our friends metaphorically evaporate into the background as they, too, grow more comfortable (or drunk) together and their laughter tells me they're no longer listening to everything we're saying. Eventually they head to the blackjack tables just outside the bar, leaving us alone together only after delivering their meaningful *be careful* stares to me and *don't be pushy* stares to Ansel.

He finishes his drink and puts the empty glass down on the bar. "What did you love most about dancing?"

I'm feeling brave, whether from the gin or Ansel, I don't care. I take his hand and pull him to his feet. He steps away from the bar and walks beside me.

"Getting lost in it," I say, leaning into him. "Being someone else." *That way I could pretend to be anyone*, I think, *in their body, doing things maybe I wouldn't do with mine if I thought about it too much.* Like leading Ansel down a dark hallway—which, though I might have needed to take a deep breath and count to ten first, I *do*.

When we round the corner and stop, he hums, and I press my lips together, loving how the sound makes my lungs constrict. It shouldn't be possible for my legs and lungs and brain to all quit working at the same time.

"You could pretend *this* is a stage," he says quietly, leaning his hand against the wall beside my head. "You could pretend to be someone else. You could pretend to be the girl who pulled me down here because she wanted to kiss me."

I swallow, forming the words carefully in my head. "Then who will *you* be tonight?"

"The guy who gets the girl he wants and doesn't have any fires to put out back home."

He doesn't look away, so I feel like I can't, either, even though my knees want to buckle. He could kiss me right this second and it wouldn't be soon enough.

"Why *did* you get me over here? Away from everyone?" he asks, smile slowly fading.

I look past him, over his shoulder into the club, where it's only slightly lighter than where we're standing.

When I don't answer, he bends to catch my eyes. "Am I asking too many questions?"

"It always takes me a while to put words together," I tell him. "It's not you."

"No, no. Lie to me," he says, moving closer, his

heart-stopping smile returning. "Let me pretend when we're alone like this I render you speechless."

And still, he waits for me to find the words I want to say in reply. But the truth is, even with a bowl full of words to choose from, I'm not sure it would make sense if I told him why I wanted him down here, away from the safety of my friends, who are always able to translate my expressions into sentences, or at the very least change the subject for me.

I'm not nervous or intimidated. I simply don't know how to slip into the role I want to play: flirty, open, brave. What is it about another person's chemistry that makes you feel more or less drawn to them? With Ansel, I feel like my heartbeat is chasing his. I want to leave my fingerprints all over his neck and his lips. I want to suck on his skin, to see if it's as warm as it looks, and decide if I like what he was drinking by tasting it on his tongue. I want to have an entire conversation with him where I don't second-guess or struggle with a single word, and then I want to take him back to the room with me and not use any words at all.

"Ask me again," I say.

His brows pull together for a beat before he understands. "Why did you bring me down here?"

This time I don't even think before I speak: "I want to have a different life tonight."

His lips push out a little as he thinks and I can't help but blink down to them. "With me, *Cerise*?"

I nod. "I know what that means, you know. It means 'cherry.' Pervert."

His eyes shine with amusement. "It does."

"And I'm sure you've guessed I'm not a virgin."

He shakes his head. "Have you seen your mouth? I've never seen lips so full and red."

Unconsciously, I pull my bottom lip into my mouth, sucking it.

His eyes grow heavy and he leans closer. "I like when you do that. I want a turn."

My voice is nervous and shaking when I whisper, "They're just lips."

"They're not *just lips*. And please," he teases, and he's so close I can smell his aftershave. It smells like fresh air, like green and sharp and soothing all at once, something I've never smelled on a man before. "You wear red lipstick so that men won't notice your mouth? Surely you know what we dream about a mouth like that doing."

I don't close my eyes when he leans in and takes my bottom lip between both of his, but *he* does. His eyes fall closed, and every one of my senses picks up the gravelly sound he makes: I taste it, feel it, hear it, see the way he shivers against me.

He runs his tongue over my lip, sucks gently, and then pulls back. I realize it wasn't really a kiss. It was more a taste. And obviously he agrees: "You don't taste like cherry."

"What do I taste like?"

He shrugs a little, thoughtfully purses his lips. "I'm unable to think of a good word. Sweet. Like a woman and a girl still, too."

His hand is still planted near my head, but the other toys with the hem of my cardigan. I realize that if I want to live a different life I have to do it. I can't tiptoe along the edge of the cliff. I have to jump. I have to figure out what kind of girl would do what I want to do with him, and pretend I'm her. *She's* the one onstage. Mia watches from the audience.

I pull his fingers down to the bottom of my dress, and then under.

He's no longer looking at my mouth; we're looking directly into each other's eyes when I drag his fingers up the inside of my thigh. It feels so secluded here—darker and still—but around the corner the bar echoes with drunken voices, a bass-heavy pop song. We're hidden but anyone could find us if they wanted to. Without any more urging from me, he slips a knuckle beneath the fabric of my underwear. My eyes roll closed and my head falls back against the wall behind me as he gently slides it back and forth over my most sensitive flesh.

I don't know what I've done, or why, and I'm suddenly consumed with warring reactions. I want him to touch me— *God I want him to touch me*—but I'm mortified, too. I've been with two other guys since Luke, but there was always more lead-up: kissing, and the usual progression of top-to-bottom groping. Having Ansel near me has reduced me to a puddle of want.

"I'm not sure who is more surprised you just did that," he says before kissing my neck. "You or I."

He pulls his finger away but almost immediately returns at a better angle, this time sliding his entire hand down the front of my underwear. My breath catches as he strokes me gently with two fingers. He's careful, but confident.

"Toutes les choses que j'ai envie de te faire . . ."

I swallow back a moan, whispering, "What did you say?"

"Just thinking of all the things I want to do to you." He kisses my jaw. "Do you want me to stop?"

"No," I say, and then panic chokes me. "Yes." He freezes and I immediately miss the rhythm of his broad fingertips. "No. Don't stop."

With a raspy laugh, he bends to kiss my neck, and my eyes roll closed as he starts to move again.

———

IT TAKES FOREVER for me to open my eyes; my head is pounding. My whole body hurts. I press my hands firmly to my temples, palms flat as if, by doing so, I can hold my head together. It *must* be in pieces. It's the only thing that could explain the pain.

The room is dark, but I know somehow that behind the heavy hotel curtains the Nevada summer sun is blinding.

Even if I slept for a week, I think I'd need two more.

The night comes back to me in tiny, chaotic bursts. Drinking. Ansel. Pulling him down the hall and feeling his tongue on mine. And then, talking. So much talking. Flashes of naked skin, movement, and the loose-limbed aftereffects of a night of orgasms, one after another.

I wince, nausea sweeping through me.

Moving is torture. I feel bruised and exhausted, and it's distracting enough for me to not initially realize that I'm completely naked. And alone. I have delicate points of pain on my ribs, my neck, my upper arms. When I manage to sit up, I see that most of the bedding is on the floor, but I'm on the bare mattress, as if I've been plucked from the chaos and intentionally laid here.

Near my bare hip is a piece of paper, folded carefully in half. The handwriting is neat, and somehow easily recognizable as foreign. My hand shakes as I quickly read the note.

> Mia,
>
> I tried to wake you, but after failing decided to let you sleep. I think we only got about two hours at any rate. I'm going to shower and then will be downstairs having breakfast in the restaurant across from the elevator. Please find me.
>
> Ansel

I start shaking and can't stop. It's not just the raging hangover or the realization that I spent a night with a stranger and can't remember a lot of it. It's not just the state of the room: a lamp is broken, the mirror is smudged with hundreds of handprints, the floor is littered with clothing and pillows and—*thank God*—condom wrappers. It isn't the mortification over the dark stain from a soda bottle on the rug across the room. It's not the delicate bruises I see on my ribs or the persistent ache between my legs.

I'm shaking because of the slim gold band on my left ring finger.

Chapter THREE

I'M SHAKING BECAUSE WHAT THE FUCK DOES THAT MEAN THAT I HAVE A RING THAT LOOKS LIKE A WEDDING RING AND WHY CAN'T I REMEMBER WHAT WE DID? The only thing I remember after pulling Ansel down the hall last night is more alcohol—a lot more—and flirting.

Flashes of a weaving limo ride.

Harlow shouting out the window and Ansel's goofy smile.

I think I remember seeing Lola kiss Oliver. The pop of a camera flash. Dragging Ansel down the hall and sex. Lots of sex.

I sprint to the bathroom and lose the contents of my stomach. The alcohol coming back up is sour, tastes like shame and a hundred bad ideas poured down my throat.

I brush my teeth with a weak arm and shaking hand while giving my reflection the dirtiest look I can manage. I look like shit, have about seventeen hickeys on my neck and chest and, I'll be honest, from the looks of my mouth, I sucked dick for a long time last night.

I gulp water from the faucet and stumble back out into the bedroom, pulling on a shirt from the first suitcase I trip over. I can barely walk, collapsing on the floor after only about thirty seconds of hunting for my phone. When I spot it across the room, I stumble-crawl over, only to realize it's completely dead and I have no idea where I put my charger. Cheek pressed to the floor, I give up. Eventually someone will find my body. Right?

I really hope this story is funny in a few years.

"Harlow?" I call out, wincing at the gravelly sound of my own voice, at the scent of detergent and stale water emanating from the carpet so close to my face. "Lola?"

But the enormous suite is completely silent. Where the hell did they end up last night? Are they okay? The image of Lola kissing Oliver returns with more detail: the two of them standing in front of us, bathed in cheap fluorescent lighting. *Holy fuck, are they married, too?*

I'm almost positive I'm going to throw up again.

I take a moment to breathe in through my nose, breathe out through my mouth, and my head clears slightly, just enough to stand, get a glass of water from the tap. To not vomit all over the expensive place Harlow's dad is paying for.

I devour an energy bar and banana I find in the minibar, and then drink an entire can of ginger ale in almost two gulps. I will never get enough liquid back into my body, I can feel it.

In the shower, I scrub at my aching skin, shaving and washing everything with trembling hungover hands.

Mia, you're a disaster. This is why you're a sucky drinker.

The worst part isn't how horrible I feel or what a mess I've made.

The worst part is I want to find *him* as much as I want to find Harlow and Lola.

The worst part is the tiny curl of anxiety I feel knowing that it's Monday and we're leaving today.

No, the worst part is that I'm an idiot.

As I dry off in the bedroom and pull on some jeans and a tank top, I look over to where I've left his note on the mattress. His tidy, slanted handwriting faces the ceiling, and a slim thread of a memory pushes into my thoughts, of my hand on Ansel's clothed chest, pushing him out of the bathroom and sitting down on the toilet seat with a stack of paper and ballpoint pen. To write a letter? I think . . . to . . . me?

But I can't find it anywhere; not under the enormous pile of blankets on the floor, not in the dismantled couch cushions in the living room, not in the bathroom or in any of the chaos of the suite. It has to be here. The only other time I wrote myself a letter, it was the one thing that guided me through the hardest point in my life.

If a letter from last night exists, I need to find it.

————

AFTER THE MOST nauseating and anxious elevator ride in history, I'm finally downstairs. I see the guys in a booth across the restaurant, but Harlow and Lola aren't with them. They're arguing in that way they seem to constantly argue, where it's really all just the man version of cuddling on a couch. They yell and gesticulate and look exasperated and then laugh. None of them looks like they're recovering from some sort of massive crime spree and I feel my shoulders relax the tiniest bit, fairly confident that wherever Harlow and Lorelei are, they're safe.

Frozen near the entrance, I ignore the perky hostess asking me repeatedly if I need a table for one. My headache is returning and hopefully someday my feet will start to move and she'll go away.

Ansel looks up and sees me, and his smile vanishes for a beat before it is replaced by something much sweeter than a smile. It's happy relief. He shows everything, so easily laid bare on his sleeve.

Finn and Oliver turn to look over their shoulders and see me. Finn says something I can't hear before rapping the table twice with his knuckles and pushing away in his chair.

Ansel stays at the table as his two friends walk toward me.

"Wh-where," I start, then pause, straighten my shoulders, and say, "Where are Harlow and Lola?"

Oliver lifts his chin toward the elevators down the hall. "Slaypee. Me bee shaah."

I squint at the Aussie. "Huh?"

"'Sleeping,'" Finn translates with a laugh. "'Maybe shower.' The accent isn't quite as thick when he's not hungover. I'll tell them you're down here."

I raise my eyebrows expectantly, wondering if there is any other information they want to share.

"And?" I ask, looking back and forth between them.

Finn's eyebrows draw together. "And . . . ?"

"Did we *all* get married?" I ask, meaning I expect he'll

tell me, *Nope, it's just a game. We won these expensive gold rings playing blackjack!*

But he nods, looking far less disturbed by this turn of events than I am. "Yep. But don't worry, we'll fix it." He looks back at the table and gives Ansel a meaningful stare.

"Fix it?" I repeat, and oh my God, is this what a stroke feels like?

Turning back to me, Finn lifts a hand, rests it on my shoulder, and looks at me with dramatic condolences. When I look behind him to Ansel, I can see his . . . *my husband's?* . . . eyes are lit with amusement.

"Do you know what a Brony is?"

I blink back to Finn, not entirely sure I've heard him correctly. "A—*what?*"

"A Brony," he repeats. "It's a guy who is into *My Little Pony.*"

"Yeah, okay." *What the . . . ?*

He leans in, bending his knees so he's at face level with me. "I ask you this not because the man you married last night in a drunken haze is a Brony, but because he thinks the whole idea of Bronies is fantastic."

"I'm not sure I'm following," I whisper. Am I still drunk? Is he? What the hell kind of world have I walked into this morning?

"He also once took an actual bath in Jell-O because someone dared him to and he was curious," Finn tells me. "He loves to open wine bottles with only a shoe and a wall. And when we ran out of cash in Albuquerque and the restaurant wouldn't accept credit cards, he paid for our dinner by dancing next door at this run-down little strip club."

"I need coffee before I can understand a single thing you're telling me," I say.

Finn ignores this. "He made about seven hundred dollars that night, but that's not my point."

"Okay?" I glance back at Ansel again. There's no way he can hear what we're saying, but he clearly knows these guys well enough that he doesn't need to. He's outright laughing.

"My point is to keep all that in mind when you speak to him. My point is Ansel falls a little bit in love with everything he sees." When he says this, my chest tightens inexplicably. "It's what I love about the guy, but his whole life is basically . . ." He looks up at Oliver for guidance.

Oliver pulls a toothpick from his mouth. "Sayren deepty?" he says before sliding the toothpick back in.

"Serendipity." Finn pats my shoulder as if we've wrapped things up here—as if this conversation made any kind of goddamn sense—and steps around me. Oliver nods once, solemnly. Neon lights flash in the reflection of his glasses and I have to blink away, wondering if throwing up again might be preferable to the conversation I'm sure is about to transpire. What are they even talking about? I can barely remember how to walk, let alone figure out how to deal with the thought that I might be legally married to a guy who loves everything about life, including Bronies.

With a nervous flip in my stomach I slip between two tables and walk over to the booth where Ansel is smiling up at me. In however many minutes we've been apart—or however many I've been unconscious—I'd forgotten the effect of him up close. Nerve endings seem to rise to the surface of my skin, anticipating his hands.

"Good morning," he says. His voice is hoarse and slow. He has dark circles beneath his eyes and his skin looks a little pale. Given that he's clearly been up longer than I have, looking at him doesn't make me especially confident I'll feel better in a couple of hours.

"Good morning." I hover at the edge of the table, not sure I'm ready to sit down. "What was Finn talking about?"

He waves his hand, already dismissing it. "I saw you coming and ordered you some orange juice and what you Americans like to call coffee."

"Thanks." When I sit, I suck in a breath at the throbbing ache between my legs, and the reality of our night of wild—and maybe a little rough—sex is like a third person at the table. I wince, a full-body wince, and Ansel notices. It sets off a comical chain reaction: he blushes and his eyes drop to the marks he's left all over my neck and chest. I try to cover my throat with shaking hands, wishing I'd brought a scarf to the desert, in the summer—which is ridiculous—and he bursts out laughing. I drop my head onto my crossed arms on the table and groan. I'm never drinking again.

"About the bite marks . . ." he begins.

"About that."

"You kept asking me to bite you."

"*I did?*"

"You were very specific," he says with a grin. "And being the gentleman that I am, I *happily* obliged."

"Oh."

"Apparently we had a wild night."

I lift my head, thanking the waitress when she puts a carafe of coffee in front of me. "The details are slowly returning."

And they are, finally: the way we crashed into the hotel room, laughing and falling onto the travertine floor just inside the entryway. He rolled me over to playfully check for scrapes, kissing along my neck, my back, the backs of my thighs. He undressed me with fingers and teeth and words kissed into my skin. Far less artfully I undressed him, impatient and practically ripping the shirt from his body.

When I look up and meet his eyes, he rubs the back of his neck, smiling apologetically at me. "If what I feel today is any indication, we, ah . . . took a long time."

I feel my face heat at the same time my stomach drops. This isn't the first time I've heard this particular bit of feedback. "I'm sorry my body is sort of . . . hard to please. Luke used to work forever to get me there and when we were first together sometimes I would even just pretend to come so he wouldn't feel like he failed."

Oh my God did I actually just say all that out loud?

Ansel scrunches his nose in an expression I haven't seen on him yet and it's the portrait of adorable confusion. "What? You aren't a robot, sometimes it takes time. I quite enjoyed figuring out how to give you pleasure." He winces then, looking even more apologetic. "I'm afraid the one taking forever was me. I had a lot to drink. Besides . . . we both wanted more after each time . . . I feel like I did about a million crunches."

And as soon as he says it, I know he's right. Even now my body feels like an instrument that had been perfectly played for hours the night before, and I seem to have gotten my wish: last night I *did* have a different life. I had the life of a woman with a wild, attentive lover. Beneath the haze of my hangover, I feel stretched and worked, the kind of satisfied that seems to reach the middle of my bones and the deepest part of my brain.

I remember being carried to the couch in the living room, later, where Ansel finished what he'd started in the lounge's hallway. The feel of his hands as he pushed my underwear aside, sliding his fingertips back and forth over my sensitive, heated skin.

"You're so soft," he'd said into a kiss. "You're soft and wet and I worry I'm feeling too wild for this small, sweet body." His hand shook and he slowed himself down by pulling my underwear all the way down my legs and off, throwing them onto the floor. "First I'll make *you* feel good. Because once I get inside you, I know I'll lose myself," he'd said, laughing, tickling my hips, nibbling at my jaw as his hand slid down my stomach and back between my legs. "Tell me when it's good."

I was telling him almost immediately, when he pressed his fingers against my clit, sliding back and forth until I started to shake, and beg, and reach for his pants. I shoved them down awkwardly, without unbuttoning them, wanting only to feel the heavy pulse of him in my hand.

I shiver as my body remembers that first orgasm and how he didn't let up, pulling another one from me before I pushed him away and rolled off the couch, taking him in my mouth.

But I don't remember how that ended. I *think* he came. Suddenly I'm consumed with panic. "In the living room, did you . . . ?"

His eyes widen briefly before that light amusement fills them. "What do you think?"

It's my turn to scrunch my nose. "I think so?"

He leans forward, resting a fist on his chin. "What do you remember?"

Oh, the little fucker. "You know what happened."

"Maybe I forgot? Maybe I want to hear you tell me."

I close my eyes and remember how the carpet felt on my bare knees, the way I initially struggled to get used to the broad feel of him in my mouth, his hands in my hair, his thighs shaking against my flattened palms.

When I look up and he's still watching me, I remember exactly how his face looked the first time he came against my tongue.

Reaching for my coffee, I lift it to my lips and take a giant, scalding gulp.

And then I remember being carried into the bedroom, Ansel wildly kissing and licking every inch of my body, sucking and biting. I remember us rolling from the bed to the floor, the crash of a lamp. I remember, however many hours later, watching him roll a condom on, his bare torso looming over me. I don't think I'd ever felt so greedy for something as I had for the weight of him on top of me. He was perfect: sliding in carefully even as drunk as we were, rocking in small, perfect arcs until I was sweaty and frantic beneath him. I remember the groan he made when he got close, and how he rolled me over, my stomach flat to the mattress, his teeth bared on my neck. Leaving one of so many marks.

Ansel watches me from across the table, a tiny, knowing smile curving his mouth. "Well? Did I?"

I open my mouth to speak but with the mischievous look in his eyes, maybe we're both remembering when he lifted me against the wall, pushing roughly back into me. Where had we been that he moved me to the wall? I remember how hard the sex was then, how a painting rattled a few feet away, him telling me how perfect I felt. I remember the sound of glasses tipping over and breaking near the bar, the sweat of his exertion sliding across my breasts. I remember his face, his hand pressed flat to a mirror behind me.

But no, that was a different time.

Jesus, how many times did we have sex?

I feel my brow lift. "Wow."

He blows a breath across his drink; the steam curls in front of him. "Hmm?"

"Yeah, I guess you did . . . *enjoy*. We must have done it a lot."

"Which was your favorite? Living room, or bed, or floor, or bed, or wall, or mirror, or bar, or floor?"

"Shhh," I whisper, lifting my cup to take another, more careful sip of coffee. I smile into my mug. "You're weird."

"I think I need a cast for my penis."

I cough-laugh, nearly sending a hot mouthful of coffee through my nose.

But when I lift my napkin to my mouth, Ansel's smile disappears. He's staring at my hand.

Shit shit shit. I'm still wearing the ring. I can't see his hands below the table now, and the crazy sex we had last night is officially the least of my worries. We haven't even started talking about the real issue: how to disentangle ourselves from this drunken night. How to *fix* it. It's so much more than being relieved we used condoms and having an awkward goodbye. A wild one-night stand isn't legally binding unless you're stupid enough to get married, too.

So why didn't I take off the ring as soon as I noticed it?

"I d-don't—" I start, and he blinks up to my face. "I didn't want to put it down and lose it. In case it was real or . . . belonged to someone."

"It belongs to you," he says.

I look away, eyeing the table, and notice two wedding rings there, between the salt and pepper shakers. They're men's rings. Is one of them his? *Oh God.*

I start to slip mine off but Ansel reaches across the table, stilling mc, and then lifts his other hand, his finger still decorated with a ring, too. "Don't be embarrassed. I didn't want to lose it, either."

This is too weird. I mean, *way* too weird for me. The feeling is like being pulled under by a violent wave. I'm suddenly hit with panic knowing that we're married, and it's not just a game. He lives in France, I'm moving in a few weeks. We've just made a huge mess. And oh my God, I can't want this. Am I insane? And how much does it cost to get out of this sort of thing?

I push back from the table, needing air, needing my friends.

"What is everyone doing about this?" I ask. "The others?" As if I need to clarify who I mean.

He swipes a hand over his face, and looks over his shoulder as if the guys might still be there. Turning back to me, he says, "They're meeting in the lobby at one, I think. And then I guess you girls plan to head home."

Home. I groan. Three weeks living at home with my family, where even the adorable boy chatter of my brothers playing Xbox can't drown out the killjoy of my father. And then I groan again: my father. What if he finds out about this? Would he still help pay for my apartment in Boston?

I hate depending on him. I hate doing anything that triggers the giddy little smirk he wears when he gets to tell me I screwed up. I also hate that I might throw up right now. Panic starts like a slow boil in my stomach, and heat flashes across my skin. My hands feel clammy and a cold sweat prickles at my forehead. I should find Lola and Harlow. I should leave.

"I should probably find the girls and get ready before we . . ." I wave vaguely in the direction of the elevators and stand, feeling sick for an entirely different set of reasons now.

"Mia," he says, reaching for my hand. He pulls a thick envelope from his pocket and looks up at me. "I have something I need to give you."

And there's my missing letter.

Chapter FOUR

*A*FTER THE ACCIDENT, I'd barely cried in the hospital, still convinced it was all some horrible dream. It was some other girl, not me, who'd crossed University and Lincoln on a bike the week before high school graduation. Someone else was hit by a truck that didn't stop at the red light. A different Mia shattered her pelvis and broke her leg so thoroughly a bone extended from the skin of her thigh.

I'd been numb and in shock the first few days; the pain was dulled by a steady drip of medication. But even through the haze, I was certain it was all a mistake. I was a ballerina. I'd just been accepted to Joffrey Ballet School. Even when the room filled with my mother's sobs and the doctor was describing the extent of my injuries, I didn't cry—because it wasn't about me. He was wrong, my chart had been switched, he was talking about some other person. My fracture was minimal. Maybe my knee was sprained. Someone smarter would come in any minute and explain it all. They had to.

But they didn't, and the morning I was discharged and faced with the reality of life without dancing . . . there wasn't enough morphine in the world to insulate me from the truth. My left leg was ruined—and with it, the future I'd worked toward my entire life. The stutter I'd struggled with for most of my childhood had returned, and my father—who spent more time researching the odds of my dancing career being lucrative than he did attending my recitals—was home, pretending not to be inwardly celebrating.

For six months I barely spoke. I did what I had to: I carried on. I healed on the outside while Lola and Harlow watched over me, never treating me like I was held together with a fake smile and staples.

Ansel leads me to the same corner I took him to last night. It's decidedly less dark this morning, less private, but I barely notice with my eyes boring into the envelope he's placed in my hand. He has no idea the significance of this, that the last time I wrote myself a letter was the day I decided to start talking again, the day I told myself it was okay to mourn the things I'd lost but it was time to move on. I sat down, wrote all the things I was afraid to say out loud, and slowly began to accept my new life. Instead of moving to Chicago like I'd always planned, I enrolled at UC San Diego and finally did something my father deemed worthy: graduating with honors and applying to the most prestigious business schools in the country. In the end I had my pick of programs. I've always wondered if subconsciously I was trying to get as far away as I could, from both him and the accident.

The envelope is wrinkled and worn, creased where it's been folded and probably pulled in and out of his pocket over and over, and reminds me so much of the letter I've read and reread over the years that I have a flash of déjà vu. Something's been spilled on one corner, there's a red smudge of my lipstick on the opposite side, but the flap is still perfectly sealed, the edges not pulling away even a little bit. He didn't try to open it, though judging by his anxious expression he's most definitely considered it.

"You said to give that to you today," he says quietly. "I didn't read it."

The envelope is thick in my hand, heavy, and stuffed with what feels like a hundred pages. But when I tear it open and look, I realize it's because my handwriting is so huge and slanted and drunk, I could only fit maybe twenty words on each narrow page of hotel stationery. I'd spilled something on it, and a few of the pages are torn slightly as if I could barely fold them correctly before giving up and shoving them in a messy pile inside.

Ansel watches me as I sort them and begin to read. I can practically feel his curiosity where his eyes are fixed on my face.

DEAR MIA SELF.MIASELF.MySELF it starts. I bite back a grin. I remember tiny ticks of this moment, sitting on the toilet lid and struggling to focus on the pen and paper.

You'RE sitting on the toilet
WRiting a letter to yourself to
READ IATER bECAUSE you'RE dRunk
ENOUgh to KNOW you'll forget a lot
tomoRROW but Not so dRunk that you
CAN't WRite. But I KNOW you bECAUSE

*you're me and we both know that
you're a terrible drinker and forget
everything that happens when you've
had gin. so let me tell you:*

*he's ansel.
you kissed him
he tasted like lemon and scotch
you put his hand in your
underwear and then
you talked for hours. yes, you
talked. i talked. we talked. we told
him everything about the accident
and ~~our leg your leg~~ my leg.
this is confusing.*

I'd forgotten this. I look up at Ansel, a prickling blush rising beneath the skin of my cheeks. I can feel my lips flush, too, and he notices, his eyes smoothing over them.

"I was so drunk when I wrote this," I whisper.

He only nods at me, and then nods at the paper, as if he doesn't want me to be interrupted, even by myself.

*you told him you hate speaking but
love moving
you told him everything about
dancing before the accident and not
dancing after*

you told him about how it felt to
be trapped under the hot engine
you told him about two years
of physical therapy, and trying to
dance "just for fun" after
you told him about luke and how
he said it felt like the old mia died
under the truck
you told him about dad and how
you're sure he's going to change
broc and jeff from sweet kids into
dickheads
you told him how much you dread
the fall and moving to boston
you actually said "i want to love
all of my life as much as i love this
night" and he didn't laugh at how
stupid you sounded
and here's the weirdest part
are you ready

I close my eyes, weaving a little. I'm *not* ready. Because this memory is sliding back into my thoughts, the victory, the urgency, the relief. I'm not ready to remember how safe he made me feel, and how easy he was. I'm not ready to realize that he's witnessed something no one in my life has ever seen before. I suck air into my lungs and look back down at the letter.

you didN't stutteR. you BABBLED.

I meet Ansel's eyes when I read this, as if seeking confirmation, but he doesn't know what the letter says. His eyes go wide as he searches my expression, barely holding back from speaking. Does he remember everything I said?

so that's why you pRoposed aNd he said yes REAlly fAst with this dRuNk smile liKe it wAs the best ideA he'd EVER heARd bECAuse of couRSE we should get mARRied! Now you'RE heAded theRE but i wANted to wRite this fiRst bECAuse you might Not REMEMBER why, ANd that's why. doN't bE A jERK. hE might just bE the NiCEst pERSoN you'VE EVER KNowN.

xo
MiASEIf
ps. you hAVEN't hAd sEx with him yEt. but you wANt to. A lot. PlEASE hAVE sEx with him.
pps. you just AsKEd him if you guys wERE goiNg to ANd he sAid "WE'll sEE." :/

I fold the papers up as neatly as I can and push them back inside the envelope with shaking hands. My heart feels like it's doubled in size, maybe conjoined to another, a new one that prefers the staccato of panic. The doubled beats bounce and reverberate in my chest.

"So?" he asks. "You know I'm dying of curiosity."

"I wrote it before we . . ." I hold up my left hand, displaying the simple gold band. "The last time I wrote myself a letter . . ." I start, but he's already nodding. I feel like I'm spinning beneath the weight of this.

"I know."

"And I proposed to you?" I suppose what actually surprises me is that there was a proposal at all. It wasn't just drunk stumbling. I remember his teasing the night before that I should go with him to France, but this took discussion, and planning. Getting a car, giving directions. It required us to sign papers, and pay, and select rings, then repeat vows coherently enough to convince someone we weren't drunk off our asses. I'm actually a little impressed by that last part.

He nods again, smiling.

"And you said yes?"

Tilting his head slightly, his lips pout the words, "Of course I did."

"But you weren't even sure if you wanted to have sex with me?"

He's already shaking his head. "Be serious. I wanted to have sex with you the first time I saw you, two nights ago. But last night, we were really drunk. I didn't . . ." He looks away, down the hall. "You left to write yourself a letter because you were worried you would forget why you proposed.

And you *did* forget." His brows rise, as he waits for me to acknowledge he's made a decent point. I nod. "But we got back
to the hotel, and you were so beautiful, and you . . ." He exhales a shaky breath. It's so jagged, I imagine I can see the
slivers of it fall from his mouth. "You *wanted* it." He leans
closer, kisses me slowly. "*I* wanted it."

I shift on my feet, wishing I knew how to pull my eyes
from his face.

"We did have sex, Mia. We had sex for hours and it was
the best, most intense sex of my life. And see? There are still
details you don't remember."

I might not remember every touch, but my body certainly does. I can feel his fingertips tattooed all over my skin.
They're in the bruises I can see and they're invisible, too: the
echo of his fingers in my mouth, dragging along my legs,
pumping inside me.

But as intoxicating as the memories are, none of this is
what I really want to talk about. I want to know what he remembers from before the wedding, before the sex, when I
dropped my life in his lap. Having sex with a virtual stranger
is weird for me, but it's not unheard of. What's monumental
is for me to have opened up so much. I never even talked to
Luke about some of these things.

"Apparently I said a lot to you yesterday," I say, before
sucking on my bottom lip and working it with my teeth. It
still feels bruised and I get tiny, teasing flashes of his teeth and
tongue and fingers pinching my mouth.

He doesn't say anything, but his eyes move over my face

as if he's waiting for me to reach some understanding he reached hours ago.

"I told you about Luke? And my family?"

He nods.

"And I told you about my leg?"

"I *saw* your leg," he reminds me quietly.

Of course he did. He would have seen the scar extending from hip to knee and the tiny ant trail of staple marks along the long, silvery gash.

"Is that what has you shaking?" he asks. "That I saw your naked leg? That I touched it?"

He knows it isn't. The smile pulling at his mouth tells me he knows my secret, and he's gloating. He remembers everything, including his unique achievement: a babbling Mia.

"It was probably the gin," I say.

"I think it was me."

"I was really drunk. I think I just forgot to be nervous."

His lips are so close I can feel their shadow on my jaw. "It was me, *Cerise*. You still haven't stuttered this morning."

I press back into the wall, needing space. It isn't just that I'm surprised to find I'm so fluent with him. It's the intoxicating weight of his attention, the need I have to feel his hands and mouth on me. It's the headache that lingers and the reality that I'm married. No matter what happens, I have to deal with this and all I want is to climb back into bed.

"I feel weird that I told you everything and I don't know anything about you."

"We have plenty of time," he says, tongue slipping out to wet his lips. "Till death do us part, in fact."

He must be kidding. I laugh, relieved that finally we can be playful. "I can't stay married to you, Ansel."

"But in fact," he whispers, "you can." His mouth presses carefully to the corner of mine, tongue peeking out to taste my lip.

My heart seizes and I freeze. "What?"

"'I want to love all of my life as much as I love this night,'" he quotes.

My heart dips and spills into my stomach.

"I realize how this sounds," he says immediately, "and I'm not insane. But you made me swear I wouldn't let you freak out." He shakes his head slowly. "And, because I promised, I can't give you an annulment. At least not until you start school in the fall. I promised, Mia."

I pull back and meet his eyes just before he leans back in, opening his mouth to mine. I sense that I should be more wary of this entire situation but his effect on me hasn't diminished even with the hangover and the alarming reality of what we've done.

He sucks at my lips, pulling them in turn into his mouth before he gives me his tongue, tasting of orange juice and water and grapes. His hands brace on my hips, and he bends lower, kissing me deeper, teasing me with a rumbling moan. "Let's go back upstairs," he says. "Let me feel you again."

"Mia!" Harlow's voice cuts down the hall through the

stale smell of cigarettes. "Holy shit, we've been looking for you all morning! I was starting to worry you might be in a gutter or something."

Lorelei and Harlow jog down the hall and Harlow stops in front of us, bending to brace her hands on her knees. "Okay, no running." She groans. "I think I'm going to barf."

We all wait, anxiously scanning the vicinity for a bucket, or a towel, or maybe just a quick exit. Finally, she stands, shaking her head. "False alarm."

Reality descends in a curtain of silence as both Lola and Harlow study us with uncertainty.

"You okay, Mia?" Lola asks.

Ansel's touch and his suggestion we should remain married, my headache, and my rebelling stomach all conspire to make me want to slide down onto the floor and curl up in a tiny ball of freak-out. I don't even care how gross the carpet is. "Nothing a little death won't solve."

"Can we steal her for a few?" Harlow asks Ansel, and her tone surprises me. Harlow doesn't ask before she takes, ever.

He nods, but before I can move away he runs his hand down my arm and touches the ring on my finger. He doesn't say a word; it's just that tiny touch that asks me not to leave this city without talking to him.

Lola guides me down the hall to the lobby, where there's a cluster of enormous chairs in a quiet corner. We each collapse into the plush suede, lost in our own miserable hangovers for several long beats.

"So," I say.

"So," they reply in unison.

"What the hell happened last night?" I ask. "How did no one say, 'Wow, we probably shouldn't all get married'?"

"Ugh," Harlow says. "I knew we should have been classier."

"I'm going to blame the seven hundred shots we had," Lola says.

"I'm going to blame Finn's impressive cock." Harlow takes a sip from a bottle of water as Lola and I groan. "No, I'm serious," Harlow says. "And son is into some stuff, let me tell you. He's a bossy little shit."

"Annulment," Lola reminds her. "You can still bang him when you're single."

Harlow rubs her face. "Right."

"What happened with Ansel?" Lola asks.

"Apparently a lot." Instinctively, I rub my finger over my bottom lip. "I'm not sure we actually slept. I'm disappointed I don't remember it all, but I'm pretty sure we did everything."

"Anal?" Harlow asks in a reverent whisper.

"No! *God*. Put ten dollars in the Whore Jar," I tell her. "You're such a troll."

"I bet the French guy could get it," Harlow says. "You look like you were pounded."

Memories rise like smoke in front of me, just tiny wisps in the air.

His shoulders moving over me, fists curled around the pillowcase beside my head.

The sharp snap of his teeth when I licked across the head of his cock.

My hand splayed across the giant mirror, feeling the heat of his breath on the back of my neck just before he pushed inside.

His voice whispering, *Laisse-toi aller, pour moi. Come for me.*

I press the heel of my hands to my eyes, trying to pull myself back into the present. "What happened with you and Oliver?" I ask Lola, redirecting.

She shrugs. "Honestly, by the time we were leaving the chapel, we both started to sober up. Harlow was in their suite making all kinds of noises. You and Ansel were in ours."

"Erp, sorry," I mumble.

"We just walked around the Strip the entire night, talking."

"Really?" Harlow asks, surprised. "But he's so hot. And he has that whole Aussie thing going on. I'd love to hear him say, 'Lick my cock.'"

"Five more in the Whore Jar," Lola says.

"How did you understand a word he said?" I ask, laughing.

"Yeah, he got worse when he was hammered," she admits, and then leans her head back against her enormous chair. "He's pretty great. It's weird, you guys. Did you know he's opening a comic book store? Out of the three of us, I'm the one who should be hitting that with the fist of God. I mean, he's hot and tall and ridiculously derpy, which you know is totally my kryptonite. But we were already coordinating the annulment while we waited for the limo to pick us up after the ceremony."

This all feels a little surreal. I was expecting a weekend of sunbathing, drinks, dancing, and best friend bonding. I was *not* expecting to have the best sex of my life and wake up married. I twist the ring on my finger and then look around, realizing I'm the only one actually wearing one.

Harlow notices it, too. "We're meeting the guys at one to head to the chapel for the *annulments.*" Her voice has weight, bite, as if she already knows my situation has the added layer of feelings in the mix.

"Okay," I say.

I catch Lola watching me. "That doesn't sound like 'okay,'" she says.

"What was Ansel saying to you in the hall?" Harlow asks. Her judgment is like another person sitting in the circle of chairs with us, glaring darkly at me with arms crossed over its chest. "He kissed you. He's not supposed to kiss you *today.* We're all supposed to be mildly horrified and then start constructing the funny details about that-one-time-we-all-got-married-in-Vegas that we'll share for the next thirty years. There's no sweetness or kissing, Mia. Only hangovers and regret."

"Um . . . ?" I say, scratching my temple. I know Harlow will put her foot down at the mention of feelings in a situation like this, but I have them. I like him.

I also like the way he looks at me, and having my mouth full of his. I want to remember how he sounds when he's fucking me hard, and whether he swears in French or English when he comes. I want to sit on the couches in the bar again and let *him* talk this time.

In a weird way, I think if we hadn't gotten married last night, we'd have a better chance of being able to explore this, just a little.

"Jesus, Mia," Harlow says under her breath. "I love you, but you're killing me here."

I ignore her pressure to reply aloud. I have no idea how Lola will react to my indecision. She's far more live-and-let-live than Harlow is and falls somewhere on the spectrum between Harlow and me in terms of comfort with casual sex. Because of this, and because none of us has ever had a spontaneous wedding to a man from another country—this really has to be funny someday—Lola is likely to be more measured in her responses, so I direct my answer to her.

"He says we could . . . stay married." There. That seems a decent way to try it on.

Silence reverberates back to me.

"I *knew* it," Harlow whispers.

Lola remains noticeably quiet.

"I wrote myself a letter before we did it," I explain, wanting to tread carefully. Of anyone in the world, these two women want only what is good for me. But I don't know whether it will hurt their feelings to learn how oddly safe I feel with Ansel.

"And?" Harlow prompts. "Mia, this is huge. You couldn't have told us this *first*?"

"I know, I know," I say, sinking back into my chair. "And I guess I told him, like, my entire life story." They both know the significance of this and so they don't comment, just wait for me to finish. "And I talked for what must have been hours. I didn't stutter, I didn't filter."

"You did talk for a really long time." Lola looks impressed.

Harlow's eyes narrow. "You're not seriously considering staying married," she says, "to a stranger you met last night in Vegas and who lives over five thousand miles away."

"Well, how can it not sound shady when you say it like that?"

"How would you like me to say it, Mia?" she shouts. "Have you completely lost your mind?"

Have I? Yes, absolutely. "I think I just need more time," I tell her instead.

Harlow stands abruptly, looking around as if there is someone else in the lobby who can help convince her best friend that she's lost the plot. Across from me, Lola simply studies my face, eyes narrowed. "Are you sure about this?" she asks.

I cough out a laugh. "I'm not sure about any of it."

"But you know you don't want to annul it right now?"

"He says he won't annul it today anyway, that he promised me he wouldn't."

Her eyebrows disappear beneath her bangs and she leans back into her chair, surprised. "He *promised* you?"

"That's what he said. He said I made him swear."

"This is the most ridicul—" Harlow starts, but Lola interrupts her.

"Well, the guy just won some points with me, then." She

blinks away, and reaches to put a calming hand on Harlow's forearm. "Let's go, sweets. Mia, we'll be back in a little bit to pack up and head home, okay?"

"Are you kidding me? We—" Harlow starts, but Lola levels her with a look. "Fine."

In the distance and through a set of glass doors, I see Oliver and Finn, waiting for them near the taxi stand. Ansel is nowhere in sight.

"Okay, good luck getting unmarried," I say with a little smile.

"You're lucky I love you," Harlow calls over her shoulder, chestnut hair flying around her as Lola drags her away. "Otherwise I would murder you."

THE LOBBY SEEMS too quiet in their wake, and I look around, wondering if Ansel is watching from some dark corner, seeing that I haven't gone along. But he isn't in the lobby. I have no idea where he is. He's the only reason I stayed back. Even if I had his number, I don't have my phone. Even if I had my phone, I have no idea where I left my charger. Drunk me definitely needs to keep better track of things.

So I do the only thing I can think of: I head upstairs to the hotel room, to shower again and pack, to try to make some sense out of this mess.

One step inside and flashes of the night before seem to invade the room. I close my eyes to dig deeper, hungry for more details.

His hands on my ass, my breasts, my hips. The thick drag of him along my inner thigh. His mouth fastened to my neck, sucking a bruise into the skin.

My thoughts are interrupted by a quiet knock on the door.

Of course it's him, looking freshly showered and just as conflicted as I feel. He moves past me, into the room, and sits at the edge of the bed.

He rests his elbows on his knees and looks up at me through hair that has fallen into his eyes. Even partly filtered, they're so expressive I feel gooseflesh break out along my arms.

Without preamble or warm-up, he says, "I think you should come to France for the summer."

There are a thousand things I can say to address the absurdity of what he's offering. For one, I don't know him. Also, I don't speak French. Tickets are ungodly expensive, and where would I live? What would I do all summer living with a stranger in France?

"I'm moving to Boston in a few weeks."

But he's already shaking his head. "You don't need to move until the beginning of August."

I feel my brows inch up. Apparently I told him *every single detail* of my life. I'm not sure whether I should feel impressed that he remembers it all, or guilty that I made him sit through so much. I tilt my head, waiting. Most girls would say something here. A gorgeous man is offering something pretty amazing, and I'm just waiting to see what else he wants to say.

Licking his lips, he seems comfortable with the knowledge that he hasn't given me something I need to respond to yet. "Just hear me out. You could stay at my flat. I have a good job, I can afford to feed and shelter you for a summer. I work really long hours, it's true. But you could just . . ." He looks away, down at the floor. "You could enjoy the city. Paris is the most beautiful city, *Cerise*. There are endless things to do. You've had a really hard few years and maybe would be happy just having a mellow summer in France." Looking back up at me, he adds quietly, "With me."

I move over to the bed and sit down, leaving plenty of distance between us. Housekeeping has already changed the linens, straightened the chaos we created; it makes it easier to pretend last night was someone else's life.

"We don't really know each other, it's true," he concedes. "But I see your indecision about Boston. You'll move there to get away from your dad. You'll move there to keep marching forward. Maybe you need to just hit pause, and *breathe*. Have you done that even once in the four years since your accident?"

I want him to keep speaking because I've decided that even if I don't know him well enough to be in love with him, I love his voice. I love the rich mahogany timbre, the curling vowels and seductive consonants. His voice dances. Nothing could ever sound rough or sharp in that voice.

But as soon as I have the thought, I know it's wrong. I remember how he sounded when he was perfectly demanding last night:

Put your hands on the wall.

I can't wait much longer for you to get there, Cerise.

Show me how much you love to feel me on your tongue.

I don't have an answer for his offer, so I don't give one. I only crawl up to the pillow and lie on my back, exhausted. He joins me, lying shoulder to shoulder until I curl into him, sliding my hands up his chest and into his hair. The shape of him triggers a muscle memory: how far I have to reach to wrap my arms around him, how he feels against my palms. I press my nose into the rope of muscle between his neck and shoulder, breathe in the clean smell of him: hotel soap and the hint of ocean that pushes through.

Ansel rolls to face me, kissing my neck, my jaw, my lips just once but he lingers, eyes open. His hands slide down my back, over the curve of my ass to my thigh and lower, to the back of my knee, where he pulls it over his hip, fitting me to him. Between my legs, I can feel how much I want him. I can feel him, too, lengthening and pressing. But instead of taking it anywhere, we fall asleep.

When I wake up, there's a piece of paper on the empty pillow. He's left his number and his promise to be there the moment I need him, but he's gone.

I WONDER HOW many thousands of drives from Vegas to California have been like this: hot wind whipping through a beater car, hungover women, regret hanging in the air like a single flat chord played the entire drive.

"I need something greasy to eat," Harlow groans, and Lola pulls off the freeway and into a Denny's parking lot.

Over grilled cheese and fries, Harlow says, "I don't get why you didn't just start the annulment process while we were there." She pokes a fry into ketchup and then drops it on her plate, looking queasy. "Now you're going to have to go back there, or go through this complicated process out of state. Tell me every detail so I can stop wanting to slap you."

Objectively Ansel is amazing, and the sex was clearly ridiculous, but she knows I'm not such a swooner that good sex is enough for me to make such a rash decision. So it comes down to the letter, really. I never kept a diary. I barely write letters to Harlow when she's overseas visiting her father on set. But I read that other, post-accident letter so many times the paper became as delicate as a dried petal, the ink nearly invisible. Letter writing for me is seen as this weird, sacred occurrence, and even though I'm not sure it's the right idea, I'm giving it the weight I think I intended when I wrote it.

"What are you going to do?" Lola asks when I've finished telling them every sordid little detail I can remember about the night.

I shrug. "Spend from now until September trying to understand why I wanted to marry this person. Then probably get an annulment."

Chapter FIVE

LOLA DROPS ME at home. I find my little brothers in the family room playing Xbox, and Dad hands me a glass of wine as soon as I step out onto the veranda.

"To our brilliant daughter," he says, holding his own glass aloft. He smiles indulgently at me before pulling Mom close to his side, and the sunset behind them creates a beautifully backlit silhouette I'm sure he would be thrilled to see in a framed photograph. "I trust that your last wild weekend was perfect, and, as your father, I don't want to hear a single thing about it." He smiles at this little joke, and I would probably find it funny were our history not so perilous. "Here's to hoping your future from here on out is nothing but focus and success."

I clink my glass to his halfheartedly and watch his face as he looks me over. I've showered twice but still look like death warmed over in my black T-shirt and torn jeans. His eyes move across my mouth, down to my neck, where I've tried to cover the bite marks and red splotches with a gray jersey scarf. Dad's smile turns quickly into a look of disgust, but he doesn't seem to have noticed my wedding ring. Carefully, I slide my left hand into my pocket to keep it that way.

He places his glass on the outdoor bar and steps away from Mom. "Women who are successful in business are *ladies*," he says through clenched teeth, and I feel an odd trickle of satisfaction, knowing how much he's enjoying this moment. I've been nothing but responsible and ambitious over the last four years, making it nearly impossible for him to be constantly critical. But he's in his element now; my father is much more comfortable delivering insults than praise.

"We went to Vegas to celebrate graduation, Dad. We didn't become hookers." *No, Mia, you just got married to a stranger.*

"You have a lot of growing up to do before you deserve your admission to BU. As much as I disliked the idea of you being a dancer for the rest of your life, at least I admired your ambition. Now, as soon as you graduate from college, you come home looking like you've been . . ." He shakes his head. "I don't even know what you've been doing. No man will ever want to work for a tramp who comes to work with bruised lips and hickeys, smelling like days-old booze. Clean up your act, Mia."

Mom gasps in a shocked breath, and looks up at him as if she'll object to this absurd tirade. But her energy dissipates as he meets her eyes in challenge. He storms back inside, his mimosa forgotten. Mom stays behind, saying only, "Oh, sweetheart."

"Don't, Mom. I'm fine."

I don't want her to have to take my side. I'm leaving soon, and life is so much easier for her when she's squarely

Team David. She throws me a conflicted glance before she follows Dad back into the house.

The sliding glass door closes too hard, and I can still hear my dad. *Will she ever learn? She'll throw this opportunity away over my dead body.*

I look out over my mom's perfect yard—immaculate lawn, lush flower beds, pristine white fence—and feel like an unsightly weed in the middle of it. I've always felt just a little out of place here. I feel like a complete outsider now.

THE DISCOVERY OUTPOST at the San Diego Zoo is never the biggest draw for the crowds. But behind the Reptile House and past the Wegeforth Bowl there's a set of exhibits that remain virtually silent even when the zoo is overrun with tourists. It's always been my favorite metaphor—find the quiet in the chaos—and the place I do my best thinking.

Early Tuesday afternoon, I slip past tourists and families with green plastic zoo-issued strollers at the zoo entrance and turn left past the flamingo exhibit, heading to my secret spot. I need to think about what I'll pack for Boston, and whether I can organize everything so I can move next week instead of three weeks from now.

I need to think about what kind of job I'd like to get: Waitress. Bakery. Retail. Some sort of business assistant. Maybe a nightclub dancer, just to birdflip my father from across the country. My mind pushes forcibly away from the immediate thought of working as a dance instructor. I turn down the bend and head toward my favorite bench, sitting down and exhaling a long, heavy breath.

I most definitely do not *need* to think about how at any point today, Ansel could be flying back to Paris.

"You're right," a deep, familiar voice says from just a little farther down the path. "This part of the zoo is deserted."

I don't believe my ears. I open my eyes to see Ansel walking up the paved walkway. He lowers himself on the bench and stretches his arm across the back, letting it rest behind me. The fingers of his right hand spread across my shoulder.

I'm speechless.

It's a familiar sensation but for completely unfamiliar reasons. I'm speechless from shock, rather than restraint.

"H-h-" I start, squeezing my eyes shut.

He waits, patiently, fingertips sliding warm and smooth over my skin.

"What are you doing here? How did you know—"

"You told me you come here to think. You said you love this part of the zoo, and I'll admit," he says, looking around, "I don't understand it at all. It's mostly concrete and sleeping lizards. But I got here maybe an hour ago?" He tilts his head, smiling warmly as if he's not a terrifying stalker. "And I'm here because I can't be away from you, Mia. You're my wife."

My eyes must go wide in horror because he bursts out laughing, retrieving his arm so he can bend over and rest his elbows on his thighs. "I'm sorry. That wasn't very nice. I'm in San Diego because I'm flying out of the airport here tonight. Oliver is meeting with the architect remodeling his store, and it's the last time we'll see each other for a while. We drove down together last night, and today I came here, hoping it was true that you come here to think all the time. And maybe to do a little thinking myself," he adds, looking over at me and smiling sweetly. "I promise I was kidding."

"You still came here looking for me," I remind him, inching away slightly.

He digs into his back pocket and hands me a sheet of folded paper. I open it and realize it's a copy of our marriage license. "You didn't have a copy. You didn't even know how to spell my last name, I don't think. I would have called you, but even though I was smart enough to leave you my number, I realized I don't have yours."

I feel like a complete asshole. He's really gone out of his way to make sure I have this, and I couldn't even text him my number.

"Thanks," I say quietly.

"Of course."

I move closer again, putting my hand on his arm, and as the adrenaline in my blood slows to a steady hum, I realize how ridiculously giddy I am to see him. "So, wait, Oliver is opening a store in San Diego?" I absolutely don't think Lola knew his store was going to be in our *hometown*.

He nods as he lifts my hand, kisses it. "He's moving here in a few weeks. Anyway, I just wanted to make sure you had that before you moved." He nods to the paper I have clenched in my hand, and then stands. "I didn't want to mail it to your house and have your dad open it." I swallow heavily, stunned at how thoughtful he's been. "I'm going to head back to the hotel and relax for a bit. I have a long flight ahead of me."

"What time do you fly out?"

He blinks away, brows pulled together as he thinks. "Around eleven?"

He pushes his hands into his pockets before I can see if he's still wearing his ring. He looks at my hands and sees that I am. "My email is just my first and last name together at XMail," he tells me. "We can coordinate everything in September."

"Okay," I say, nodding.

He leans down, kisses the top of my head, and then whispers, "I'll be at the Hilton Bayfront until around eight. I bought an open, round-trip ticket for you to Paris." Standing up, he shrugs and lets a huge smile spread across his face as my jaw hits the sidewalk. "What can I say, I'm an optimist. Or insane. Depends on who you ask."

He may be insane, but that ass looks mighty fine as he walks away.

Sitting in my lizard and concrete shelter for a while, I contemplate going home and immediately discard the thought. I contemplate going to Lola's and hanging out with her and Greg for dinner, but I'm sure she's giving her dad the full rundown of our insanity over the weekend. No doubt he's laughing his ass off, and I don't really want to be the killjoy who got sentimental. I contemplate heading over to Harlow's place in La Jolla, but even though some brainless beach time sounds amazing, the genuine love and intense focus of the entire Vega clan would provide too stark a contrast to my own family's weirdness.

So I drive downtown.

ANSEL PULLS THE door open and breaks into an enormous smile, which slowly fades as he sees I've come empty-handed, no suitcase. Nothing but my tiny cross-body bag slung over my chest.

"I can't come to France with you," I start, looking up at him with wide eyes. My pulse feels like a heavy drum in my throat. "But I didn't want to go home, either."

He steps to the side to let me in and I drop my bag on the floor and turn to watch him. There's really only one reason I'm here, in this hotel room, and I think we both know it. It's easy to pretend to be the lover in a movie, coming to the hotel for one last night together. I don't have to work to be brave when it's safe like this: he's leaving. It becomes almost like a game. A play. A role.

I don't know which Mia is taking over my body, but I'm shutting out everything but how it feels to be so close to this boy. I only have to take one step closer and he meets me halfway, sliding both hands into my hair and covering my mouth with his. Ocean and green and still the lingering scent of me on his clothes.

His taste, *oh*. I want to feel so full of him that every other thought dissolves under the heat of it. I want his mouth everywhere, sucking at me like he does. I love how he loves my lips, how—after only one night together—his hands already know my skin.

He walks me back to the bed, lips and tongue and teeth all over my cheeks and mouth and jaw. I fall backward when my knees hit the bed.

He pulls at the hem of my dress and unsheathes me in a single determined tug, then reaches behind me, ridding me of my bra with a tiny slip of his fingers. He makes me feel like I'm something to reveal, something in which to revel. I'm the reward at the end of his magic trick, exposed beneath the velvet cape. His eyes rake across my skin and I can see his own impatience: shirt flung across the room, fingers tugging at his belt, tongue flicking at the air, searching for the taste of me.

Ansel gives up on undressing, instead kneeling on the floor between my thighs, spreading me, kissing me through the fabric of my underwear. He nibbles and tugs, sucking and licking impatiently before he slides my last remaining article of clothing down my legs.

I gasp when he leans forward, covering my most sensitive skin in a long, slow lick. His breath feels like tiny bursts of fire where he kisses my clit, my pubic bone, my hip. I push up, leaning back on my hands to watch him.

"Tell me what you need," he says, his voice raspy against my hip.

With this, I remember weakly that he made me come with his hands and body, but not his mouth. I can sense the need to conquer this, and wonder how long he tried before I grew impatient, pulling him up and into me.

The truth is I'm not sure what I need. Oral sex has always been a stop on the way to somewhere else. A way to get me wet, to make the circuit of my body. Never something done until I shook and sweated and swore.

"S-suck," I say, guessing.

He opens his mouth, sucking perfectly for a breath of time and then too much. "Not so hard." I close my eyes, finding the bravery to tell him, "Like you suck on my lip."

It's exactly the direction he needed and I fall back against the mattress without thinking, my legs spreading wider, and with this he grows wild. Palms firmly planted on my inner thighs to keep my legs open, sounds pressed into me, vibrating through me.

One of his hands leaves me and I can feel him moving, can sense the shifting of his arm. Propping myself on an elbow I look down and realize he's touching himself, eyes on me, fevered.

"Let me," I tell him. "I want to taste you, too."

I don't know where these words are coming from; I'm not myself right now. Maybe I'm never myself with him. He nods but doesn't stop moving his hand. I love it. I love that it's not weird or taboo. He's lost in me, he's hard, he's giving in to the need for his own pleasure while he gives me mine.

As he kisses and sucks and licks with such uninhibited hunger, I'm afraid I won't be able to come and his enthusiasm and effort will be wasted. But then I feel the tight pull, the edge of something that grows bigger and bigger with every breath across my skin. I thread my hands in his hair, rock up into him.

"Oh, God."

He groans, mouth eager, eyes on me wide and thrilled.

I relish the tight swell of my tendons, my muscles, the blood rushing so heated and urgent in my veins. I can feel it build, spread out, and race through my limbs, exploding between my legs. I'm gasping, hoarse and senseless, offering no words, just sharp sounds. The echo of my orgasm rings around us as I fall back onto the pillow.

I feel drugged, and with effort I push him away from where his lips press to my thigh so I can sit up. He stumbles to his feet, pants undone and slung low over his hips. I look up at him, and from the light coming out of the bathroom I can see how wet his mouth is, from me—as if he was hunting, as if I was caught and devoured.

He wipes a forearm across his entire face, and steps closer to the bed just as I lean forward and take him in my mouth.

He cries out, desperate. "Already close."

It's a warning. I can feel it in the jutting thrusts of his hips, the tense swelling of the head of his cock, the way he grips my head like he wants to pull back, make this last longer, but can't. He fucks my mouth, seeming to know already that it's okay, and after only six sharp jabs across my tongue and teeth and lips, he's holding steady, deep inside and coming with a low, rasping groan.

I pull my mouth away from him and he runs a shaking finger across my lip as I swallow.

"So good," he exhales.

I fall back on the pillow and feel like my muscles have been completely silenced after the frenzy of my entry into the room. I'm leaden and numb, and other than the heavy echo of pleasure between my legs, the only thing I can feel is my smile.

The room has turned pink in the late afternoon sun pouring through the window, and Ansel hovers over me on rigid arms, breathing heavily. I feel the rake of his gaze move across my skin, come to settle on my breasts, and he smiles at the same time I feel my nipples grow tight.

"I left marks all over you the other night." He bends, blowing air across one peak. "I'm sorry."

I laugh and tug his hair playfully. "You don't sound sorry."

He grins up at me, and when he pulls back to admire his handiwork again, I give in to the unfamiliar instinct to cross my arms over my chest. In dance, my small frame was a benefit; my small breasts were an ideal nonhindrance. But in the bare skin world of sex, I can't imagine my 32Bs cut it.

"What are you doing?" he asks, tugging on my forearm as he kicks off his pants. "It's too late to be shy with me now."

"I feel tiny."

He laughs. "You are tiny, *Cerise*. But I like every tiny inch of you. I haven't seen your skin in hours." Bending, he circles my nipple with his tongue. "You have sensitive breasts, I discovered."

I suspect I have sensitive *everything* when he's the one touching me.

His palm spreads across one breast while he sucks at the other and his tongue begins to move in small, flat, pressing circles. It revives the delicious throb between my legs.

I think he knows it, too, because the hand cupping my breast slides down over my ribs, across my stomach, down my navel, and between my legs, but he never stops circling with his tongue.

And then his fingers are there, two of them pressed flat, and he's making the same circles in the same rhythm, and it's as if a tight band connects between where his tongue and fingers are, pulling tighter and tighter, warmer and warmer. I'm bowing up off the bed and gripping his head, begging him in a hoarse voice to *please please please*.

The same rhythm, both places, and I'm worried I'll fall apart, melt into the bed or simply dissolve into nothing when he hums over my nipple, his fingers pressing harder, and then he lets up only long enough to ask me, "Won't you let me hear you one more time?"

I don't know if I could survive it. I can't survive without it.

With him, my sounds are hoarse and free, I don't seem to hold back words of pleasure, and it's completely without thought. I offer up everything and my sounds spur him on until he's sucking frantically and I'm arching into his hand crying out—

Coming

Coming

Three fingers plunge into me, the heel of his hand taking over outside. It's pleasure so intense it hurts. Or maybe it's knowing how easy this is and how good, and that I have to either give him up or do something crazy to keep him. My orgasm lasts so long I run through both of these scenarios multiple times during the most intense pleasure of it. It lasts long enough for him to unlatch his lips from my breast and move to my face and kiss me, sucking all of my sounds into his mouth. It lasts long enough for him to tell me I'm the most beautiful thing he's ever seen.

My body quiets and his kisses slow until it's just the small slide of his lips over mine. I taste like him and he tastes like me.

Ansel leans over the side of the bed to pull a condom from the pocket of his jeans. "Are you too sore?" he asks, holding it up in question.

I'm sore, but I don't think I could ever be too worn-out to feel him. I need to remember exactly what it's like. The scattered shrapnel of my memory won't suffice if I have to let him go tonight. I don't answer aloud, but I pull him over me, bending my knees at his sides.

He kneels, brows drawn as he rolls the condom down his length. I want to pull out my phone, take pictures of his body and his serious, focused expression. I need the pictures so I can say, *See, Mia? You were right about his skin. It's as smooth and perfect as you remember.* I want to somehow capture the way his hands are shaking with urgency.

When he's done he places a hand by my head and uses

the other to guide himself to me. The moment I can feel the heavy press of him, it occurs to me that I've never felt so impatient in my life. My body wants to devour his.

"Come back with me," he says, moving barely in, and back out again. A torture. "Please, Mia. Just for the summer."

I shake my head no, unable to find words, and he groans in frustration and pleasure as he slowly pushes inside. I lose my breath, lose my ability to breathe or even care that I need to, and pull my legs up high, wanting him deeper, wanting to feel him entering me forever. He's heavy, thick, so hard that when his hips meet my thighs I hover at the edge of discomfort. He's the one making me lose my breath, making me feel like there's not enough room in my body for him and air at the same time, but nothing has ever felt so good.

I'd tell him I changed my mind, I'll come with him, if I could find words, but with his arms braced beside my head he starts to move and it's unlike anything else. It's unlike *everything* else. The slow, solid drag of him inside me builds an ache so good it's enough to make me feel a little unhinged at the thought that the feeling will end at some point.

He's giving me a gentle warm-up, his eyes on mine as he pulls slowly out, even more slowly pushes back in, occasionally ducking down to slide his mouth over mine. But when I scrape my tongue over his teeth, and he jerks forward, sharp and unexpected, I hear my own tight gasp, and it unleashes something in him. He starts to move, hard and smooth over me, perfect curling thrusts of his hips.

I don't really know how many times we had sex the other night, but he must have figured out what I need, and he seems to love to watch himself giving it to me. He pushes up on his hands, kneeling between my spread legs, and already I know that when I come it will be unlike anything I've felt before. I can hear his grunting breaths and my own sharp exhales. I can hear the slap of the front of his thighs against the inside of mine and the slick, smooth strokes of him moving in and out of me.

I won't need his fingers or mine or a toy. We fit. His skin slides across my clit again and again and again.

Lola was right when she teased about how it would be with Ansel and me: it *is* missionary, and there's eye contact, but it isn't precious or soft-focus the way she meant. I can't imagine not looking at him. It would be like trying to have sex without touching.

The pleasure climbs up my legs like a vine, building into a flush I can feel spreading across my cheeks, across my chest. I'm terrified I'll lose this sensation, that I'm chasing something that doesn't really exist, but he's moving faster, and harder, so hard he has to hold my hips with his hands so he doesn't push me off the bed. His eyes rake over my gasping lips and my breasts that bounce with his thrusts. The way he fucks me makes my slight body feel voluptuous for the first time in my life.

I open my mouth to tell him I'm falling and nothing comes out but a cry for *more* and *yes* and *this* and *yes* and *yes*. Sweat drops from his forehead onto my breast and rolls onto my neck. He's working so hard, holding so much back, *wait-ing waiting waiting* for me. I love the restraint and hunger and determination in his beautiful face and I'm at the edge, right there.

Warmth rushes throughout my body a split second before I fall.

He sees it happen. He watches, mouth parting in relief, eyes blazing in victory. My orgasm crashes over me so hard, so consuming, I'm not myself anymore. I'm the savage pulling him down onto me, rutting up into him and gripping his ass to pull him in deeper. I'm pure desperation beneath him, begging, biting his shoulder, spreading my legs as wide as they'll go.

The wildness unhinges him. I can hear the sheets pop away from the mattress and feel them bunch behind me as he grips them for leverage, moving hard enough that the head-board cracks into the wall.

"Oh," he groans, rhythm growing punishing. He buries his face in my neck, groaning, "Here. Here. Here."

And then he opens his mouth on my neck, sucking and pressing, shoulders shaking over me as he comes. I slide my hands over his back, relishing the bunching definition of his tense posture, the curve to his spine as he stays as deep as he can. I shift beneath him to feel his skin on mine, mixing my sweat with his.

Ansel pushes up to his elbows and hovers over me, still pulsing inside as he presses his palms to my forehead and slides them over my hair.

"It's too good," he says against my lips. "It's so good, *Cerise*."

And then he reaches between us to grip the condom, pulling out and slipping it off. He drops it blindly in the vicinity of the bedside table and collapses beside me on the mattress, dragging his left hand down his face, across his sweaty chest, where it comes to rest over his heart. I'm unable to look away from the gold band on his ring finger. His stomach tightens with each jagged inhale, jerks with each forceful exhale.

"Please, Mia."

I have one last refusal in me, and I squeak it out: "I can't."

He closes his eyes and my heart splinters, imagining not seeing him again.

"If we hadn't been drunk and crazy and ended up married . . . would you have come with me to France?" he asks. "Just for the adventure of it?"

"I don't know." But the answer is, I might have. I don't need to move to Boston yet; I plan to—soon—because I had to leave my campus apartment but don't want to move back in with my parents for the entire summer. A summer in Paris after college is what a woman my age *should* do. With Ansel— only as a lover, maybe even just as a roommate—it would be a wild adventure. It wouldn't carry the same weight of moving in with him for the summer, as his *wife*.

He smiles, a little sadly, and kisses me.

"Say something to me in French." I've heard him say a

hundred things while he's lost in pleasure, but this is the first time I've requested it, and I don't know why I do it. It seems dangerous, with his mouth, his voice, his accent like warm chocolate.

"Do you speak any French?"

"Besides, '*Cerise*'?"

His eyes fall to my lips and he smiles. "Besides that."

"*Fromage. Château. Croissant.*"

He repeats "croissant" in a small laughing voice, and when he says it, it sounds like a completely different word. I wouldn't know how to spell the word he just said, but it makes me want to pull him on top of me again.

"Well, in that case I can tell you, *Je n'ai plus désiré une femme comme je te désire depuis longtemps. Ça n'est peut-être même jamais arrivé.*" He pulls back, studies my reaction as if I'd be able to decode a word of it. "*Est-ce totalement fou? Je m'en fiche.*"

My brain can't magically translate the words, but my body seems to know he's said something wildly intimate.

"Can I ask you something?"

He nods. "Of course."

"Why won't you just annul it?"

He twists his mouth to the side, amusement filling his eyes. "Because you wrote it into our wedding vows. We both vowed to stay married until the fall."

It's several long seconds before I get over the shock of that. I sure was a bossy little thing. "But it's not a real marriage," I whisper, and pretend I don't see it when he winces a little. "What does that vow mean anyway if we plan to break all the others about 'until death do us part'?"

He rolls over and sits up at the edge of his bed, his back to me. He curls over, pressing his hands onto his forehead. "I don't know. I try not to break promises, I suppose. This is all very weird for me; please don't assume I know what I'm doing just because I'm holding firm on this one point."

I sit up, crawl over to him, and kiss his shoulder. "It seems I fake-married a really nice guy."

He laughs, but then stands, moving away from me again. I can sense he needs distance and it pushes a small ache between two of my ribs.

This is it. This is when I should go.

He pulls on his underwear and leans against the closet door, watching me as I get dressed. I pull my panties up my legs, and they're still wet from me, from his mouth, too, though the wetness feels cold now. Changing my mind, I drop them on the floor and put on my bra and my jersey dress and step into my flip-flops.

Ansel wordlessly hands me his phone and I text myself so he has my number. When I hand it back, we stand, looking at anything but each other for a few painful beats.

I reach for my bag, pulling out gum, but he quickly moves to me, sliding his hands up my neck to cup my face. "Don't." He leans close, sucking on my mouth the way he seems to like so much. "You taste like me. I taste like you." He bends, licking my tongue, my lips, my teeth. "I like this so much. Let it stay, just for a bit."

His mouth moves lower, down my neck, nibbling at my collarbone, and to where my nipples press up from beneath my dress. He sucks and licks, pulling them into his mouth until the fabric is soaked. It's black, so no one but us will know, but I'll feel the cool press of his kiss even after I walk out of the room.

I want to pull us back to the bed.

But he stands, studying my face for a beat. "Be good, *Cerise*."

It occurs to me only now that we're married, and I would be cheating on my husband if I slept with someone else this summer. But the idea of anyone else getting this man makes something simmer in my belly. I don't like the thought at all, and I wonder if that's the same fire I see in his expression.

"You, too," I tell him.

Chapter SIX

I'M SURE I know what the phrase "weak in the knees" means now because I'm dreading having to get out of my car and use my legs. I've been with three people other than Ansel, but even with Luke, sex was never like that. Sex where it's so wide open and honest that I know even after it's over—and the heat has dissipated and Ansel isn't even here beside me anymore—that I would have let him do anything.

It makes me wish I remembered our night in Vegas better. We had hours together then, rather than the paltry cupful of minutes tonight. Because somehow I know it was more honest and free and doubtless than even *this* was.

The heavy thunk of my car door slamming echoes down our quiet, suburban street. My house looks dark, but it's too early for them to all be in bed. With the warm summer weather it's most likely that my family is out on the back patio, having a late dinner.

But once I'm inside, I hear nothing but silence. The house is dark everywhere: in the living room, family room, kitchen. The patio is quiet, every room upstairs deserted. My footsteps slap quietly on the Spanish tile in the bathroom but fall silent as I move along the plush hallway carpet. For some reason I walk into every single room . . . finding no one. In the years since I started college—before I moved my things back into my old bedroom only days ago—I haven't once been alone in this house, and the realization hits me like a physical shove. Someone is always here when I am: my mother, my father, one of my brothers. How *strange* that is. Yet now I've been given some quiet. It feels like a reprieve. And with this freedom, a current of electricity curls through me.

I could leave without having to confront my father.

I could leave without having to explain anything.

In an impulsive, hot flash, I'm certain this is what I want. I sprint to my room, find my passport, tear off my dress, and pull on clean clothes before hauling the biggest suitcase from the hall closet. I shove everything I can find from my dresser into it, and then practically clear my bathroom counter with a sweep of my arm into my toiletries case. The heavy bag thuds down the stairs behind me, falls over in the hallway as I begin to scribble a note for my family. The lies tumble out, and I struggle to keep from trying to say too much, sounding too manic.

> I have an opportunity to go to France for a few weeks! A free ticket, too. I'll be with a friend of Harlow's Dad. She owns a small business. I'll tell you about it later but I'm okay. I'll call.
>
>   Love you,
>   Mia

I don't ever lie to my family—or anyone for that matter—
but right now, I don't care. Now that the idea is in my head,
the idea of not going to France pushes me into a full-on panic
because not going to France means staying here for a few
weeks. It means living under the dark cloud of my father's
controlling bullshit. And then it means moving to Boston and
starting a life I'm not sure I want.

It means the possibility of never seeing Ansel again.

I look at the clock: I only have forty-five minutes until the
plane leaves.

Lugging my bag to my car, I hurl it in the trunk and run
to the driver's side, texting Harlow: Whatever my dad asks
you about France, just say yes.

Only three blocks away from my house I can hear my
phone buzz on the passenger seat, no doubt with her reply—
Harlow rarely puts her phone down—but I can't look now. I
know what I'll see anyway, and I'm not sure when my brain
will quiet down enough for me to answer her WHAT??

Her, WHAT THE FUCK ARE YOU DOING??

Her, CALL ME RIGHT THE FUCK NOW, MIA HOLLAND!!

So instead, I park—I'm being optimistic, and pull into
the long-term parking lot. I drag my bag into the terminal. I
check in, silently urging the woman at the ticketing counter
to move faster.

"You're cutting it very close," she tells me with a disap-
proving frown. "Gate forty-four."

Nodding, I tap a nervous hand on the counter and
sprint away once she's handed me my ticket, folded neatly in

a paper sleeve. Security is dead at night on a Tuesday, but once I'm through, the long hallway to the gate at the end looms ahead of me. I'm running too fast to be worried about Ansel's reaction, but the adrenaline isn't enough to drown out the protesting of my permanently weak femur as I sprint.

At the gate, our flight is already boarding, and I have a panicked moment thinking maybe he's already on the plane when I can't pick him out of the mass of heads lined up to head down the jetway. I search wildly, self-consciously, and it's a horrible, anxious feeling now that I'm here: telling him I changed my mind and want to come to France and

live with him

rely on him

be with him

requires a type of bravery I'm simply not sure I have outside of a hotel room where it's all a temporary game, or in a bar where liquor let me find the perfect role to play all night. It's possible I mentally calculate the danger of being relatively drunk for the entirety of the next few weeks.

A warm hand curls around my shoulder and I turn, finding myself staring up at Ansel's wide, confused green eyes. His mouth opens and closes a few times before he shakes his head as if to clear it.

"Did they let you come down here to say goodbye?" he asks, seeming to try out the words. But then he looks closer: I've changed into white jeans, a blue tank top under a green hoodie. I have a carry-on slung over my shoulder, I'm out of breath and wearing what I can only imagine is a look of sheer panic on my face.

"I changed my mind." I hitch my bag higher on my shoulder and watch his reaction: his smile comes a little too slowly to immediately put me at ease.

But at least he *does* smile, and it seems genuine. Then he confuses me even more, saying, "I guess I can't stretch out and sleep on your seat now."

I have no idea what to say to that, so I just smile awkwardly and look down at my feet. The gate attendant calls out another section of the plane to board and the microphone squawks sharply, making us both jump.

And then, it seems like the entire world falls completely silent.

"Shit," I whisper, looking back down the way I came. It's too bright, too loud, too far away from Vegas or even the enclosed privacy of his San Diego hotel room. *What the hell am I doing?* "I don't have to come. I didn't—"

He shushes me, taking a step closer and bending to kiss my cheek. "I'm sorry," he says carefully, moving from one cheek to the other. "I'm all of a sudden very nervous. That wasn't funny. I'm so glad you're here."

With a heavy exhale, I turn when he presses his hand to my lower back, but it's as if our heated bubble has been punctured and we've stepped offstage and into the even more glaring lights of reality. It presses down on me, suffocating. My feet feel like they're made of cement as I hand my ticket to the gate attendant, forcing a nervous smile before stepping onto the jetway.

What we know is dimly lit bars, playful banter, the clean, crisp sheets of hotel rooms. What we know is the unrequited possibility, the temptation of the idea. The make-believe. The adventure.

But when you choose the adventure, it becomes real life.

The jetway is filled with a strange buzzing sound I know will stay in my head for hours. Ansel walks behind me, and I wonder if my jeans are too tight, my hair too messy. I can feel him watching me, maybe checking me out now that I'll be invading *his* real life. Maybe reconsidering. The truth is, there's nothing romantic about boarding a plane, flying for fifteen hours with a virtual stranger. It's the *idea* that's exciting. There's nothing escapist or glossy about overlit airports or cramped airplanes.

We stow our bags, take our seats. I'm in the middle, he's in the aisle, and there's an older man reading a paper next to the window whose elbows press into my space, sharp but oblivious.

Ansel adjusts his seat belt and then adjusts it again before reaching above us for the vent. He aims it at himself, then at me, then back at himself before turning it down. He turns on the light, and his hands drop back into his lap, restless. Finally, he closes his eyes and I count as he takes ten deep breaths.

Oh, shit. He's a nervous flyer.

I am the worst possible person in this moment because I don't speak freely, not even in moments like this when some easy reassurance is required. I feel frantic inside, and my reaction to "frantic" is to go completely still. I'm the mouse in the field and it feels like every unknown situation in my life is an eagle flying overhead. It's suddenly comical that I've chosen to do this.

Announcements are made, disasters prepared for, and the plane is off, climbing heavily through the night sky. I take Ansel's hand—it's the least I can do—and he grips it tightly.

God, I want to make this better.

About five minutes later, his hand goes slack, and then slides dully away from mine, heavy with sleep. Maybe if I'd given him more notice—or if I'd let him talk more the first night we met—he would have been able to tell me how much he hates to fly. Maybe then he would have been able to tell me he took something to help him sleep.

The cabin lights dim and both men beside me are dead asleep, but my body seems to be unable to relax. It's not a normal feeling, being wound up like this. It's a bit like having a fever, being restless in my own skin, unable to find a comfortable position.

I pull out the book I blindly shoved into my carry-on; unfortunately, it's the memoir of a famous female CEO—a graduation gift from my father. The cover alone—a photo of her standing in a sensible suit against a stark blue background—does nothing to settle my sour stomach. Instead I read every word of the airplane safety insert and *SkyMall* in the seat pocket in front of me, and then steal the airline magazine from Ansel's pocket and flip through it.

I still feel like hell.

Pulling my legs up, I press my forehead to my knees, turn my air up as far as it will go. I try to breathe deeply, but nothing seems to help. I've never had a panic attack before, so I don't know what one feels like, but I don't think it's this.

I hope that's not what this is.

It's only when the flight attendant hands me a menu, and both options—salmon or tortellini—make my stomach revolt, that I realize what I'm feeling isn't just nerves. It isn't even the renewed rearing of my hangover's head; this is something else. My skin is hot and oversensitive. My head swims.

The food is wheeled into the cabin, the smell of salmon and potatoes and spinach so pungent and thick that I'm gasping, stretching on my seat to get closer to the thin stream of cool air. It's not enough. I want to escape to the bathroom, but immediately know I won't make it. Before I can wake Ansel, I'm frantically digging in the seat pocket in front of me for the airsickness bag, barely getting it open before bending over and violently hurling inside.

It doesn't get any worse than this moment right here, I'm sure of it. My body is in charge, and no matter how much my brain tells it to be quiet, to throw up like a proper lady—fucking *quietly*—it won't. I groan, feeling another wave hit me, and beside me Ansel comes awake with a jerk. He presses a hand to my back and his sharp "Oh, no!" brings my humiliation fully to the surface.

I really can't let him see me like this.

I push to stand, tripping over him before he has time to get out of his seat and practically falling into the aisle. I'm getting looks from other passengers—looks of shock and pity and disgust—but they should just be glad I managed to hold on to my bag of vomit when I launched myself into the aisle. Even though I have to concentrate fully on walking as I trip down toward the bathroom, in my head I'm glaring back at them. Have they ever been sick on a plane full of five hundred people, including their new stranger-husband? No? Then they can shut the hell up.

One small mercy is the empty lavatory just a few rows up and I shove the door open, practically collapsing inside. I throw away the bag in the tiny garbage can and crumple to the floor, bending over the toilet. Cold air blows up into my face, and the deep blue liquid in the bowl is enough to make me retch again. I'm shivering with fever, involuntarily moaning with every exhale. Whatever bug I have came on like a train barreling down the track and hitting a building full speed.

There are moments in life where I wonder whether things can get worse. I'm on a plane, with my new husband, whose enthusiasm for this whole thing seems to be flagging, and it's in this deep moment of self-pity that I register—with absolute horror—that I've also just started my period.

I look down at my white jeans and stifle a sob as I reach for some toilet paper, folding it and shoving it into my underwear. I push to stand and my hands are jerky and weak when I pull my hoodie off, tying it around my waist. I splash some water on my face, brush my teeth with my finger, and almost gag from it, my stomach rolling in warning.

This is a nightmare.

A quiet knock lands on the door, followed by Ansel's voice. "Mia? Are you okay?"

I lean against the tiny counter as we hit a small batch of turbulence and the effect inside my body is magnified. I nearly pass out from the sensation of my stomach dropping in air. After a beat, I open the door a crack. "I'm okay."

Of course I'm not okay. I'm horrified, and if I thought I could escape from the plane by crawling into this toilet, I might try.

He looks worried . . . and drugged. His eyelids are heavy, his blinks slow. I don't know what he took to sleep, but he was only out for about an hour, and he weaves a little as if he might fall over. "Can I get you anything?" His accent is thicker with his drowsiness, his words harder to follow.

"Not unless you have a pharmacy in your carry-on."

His brows pull together. "I have ibuprofen, I think."

"No," I say, closing my eyes for a beat. "I need . . . girl things."

Ansel blinks slowly again, confusion making his brow furrow further. But then he seems to understand, eyes going wide. "Is that why you're throwing up?"

I nearly laugh from the look on his face. The idea that I would suffer a period *and* throw up every month seems to horrify him on my behalf.

"No," I tell him, feeling my arms start to shake from the effort it's taking to stand. "Just a fabulous coincidence."

"You don't . . . have anything? In your purse?"

I let out what has to be the heaviest sigh known to man. "No," I tell him. "I was a little . . . distracted."

He nods, rubbing his face, and when his hand is gone he looks more awake, and resolute. "Stay here."

He closes the door with a determined click, and I hear him call to a flight attendant. I sink down onto the toilet seat, resting my elbows on my knees and my head in my hands as I listen to him through the door.

"I'm sorry to bother you but my wife," he says, and then pauses. With the last word he says, my heart begins to hammer. "The one who now got sick? She's started her . . . cycle? And I'm wondering if you keep any, or rather if you have . . . something? You see this all happened a bit fast and she packed in a hurry, and before that we were in Vegas. I have no idea why she came with me but I really, *really* don't want to screw this up. And now she needs something. Can she, uh," he stutters, finally saying simply, "borrow *quelque chose*?" I cover my mouth as he continues to ramble, and I would give anything in this moment to see the expression of the flight attendant on the other side of this door. "I meant *use*," he continues. "Not to borrow because I don't think they work that way."

I hear a woman's voice ask, "Do you know if she needs tampons or pads?"

Oh God. Oh God. This can't be happening.

"Um . . ." I hear him sigh and then say, "I have no idea

but I'll give you a hundred dollars to end this conversation and give me both."

This is officially the worst. It can only get better than this.

———————————

AND YET. THERE are no words for the humiliation of being pushed in a wheelchair through customs to baggage claim and sitting in the middle of Charles de Gaulle, holding an airsickness bag up to my face in case I lose the two sips of water I've managed in the past hour. The world feels too bright and bustling, rapid-fire French squawks in sharp bursts from loudspeakers all around me. After an eternity, Ansel comes back with our luggage and the first thing he asks is whether I've thrown up again.

I tell him he should just put me on a plane headed back to California.

I *think* he laughs and says no.

He spills me into the back of a cab before climbing in after me and speaking in a burst of French to the driver. He's speaking so fast I'm sure there's no way anyone can understand him, but the driver seems to. We lurch from the curb, and take off at an unreal speed from the beginning. Getting out of the airport is all jerks and starts, acceleration and swerving.

Once we get into the thick of the city, and buildings rise and loom above narrow, curved streets, it's harrowing. The cab driver doesn't seem to know where his brake pedal is but he sure knows his horn. I curl into Ansel's side, trying to keep what's left of my stomach from crawling up my throat. I'm sure there are a million things I want to see from the window—the city, the architecture, the vibrant green I can almost feel in the light coming into the cab—but I'm shaking and sweaty and barely conscious.

"Is he driving a cab or playing a video game?" I mumble, barely coherent.

Ansel laughs quietly into my hair, whispering, *"Ma beauté."*

In a beat, the world stops churning and jerking and I'm pulled from the seat, strong arms behind my knees and around my back, under my arm, lifting me.

Ansel easily carries me into a building and directly into a tiny elevator. He waits as the cabbie pulls our bags behind him and shoves them in with us. I can feel Ansel's breath on my temple, can hear the gears of the lift taking us higher and higher.

I turn into him, my nose in the soft, warm skin of his neck, relishing his smell. He smells like man and ginger ale and the tiny remnant of soap from so many hours ago, since he showered clean of me in the hotel room.

And then I remember: *my* present smell must be *revolting*. "I'm sorry," I whisper, turning my head and trying to pull away, but he squeezes me, saying, "Shh," into my hair.

He struggles to find his keys in his pocket while carrying me, and once we're inside, he sets me down on my feet and it's only now that my body seems to get permission to respond to the cab ride: I turn, crumple to my knees, and throw up whatever water I have in my stomach into the umbrella bucket near the door.

Seriously, it is not possible for my humiliation to grow.

Behind me, I hear Ansel lean back heavily against the door before he slides down behind me, pressing his forehead to my back just between my shoulder blades. He's shaking with silent laughter.

"Oh my God," I groan. "This is the worst moment in the history of ever." Because it is, and it turns out my humiliation can grow plenty.

"You poor girl," he says, kissing my back. "You must be miserable."

I nod, trying—but failing—to pull the bucket with me when he lifts me around my ribs.

"Leave it," he says, still chuckling. "Come on, Mia. Leave it. I'll take care of it."

When he lays me down on a mattress, I'm barely aware of the light, the smell of him everywhere. I'm too incoherent to be curious about his apartment but I make a mental note to look around and compliment it as soon as I no longer want to die. I add this task to the to-do list where I also thank him profusely, and then apologize, and then get on a plane and fly back to California in mortification.

With a small pat to my back, he's gone and almost immediately I fall fast asleep and have intricate, fevered dreams about driving through dark, narrow tunnels.

Beside me, the mattress dips where he sits and I jerk awake, knowing somehow it's been barely a minute since he left.

"Sorry," I groan, pulling my knees to my chest.

"Don't be." He puts something down on a table near the pillow. "I've put some water here. Approach it with caution." I can still hear the smile in his voice, but it's easy, unmocking.

"I'm sure this isn't how you pictured our first night here."

His hand smooths over my hair. "Nor you."

"Probably the least sexy thing you've ever seen," I babble, rolling into the warm, clean Ansel smell of the pillowcase.

"'Least sexy'?" He repeats with a laugh. "Don't forget I biked across the United States with sweaty, dirty people."

"Yeah, but you never wanted to have sex with any of them."

His hand stills where it's gently rubbing my back, and I realize what I've just said. It's laughable, this assumption that he will ever touch me sexually again after the past fifteen hours. "Sleep, Mia."

See? Proof. He called me Mia, not *Cerise*.

I WAKE UP to morning of some bright, unknown hour. Outside there are birds and voices and trucks. I smell bread, coffee, and my stomach clenches, quickly protesting that I'm not ready for food yet. And as soon as I remember the day before, a hot wave covers my skin; whether it's embarrassment or fever, I have no idea. I kick off the covers and see that I'm dressed only in one of his T-shirts and my underwear.

And then I hear Ansel in the other room, speaking English. "She's sleeping," he says. "She's been very sick, this past day."

I sit up in response to the words, but I'm thirstier than I've ever been in my life. Grabbing the glass of water on the bedside table, I lift it to my lips, drink it in four long, grateful swallows.

"Of course," he says, closer now. He's just outside the door. "Just a moment."

His feet quietly pad into the room and when he sees that I'm awake his face cycles through relief, then uncertainty, then regret. "In fact, she's already awake," he says into the phone. "Here she is."

It's my phone he's handing me, and the display tells me my father is on the line. Ansel covers the receiver briefly, whispering, "He's called at least ten times. I've charged it, so fortunately . . . or not," he says with an apologetic smile, "you have plenty of battery left."

My chest aches, stomach twisting with guilt. Pressing the phone to my ear, I manage only, "Dad, hi. I—" before he cuts me off.

"What the hell is *wrong* with you?" he yells, but doesn't wait for a reply. I pull the phone a few inches from my ear to relieve the pain of his shouting. "Are you on drugs? Is that what this Ansel person means when he says you're sick? Is that your drug dealer?"

"What?" I blink, my heart pounding so fast I'm terrified that I'm going to have some sort of cardiac event. "Dad, *no*."

"Who other than a druggie flies to France with no warning, Mia? Are you doing something illegal?"

"No, Dad. I—"

"You're unreal, Mia Rose. *Unbelievable.* Your mother and I have been worried sick, calling constantly for the last two days!" The rage in his voice comes through as clear as if he's in the next room. I can just imagine how red his face is, lips wet with spittle, hand shaking where he grips the phone.

"You'll never get it. You'll *never* get it. I just hope your brothers do better when they're your age."

I close my mouth, close my eyes, close my thoughts. I have the vague sense of Ansel sitting down beside me on the bed, his hand rubbing soothing circles on my back. My father's voice is booming, always authoritative. Even if I pressed the phone flat to my ear I know Ansel would be able to hear every word. I can only imagine what he said to Ansel before I got on the line.

In the background, I can hear my mother's pleading voice murmuring, "David, honey, don't," and know she's carefully trying to pry the phone away. And then her voice is gone, muffled voices behind his hand over the receiver.

Don't, Mom, I think. *Don't do this for me. Defending me right now isn't worth the days of silent treatment followed by more days of snide, underhanded insults.*

Dad returns to the line, his voice heated and sharp as a knife. "You do realize, Mia, that you are in a world of trouble. Do you hear me? A *world.* If you think I'm going to help you move to Boston after this, you're delusional."

I drop my phone on the mattress, Dad's voice still hurtling through the line, but the glass of water I've had doesn't want to stay down. The bathroom opens off Ansel's bedroom, and I'm tripping across the room, falling onto my knees in front of the toilet, and now not only do I have to suffer the humiliation of having Ansel hear my father berate me on the phone, but he gets to watch me throw up. Again.

I try to pull myself up so I can go wash my face, fumbling to find where I'm supposed to push to flush the toilet and failing, falling to the side in exhaustion and landing on the cool tile.

"Mia," Ansel says, bending one knee beside me, rubbing my arm.

"I'll just sleep here until I die. I'm pretty sure Harlow will send one of her manservants to retrieve my body."

Laughing, he lifts me into a sitting position and then tugs his shirt up and over my head. "Come on, *Cerise*," he murmurs, kissing just behind my ear. "You are burning up. Let me put you in the shower and then we are going to the doctor. I worry. You are making me worry."

THE DOCTOR IS younger than I expect: a female in her thirties with an easy smile and reassuring competency with eye contact. While a nurse takes my vitals, the doctor speaks to Ansel and, presumably, he explains what's going on with me. I catch only when he says my name, but otherwise have to trust that he's relaying everything accurately. I imagine it goes something like, "The sex was great and then we got married and now she's here! Help me! She won't stop throwing up, it's incredibly awkward. Her name is MIA HOLLAND. Is there a service by which we ship wayward American girls back to the States? *Merci!*"

Turning to me, the doctor asks me some basic questions in broken English. "What are the symptom?"

"Fever," I tell her. "And I can't keep any food down."

"What is your highest, ah . . . temperature before you come here?"

I shrug, looking at Ansel. He says, "*Environ, ah, trente-neuf ? Trente-neuf et demi?*" I laugh, not because I have any idea what he's just said, but because I still have no idea what my temperature is.

"Is it possible you are pregnant?"

"Um," I say, and both Ansel and I laugh. "No."

"Do you mind if we do an exam and take some blood?"

"To see if I'm pregnant?"

"No," she clarifies with a smile. "For tests."

I stop short when she says this, my pulse hauling off in a full sprint. "Do you think I have something I need a blood test for?"

She shakes her head, smiling. "Sorry, no, I am thinking you just have a stomach virus. The blood is . . . ah . . ." She searches for the word for several seconds before looking up at Ansel for help. "*Ça n'a aucun rapport?*"

"Unrelated," he translates. "I thought . . ." he begins and then smiles at the doctor. I gape at this shy version of Ansel.

"I thought since we are already here we can do the standard tests for, ah . . . sexually—"

"Oh," I mumble, understanding. "Yeah."

"It's okay?" he asks. "She will do my tests at the same time."

I'm not sure what surprises me more: that he looks nervous about my answer or that he's asking the doctor to test us for STDs in case someday I stop throwing up and we actually have sex again. I nod, numbly, and hold out my arm when the nurse pulls out a rubber strip to tie below my bicep. If this was any other day, and I hadn't just vomited up half of my body weight, I'm certain I'd have something smart to say. But right now? I'd probably promise her my firstborn if she could make my stomach settle for just ten blessed minutes.

"Are you on birth control or would you like to arrange?" the doctor asks, blinking from her chart up to me.

"Pill." I can feel Ansel look at the side of my face and wonder what a blush looks like on skin as green as mine.

Chapter SEVEN

I WAKE TO THE feeling of lips pressed carefully to my forehead, and force my eyes open.

The sky directly above me isn't an illusion I've been imagining all week. Ansel's bedroom is on the very top floor of the apartment building, and a skylight over the bed lets in the early morning sun. It curls across the footboard, bright but not yet warm.

The far wall slants down from a lofted ceiling of about fifteen feet, and along the low wall of his bedroom are two French doors that Ansel has left open to a small balcony outside. A warm breeze stirs through the room, carrying the sounds of the street below.

I turn my head, my stiff neck protesting.

"Hey." My voice sounds like sandpaper rubbed across metal.

His smile makes my chest do a fluttery, flipping thing. "I'm glad your fever has finally broken."

I groan, covering my eyes with a shaking hand as my memory of the past few days returns to me. Throwing up everywhere, including on myself. Ansel carrying me into the shower to clean me up, and later, to cool me down. "Oh my God," I mumble. "And the mortification sets in."

He laughs quietly into another kiss, this one to my temple. "I worried. You were very sick."

"Is there any surface of your apartment that remained untouched by my vomit?"

He lifts his chin, eyes shining in amusement, and nods to the corner. "Over there, the far side of the bedroom is clear."

I cover my face again, my apology muffled by my hand.

"*Cerise*," he says, reaching out to touch my face. Instinctively I shrink away, feeling revolting. I immediately want to correct the flash of hurt in his eyes, but it clears before I'm sure I believe it was really there. "I need to work today," he says. "I want to explain, before I leave."

"Okay." This sounds ominous, and I take a moment to look lower than his face. He's wearing a dress shirt. After a quick mental calculation, I realize he's feeling the need to explain because it's *Saturday*.

"When I ran into the office on Thursday to retrieve some files to bring home, the senior partner I work most closely with saw my wedding ring. She was . . . displeased."

My stomach drops, and this is the moment the reality of what we're doing hits me like an enormous wave. Yes, he invited me here, but I've crashed directly into his life. Once again I'm reminded how little I know about him. "Are you two . . . involved?"

He freezes, looking mildly horrified. "Oh, no. God, no." His green eyes narrow as he studies me. "You think I would have slept with you, married you, and *invited* you here if I had a girlfriend?"

My answering laugh comes out more like a cough. "I guess not, sorry."

"I've been her little slave boy these past few months," he explains. "And now that I'm married, she's convinced I'll lose focus."

I wince. What we've done is so rash. So stupid. Not only is he married now, but soon he'll be divorced. Why didn't he bother to hide our Vegas mishap at his job? Does he approach *anything* with caution? "I don't need you to change your work schedule while I'm here."

He's already shaking his head. "I only need to work this weekend. It will be fine. She'll get over her panic. I think she got used to having me in the office whenever she wanted."

I bet she did. I feel my frown deepen as I look him over, and I'm not so ill that a hot slide of jealousy doesn't slip through my bloodstream. With the sunlight streaming down from the ceiling and lighting up the sharp angles of his jaw and cheekbones, I'm struck all over again by how amazing his face is.

He continues, "I'm almost done with this enormous case and then I'll have more flexibility. I'm sorry I'm not really here for your first weekend."

God, this is so, *so* weird.

I wave him off, unable to say more than "Please don't worry." He's practically been serving me since I arrived, and the mortification and guilt commingle into a sour mix in my stomach. For all I know, he's seen enough of me at my worst to put him off this game we're playing entirely. I wouldn't be all that surprised if, after I've fully recovered, he suggests a few hotels I might find fitting for the remainder of my stay.

What a horrible start to our . . . whatever this is.

Since the opportunities might eventually be limited, when he walks across the room I ogle the hell out of him. He's so long, thin but toned. Suits were made for exactly his type of body. His light brown hair is combed neatly off his face, his tan neck disappearing beneath the collar of his shirt. He no longer looks like the casual and playful man I met in Vegas; he looks like a young, badass lawyer and he's eminently more fuckable. How is it even possible?

I push up onto an elbow, wanting a sharper memory of how it felt to draw my tongue down his chin and over his Adam's apple. I want to remember him unhinged and desperate, rumpled and sweaty, so I can relish knowing that the women he sees today will only know this put-together, clothed side of him.

The pants are deep blue, the shirt a crisp white, and he stands in front of a slim mirror, knotting a beautiful silk blue and green tie.

"Eat something today, hmm?" he says, smoothing his hand down his front before reaching for a blue suit jacket hanging on a small stand in the corner.

For once, I want to be the woman who climbs up on her knees, beckons him to the bed, and pretends his tie needs to be fixed before using it to pull him back under the covers.

Unfortunately for this seduction plan, I was already slim but I feel skeletal now. My legs are shaky and weak when I push myself out of bed. Not sexy. Not even a little. And before I shower, before I even approach a mirror—and definitely before I attempt to seduce this hot husband/stranger/person-I'd-like-to-be-naked-with-again—I do need something to eat. I smell bread, and fruit, and the sweet nectar of the gods: I haven't had coffee in days.

Ansel walks back over and his eyes make the circuit of my face and down over my entire body, hidden to mid-thigh beneath one of his T-shirts. I forgot to pack pajamas, apparently. He confirms my suspicion that I look like death barely warmed over when he says, "There's food in the kitchen."

I nod and hold on to the lapels of his jacket, needing him to linger just a second longer. Other than Ansel, I know no one here, and I've barely been able to process my decision to get on that plane nearly four days ago. I'm struck with a confusing mix of elation and panic. "This is the weirdest situation of my life."

His laugh is deep, and he bends so it rumbles past my ear as he kisses my neck. "I know. It's easy to do, harder to follow through. But it's fine, okay, Mia?"

Well, that was cryptic.

When I let him go, he turns to pack his computer into a leather messenger tote. I follow him out of the bedroom, freezing as I watch him grab a motorcycle helmet from where it rested on a table near the door.

"You drive a motorcycle?" I ask.

His smile stretches from one side of his face to the other as he nods, slowly. I've seen how cars drive in this city. I'm really not all that confident he'll return in one piece.

"Don't make that face," he says, lips pouting out the quiet words and then curling into a panty-dropping smile. "Once you ride with me, you'll never get in a car again."

I've never been on a motorcycle in my life—never wanted to—and I've sworn off two-wheeled vehicles forever in general. But something about the way he says it, the way he comfortably tucks the helmet under his arm and hitches his bag over his shoulder, makes me think maybe he's right. With a wink, he turns and leaves. The door closes with a quiet, perfunctory click.

And that's it. I've been in a haze of stomach flu for days, and now that I'm better, Ansel is gone and it's not even eight in the morning.

Outside the bedroom the apartment spreads before me with a continuous kitchen, living room, and dining room. Everything feels so *European*. The furniture is sparse—a black leather couch, two armless, modern red chairs, a low coffee table. On the other side of the room is a dining room table with four matching seats. The walls bear an eclectic mix of framed photographs and colorful paintings. For a bachelor pad, the apartment is impressive.

The space is open, but not very big, and the same slanted ceiling is present here. But instead of French doors, the far wall is lined with windows. I walk to the one closest to me, press my hands to the glass, and look down. On the street, I watch Ansel climb onto a shiny black bike, put on his helmet, kick the bike into gear, and pull away from the curb. Even from this vantage, he looks ridiculously hot. I wait until I can no longer see him in the blur of traffic before looking away.

My breath catches and I close my eyes, weaving a little. It isn't the residual memory of the gripping nausea or even the hunger that makes me a tiny bit dizzy. It's the fact that I'm *here*, and I can't just walk a few blocks and get home. I can't just pick up the phone and make everything okay with a quick call to my family. I can't find an apartment or a job in Boston while I'm living in *Paris*.

I can't call my best friends.

I find my purse across the room and frantically dig around in it for my phone. Stuck to the screen is a sticky note with Ansel's neat script telling me he's set me up on his international cellular plan. It actually makes me laugh—maybe a little maniacally in my relief—because that really was the thought that sent my heart hammering into near-panic mode: *How will I call my girls from France?* I mean, it's so indicative of my absurd priorities. Who cares if I don't speak French, I'm married, I'm going to have to dip into my savings, and my stranger-husband seems to work constantly? At least I won't get charged my firstborn child in AT&T minutes.

I wander the flat as Harlow's phone rings thousands of miles away through the line. In the kitchen, I see Ansel has left me breakfast: a fresh baguette, butter, jam, and fruit. A carafe of coffee sits on the stove. He is a saint and deserves some kind of ridiculous award for the past few days. Maybe just a constant offering of blowjobs and beer. He's apologizing for working, when I really should be apologizing that he had to clean up my vomit and go buy me tampons.

The lingering memory is so horrifying that I'm pretty sure I can never let him see me naked again without wanting to throw up.

The phone rings and rings. I do a blurry calculation, knowing only that when it's mid-morning here, it must be really late there. Finally, Harlow answers with only a groan.

"I have the most embarrassing story in the history of embarrassing stories," I tell her.

"It's middle-of-the-night-thirty here, Mia."

"Do you or do you not want to hear the greatest humiliation of my life?"

I hear her sit up, clear her throat. "Just realizing you're still married?"

I pause, the weight of that panic settling in a little more each minute. "It's worse."

"And you flew to Paris to be this guy's sex toy all summer?"

I laugh. If only. "Yes, we'll discuss the insanity of all of this, but first, I need to tell you about the trip here. It's so bad, I want someone to drug my coffee so I'll forget."

"You could just have some gin," she quips, and I laugh before my stomach turns with nausea.

"I got my period on the plane," I whisper.

"Oh no!" she says, sarcastically. "Not *that*."

"But I had nothing with me, Harlow. And I was wearing

white jeans. Any other time I'd be like, 'Yep, I menstruate.' But this? We just met and I can think of about fifteen hundred conversations I'd rather have with a hot semi-stranger other than 'I just started my period and I'm an idiot so let me just tie my sweatshirt around my waist to be really obvious about what's going on. Also, you being a dude, I realize it's unlikely but do you happen to have a spare tampon?'"

This seems to sink in because she falls quiet for a beat before saying a quiet, "Oh."

I nod, my stomach twisting as I reel through the remaining memories. "And layered all throughout that, I was barfing on just about everything thanks to the stomach flu."

"Lola has it, too," she says through a yawn.

"That explains a few things," I say. "I threw up on the plane. Getting off the plane. In the terminal . . ."

"Are you okay?" The concern rises in her voice, and I can tell she's about five minutes from booking a flight and coming to me.

"I'm fine now," I reassure her. "But we got back to his apartment after this cab ride that was . . ." I close my eyes when the floor weaves in front of me at the memory. "I swear crazy Broc as a toddler would be a better driver. And as soon as we got here I threw up in Ansel's umbrella bucket."

She seems to miss the most important piece of information here when she asks, "He keeps a bucket for his umbrella? Men do that?"

"Maybe he put it there for guests to puke in," I suggest. "And I've been sick since Tuesday night and I'm pretty sure he's seen me throw up about seven hundred times. He had to help me shower. Twice. And not the sexy kind, either."

"Yikes."

"Yeah."

"By the way, you can thank me for covering for you with your dad," she says, and I can practically hear the venom in her voice. "He called, and I confirmed everything from your little story while I plucked each and every hair from my Dave Holland voodoo doll. You're in Paris working as an intern for one of my dad's movie-finance colleagues. But play dumb when you come home to your father's sudden male pattern baldness."

"Ugh, sorry about that." The idea of talking to my father right now makes me feel sick all over again. "He talked to Ansel, too. Actually, 'screamed' would be a more accurate description. It didn't even seem to faze Ansel, though."

She laughs, and at the familiar sound I miss her so it squeezes my ribs together painfully. "Mia, you're going to need to really up your game in order to bring sexy back."

"I know. I can't imagine he'll ever want to touch me again. *I* don't want to touch me again. Even that enormous battery-powered rabbit sex toy you got me for my twenty-first birthday probably won't ever want to touch me again."

But the humor evaporates and my fear returns, roaring through my veins, heart pounding and limbs shaking. I haven't just tipped my world. I've propelled myself into a completely new orbit. "Harlow? What *am* I doing here? Was this a horrible mistake?"

It's a long time before she answers, and I pray she hasn't fallen asleep on the other end of the line. When she does speak, though, her voice is more awake, stronger and thoughtful . . . just the way I need her. "It's funny you're asking me this *now*, Mia. And what's even funnier, is *you're* wondering if it's a mistake, and I'm over here mentally high-fiving you all over the place."

"What?" I ask, sliding down onto the couch.

"When you didn't want to annul the stupid fucking marriage, I was pissed. When you got all schmoopy over Ansel, I thought you'd lost your mind and would be better off just banging the dimples off him for a couple of nights. But then you took off to Paris for the *summer*. You don't do crazy things, Mia, so I just have to assume you found some wild oats, and you're sowing them." She pauses, adding, "I assume you have *fun* with him."

"I do," I admit. "Or, I did. Before the bleeding on planes and vomiting in buckets."

"You've found your adventure, and are going to chase it," she says, and I hear sheets rustling in the background, the familiar sounds of Harlow curling onto her side on her bed. "And why not? I'm super proud of you, and I hope you have the time of your life out there."

"I'm terrified," I admit in a small voice.

She reminds me I have savings, she reminds me I'm twenty-three. She reminds me there is nothing I have to be doing here other than enjoying myself, for the first time in . . . *ever*.

"It doesn't *really* have to be about fucking Ansel all summer," she says. "I mean it totally could but there's more to do than worry about what he's thinking. Get out of the house. Eat some *macarons*. Drink some wine—just not yet because you are officially banned from barfing until September. Go stock up on experiences."

"I don't know where to start," I admit, looking out the window. Beyond our narrow street the world outside is an almost blinding intrusion of greens and blues. I can see for miles: a cathedral, a hill, the top of a building I know I've seen in pictures. Rooftops are tile and copper, gilded golden and stone. Even from the window of Ansel's little flat, I'm convinced I've just stepped into the most beautiful city in the world.

"Today?" she says, thinking. "It's Saturday in June, so the crowds will be ridiculous; skip the Louvre and the Eiffel Tower. Hit Luxembourg Gardens." She yawns loudly. "Report in tomorrow. I'm going back to sleep."

She hangs up.

––––––––––

NOTHING IS MORE surreal than this, I swear it. I eat at the window, staring out at the view, and then move into the small, tiled shower, where I shave and wash and shampoo until I feel like every inch of me has been sufficiently scrubbed. When I step out, the steam begins to clear and in a rush, it hits me that I can't just go home and grab the things I forgot to pack. I have no blow-dryer, no flatiron. I can't meet up with the girls tonight to tell them everything. Ansel is gone for the day and I have no idea when he'll be back. I'm alone, and for the first time in five years I'm going to have to dip into the savings account I've watched grow with pride. Every one of my paychecks from the coffee shop I worked in throughout college went directly into that account; Mom insisted on it. And now, it's going to allow me to have a summer in France.

A summer. In *France*.

My reflection in the mirror whispers, *What the fuck are you doing?* I blink my eyes closed, pushing myself into autopilot mode.

I find my clothes; he's made room for my things in his dresser and closet.

You're married.

I brush my hair. My toiletries are unpacked, tucked into one of the drawers in the bathroom.

You're living with your husband in Paris.

I start to lock up the apartment using the spare key Ansel left for me right next to a small bundle of euros.

I find myself staring down at the unfamiliar paper bills, unable to quell the unease I feel at Ansel having left me money. It's such a visceral reaction, the way my stomach tightens at the thought of living off someone else—someone other than my parents, I guess—that I have to push it aside until he's home and we can have a conversation that doesn't involve me with my head in the toilet.

In Las Vegas, and then in San Diego, we were on even footing. At least, it *felt* more even than it does now. We were both on vacation, carefree. After, I was headed to school, he was headed back here to his job, and life, and well-decorated flat. Now I'm the post-college squatter with no plans, the girl who needs directions to the métro, and snack money left by the door.

I leave the money where it is and cross the narrow hall to the elevator. It's tiny, and with barely more than two feet on either side of me, I reach out and press the button marked with a star and the number one. The lift groans and shudders as it makes its descent, wheels and gears whirring above me until it lands with a thunk on the ground floor.

Outside the apartment it's loud and windy, hot and chaotic. The streets are narrow, the sidewalks made of pavers and cobblestone. I start walking, stopping at the corner where the narrow road opens up into what must be a wider, main street.

There are crosswalks, but no clear pedestrian rules. People step off the curb without looking. Cars use their horns as frequently as I take a breath but they don't seem the slightest bit annoyed. They honk, they move on. There don't really seem to be lanes, just a steady stream of cars that stop and go and yield in a pattern I don't understand. Street vendors offer pastries and bottles of bright, sparkling sodas, and people in suits and dresses, jeans and track pants rush past me as if I'm a stone in a river. The language is lyrical and fast . . . and completely incomprehensible to me.

It's as if the city is spread lusciously before me, prepared to pull me fully into its intricate heart, into mischief. I'm instantly, deeply enamored. How could I not be? Everywhere I turn the streets look like the most beautiful sets I've ever imagined, as if the entire world here is a stage, waiting to see my story unfold. I haven't felt this kind of buzz since I was dancing, lost in it, living for it.

I use my phone to find the métro station at Abbesses, only a few blocks from Ansel's apartment, manage to locate the line I need to take, and then I'm left waiting for the train, struggling to take in my surroundings. I send Harlow and Lola pictures of everything I see: the French posters for a book we all loved, six-inch heels on a woman who would already be taller than most men on the platform, the train as it blows into the station, carrying hot summer air and the smell of brake dust.

It's a short ride to the sixth arrondissement, where Luxembourg Gardens are located, and I follow a group of chattering tourists who seem to have the same destination in mind. I was prepared for a park—grass and flowers and benches—but I wasn't prepared to find such huge stretches of open space nestled in the center of this busy, cramped city. I wasn't expecting the wide lanes lined with perfectly manicured trees. There are flowers everywhere: row after row of seasonal blooms, cottage beds and wildflowers, hedges and lacy blossoms of every imaginable color. Fountains and statues of French queens offer contrast to the foliage, and the tops of buildings I've seen only in movies or pictures loom in the distance. Sunbathers stretch out on metal chairs or benches under the sun, and children push small boats across the water while Luxembourg Palace watches over it all.

I find an empty bench and take a seat, breathing in the fresh air and the scent of summer. My stomach growls at the smell of bread from a nearby cart but I ignore it, waiting to see how it handles breakfast first.

It's then that I realize *again* that I'm in Paris. Five thousand miles from everything I know. This is the last chance I'll have to relax, soak it in, create my own adventure, before I begin school and the regimented march from student to professional.

I walk every inch of the park, throw pennies into the fountain, and finish the paperback I had tucked in the bottom of my bag. For the span of an afternoon, Boston, my father, and school don't even exist.

Chapter EIGHT

I'M ON SUCH a high from my day, I stop at the small market on the corner, intent on making Ansel dinner. I am all over this Paris thing, check me out. I'm learning to make do with the language barrier and find that the Parisians aren't nearly as frustrated that I don't speak French as I'd expected. They just seem to hate it when I try and then mangle it. I've been able to get by just fine with some pointing, smiling, innocent shrugging, and *s'il vous plaît,* and manage to buy some wine and prawns, fresh pasta, and vegetables.

But my nerves creep back in as I walk to the rickety elevator and as it noisily ascends to the seventh floor. I'm not sure if he'll be home yet. I'm not sure what to expect at all. Will we pick up where we left off in San Diego? Or is now when we start . . . uh . . . dating? Or has the experience of our first few days put him off this little experiment altogether?

I lose myself in cooking, impressed with Ansel's small kitchen. I've figured out his stereo and have some French dance music on as I happily bounce around the kitchen. The apartment smells of butter and garlic and parsley when he walks in, and my body grows tight and jittery when I hear him drop his keys in the little bowl on the entry table, put his helmet on the floor beneath.

"Hello?"

"In the kitchen," I reply.

"You're cooking?" he calls, rounding the corner into the main loft of the apartment. He looks good enough to devour. "I'm guessing you feel better."

"You have no idea."

"It smells wonderful."

"It's almost ready," I say, begging my pulse to slow. Seeing him makes the thrill inside me bloom so wide my chest grows tight.

But then his face falls.

"What is it?" I follow the path of his eyes to the pan on the stove where I've tossed the prawns with the pasta and vegetables.

He winces. "It looks unbelievable. It's just . . ." He swipes a palm across the back of his neck. "I'm allergic to shellfish."

I groan, covering my face. "Holy crap, I'm sorry."

"Don't be sorry," he says, clearly distressed. "How would you have known?"

The question hangs between us and we both look anywhere but at each other. The amount of things we know about each other seems dwarfed by the amount of things we don't. I don't even know how to go back to the introduction phase.

He takes a step closer, telling me, "It smells so good."

"I wanted to thank you." It takes a beat before I can get the rest out, and he looks away for the first time I can remember. "For taking care of me. For bringing me here. Please wait, I'll go get something else."

"We'll go together," he says, walking closer. He puts his hands on my hips but his arms are stiff and it feels forced.

"Okay." I have no idea what to do with my own arms, and instead of doing what I think a normal woman would do in this situation—put them around his neck, pull him closer—I fold them awkwardly across my chest, tapping my collarbone with my finger.

I keep waiting for his eyes to flare with mischief or for him to tickle me, tease me, do something ridiculous and Ansel-like, but he seems beat and tense when he asks, "Did you have a good day?"

I start to answer but then he pulls one hand away, digging into his buzzing pocket and pulling out his phone, frowning at it. *"Merde."*

That word I know. He's been home for less than three minutes, and I already know what he's going to say.

He looks back up at me, apology filling his eyes. "I have to go back into work."

ANSEL IS GONE when I wake up, and the only evidence I have that he came back at some point is a note on the pillow beside mine telling me he was only home for a couple of hours and slept on the couch, not wanting to wake me. I swear I can feel something inside me splinter. I went to bed in one of his clean T-shirts and nothing else. New husbands don't sleep on the couch. New husbands don't worry about waking up their new, jobless, tourist wife in the middle of the night.

I don't even remember if he kissed my forehead again before he left, but a very large part of me wants to text him and ask, because I'm starting to think the answer to that question will tell me if I should stay, or book the flight for my return trip home.

It's easy to distract myself and fill my second day alone in Paris: I wander around the exhibits and gardens at the Musée Rodin, and then brave the interminable lines at the Eiffel Tower . . . but the wait is worth it. The view from the top is *unreal*. Paris is stunning at street level, and hundreds of stories up.

Back in the apartment Sunday night, Lola is my companion. She's sitting on her couch at home in San Diego, recovering from whatever virus we both got, and replying to my texts with reassuring speed.

I tell her, I Think he regrets bringing me back with him.

That's insane, she replies. It sounds like work sucks for him right now. Yes he married you, but he doesn't know if it will last and he has to take care of the job, too.

Honestly, Lola, I feel pretty moochy, but I don't want to leave yet! This city is ahhh-mazing. Should I stay at a hotel, do you think?

You're being sensitive.

He slept on the COUCH.

Maybe he was sick?

I try to remember if I heard anything. He wasn't.

Maybe he still thinks it's shark week?

I feel my eyebrows inch up. I hadn't considered this. Maybe Lola is right and Ansel thinks I'm still on my period? Maybe I really do need to be the one to initiate some sex-type things?

OK that's a good theory.

Test it out, she replies.

Forget the T-shirt. Tonight, I'm going to sleep naked, no covers.

I WAKE, GLANCING at the clock. It's nearly two thirty in the morning and I immediately sense that he's not home yet. The lights are all out in the apartment, and beside me, the bed is empty and cold.

But then I hear a shuffle, a zipper, a tight moan coming from the other room.

I climb out of bed, pull on one of his T-shirts he's left in the laundry bin and which smells so acutely of him that for a beat, I have to stop, close my eyes, find my balance.

When I step into the living room and look to the kitchen, I see him.

He's bent over, one hand braced on the counter. His dress shirt is unbuttoned, tie hanging loosely around his neck and pants pushed down his hips as his other hand flies over his cock.

I'm mesmerized at the sight, the sheer eroticism of Ansel pleasuring himself in the dim light coming in from the window. His arm moves quickly, elbow bent, and through his dress shirt, I can see the tension of the muscles in his back, the way his hips begin to move into his hand. I step forward, wanting to see better, and my foot catches a squeaky board. The sound groans through the room, and he freezes, his head snapping to look over his shoulder.

When his eyes meet mine, they flash with mortification before slowly cooling to defeat. He lets his hand fall away and his head drops, chin to chest.

I approach him slowly, not sure if he wants me, or wants anything *but* me. Why else would he be out here doing this, when I was naked in his bed?

"I hope I didn't wake you," he whispers. In the light coming in through the window, I can see the sharp line of his jaw, the smooth expanse of his neck. His pants are slung low on his hips, his shirt unbuttoned. I want to taste his skin, feel the soft line of hair that travels down his navel.

"You did, but I wish you had *tried* to wake me if you wanted . . ." I want to say "me" but again, I'm not at all sure that's what he wanted. "If you needed . . . something."

God, could I be less smooth?

"It's so late, *Cerise*. I came in, started to undress. I saw you naked in my bed," he says, gaze fixed on my lips. "I didn't want to wake you."

I nod. "I *assumed* you would see me naked on your bed."

He exhales slowly through his nose. "I wasn't sure—"

Before he finishes the sentence, I'm already lowering my-self to my knees in the darkness, moving his hand away so I can lick him, bring his need back to life. My heart is beating so hard, and I'm so nervous I can see my hand shaking where I touch him, but fuck it. I tell myself I'm channeling Harlow, confident sex goddess.

I tell myself I have nothing to lose. "I went to bed naked on *purpose*."

"I don't want you to feel obligated to be with me like this," he croaks.

I look up at him, flabbergasted. What happened to the delightfully pushy guy I met only a week ago? "I don't feel *obligated*. You're just busy . . ."

He smiles, gripping his base and painting a wet line across my lips with the bead of moisture that appears at his tip. "I think we're both being too tentative, maybe."

I lick him, playing a little, teasing. I'm greedy for the breathless noises he's making, the rough eager grunts when I almost take him in and then pull away to kiss and play some more.

"I was thinking about you," he admits in a whisper, watching me draw a long wet line from base to tip with my tongue. "I can barely think about anything else anymore."

This admission uncoils something that had grown tight and tense in my gut, and I only realize how anxious I'd been about this when he says it. I feel like I've melted. It makes me eager to give him pleasure, sucking more of him, giving him the vibrations of my voice around him as I moan.

Seeing him like this—impatient, relieved at my touch—makes it easier for me to keep playing, keep being this brave, brazen seductress. Pulling back, I ask, "In your mind, what were we doing?"

"This," he says, tilting his head as he slides a hand into my hair, anchoring me. I prepare myself to feel the full invasion of him into my mouth only a second before he pushes in deep. "Fucking these lips."

His head falls back and he closes his eyes, hips rocking in front of my face. *"C'est tellement bon, j'en rêve depuis des jours . . ."* With apparent effort, he straightens, leaning over a little, growing rougher. "Swallow," he whispers. "I want to feel you swallowing." He pauses so I can do what he's asked and he moans hoarsely as I pull him deeper into my throat with the movement.

"Will you swallow when I come? Will you make a little hungry sound when you feel it?" he asks, watching me intently now.

I nod around him. For him, I will. I want anything he'll give me; I want to give him anything just the same. He's the only anchor I have to this place, and even if this marriage is only pretend, I want that feeling back, when it was free and easy between us that night in San Diego, and the one before that, which I only remember in tiny fragments, flashes of skin and sounds and pleasure.

For several minutes he moves, treating me to his quiet growling sounds and whispers that I'm beautiful, giving me every inch along my tongue before pulling almost all the way out and jerking his length with his fist, the crown of his cock tapping against my lips and tongue.

It's like this that he comes, messily, spilling in my mouth, on my chin. It's intentional, it has to be, and I know I'm right when I look up and see his eyes darken at the sight of his orgasm on my skin, my tongue swiping out, instinctively. He steps away, running his thumb over my lower lip before bending to help me up. With a damp towel, he gently wipes me clean and then steps back, preparing to lower himself to his knees, but he weaves slightly and when the streetlight outside catches his profile, I can tell he's about to fall over in exhaustion. He's barely slept in days.

"Let me make you feel good now," he says, instead leading me toward the bedroom.

I stop him with my hand on his elbow. "Wait."

"What?" he asks, and my thoughts trip on the rough edge in his voice, the simmering frustration I've never before heard from him.

"Ansel, it's nearly three in morning. When was the last time you slept?"

His expression is unreadable in the shadow, but it isn't so dark that I can't see how his shoulders seem too heavy for his frame, how tired he looks "You don't want me to touch you, too? I come on your lips and you're ready for sleep?"

I shake my head and don't resist when he reaches for me, slides his hand under his shirt, up my thigh. He spreads me with his fingers and groans. I'm drenched and now he knows it, too. With a quiet hiss he begins to move his hand, bending to suck on my neck.

"Let me taste this," he growls, his breath warm on my skin, fingers slipping easily over my clit before pushing down and into me. "It's been a week, Mia. I want my face covered in you."

I'm shaking in his arms with how much I want him. His fingertips feel like heaven, his breath is hot on my neck, kisses sucking and urgent all along my neck. What's another fifteen minutes of lost sleep? "Okay," I whisper.

I wait until he's finished brushing his teeth and slides into bed wearing only his boxers before I slip into the bathroom after him. "Be right there."

I brush my teeth, wash my face, and tell my reflection to stop overthinking everything. If the man wants sex, give him sex. *I* want sex. Let's have sex! I quietly pad out into the darkness. My stomach is warm, the space between my legs slick and ready and *this is it,* I think. *This is when the fun starts, when I can enjoy him and this city and this tiny slice of life where I don't have anyone else I need to worry about but me, and him.*

The moon lights a path from the small bathroom to the foot of the bed, and I flip off the bathroom light, pulling the light covers back so I can climb into bed beside him. He's warm, and his soap and aftershave immediately trigger the hunger I've missed for days now, that desperate need for the urgent grip of his hands, the feel of him kissing me and moving over me. But even when I slide my hand up his stomach and over his chest, he remains still, limbs heavy beside me.

Nothing comes out when I open my mouth the first time, but the second time I manage to whisper, "Do you want to have sex?" I wince at the stark words, blown free of nuance or seduction.

He doesn't answer and I shift closer, heart hammering as I curl around his hard, warm body. He's fast asleep, breaths solid and steady.

HE'S UP BEFORE me again, this time in a charcoal suit, a black shirt. He looks ready for a photo shoot: black and white stills of him caught unaware on the street corner, sharp jaw carving a shadow through the sky behind him. He's bent over me, about to deliver a chaste kiss to my lips, when my eyes open.

He steers himself from my mouth to my temple, and my stomach sinks when I realize it's Monday, and again, he'll be working all day.

"Sorry about last night," he says quietly into my ear. When he pulls back, his gaze flickers away from mine and he focuses instead on my lips.

I had dreams, though—*sexy dreams*—and am not ready for him to leave yet. I can still imagine the feel of his hands and lips, his voice grown hoarse after hours over and behind and beneath me. Sleep still clouds my thoughts, makes me brave enough to act. Without thinking, I pull at his arm and bring it beneath the covers with me.

"I had dreams about you," I rasp, smiling sleepily up at him.

"Mia . . ."

He's unsure what I'm doing at first and I watch when understanding dawns as I drag his hand down my ribs, over my navel. His lips part, eyes grow heavy. Ansel meets my hips halfway with his hand, sliding his fingers between my legs and cupping me.

"Mia," he groans with an expression I can't quite read. It's part longing and part something that looks more like anxiety. At the border, awareness trickles in.

Oh shit.

His suit jacket is folded over his other forearm, laptop bag still slung over his shoulder. He was rushing out the door.

"Oh." The flush of embarrassment creeps up my neck. Pushing his hand away from my body, I begin, "I didn't—"

"Don't stop," he says, jaw clenching.

"But you're leavi—"

"Mia, please," he says, his voice so low and soft it drips over me like warm honey. "I want this."

His arm shakes, eyes roll closed, and I let mine do the same before I fully wake up, before I lose my nerve. What had I thought in Vegas? That I wanted a different life. That I wanted to be brave. I wasn't brave then, but I pretended to be.

With my eyes closed, I can pretend again. I'm the sex-bomb who doesn't care about his job. I'm the insatiable wife. I'm the only thing he wants.

I'm drenched and swollen and the noise he makes when he slides his fingers over me is unreal: a deep, rumbling groan. I could come with barely an exhale across my skin I'm so keyed up, and when he seems to want to explore me, to *tease,* I rise into his fingers, seeking. He gives me two, pushed straight into me, and I grip his forearm, rocking up, fucking his hand. I can't stop long enough to care how desperate I seem.

Heat crawls up my skin and I pretend it's the heat of the spotlight.

"Oh, let me see," he whispers. "Let go."

"Aah," I gasp. My orgasm takes shape around the edges, the sensation crystallizes and then builds, crawling up from where his thumb now circles frantically against my skin until my orgasm is hammering through me. Clutching his arm in both hands, I cry out, rippling around his fingers. My legs and arms and spine feel fluid, filled with liquid heat, molten as relief floods my bloodstream.

I open my eyes. Ansel holds still, and then slowly pulls his fingers from me, slipping his hand back out from under the covers. He watches me as consciousness eventually pushes sleep completely aside. With his other hand, he hitches his bag higher on his shoulder. The room seems to tick in the quiet, and even though I try to grasp on to my feigned confidence, I can feel my chest, my neck, my face grow warm with heat.

"Sorry, I—"

He silences me with his wet fingers pressed to my mouth. "Don't," he growls. "*Don't* take it back."

He traps his fingers with his lips pressed to mine, and then slips his tongue across his fingers, across my mouth, tasting me and releasing a sweet, relieved exhale. When he pulls back enough for me to focus on his eyes, they're full of determination. "I'm coming home early tonight."

Chapter NINE

*I*T SEEMS HARDER to keep track of what I'm spending when euros still feel like play money. Given how different things feel with Ansel from how they did in the States—and even though I'm in love with this place—part of me thinks I should stay for two weeks, see everything I possibly can in that time, and then fly home to make amends with my father so I don't have to resort to prostitution or stripping when I move to Boston and begin apartment hunting.

But the idea of facing my father now makes my skin go cold. I know what I've done was impulsive and maybe even dangerous. I know any loving father in this situation would have a right to be angry. It's just that *everything* makes my father angry; we've all grown desensitized over time. I've been sorry enough times when I didn't need to be; I can't find it in me to be sorry this time. I may be scared and lonely, not knowing whether Ansel's schedule will let up, what will happen with us tonight, tomorrow, next week, or what will happen when I find myself in a situation where I can't communicate with someone, but this was the first decision in my life that feels like it's only mine.

I'm still completely lost in my head, overthinking my

wake-up call with Ansel, when I step out of the shower. In front of me, the bathroom mirror dries perfectly, clear of any stray water droplets, any streaks, as if it's been treated with something. I'd offer to clean to pull some of my weight but there's absolutely nothing that needs to be done. The bathroom window gleams, too, sun shining directly inside. Curiosity prickles at the edges of my thoughts, and I walk around, inspecting everything. The apartment is spotless, and—in my experience—for a man, strangely so. Before I get to the living room windows, I know what I'll find.

Or, rather, what I *won't* find. I know I pressed my hand to the glass my first real day here, watching him climb onto his motorcycle. I know I did it more than once. But there's no handprint there, only more unblemished, crystal-clear glass. No one has been here but us. At some point, in his sliver of time at home, he took a minute to wipe the windows and mirrors clean.

———

THE OLD WOMAN who lives on the bottom floor is sweeping the doorstep when I walk out of the elevator and I spend at least an hour with her on my way out. Her English comes in fragments, mixed with French words I can't translate, but somehow we make what could be an awkward conversation into something surprisingly easy. She tells me the elevator was added in the seventies, after she and her husband moved in here. She tells me the vegetables are much better down Rue de Rome than in the market on the corner. She offers me tiny green grapes with bitter seeds that give me goose bumps but I can't seem to stop eating them. And then she tells me she's happy to see Ansel smiling so much now, and that she never really liked *the other one.*

I push this bit of information and the twisting, dark curiosity out of my head and thank her for her company. Ansel is gorgeous and successful and charming; of course he had a life before I followed him to the airport, a life that no doubt included women. It doesn't surprise me to know someone was with him before. It's just that I realize I'm still waiting to learn *anything* about him, other than what he looks like with no clothes on.

I SPEND MOST of the day looking around our neighborhood and making a mental map of the area. Streets go on endlessly, shop after shop, tiny alley after tiny alley. It's a bit like diving down the rabbit hole, but here I know I'll find my way out; I simply need to find the telltale *M* of the Métropolitain and will be able to get back to Ansel's street easily.

My street, I remind myself. Ours. Together.

Thinking of his home as mine is a little like pretending a movie set is home or learning that euros are real money. And every time I look down at my wedding ring, it only feels more surreal.

I like this view of the street at dusk. The sky is bright high above me, but beginning to fade where the sun has started to slip low on the horizon. Long shadows cut across the sidewalk, and colors somehow seem richer, more saturated than I've ever seen before. Buildings crowd the narrow road and the cracked, uneven sidewalk feels like a path to an adventure. In daylight, Ansel's building looks a little shabby, touched with dust and wind and exhaust. But at night it seems to brighten. I like that our home is a night owl.

As I follow the crooked sidewalk, I realize this is the first time I've walked all the way from Rue St.-Honoré to the métro, gotten off at the right stop, and then made it all the way home without needing to check the app on my phone.

Behind me I hear cars on the road, motorcycles, a bicycle bell. Someone laughs from an open window. All the windows are open here, balcony doors and shutters thrown wide to catch the cooler evening air, curtains billowing out into the breeze.

There's a lightness in my chest as I near our building, followed by a distinct jump in my pulse when I spot Ansel's motorcycle parked on the sidewalk just out front.

I fill my lungs as I step into the tiny lobby and walk toward the elevator. My hand shakes as I press the button for our floor and I remind myself to breathe. *Deep breath in. Deep breath out. Keep it together.* This will be the first time Ansel has arrived home before me; the first time we'll actually be in the apartment together without one of us half asleep or vomiting or working into the early hours of the morning. My cheeks burn as I remember him growling, "*Don't* take it back," only this morning after I got myself off with his hand.

Oh dear God.

My stomach erupts into butterflies, and a mix of nerves and adrenaline propels me out of the elevator. I fit my key into the lock, take a deep breath, and swing open the door.

"Honey, I'm home!" I bounce into the entryway and stop at the sound of Ansel's voice.

He's in the kitchen, phone pressed to his ear and speaking in such rapid-fire French I'm not sure how the person on the other end of the line can possibly understand him. He's clearly agitated, and repeats the same phrase, louder and more irritated each time.

He hasn't noticed me yet and although I have no idea what he's saying or who he's talking to, I can't help but feel like I'm intruding. His annoyance is like another person in the room and I quietly set my key on the table and wonder if I should step back into the hall or maybe excuse myself to the bathroom. I see the moment he catches my reflection in the living room window: he stiffens and his eyes go wide.

Ansel turns, tight smile in place, and I lift my hand, offering a small, awkward wave.

"Hi," I whisper. "Sorry."

He waves back, and with another apologetic smile holds up a finger signaling for me to wait. I nod, thinking he means for me to wait while he ends his call . . . but he doesn't. Instead he nods toward the back of the flat and then moves across the floor and into the bedroom, closing the door behind him.

I can only stare, blinking at the simple white door. His

voice filters out into the living room and, if possible, is even louder than it was before.

Deflating, I let my bag slip from my shoulder to land in a heap on the couch.

There are groceries on the counter: a bag of fresh pasta, some herbs, and a wedge of cheese. A baguette wrapped in brown paper sits next to a pot of water that's just starting to boil. The simple wooden table is set in bright red dishes, a bouquet of purple flowers spilling from a small vase in the center. He was making us dinner.

I open a few of the cupboard doors, searching for a wineglass, and try to ignore the words I can still hear in the other room. To a person I don't know. In a language I don't speak.

I also try to tamp down the thread of uneasiness that's begun winding tightly in my gut. I remember Ansel telling me his boss was concerned he'd become *distracted,* and wonder if that's who he's talking to. It could be one of the guys— Finn or Oliver—or Perry, the one who couldn't make it to Vegas. But would he sound this frustrated speaking to his boss, or a *friend*?

My eyes dart to the bedroom just as the door opens, and I jump, startling slightly before trying to look busy. I reach for a bunch of basil and search in the drawer nearest my hip for a knife.

"I'm so sorry," he says.

I wave him off, and my voice comes out a little reedy: "Don't worry! You don't have to explain anything to me. You had a life before I got here."

He leans forward, placing a kiss on each of my cheeks. God he smells good. His lips are so soft and I have to grip the counter to keep myself steady.

"I *did* have a life," he says, taking the knife from my hand. "But so did you." When he smiles it doesn't quite reach his eyes. There's no dimple. I miss it.

"Why does your job kill your joy?" I ask him, wishing he would touch me again.

With an amused grin, he shrugs. "I'm very junior at the firm still. We're representing a huge corporation in a very big case, so I have thousands and thousands of pages of documents to go through. I don't even think the attorneys who have been there for thirty years remember being this busy."

I lift a small tomato to my lips, humming against it and saying, "That stinks," before popping it in my mouth.

He watches me chew, nodding slowly. "It does." His eyes darken and he blinks once, and then again, harder, his eyes clearing as his gaze meets mine again. "How was your day?"

"I feel guilty I'm out there having so much fun and you're stuck in the office all day," I admit.

He puts the knife down and turns to face me. "So . . . you're staying?"

"Do you *want* me to stay?" I ask, voice thick with awkwardness and my pulse heavy in my throat.

"Of course I want you to stay," he insists. With a fumbling hand, he pulls his tie loose and off, dropping it on the far end of the counter. "On vacation it's easy to pretend real life doesn't exist. I didn't consider how my job would affect this. Or maybe I just figured you were smarter than I am and less impulsive."

"I promise. I'm fine. Paris doesn't exactly suck." I give him a bright smile.

"The problem is, I'd like to be enjoying you while you're here."

"You mean my sparkling wit and big brain, don't you?" I ask with a grin, reaching for the basil on the counter.

"No, I don't care about your brain. I mean your boobs. I really only care about boobs."

I laugh, relief trickling into my bloodstream. There he is. "Who let you graduate from law school, you oaf?"

"It took some convincing, but my father is a wealthy man."

I laugh again and he takes a step closer but as soon as he does, the moment explodes into awkward again as I reach for him and our hands collide in midair. We apologize in unison and then stand there, staring at each other.

"You can touch me," I tell him just as he asks, "Why don't you ever take the money I leave on the table?"

I pause for a beat before whispering, "I'm getting a weird prostitute vibe from that sequence."

Ansel bends over, laughing with me. "I'm sorry. I don't know how to say everything I've been practicing all day." He runs a hand through his hair and it leaves it sticking up and ridiculous and *damn*. I want to run my fingers through it, too. "I just have so much guilt that I'm not around much since you arrived, and I want to make sure you're having fun."

Ah. Guilt is making him the robot version of the adoraboy I married. "Ansel, you don't have to take care of me."

His face falls a little but he puts it back together. "I want to contribute somehow."

"You brought me here," I remind him.

"But I've barely seen you. And last night, I fell asleep . . . and you . . ." I watch as his tongue slips out and wets his lips. He stares at my mouth, lips parted. "This is so weird," he whispers.

"The weirdest," I agree. "But I'm not taking your money."

"We're *married*."

"We aren't *that* married."

He laughs, shaking his head in mock exasperation, but amusement digs his dimple into his cheek and it makes my heart grow ten sizes too big for my chest. *Hello, lover.*

Legally, yes, we're married. But I'm already relying on him for shelter, and food. There is no way I'm comfortable taking his money when I don't even know his middle name.

Holy shit I don't even know his middle name.

"I think it's great you're having such a good time," he says, carefully. "Have you been to the Musée—?"

"What's your middle name?" I blurt.

He tilts his head, letting a tiny smile tease at the corner of his lips. "Charles. After my father."

Exhaling, I say, "Good. Ansel Charles Guillaume. A good name."

His smile slowly straightens as he seems to catch up with me. "Okay. What is *your* middle name?"

"Rose."

"Mia Rose?"

I love the way he says Rose. The *r* sound comes out more purr than actual letter. "You say my name better than anyone ever has."

"I should," he murmurs, winking. "It's officially my new favorite name."

I watch him for a beat, feeling a smile slowly curve my mouth. "We're doing everything backwards," I whisper.

Taking a small step closer, he says, "I need to seduce you all over again, then."

Oh, the flutters. "You do?"

His smile curls up, dangerous. "I want you in my bed tonight. Naked beneath me."

He's talking about having *sex,* and suddenly there is no way I would be able to eat a bite of food. My stomach crawls up my throat and my panties practically drop in anticipation.

"It's why I wanted to start by making you dinner," he continues, oblivious. "And my mother would skin me alive if she knew how much takeout I eat."

"Well, I can't imagine you coming home at midnight and making yourself something to eat."

"True," he says slowly, drawing the word out into several syllables as he takes another step closer to me. "I wanted to make up for last night." He smiles and shakes his head before glancing down at me. "And having to leave so quickly this morning after you used my fingers so ingeniously." He pauses, making sure he has my undivided attention before adding, "I wanted to stay."

Oh. I wonder if he can hear the way my heart suddenly drops into my stomach because it feels like the crash it makes reverberates around the room. My head is full of words but there must be some disconnect between my brain and my mouth because *nothing* comes out. Every hair along my arms stands on end and he's watching me, waiting for a reaction.

He wants to have sex tonight. *I* want to have sex tonight. But what was easy before suddenly feels so . . . complicated. Do we do it now? The couch would be nice, maybe even the table . . . Or should we finish dinner and go into the bedroom to be civilized? I glance out the window and see that the sun still filters through the skylight above the bed. He'll see my scars. All of them. Logically, I know he's seen them before— felt them along my skin—but this is different. It's not sponta- neous maybe-it-won't-ever-happen-again sex. It's not you-have-no-idea-who-I-am-so-I-can-be-anyone-I-want sex. Not lottery-ticket, just-happened-upon-a-perfect-opportunity sex. This is sex we plan, sex we can have whenever we want. Accessible sex.

All these thoughts and more flash through my head and he's still watching me, waiting with unsure eyes. I'm thinking too much and panic that I'll screw this up rises like smoke in my chest, my throat.

"Are you hungry?" he asks, hedging.

"I don't have to be." *What does that even mean, Mia?*

"But . . . you are now?" He scratches his temple, understandably confused. "I mean, we can eat first if you prefer."

"I don't. We shouldn't. Let's not? I'm okay not eating first."

With a quiet laugh, Ansel shuts off the stove and turns. He takes my face in his hands, palms warm against my cheeks, and kisses me. His lips tease at mine, teeth gently scraping across. I feel his fingers thread in my hair and he tips my head back, pulling away just long enough to brush his nose along mine and tilt my chin up to him. Against my skin, his fingers tremble with restraint and his noises come out tight, barely controlled.

I suck in a breath as the tip of his tongue pushes inside and he moans into my mouth. My nipples harden as he begins walking us back to the bedroom, and I feel the heaviness of my breasts, the heat between my legs.

His foot lands on top of mine and he whispers an apology, wincing as I say, "It's okay, it's okay," into his kiss.

My eyes are closed but I feel the moment he kicks off his shoes, hear them tumble along the wood floor. The edge of a wall connects with my back and he whispers another apology into my mouth, sucks on my tongue, and tries to distract me. His fingers run along my spine, under the hem of my shirt, and soon it's up and over my head, forgotten somewhere behind us. My hands tug at his shirt until his skin is bare and warm and pressed against mine.

Clothes come off, he—literally—trips out of his pants, the room tips, and when I open my eyes again I see the ceiling above and feel the soft sheets at my back. He kisses down my neck and along my shoulder, licks a path down to my breast. It's darker back here than I'd expected and I almost forget we're naked until Ansel moves to his knees and stretches across me, fumbling with the bedside table and returning with a condom.

"Oh," I say, pulling my eyebrows together. I guess we're ready to go. Also, I guess the blood test results aren't in yet. "Are we . . . ?"

He looks down to the foil packet. "I checked the mail and . . . we didn't . . . I mean. If . . ."

"No," I blurt. "Good. It's fine." And could this be more awkward? Is he thinking I have something? Does he think Vegas was, like, an everyday occurrence for me? And what about him? What about *the other one*? Miles of naked chest and arms are in front of me, his flat stomach, his cock hard as it juts out between us—how many other women have enjoyed this exact view? "We definitely should use one, to be grown-up about it until we know."

He nods and I don't miss the way his hands shake as he tears open the wrapper, when he reaches for himself and rolls the latex down his length. My legs are open and he settles between them, his eyes flickering up to me.

"Okay?" he asks.

I nod and choke on a little breath when his fingers find where I'm wet, moving in small circles before he replaces them with his cock.

And *oh* . . . okay. That feels . . . nice.

"Still okay?" he asks again, and this time I bring my legs around his hips and tighten, pulling him forward.

He exhales as he pushes inside, stilling when his body is flush with mine. His small sounds vibrate along my skin and I nod to tell him I'm good, to keep going. He pulls out, pushes back in. His hair brushes along my chest when he looks down between us, watching the way he moves in me. Over and over.

I'm aware of every breath he takes, every word and grunt as it leaves his lips, the sound of his skin where it slaps against mine. There's a shout from outside and I look over toward the window. Ansel touches my chin, smiles as he brings my attention back, and kisses me. I can still taste the wine he must have had while he started dinner; I can smell the lingering trace of his aftershave. But I can also hear sounds on the street, feel the heavy, humid air in the apartment pressing down over us.

It occurs to me that I didn't notice any of those things before, not when we were together in Vegas or his hotel room. I was so lost in the fantasy of where we were and what we were doing, pretending to be someone else with a different life, that I forgot to think or worry; all I wanted was *him*.

Ansel speeds up and reaches between us, his fingers slipping to where he's inside me before moving up to my clit. And it feels good, it does. Being with him feels good and his sounds are amazing and it's only been a few minutes but . . . oh . . . I feel something.

There? *There*.

"Yes," I breathe, and he curses in response, hips accelerating. And wow, that is definitely helping because there it is again, a flicker, a tightening deep in my stomach. Pressure builds, heavy and *there* again and I'm close.

I think?

Yes.

No.

. . . maybe?

I shift my hips and he shifts his in response, harder again and faster until the headboard begins tapping steadily against the wall behind me and . . .

That might be hard to tune out. What about the neighbors?

Ugh, brain, shut up. I squeeze my eyes closed and refocus, take a deep breath and look up. Ansel is gorgeous above me, whispering dirty little things in my ear, some of them I understand and others, hell, he could probably read me his grocery list and it would be hot.

"I can practically hear you thinking, *Cerise*," he says into my ear. "Stop."

God I'm trying. I slide my legs higher up his sides and try to guide him, silently begging my body to get back to that place where my limbs melt and I hear nothing but white noise and the sound of him coming and coming but . . . shit, that is so not happening. Stupid body. Stupid brain. Stupid temperamental orgasm.

"Let me hear you," he says, but it sounds a lot like a question. Like he's asking me. "You don't have to be quiet."

Am I being quiet? I groan at how awkward I feel and

close my eyes, wondering if I should just tell him he doesn't have to wait for me, remind him that sometimes my body takes too long or, I can't believe I'm thinking this, if I should fake it.

"Ansel," I say, and tighten my grip on his shoulders because frankly, I have absolutely no idea what's about to come out of my mouth. "You feel so good, but—"

Apparently that's all he needed.

"Oh God," he moans. "Not yet, not yet."

He bites his lip, twists the fingers of one hand into my hair while the other moves to cup my ass, lifting me to him. Closer. He leans down and groans into my mouth and if I wasn't so lost in my own head *dear God* all of this would be hot.

"Fuck, fuck, *fuck*," he growls and pushes into me one final time, so deep I feel like I'm practically folded in half. The air escapes my lungs in a whoosh as he collapses against me and I blink up at the ceiling.

I'm familiar with this moment; it's the same one I've had over and over throughout my life. The moment when my body didn't quite get there and I'm left with this worry that there's something wrong with me. That maybe I'll never have routine orgasms with another person.

Ansel kisses me once on the lips, warm and lingering, before he grips the condom and pulls out. "You okay?" he asks, bending to catch my eyes.

I stretch, do my best to look thoroughly wrecked, and smile up at him. "Absolutely. Just"—I pause for a very dramatic yawn—"*sorelaxednow*," I say sleepily.

I can see the words on the tip of his tongue, the question: *Did you?*

"Do you want dinner?" he asks instead, kissing my chin. His voice has a slight shake to it, a breath of uncertainty.

Nodding, I watch as he rolls out of bed, puts his clothes back on, and smiles sweetly at me before ducking out of the bedroom.

Chapter TEN

THREE MORE DAYS pass in a blur of sightseeing, rich food, coffee, and worn-out feet, with only a few hours at home, awake with Ansel. He's easy to be near, his goofiness returning after he's had time to decompress from his day, and he has the rare ability to get me talking and laughing about anything: vegetables, sports, film, shoe size/penis size correlations, and my favorite places to be kissed.

But neither of us seems to know how to get the comfort of *touching* back. On the couch Wednesday night, he cuddles me, kisses the top of my head, translating a French crime drama in quiet whispers. He kisses my temple when he leaves for work and calls at noon and four every day.

But he seems to have put the sex in my hands . . . so to speak. And I am failing big-time. I want to tell him I'll never be the seductive sexbomb, and he needs to unleash some of the wild Ansel to get me comfortable, but he's too exhausted to do much more than take his shoes off when he gets home.

I pretend I'm in a movie montage, developing a new morning routine in my fabulous life in Paris. I stare out the window and sip the coffee Ansel made before he took off, de-

ciding what I'm going to do all day and going over the small
list of translations he's left for me.

How are you? *Comment allez-vous?*
Thank you. *Merci.*
Do you speak English? *Parlez-vous anglais?*
Which way to the métro? *Où se trouve le métro?*
Where is the toilet? *Où sont les toilettes?*
How much? *Combien ça coûte?*
Why no, I'm not interested. My husband is perfect.
*Comment, non, ça ne m'intéresse pas. Mon mari est
parfait.*

Once I've showered and dressed, I get a pastry at the tiny
patisserie two blocks from our building, where I chat with the
American girl who works there, Simone, and then either walk
or take the métro to a place I've never been before. The Latin
Quarter, Montmartre, Musée d'Orsay, the Catacombs. I even
plan a bike tour of Versailles, where I can see the expansive
gardens and the palace.

It's a dream life, I know this. It's such a dream life that
future-me almost hates present-me for having so much time
and freedom and ever feeling lonely. It's ridiculous. It's
just . . . I *like* Ansel. I'm greedy for more time with him.

At least there's comfort in knowing I can call Lola or
Harlow around the time they're getting out of bed, and
they're both living vicariously through me. Friday afternoon I
find a sunny bench outside the d'Orsay and call Harlow, to
catch her up on everything Paris Adventure.

Even though Harlow has been here more times than I can remember, I tell her about our flat, about the métro, about the pastry and coffee and unending, curving streets. I tell her it's easy to walk for miles and not realize it, that the most amazing landmarks are often tucked into the most ordinary places . . . though nothing about Paris is ordinary.

"And I'm meeting people!" I tell her. "Other than Ansel, that is."

"Example, please. Would we approve?"

"Maybe?" I say, thinking. "There's this American girl here, she works at the bakery where I get my breakfast. Her name is Simone, she's from the Valley—"

"Ew."

I laugh. "But she used the word *gruesome* to mean 'cool' and ever since then I can't think of her as anyone other than Gruesimone."

"This is why I would go gay for you, Mia," Harlow says. "You hardly say anything and then shit like this comes out of your mouth. Like the time you called me Whorelow when we had that fight in seventh grade and I started laughing and couldn't stop until I peed my pants? We are terrible fighters."

"Listen," I say, cracking up at the memory. "She's not speaking to her best friend since fifth grade because she chose the same song for her first dance at her wedding."

Harlow pauses for a beat. "Give me another example, I can maybe see that one."

"Seriously?" I pull my phone away from my ear and look at it as if she can see my judgment through the call. "And don't worry, Harlow, neither Lola nor I will pick anything by Celine Dion."

"I realize you're mocking me but the woman is amazing. And in concert? Don't even get me started."

I groan. "Okay, so another example." I sort through some options. I could talk about the other barista, the non-verbal Rhea—whom I've started thinking of as Rheapellent—but then I remember Simone's weirdest habit. "Gruesimone says 'FML' for everything. Like—"

"Wait," she interrupts me. "What's 'FML'?"

"Fuck my life."

"Wow, okay," she says. "And people use this for reasons other than 'I have cancer' or 'I am trapped under a truck'?"

"Apparently," I say, nodding. "She drops some change, 'FML.' She slops some coffee on her hand: 'FML.' She chips a nail and, I kid you not, 'FML.' And outside on the street, this city is *insane*. Cars drive *crazy* here but pedestrians will just step into the street like, 'I've had a nice life, it's okay if it all ends here.'"

Harlow is cackling on the other end of the line and it warms me, makes my world feel big again. "And lunch with a bottle of wine and four espressos?" I ask, giggling. "Why not?"

"Sounds like my kind of city," Harlow says.

"You've been here, why am I describing it?"

"Because you miss me?"

I slump against the back of the bench. "I do. I really do."

She pauses for a beat before asking, "And the husband?"

Ah. There it is. "He's good."

"That's it?" she asks, voice going quieter. "That's really all I get? You've been gone for two weeks, living with Baby Adonis, and all you can tell me is 'he's good'?"

I close my eyes and tilt my head into the sun. "He's so sweet but he works *constantly*. And when he's home, I'm basically as seductive as a cardboard box."

"Well, have you made any *other* friends? Hot friends. You know, for me?" she asks, and I can hear the smile in her voice.

I hum. "Not really. I mean, it's been a week and a half, and I was sick for a lot of that. I met the woman downstairs, and she barely speaks English but we make it work."

"Have Ansel introduce you to some people for when he's gone."

"Yeah, I haven't even heard about any of his friends." My thoughts trip on this a little. "I mean don't get me wrong, we get so little time together that I'm not really sure I want to share him. But . . . is that weird? Do you think it's strange that he hasn't mentioned getting together with some people here?"

"Hmm, well . . . either he has a stack of dead girlfriends somewhere that he's trying to keep hidden—"

"Ha ha."

"—or it's like you said and he's just *busy*. There were literally weeks at a time where we barely saw my mom growing up because she was on set."

I pull at a thread on my T-shirt, wondering if she could be on to something. "Yeah, I guess you're right."

"*Orrrrr,*" she starts, "he's a boy and therefore likes to

pretend you're happy just walking around his apartment naked all day. That's the hypothesis that gets my vote."

"I'll take it."

"You'll be on a plane in a few weeks. Enjoy the freedom. Fill your days with sun and wine. Naked times with hot French boys. One in particular."

"We had the most awkward sex in the history of the world the other night. I couldn't stop overthinking everything. And nothing else for the past three days and I *want* to touch him constantly. It's torture." And it is. As soon as I say it, I think of the smooth skin of his neck, the gentle bite of his teeth, the clean lines of his chest and stomach.

"So get out of *your* head," she says in a dramatic Russian accent, "and give *his* head some attention, if you catch my drift."

"I don't, Whorelow. Can you explain that to me? His . . . 'head'? Do you mean his penis? I wish you would stop speaking in riddles."

"Well, tell me something. Why was it easy in Vegas, and not easy there?"

"I don't know . . ." I wrinkle my nose, thinking. "I just pretended to be the kind of girl who would do something like that. One-night stand and sexy and blah blah."

Laughing, she asks, "So be that girl again."

"It's not really that easy. It's weirder here. Like, everything is loaded. 'We should have sex because I am very attracted to you and also we are married. Married people have sex. Beep boop boop, system reboot failure.'"

"You're doing the robot right now, aren't you?"

I look at my hand raised at my side, fingers pointed and pressed together. "Maybe."

Her laugh gets louder and she pushes the words out: "Then be someone less neurotic, you troll."

"Oh, dude, I should have thought of that, Whorelow. I could totally just be someone less neurotic. Thanks so much, my problems are solved."

"Okay, fine," she says, and I can just see her face, can just *see* the way she would lean in and grow serious about her favorite topic ever: sex. "Here's a suggestion just for you, Sugarcube: get a costume."

I feel like the sky has just opened up and the universe has dropped an anvil on my head.

Or a gauntlet.

I close my eyes and remember Vegas, how easy it was to be playful rather than earnest. To pretend to be someone braver than I am. And the morning I used his hand as a sex toy. It worked then, too. Being someone else, getting lost in the part.

I feel the idea tickling in my thoughts before it spreads, wings expanding with a rush.

Play.

What did you love most about dancing, he'd asked me.

The ability to be anyone up onstage, I told him. *I want a different life tonight.*

And then I chose a different life but it sits here, wilting.

"Do I know you or what?" Harlow asks, her smiling pushing all the way across the ocean through the phone line.

———————

EVEN AFTER MY epiphany that it helps me relax when I'm pretending, I'm still not really sure how to tackle this. A costume . . . like sexy underwear to get me in the right headspace? Or is Harlow really suggesting I pull out all the stops and go full-on, jazz-hands, showtime? My phone continually buzzes with texts from her, all of them filled with links and addresses within an area known as Place Pigalle.

And of course they're all in the neighborhood near our apartment, lending even greater sense of destiny to this plan. *Make it easy on me why don't you, Harlow?*

But none is exactly what I'm looking for: they're either dark and cavelike, or advertised with bright neon lights and posed mannequins dressed in scraps of frightening lingerie in the window. I continue to walk, following the last address Harlow sent and wandering down one narrow alley and then another. In the shadows it's quiet, nearly damp, and I continue for what feels like blocks before the sky appears in a tiny courtyard. And only about ten yards down, there is a little, understated shop with lace and velvet and leather in the window.

I feel like I've been transported to Diagon Alley.

I open the door and am hit with the smell of iris and sage, a scent so warm and earthy, I immediately feel myself relaxing. A woman inside steps out from behind the counter and somehow knows to give me a "Hello," and not a "*Bonjour*."

She wears a leather corset, her breasts pushing up enviably. Dark denim wraps around her legs and her heels have to be at least five inches of screaming, fire engine red.

All around me there are cases of toys—dildos and vibrators, rubber fists and handcuffs. Near the back of the store are shelves of books and videos, and along the side walls are racks of costumes of every color and for nearly every fantasy.

"You are looking for a costume to wear or play?" she asks, noticing where I've turned my attention. Even though her question, as phrased, is a little confusing, and even though my brain wants to linger on the sweetness of her accent curling around "costume," I know what she meant. Because it's exactly why I walked in here.

"Play," I say.

Her eyes turn up in a warm smile. A real smile in a tiny store buried in an enormous city.

"We start you out easy, okay?" She walks over to a rack with costumes I recognize: nurse, maid, schoolgirl, cat. I run my hand over the rack, feeling excitement bloom beneath my ribs. "And then you come back when he will like some more."

Chapter ELEVEN

I GET HOME, RELIEVED that Ansel isn't here yet. Dropping a bag of takeout on the kitchen counter, I move to the bedroom and pull the costume from the garment bag. When I hold it up in front of me, I feel the first pang of uncertainty. The saleswoman measured my bust, my waist, and my hips so she could calculate my size. But the tiny thing in my hands doesn't look like it will fit.

In fact, it *does* fit, but it doesn't look any bigger once it's on. The bodice and skirt are pink satin, overlaid with delicate black lace. The top pushes my breasts together and up, giving me cleavage I don't think I've ever had before. The skirt flares out, ending many inches above my knees. When I bend over, the black ruffle panties are supposed to show. I tie the tiny apron, fix the little cap on my head, and pull on the black thigh-highs, straightening the pink bows at my knees. Once I slip on the spiked heels and hold my feather duster, I feel both sexy and ridiculous, if the combination is even possible. My mind seesaws between the two. It's not that I don't look good in the costume, it's that I can't honestly imagine what Ansel will think when he comes home to this.

But it isn't enough for me to just dress up. Costumes alone do not a show make. I need a plot, a story to tell. I sense that we need to get lost in another reality tonight, one where he doesn't have the stress of his job looming over his daylight hours, and one where I don't feel like he offered an adventure to a girl who left her spark back in the States.

I could be the good maid who has done her job perfectly and deserves reward. The idea of Ansel thanking me, rewarding me, makes my skin hum with a flush. The problem is Ansel's flat is spotless. There's nothing I can do to make it look better, and he won't pick up on what role he's supposed to play.

That means I need to get in trouble.

I look around, wondering what I can mess up, what he'll immediately notice. I don't want to leave food on the counter in case this plan is successful and we end up in bed all night. My eyes move across the apartment and stop at the wall of windows, pinned there.

Even with only the light of the streetlamps coming through the glass, I can see how it gleams, spotless.

I know he'll be here any second. I hear the grind of the elevator, the metal clanking of the doors closing. I close my eyes and press both palms flat to the window, smearing. When I pull back, two long smudges stay behind.

His key fits into the lock, creaking as it turns. The door opens with the quiet skid of wood on wood, and I move to the entryway, back straight, hands clasped around the feather duster in front of me.

Ansel drops his keys on the table, places his helmet beneath it, and then looks up, eyes going wide.

"Wow. Hello." He tightens his grip on two envelopes in his hand.

"Welcome home, Mr. Guillaume," I say, voice breaking on his name. I'm giving myself five minutes. If he doesn't seem to want to play, it won't be the end of the world.

It won't.

His eyes first move up to the tiny, frilled cap pinned in my hair and then down, tripping as they always do over my lips before sliding down my neck, to my breasts, my waist, my hips, my thighs. He eyes my shoes, lips parting.

"I thought you might want to look over the house before I leave for the night," I say, stronger now. I'm bolstered by the flush in his cheeks, the heat in his green eyes when he looks back at my face.

"The house looks good," he says, voice nearly inaudible from the rasp of it. He hasn't even looked away from me to the room beyond, so at least I know so far he's playing along.

I step aside, curling my hands into fists so my fingers don't shake when the real game begins. "Feel free to check everything."

My heart is beating so hard I swear I can feel my neck move. His gaze instinctively moves past me to the window just behind, his brow drawing together.

"Mia?"

I move to his side, biting back my excited grin. "Yes, Mr. Guillaume?"

"Did you . . ." He looks at me, searching, and then points to the window, using the envelopes in his hand. He's embarrassed I've discovered this compulsion. He's trying to understand what's going on, and the seconds tick by, painfully slow.

It's a game. Play. Play.

"Did I miss a spot?" I ask.

His eyes narrow, head jerking back slightly when he understands, and the nervous tickle in my stomach turns into a lurching roll. I have no idea if I've made an enormous mistake by trying to do this. I must look like a lunatic.

But then I remember Ansel in the hall in his boxers, flirting. I remember his voice hot in my ear, sneaking up on me, and Finn sneaking up on *him,* nearly pulling his pants around his ankles. I remember what Finn told me about Bronies and serendipity. I know that at his core, beyond the stress of work, Ansel is game for some fun.

Shit. I just hope he's game for *this.* I don't want to be wrong. Wrong will send me back to the dark ages of awkward silence.

He turns slowly, wearing one of his easy smiles I haven't seen in days. He looks me over again, from the top of my head to my tiny, dangerous heels. His gaze is tangible, a brush of heat across my skin. "Is this what you need?" he whispers.

After a beat, I nod. "I think so."

A cacophony of horns blares up from the street below and Ansel waits until the flat is silent again before he speaks.

"Oh yes," he says slowly. "You missed a spot."

I pull my brows together in mock concern, my mouth forming a soft, round O.

With a dramatic scowl he turns, stomping to the kitchen and pulling out an unlabeled bottle. I can smell the vinegar, and wonder whether he has his own glass-cleaning recipe. His fingers brush mine when he hands me the bottle. "You may fix it before you leave."

I feel my shoulders straighten confidently as he follows me to the window, watching as I spray a cloud over the handprints. There's a heavy buzz in my veins, a sense of power I hadn't expected. He's doing what I want him to do, and though he's handing me a cloth to wipe the window clean, it's because I've orchestrated it. He's just playing along.

"Go over it once again. Leave no streaks."

When I'm finished, it gleams, spotless, and behind me he exhales slowly. "An apology seems appropriate, no?"

When I turn to face him, he looks so sincerely displeased that my pulse trips in my throat—hot and thrilled—and I blurt, "I'm sorry. I—"

He reaches up, eyes twinkling as his thumb strokes across my bottom lip to calm me. "Good." Blinking toward the kitchen, he inhales slowly, smelling the roasted chicken, then asks, "Have you made dinner?"

"I ordered—" I pause, blinking. "Yes. I cooked you dinner."

"I'd like some now." With a tiny smile, he turns and

walks across the room to the dining table, sitting down and leaning back in the chair. I hear the rip of paper as he opens the mail he'd been holding and a long, quiet exhale as he places it on the table beside him. He doesn't even turn around to look at me.

Holy shit is he good at this.

I move to the kitchen, pulling food from the takeout container and arranging it as neatly as I can on a plate for him between stolen glances in his direction. He's still waiting and reading his mail, patiently, completely in character while he waits for me—*his maid*—to bring him his dinner. So far, so good. Spotting a bottle of wine on the counter, I pull out the cork and pour him a glass. The red shines decadently, climbing up the sides as it sways in my hand. I pick up the plate and carry his dinner out to him, setting it down with a quiet *thunk.*

"Thank you," he says.

"You're welcome."

I hover for a beat, staring down at the letter I think he's left for me to see. It sits, faceup, on the table and the first thing my gaze snags on is his name at the top, and then the long list of checkmarks beneath the *Negatif* column for every sexually transmitted disease we were tested for.

And then I see the unopened envelope beside his, addressed to me.

"Is this my paycheck?" I ask him. I wait until he nods before sliding it off the table. Opening it quickly, I scan the letter and smile. Good to go.

He doesn't ask what mine says, and I don't bother to tell him. Instead, I stand to the side and just behind him, my heart jackhammering in my chest as I watch him dig into his dinner. He doesn't ask if I've eaten, doesn't offer anything to me.

But there's something about playing this game, a mild domination role for him, that makes my stomach flutter, my skin hum with warmth. I like to watch him eat. He curls over his plate and his shoulders flex, muscles in his back defined and visible through his light purple dress shirt.

What will we do when he's done? Will we continue to play? Or will he drop the act, pull me to the bedroom, and touch me? I want both options—I especially want him now that I know I'll feel every inch of his skin—but I want to keep playing even more.

He seems to drink his wine quickly, washing down every bite with long gulps. At first, I wonder if he's nervous and just hiding it well. But when he puts his glass down on the table and gestures for me to refill it, it occurs to me that he's simply wondering how far I'll go serving him.

When I bring the bottle out and refill his glass, he says only a quiet *"Merci,"* and then returns to his food.

The silence is unnerving, and it *has* to be intentional. Ansel may be a workaholic, but when he's home the flat is not ever quiet. He sings, he chatters, he makes everything into a drum with his fingers. I realize I'm right—it *is* intentional—when he swallows a bite and says, "Talk to me. Tell me something while I eat."

He's testing me again, but unlike refilling his wine, he knows this one is more of a challenge.

"I had a nice day on the job," I tell him. He hums as he chews, looking over his shoulder at me. It's the first time I catch a glimpse of hesitation in his eyes, as if he wants me to be able to tell him everything I did today, and truthfully, but can't while we play.

"Cleaned for a while over near the Orsay . . . then near the Madeleine," I answer with a smile, enjoying our code. He returns to his food, and his silence.

I sense that I'm meant to keep talking, but I have no idea what to say. Finally, I whisper, "The envelope . . . my paycheck looks good."

He pauses for a moment, but it's long enough for me to notice the way his breath catches. My pulse picks up in my throat when he carefully wipes his mouth and puts his napkin down beside his plate, and I can feel it along the length of my arms, deep down in my belly. He pushes back from the table, but doesn't stand. "Good."

I reach for his empty plate but he stops me with his hand on my arm. "If you're to remain my maid, you should know I'll never overlook the windows."

I blink, trying to unscramble this code. He licks his lips, waiting for me to say something.

"I understand."

A tiny, playful smile teases at the corner of his mouth. "Do you?"

Closing my eyes, I admit, "No."

I feel his fingertip run up the inside of my leg, from my knee to the middle of my thigh. Every sensation is as sharp as a knife.

"Then let me help you understand," he whispers. "I like that you fixed your mistake. I like that you served me dinner. I like that you wore your uniform."

I like that you wanted to play, he means, and he says it with his tongue wetting his lips and his eyes raking over my body. *I'll understand next time,* he's saying.

"Oh." I exhale, opening my eyes. "I may not forget the window every night. Maybe some nights I'll forget other things."

His smile appears and is gone as soon as he can control it. "That's okay. But uniforms, in general, are appreciated."

Something inside my chest unknots, as if seeing this confirmation that he understands this about me. Ansel is comfortable in his skin, a portrait of ease. Unless dancing, I've never been that girl. But he makes me feel safe exploring all the ways I can wrestle my way out of my own head.

"Did serving me dinner make you wet?"

With this blunt question, my eyes fly to his and my heart takes off in a frantic sprint. "What?"

"Did serving. Me dinner. Make you *wet*."

"I . . . think so."

"I don't believe you." He smiles, but it has a deliciously sinister curve to it. "Show me."

I reach down, pushing my shaking hand into my underwear. I *am* wet. Embarrassingly, wantonly so. Without thinking, I stroke myself while he watches, eyes growing darker.

"Feed it to me."

The words burst something open inside me and I moan, pulling my hand free. He watches its path from between my legs to just in front of his mouth, the slickness visible in the dim light.

I paint his lips until he parts them and I press two fingers inside. His tongue is warm and curls around my fingers; it's torture—I want to feel his mouth between my legs now—and he knows it. He holds me by the wrist so I can't pull away as he sucks my fingertip, licking it like he would my clit, teasing me until my entire body aches. It's the kind of ache that comes with pleasure on its heels, promising more.

"Again."

I whimper a little, not wanting to feel the pressure of my hand there again without relief. I don't remember the last time I've wanted sex so intensely. If possible, I'm even more soaked. He lets me glide my fingers back and forth longer this time, long enough that I can feel my orgasm in the distance, know how much my body wants to let go.

"Stop," he says sharply, this time reaching for my arm and pulling my hand out. He sucks each finger in turn, eyes fixed to mine. "Climb on the table."

I move around him, pushing his plate far out of the way and lifting my butt onto the dining table so I'm sitting in front of him, his thighs bracketing mine.

"Lie back," he tells me.

I do as he says, exhaling a shaky breath when his hands run up my legs and back down again, before taking off my sleek, black, sky-high heels. He rests my feet on his thighs and leans forward, kissing the inside of my knee.

The fabric of his dress pants is soft against the soles of my feet, and his breath slides up my leg, over my knee, and along my thigh. His soft hair brushes against my skin, his hands curl around my calves, steadying my legs.

I feel *everything* and it's as if I'm made of pure hunger. It's hot and liquid, filling my limbs and tamping down my patience. *Touch me,* my body screams. I squirm on the table and Ansel stills me with a firm hand on my abdomen.

"Be *still*." He exhales once, a long stream of air blown directly between my legs.

"Please . . ." I gasp. I love this side of him, I want more, want to provoke the sharp edge to his tone, but I want his satisfaction in me, too. I'm torn between trying on petulance and delving further and further into this easy, obedient place.

"'Please' what?" He kisses the delicate skin just beside the fabric of my frilly underwear. "Please reward you for being such a good maid?"

I open my mouth but only a low, pleading sound comes out as he noses at my pussy beneath the fabric, pressing, kissing, teeth bared and gliding over my lips, my pubic bone, over to my hip.

"Or 'please' punish you for being so very wicked, putting your hands on my windows?"

Both. Yes. Please.

I'm unbelievably wet, hips pushing up, tiny noises escaping from my throat every time I feel the hot press of his breath into my skin.

"Touch me," I beg. "I want your mouth on me."

Hooking a finger beneath the fabric, he pulls my soaked underwear aside, licking me directly in a long, firm drag of his tongue. I gasp, arching up beneath him.

He opens his mouth, sucking, urgent, and

good,

God

so good

licking me with a flattened tongue, fingers pressing into me and curling. He pulls back with a quiet grunt and tells me, "Watch me." The next four words are spoken into the delicate skin of my clit: "Watch me kiss you."

His demand is more a preemptive threat than an order because I couldn't tear my eyes away from his ownership of my body even if I wanted to.

"You taste like the ocean," he groans, sucking, pulling at me with his lips and tongue. The feeling is too intense to be called pleasure. It's something bigger, pushing all of my inhibitions away, making me feel strong and bold enough to push onto my elbow, run my other hand into his hair to gently guide him as I roll my hips.

It seems impossible that I can feel *more,* but when he realizes I'm close, he begins to moan against me, encouraging with the vibration of his voice, the solid thrusting of two fingers and the wet slide of his tongue around and around and around . . .

I grow dizzy for a beat before I tumble, floating, shaking through the blissful spasms that feel so good it's the razor-sharp line of pleasure edging pain. It's an orgasm so intense my legs want to pull closed, my hips arch off the table.

But he holds me open, fingers pumping between my legs until I'm gasping, boneless, struggling to sit and pull him up to me.

He staggers to his feet, pulling his arm across his mouth. "*That* is what you sound like when you come."

His hair is a mess from my hands, his lips swollen from sucking me so thoroughly. "I'm taking you to my bed," he says, pushing his chair back and out of the way. He holds out a hand to me, helps me down from the table on shaky legs. As he walks, he loosens his tie, unbuttons his shirt, steps out of his shoes. By the time we've made it to his room, he's pushing his pants down his legs and gesturing for me to sit at the edge of the bed.

In two steps, he's in front of me, hand curled around the base of his cock as he holds it to me, saying only, "Suck."

As he leans in, my teeth clench with how much I want to taste him. The pillow I sleep on every night has nothing on the reality of his scent. It's clean sweat and grass and saltwater. The smell of him is edible, and *hard* doesn't describe how he feels when I wrap my hand around his shaft. He's like steel in my palm, his body wound so tight I don't know how much longer he can wait.

I lick him, and then again, over and up and down his length until he's slick and wet and slides easily into my mouth. I'm shaking; wild from the earth taste of him and the way he looms over me. Never before has he looked so strong, almost savage the way his hand slides into my hair, guiding me carefully at first and then holding so he can push deeply, once with a jagged, relieved groan. Otherwise he's silent, fingertips pressed to my scalp as he lets me take over again, only occasionally pushing deep. In my mouth he feels as swollen as my abused lips do, fat and needing to be devoured. And I *do* devour him. I've never loved doing this as much as I do with him, his thick shaft and smooth skin stretched tight over the engorged tip. I curl my tongue around the ridge, sucking, wanting more.

He releases a husky feral sound before pulling back, wrapping a fist around his cock. "Undress."

I stand on shaky legs, peeling the stockings off, removing the skirt, the bustier, and finally, the frilly underwear. He watches me, eyes dark and impatient, and growls, *"Allonge-toi."* He lifts his chin, repeating quietly in English, "Lie back."

I scoot farther up on the bed, eyes wide and pinned to him as I lie back and spread my legs. I want to feel him. Just him. Right now—I can see it in his eyes—he knows I'll give him anything, give him everything. He lurches forward, bracing a hand on my spread inner thigh and entering me in a single, long push.

All the air leaves me and for a few overwhelmed seconds,

I can't get it back. I try to remember how to inhale then exhale, try to remind myself that his cock isn't *actually* pushing all of the air out of me, it only feels that way. I'd forgotten what it feels like to have him inside me like this: confident, commanding. But the feel of his warmth, nothing between us . . . it steals my air, my thoughts, my clarity.

He doesn't move for an eternity, just stares down, eyes moving over every inch of me he can see from his vantage. He's so hard it has to be edging discomfort for him, and I can feel the shake of his hand gripping the sheet near my head.

"You need to be reminded?" he whispers.

I nod frantically, hands grasping his sides as my hips move off the bed, hungry. He pulls back so slowly I feel my nails digging into the skin of his sides before I even realize what I'm doing. He hisses, stabbing back into me with a low groan.

And then he snaps back again, and then forward, hard and tormenting, his pace nearly punishing. Punishing me for the handprint, punishing us both for the distance that got between us. Punishing me for forgetting sex with us is like this, and *nothing* is better. He leans over me, his skin rubbing mine where I need him, sweat dampening his brow and the smooth expanse of his chest. I curl into him, licking his collarbone, his neck, pulling his head to mine to feel the deep rumble of his pleasure against my teeth, my lips, my tongue.

My thighs shake at his sides, pleasure climbing, and I need harder and more of him, my fingers are desperately pulling at his hips, my words begging and unintelligible. I feel my release twisting in me, tighter and tighter until it snaps, bursting wide open in a jerking, clutching lash of sensation and I'm arching from the bed, crying his name over and over.

He pushes up on his hands, watching me come apart under him, and through the fog of my orgasm, I watch him climb. His strokes are long and hard, our skin slapping together in a crude sound that makes me wilder, makes me wonder if I really am on the verge of coming again so soon.

"Aah," I cry out. "I'm . . ."

"*Show* me," he growls, dropping a hand between us, petting my clit in tiny, perfect circles.

I bow off the bed, my entire body clenching in a second orgasm so sharp my vision blurs.

Ansel's neck becomes corded and tense, teeth clench and eyes narrow and he hisses, *"Fuck,"* before his hips become brutal, loudly pounding against my thighs. He collapses on top of me and I can feel the way he twitches inside, the way he shudders under my hands.

I let out a shaky gasp, winding my legs around his hips when he begins to pull back. "No," I say into the skin of his neck. "Stay."

He bends, his mouth latching on to my breast, sucking, tongue roaming up my neck to my jaw as his hips rock slowly back and forth. He seems insatiable, and even though I know he's already come, I don't sense that we're done. Once his mouth finds mine, I'm lost again, lost in the wet slide of his tongue, the slow press of him in and out of me. It feels like only a second that his body relaxes inside before I feel him stirring again, lengthening until he's moving in earnest, long curling thrusts with his body pressed all along mine.

This time it's slow, and he kisses me every second of it, deep and searching, letting me hear the agony and pleasure of our bodies so thoroughly that it makes me delirious.

HE ROLLS OFF me, groaning in relief. I curl to him in the dark, my heart racing still, skin damp with sweat.

"Ah," he whispers, kissing the top of my head. "There she is."

I kiss his throat, tongue sliding over the hollow where I taste the faint salt of his sweat and mine.

"Thank you for this," he says. "I love that you did this tonight."

My hand drifts up his stomach, across his chest, and I close my eyes as I ask, "Tell me about the window."

Beside me he freezes for a beat, before exhaling a long, slow breath. "It is complicated, maybe."

"I don't have anywhere I need to be," I say, smiling into the darkness.

His lips press to my temple before he says, "My mother, as I mentioned, is American." I look up at his face from where I rest on his chest, but it's hard to make out his features in the dark. "She moved to France when she was just out of high school, and worked as a maid."

"Oh," I say, laughing. "Maybe my costume choice was a little weird for you."

He groans, tickling my side. "I assure you, you did not make me think of my mother tonight at all." After I've stilled at his side, he says, "Her first job was working in the very regal house of a businessman named Charles Guillaume."

"Your father," I guess.

He nods. "My mother is a wonderful woman. Caring, fastidious. I imagine she was a perfect housekeeper. I suppose I get those tendencies from her, but also my father. He required the house to be spotless. He was obsessive about it. He required that I never leave a mark, anywhere. Not on mirrors, or windows. Not a crumb in the kitchen. Children were neither to be seen *nor* heard." He pauses, and when he speaks again, his voice is lighter. "Perhaps our fathers are not very nice, but would get along well?"

I hold my breath, not wanting to move or blink or do anything to break this moment. Each word feels like a gift and I'm so hungry for every little piece of his history. "Tell me more about them?"

He shifts me closer, sliding his hands into the hair at the back of my head. "They began to have an affair when my mother was only twenty, and my father was forty-four. From what my mother has told me, it was very passionate. It consumed her. She never planned to stay in France for so long, but she fell in love with Charles and I don't think she has ever recovered."

"'Recovered'?"

"My father is an asshole," he says, laughing a little dryly. "Controlling. Obsessive about the house, as I mentioned. As he's aged, he's only gotten worse. But I think he must have a charisma, a charm that drew her in." I smile into the dark when he says this, knowing he may be a better man, but he certainly got charm from his father. "During this time that he and my mother were together, he was married to another woman. She lived in England, but my father refused to leave his home to live with her, and my mother didn't know this wife existed. When Maman became pregnant with me, my father wanted her to remain in the servants' quarters, and didn't let her tell anyone it was his child." He laughs a little. "Everyone knew anyway, and of course I turned three or four, and I looked exactly like him. Eventually, the wife found out. She divorced my father, but he did not choose to marry my mother."

I feel my chest tighten. "Oh."

"He loved her," he says quietly, and I'm obsessed with the way he speaks. His English is perfect, but his accent lifts the words, tilts them so his *h*'s comes out nearly inaudible, his *r*'s always slightly guttural. He manages to sound both polished *and* crude. "He loved her in his strange way, and made sure to always provide for us, even insisting on paying when my mother wanted to attend culinary school. But he's not a man who loves very generously; he's selfish and didn't want my mother to leave him, even though he had many other women in those years. They were at the house, or at his work. He was very unfaithful, even while he was possessive and crazy for my mother. He said he loved her like no other. He expected her to understand that his appetites for other women were not personal against her. But of course *she* was never to sleep with another man."

"Wow," I say quietly. In truth, I can't imagine knowing so much about my parents' marriage. Theirs feels like a bleached, sterile landscape compared to this.

"Exactly. So, when my grandmother became sick, my mother took the chance to leave France, to go home to Connecticut and tend to her until she died."

"How old were you when she left?"

He swallows, saying, "Sixteen. I lived with my father until I began university."

"Did your mother come back?"

I can feel him shake his head beside me. "No. I think leaving was very hard for her, but once she was gone she knew it was the right thing. She opened a bakery, bought a home. She wanted me to finish school here, with my friends, but I know being so far away ate at her. It's why I came to the States for law school. Maybe she would have come back here if I asked her to, but I couldn't, no?"

When I nod, he continues, "I went to Vanderbilt, which is not so very close to her, but much closer than France." He turns his head, pulling back so he can look at me. "I do intend someday to live there. In the States. She doesn't have anyone else."

I nod, tucking my face into the crook of his neck and overcome with a relief so enormous I feel light-headed.

"Will you stay with me?" he asks quietly. "Until you need to be in Boston?"

"Yes. If it's what you want, too."

He answers with a kiss that deepens, and the sensation of his hands in my hair and his groan on my tongue fills my head with an emotion that feels a little like desperation. In a flash, I'm terrified of having true, intense feelings for him, of having to end this marriage game at some point, let real life back in and try to get over him. But I push it aside, because it feels too good to let the moment turn down at any corner. His kisses slow and tame until he's just pressing his smile to mine.

"Good," he says.

It's enough for now. I can feel the heavy weight of sleep behind my eyes, in my thoughts. My body is sore and feels perfectly used. Within only seconds, I hear the slow, steady rhythm of his sleeping breath.

Chapter TWELVE

I'M DIMLY AWARE of a fist pounding heavily on the door and I sit up, disoriented. Beside me, Ansel bolts upright, looking at me with wide eyes before tossing back the covers, pulling on boxers, and sprinting out of the room. I hear his voice speaking to whoever is there, thick with sleep and so deep. I've never heard him sound stern before. He must have stepped out into the hallway and close the door behind him because his voice disappears after a heavy click. I try to stay awake. I try to wait for him and make sure everything's okay and tell him how much I enjoy his voice. But I must be more exhausted than I thought and it's the last groggy thought I have before my eyes fall closed again.

I FEEL THE air slide under the sheets and sweep over my skin as Ansel climbs back into bed. He smells like *him,* like grass, like salt and spice. I roll to his side, my mind still foggy and full of heated dream images . . . and as soon as his cool skin touches mine, longing flares low in my stomach. I want him with a kind of instinctive, barely awake yearning. The clock beside the bed tells me it's nearly four in the morning.

His heart is pounding under my palm, chest smooth, hard, and bare, but he traps my wandering hand with his, stilling it so that I can't slide it down his stomach and lower.

"Mia," he says quietly.

I gradually recollect that he had to go to the door. "Is everything okay?"

He exhales slowly, clearly trying to calm down, and I sense more than see his nod in the darkness. The skylight over his bed lets in a bright slice of moonlight, but it cuts across our feet, illuminating only the very edge of the bed.

I press my body along his side, sliding my leg up over his. The muscles of his quads are defined and firm beneath smooth, warm skin, and I stop when I've reached his hip, gasping slightly when he arches up into me and groans. He's still wearing only boxers, but beneath my thigh he's semi-hard. Beneath my palm, his heart is slowly returning to normal.

I can't be this close to him—even half asleep—and not want to feel more. I want the blankets tossed away and his boxers shoved down. I want the heat of his hips pressing to mine. As I hum quietly against his skin and rock against him—half conscious, half instinct—it's several long beats before I feel his body fully stir.

But it does, and with another quiet groan he rolls to face me, shoving his boxers down his hips just far enough for him to pull his erection free.

"J'ai envie de toi," he says into my hair and rubs the head of his cock over me, testing, before pushing inside with a tight sound of hunger. "I *always* want you."

It's sex without words or pretense, just both of us work-ing to get to the same place. My movements are slow, full of lazy sleepiness and that middle-of-the-night bravery that makes me roll on top of him, rest my head on his shoulder as I slide along his length. His movements are also slow, but be-cause he's being intentionally gentle, careful with me.

He's usually so much more talkative. Maybe it's that it's so late, but I can't shake the feeling that he's working to pull himself out of the hallway and back into the bedroom.

But then Ansel's hands drift down my sides, clutching my hips, and any uneasiness dissolves, replaced with a mounting, crawling pleasure.

"You fuck so good," he growls, rocking up into me, meeting my movements halfway. It's no longer sleepy and re-laxed. I'm close, he's close, and I'm chasing the sound of his orgasm as much as I am the pleasure I can feel sliding up my legs and down my spine. I'm so full of him, so full of sensa-tion, it's all I am anymore: crystalline and hot, hungry and wild.

He pushes me so I'm sitting upright, his hands jerking my hips back and forth over him, urging me to ride him roughly as he shoves himself deeper and harder into me.

"*Fuck* me," he growls, reaching up with one hand to grip my breast roughly. "Fuck me *harder*."

And I do. I find anchor with my hands on his chest and let go, slipping down onto him over and over again. I've never been so wild on top, never moved so fast. The friction between us is amazing, slick and rough, and with a sharp gasp

I start to come, my fingernails digging sharply into his skin and tight, desperate sounds falling from my lips.

I want

So

Coming so

Hard oh

Oh my God

My incoherence tears a savage growl from his throat and he sits up, fingers clamped to my hips and his teeth pressed to my collarbone as he pushes roughly up into me, coming with a hoarse shout after a final, brutal thrust.

His arms form a tight band around my waist as he presses his face to my neck, catching his breath. I feel dizzy; my legs are sore already. He doesn't seem to want to let me go but I need to shift my position, and I gingerly lift myself off and slide down next to him on the bed. Without speaking, he rolls to face me, pulling my leg over his hip and slowly rocking his still-hard cock along my clit as he kisses my chin, my cheeks, my lips.

"I want more," he admits into the dark room. "I don't feel done."

I reach down, slide him carefully back inside me. It won't last long, but there's something about feeling him like this— just barely rocking, no space between us, the black of night spread across the bed like a velvet blanket—that makes my bones ache with how intense it is between us.

"I just want to make love to you all day," he says against my mouth and rolls on top of me. "I don't want to think about work or friends or even eating. I want to exist on you alone."

With this, I remember wanting to ask him what happened at the door. "Are you okay?"

"Yes. I just want to fall asleep inside you. Maybe our bodies will make love again while our brains sleep."

"No, I mean," I start carefully, "who was at the door?"

He stills. "Perry."

Perry. The friend who wasn't in Vegas with the rest of them. "What did he want?"

He hesitates, kissing my neck. Finally, he says, "I don't know. In the middle of the night? I don't know."

Chapter THIRTEEN

I DON'T HAVE TO open my eyes to know it's still dark out. The bed is a nest of warm blankets; the sheets are smooth and smell like Ansel and laundry detergent. I'm so tired, floating in that place between awake and dreams, and so the words being whispered into my ear sound like bubbles rising up from underwater.

"Are you frowning in your sleep?" Warm lips press to my forehead, a fingertip smoothing the skin there. He kisses one cheek and then the other, brushing his nose along my jaw on his way back to my ear.

"I saw your shoes by the door," he whispers. "Have you walked all of Paris by now? They look nearly worn through on the bottom."

In truth he's not that far off. Paris is an unending map that seems to unfurl right in front of me. Around each corner is another street, another statue, another building older and more beautiful than anything I've seen before. I get to one place and that only makes me want to see what's beyond it, and beyond that. I've never been so eager to become lost in a *place* before.

"I love that you're trying to learn my city. And God help

the poor boys who see you walk by in that little sundress I saw hanging in the bathroom. You'll have admirers following you home and I'll be forced to chase them off."

I feel him smile against the side of my face. The bed shifts and his breath ruffles my hair. I keep my features relaxed, my exhales even, because I never want to wake up. Never want him to stop talking to me like this.

"It's Saturday again . . . I'm going to try and be home early tonight," he sighs, and I hear the exhaustion in his words. I'm not sure I've fully appreciated how difficult this must be for him, to balance what he sees as his responsibility to me, and to his job. I imagine it must feel like being pulled in every direction.

"I asked you to come here and I'm always gone. I never meant it to be this way. I just . . . I didn't think it through." He laughs into my neck. "Everyone I know would roll their eyes at that. Oliver, Finn . . . *especially* my mother," he says fondly. "They say I'm impulsive. But I want to be better. I want to be good to you."

I almost whimper.

"Won't you wake up, *Cerise*? Kiss me goodbye with that mouth of yours? Those lips that get me in trouble? I was in a meeting yesterday and when they called my name I had no idea what anyone was talking about. All I could think about was the way your cherry lips look stretched around my cock, and then last night . . . *oh*. The things I'll imagine today. You're going to get me fired and when we're penniless on the street you'll have no one to blame but that mouth."

I can't keep a straight face anymore and I laugh.

"Finally," he says, growling into my neck. "I was beginning to contemplate pulling the fire alarm."

EVEN AS I wake alone, a couple of hours later, I remember the way he whispered against my shoulders, and finally into my ears. I'd rolled to my back, eyes still closed as I wrapped myself around him in a drowsy hug, the fabric of his suit rough, the silk of his tie suggestive as it dragged between my naked breasts. Had I been more awake I would have pulled him down, watched as he matched his fingertips to the bruises pressed into my skin.

Ansel left me breakfast. There's coffee and a wrapped croissant waiting on the counter, and along with the lace cap that went with my maid costume, a new list of scribbled phrases rests beneath my plate.

What time is it? *Quelle heure est-il?*
What time do you close? *A quelle heure fermez-vous?*
Take your clothes off, please. *Déshabille-toi, s'il te plaît.*
Fuck me. Harder. *Baise-moi. Plus fort.*
I need the large dildo, same size as my husband. *Je voudrais le gros gode, celui qui se rapproche le plus de mon mari.*
That was the best orgasm of my life. *C'était le meilleur orgasme de ma vie.*

I'm going to come in your mouth, you beautiful girl.
Je vais jouir dans ta bouche, beauté.

I'm still smiling as I step into the bathroom and shower, memories of last night running on a reel inside my head. The water pressure in Ansel's apartment is terrible and the water is barely lukewarm. I'm reminded once again that I'm not back in San Diego, where the only person I needed to battle for hot water this late in the morning was my mom after her morning yoga class. There are seven floors of people to take into account here, and I make a mental note to get up earlier tomorrow, and sacrifice an extra hour of sleep for a hot shower. But that's not the only thing I'd miss out on. Those few, unguarded moments in the morning when Ansel thinks I'm still sleeping might just be worth a cold shower. Lots of them.

———————

GRUESIMONE IS OUTSIDE having a cigarette when I walk past the patisserie toward the métro. "Today has already been a *fucking* nightmare," she says, blowing a plume of smoke out the side of her mouth. "We sold out of the scones everyone loves and I spilled a *fucking* coffee on myself. FML."

I'm not sure why I sit with her for the duration of her break, listening to her vent about the trials of being a poor twenty-something in Paris, how her boyfriend can never seem to shut the coffee off before he leaves, or how she'd give up smoking but it's cigarettes or customer homicide—their choice. She isn't very nice, to anyone, really. Maybe it's that she's American, and it's comforting to have regular conversations with someone who isn't Ansel in a language I actually understand. Or maybe I really am that starved for outside human contact. Which is . . . really depressing.

When she's finished her last cigarette and my coffee has long grown cold, I tell her goodbye and head toward the métro, and then explore as much of Le Marais as I can in a morning.

Here there are some of the oldest buildings in the city, and it's become a popular neighborhood for art galleries, tiny cafés, and unique, pricy boutiques. What I love most about the neighborhood are the narrow winding streets, and the way tiny courtyards pop up out of nowhere, begging to be explored, or simply for me to sit and fly through a novel, getting lost in someone else's story.

Just when my stomach is rumbling and I'm ready for lunch, my phone vibrates in my bag. I'm still surprised by the delicious lurch in my chest when I see Ansel's name and face—the dorky selfie of him with pink cheeks and wild grin—flash across my screen.

Is it fondness I feel? Sweet Jesus, I'm definitely fond, and whenever he's close I basically want to molest him. It isn't just that he's gorgeous, and charming, it's that he's kind and thoughtful, and that it would never occur to him to be sharp or judgmental. There's an inherent ease to him that's disarming, and I have no doubt he leaves a trail of unintentionally broken hearts—male *and* female—wherever he goes.

I'm almost positive the old woman who runs the store around the corner from our apartment is a little in love with him. In truth, I'm pretty sure almost *everyone* Ansel knows is a little in love with him. And who could blame her really? I watched her one evening tell him something in rapid-fire French and then pause, pressing her wrinkled hands to her face like she just told the cute boy about her crush. Later, as we'd walked down the sidewalk eating our gelato, he'd explained that she told him how much he looks like the boy she fell in love with at university, and how she thought about him for a moment every morning when he stopped by for coffee.

"She thanked me for making her feel like a schoolgirl again," he'd said a little reluctantly and then turned to me with a flirty little smile. "And was glad to see me married to such a pretty girl."

"So basically you make the old ladies a little frisky."

"I really only care about *this* lady." He'd kissed my cheek. "And I don't want to make you frisky. I want you naked and begging to come all over my mouth."

I've never known someone who is such a mixture of brazen sexuality and feigned innocence before. So it's with a combination of excitement and fear that I read his message now, while traversing the busy sidewalk.

Last night was fun, it reads.

I chew my lip as I contemplate my response. The fact that he understood what I was doing, that he played along and even suggested we do it again, well . . .

I take a deep breath. So fun, I reply.

Was it nice to get outside your head a little?

The sun is high overhead and it's got to be close to eighty-five degrees outside, but with one sentence he's managed to make goose bumps erupt along my arms and legs, my nipples tighten. Somehow talking about it like this, acknowledging what we did, feels as dirty as seeing that tiny costume hanging in the closet this morning, beside the clothes he wears to work every day.

It was, I type, and if a text could come across breathy, that is exactly how this would sound.

There's a long pause before he begins typing again and I wonder if it's possible he's wound as tight as I am right now. Think you'd want to do it again?

I don't even have to think about it. Yes.

His answer comes slowly; it feels like he's typing for an eternity. Go to the Madeleine station, line 14 to Chatelet. Walk to 19 Rue Beaubourg-Centre Georges Pompidou (the large museum, you can't miss it). Take the escalators to the top floor. Wait at the bar at Georges Restaurant 19h00 (7:00 pm). Best view around.

I'm close enough to walk there, and a giddy thrill inches its way up my spine and slips like a warm bath along my skin. My limbs suddenly feel heavy, my body aches, and I have to step into an alcove in front of a small bookstore to pull myself together. I imagine this is what a sprinter feels like in those last moments before the starter pistol cracks through the air.

I have no idea what Ansel is planning, but I'm ready to find out.

THE CENTRE POMPIDOU is easy to find. Thanks to Google, I know it's centered on Paris's Right Bank, and sits in an area known as the Beaubourg neighborhood. After my days of exploring, I have a pretty good sense of where I am. But although I saw a photo of the museum online, I'm in no way prepared for the monstrous, skeletal curiosity that seems to rise up from the city around it.

It's as if the massive building has been stripped of its outer layers, revealing the very pieces that keep it erect just underneath. Brightly colored tubes in green, blue, yellow, and red are interspersed with metal beams, and look as much like a piece of art as the items housed inside.

I follow a sign that leads me to a large paved plaza, filled with students and families and groups of tourists strolling about. Performers sit surrounded by small crowds and children rush by, their laughter echoing in the hulking empty spaces created by the enormous building.

Just as Ansel instructed, I take the largest escalators I've ever seen to the top floor. The entire ride up is encapsulated in Plexiglas tunnels, giving me a view of an enormous expanse of Paris, with buildings in the distance I've only ever seen in books. I spot the Eiffel Tower immediately, set against a backdrop of bright blue sky.

My reflection winks back at me, dressed in my simple jersey shift dress, my dark hair glossy in the late afternoon sun. My face is flushed with anticipation and I'm pushing away the tremor of anxiety that I have no idea what is happening, and I've left Ansel completely in charge. Am I still his maid? I pause, mid-step between one escalator and the next, as the possibility sinks in. Our balance of power is already skewed since we arrived here. What am I heading into?

But, I reason, *when you let go last night, he took over and gave you the most intensely erotic night of your life. Trust him.*

With a deep breath, I step off at the top and make my way into the trendy restaurant. A beautiful woman with tomato-red hair and a short white dress leads me through a space that looks more like a sci-fi movie set than a place to have dinner. Everything is brushed metal and gleaming white, steel beams and polished cavelike sculptures. The tables are sleek and industrial, each one topped with a ruby-red long-stemmed rose. The outdoor dining area is protected by low-slung glass so as not to hinder the view because wow . . . what a view it is.

I thank her and take a seat at the bar, checking my phone for any messages. I've just begun a text to Ansel when I feel a slight tap on my shoulder.

"Would you mind if I sat here?" he asks, nervous. And *oh*. This isn't the same game as last night. The confusion must show in my expression because he continues, "Unless you're waiting for someone, of course."

Strangers. This I can do. This we know.

"No. Um . . . not at all. Be my guest," I say, and gesture to the seat on my right.

Ansel folds all six feet, two inches of his frame onto the brushed aluminum stool and toys with the neatly folded cloth napkin. I didn't get to fully drink in the sight of him before he left this morning, and try to covertly check him out as he fidgets, playing this new role.

He's wearing a shirt I've never seen on him, deep green with a pattern so delicate I have to peer closely to even make it out. His black dress pants fit him perfectly; there's a touch of stubble lining his jaw and his hair seems a bit more disheveled than normal, falling forward over his forehead. I have the sudden desire to twist my fingers in it while I pull his face between my legs.

I actually have to look away to catch my breath. This guy is my *husband*.

You look amazing, I want to say.

How did I find someone so easy and perfect in Las Vegas of all places? I want to ask.

But instead, I stay quiet and let him show me how this night is supposed to go.

"I think I was stood up," he says, and now that I've composed myself, I turn back to face him.

"That's terrible. They didn't call or text?"

He shakes his head and runs a hand through his hair, righting it again. "It's probably for the best," he says with a resolute lift of his chin. "I don't think we are that compatible anyway."

I angle myself toward him. "Was this supposed to be the first date?"

He shakes his head and opens his mouth to speak, pausing when the bartender stops in front of us. *"Un whisky-soda, s'il vous plaît,"* he says to the man before turning to me expectantly.

"Um . . . gin *et* . . . tonic?" I phrase it as a question and the bartender smirks before walking away.

Ansel gives a lingering stare to the bartender's back, then clears his throat before continuing. "We've been together for a while but—" He stops abruptly, shaking his head. He leans closer, dropping his voice when he says, "No, ignore that. I don't want to pretend to cheat."

I bite my lip to hold in my grin. Jesus, he's cute.

"What I mean to say is that we had talked on the phone a few times?" he says, his eyes searching mine as if this cover story works better. "It never felt totally right but I thought if we met in person . . ."

I hum in response, shaking my head in sympathy. "Sorry she's not here."

He takes a deep breath before relaxing his shoulders, and his lips push out in an edible pout. "What about you? You said you're not meeting anyone. Are you dining alone?" Holding up his hands, he adds, "And I ask that in the least stalkerish way possible. Please don't call security."

I laugh, spinning my phone on the bar in front of me. "I'm new to town," I say. "It was a long day at work and I needed a drink. A friend said this place had the best view around."

"'A friend'?"

"Just this guy I know," I tease.

Ansel smiles and looks over his shoulder. "Your friend might be wrong. Not sure you could beat the view on top of that," he says, motioning to the Eiffel Tower.

The bartender sets our drinks in front of us and I reach for my glass. "No alcohol up there, though."

"Ahhh, but yes. There's champagne on the top level. Served in the finest plastic stemware around. Don't want to miss that while you're here."

"You make me want to brave the terrifying lines and claustrophobic elevators."

"You must make sure to do it before you leave," he says. "It's a touristy thing, but it's sort of required at least once in your lifetime."

"Actually, I *did* see the top," I admit, and take a sip of my drink. "I went alone on one of my first days in town. I didn't know they had booze there, though, or I'd have stayed a *lot* longer."

"Maybe someone can go with you next time," he says quietly, apology darkening his expression. He's guilty that I'm alone so much. I'm guilty for interrupting him. We're both living so much in our own heads, no wonder we pretend.

"Maybe," I answer with a smile. "And you live here? In Paris."

Ansel nods and takes another sip of his drink. "I do. But my mother is American. And I traveled around the States after college."

"Just traveled around?" I tease. "Backpacked your way across America?"

"Close," he says with a laugh. "The summer before law school I participated in a program called Bike and Build. Have you heard of it?"

I shake my head a little, saying only, "I've heard the name . . ." Of course Ansel has mentioned it before, but I feel a bit guilty never having asked him more about it.

"It's basically a group of people—mostly university-aged—cycling across the country for three months, stopping en route to work on various building sites."

"I went to *Vegas* after I graduated from college. I think you win."

"Well *that* could be fun, too," he says meaningfully, eyes teasing as he takes a drink from his glass. "I hear there is plenty of adventure to be had in Vegas."

"Yes," I say and smile. "But three months? On a *bike*?"

Ansel laughs. "Three months. Well, eleven weeks to be exact. Riding about seventy miles a day."

"I would be dead. You'd have to call my mother to collect me by about day four."

He makes a show of looking me up and down appreciatively. "You look like you could handle it."

I shake my head. "I assure you, I am not good on two wheels. So, tell me. Did you sleep in hotels or . . . ?"

"Sometimes," he answers with a shrug. "Some groups stay in churches or other places. Maybe a group of families. My group had a sort of . . ." He pauses to search for the word, his brows drawn together. "Sleeping outside in a tent?"

"Camping," I say with a laugh.

He snaps his fingers. "Right. We'd usually be in one place for a few days while we worked, and so we'd set up a kind of traveling camp. Three or four of us sharing a canvas tent, sleeping on the worst cots you can imagine."

I look at him now, in his crisp shirt and pressed dress pants, and have a hard time imagining him even as he was, dressed down in Vegas, let alone sweaty and working on construction sites. I let my eyes linger on his neck and enjoy the fantasy for a beat. "That's pretty intense."

He nods in agreement. "Four of us, together all day long. Sometimes it was excruciating, the heat. How humid it could be and we would all just keep pushing until night. It was hard, but it was the most fun I'd ever had. I don't know that I'll ever know anyone in the way I know those three friends."

Fascinated, I break character for just a moment. "You mean Oliver and Finn and Perry."

A shadow falls over his face and he nods slowly.

Shit. "I'm sorry, I didn't mean to—"

But he's already holding up his hand. "No. Those relationships are some of the best and . . . complicated of my life. Does that make sense?" I nod. "I rode next to them for sometimes eight or ten hours a day. I slept three people deep in a space no bigger than your average bathroom. We missed our families together, we comforted each other, we celebrated some of the proudest moments of our lives. Practically living in each other's pockets at that age made three months feel like a lifetime, and it . . . I guess maybe it's hard when lives change in ways that aren't how we imagined or hoped."

Whatever this Perry is going through, it's obviously something Ansel is having a hard time dealing with. He's quiet for a moment, attention zeroed in on his glass. I'm not used to seeing him like this, and it presses like a bruise in my chest. I didn't realize how hungry I was for more details of his life until we were here, pretending to be sharing these pieces with the safety of a stranger. "You don't have to talk about it," I say quietly.

"It's just that there's nothing I can really do to *fix* what Perry's going through, and . . . I don't mean to sound self-important, but that's not a situation I'm familiar with."

"Whatever he's dealing with," I say, "you can be there, but it is *his* life. You can't make it perfect for him."

He studies me for a silent beat, opening his mouth and then closing it again. "No . . . It's just that"—he pauses and draws in a deep breath—"I know. You're right."

I want to tell him I understand, that I know what it's like to be so close to someone, to feel them drift away and be unable to pull them back, but I can't. The closest people in my life have always been Harlow and Lorelei. They're my constants, and have been since we were in elementary school. By the time Luke and I broke up after the accident, I was ready to let him go. And while I might feel the occasional hollow spot from where he used to fit into my life, I think I always knew I wasn't going to be with him forever.

Wanting to change the subject, I whisper, "Well, from where I'm sitting, whoever stood you up tonight was a total idiot."

Understanding washes over his expression and he turns on his stool to face me completely, one elbow propped up on the bar.

"I don't know," he says finally, biting his bottom lip. "I'm beginning to think she might have done me a favor . . ." He leaves the sentiment hanging meaningfully between us, and we continue to sit there in silence, the pulsing bass of music overhead thumping all around us. "Do you have a boyfriend?" he says suddenly.

"Boyfriend?" I shake my head, fighting a grin. "No." It's technically true. "Girlfriend?" I ask in return.

He shakes his head, eyes flickering to my mouth before blinking up to meet mine again.

Once the conversation about Bike and Build moves on, all traces of sadness and regret seem to disappear from Ansel's eyes and it's just like the first night we were together: the two of us, talking for hours. It helps me remember every detail that hadn't yet returned. Like the way he talks with his hands, pausing only when he forgets a word, his brow furrowed in concentration, before I laugh, a mini-game of Charades breaking out as I help him find the right one. Or the way he listens so carefully he tilts his head toward me, eyes continually inspecting my expression. He makes me feel like I'm the only person on the planet. He looks at me like he's one second away from devouring me.

No wonder I proposed.

He asks me about my life in San Diego, and listens with the same rapt attention as if the night in Las Vegas never happened, and he hasn't heard every detail before.

"And you loved dancing," he says, smiling, his empty glass abandoned on the bar in front of him. It's not posed as a question, but an observation.

"I did."

"And performing."

I sigh. "I *loved* performing."

Ansel's eyes narrow, a beat of meaningful silence stretching between us before he says, "I'm *sure*."

He's completely unashamed by the way he scans my body, gaze lingering at my breasts. I feel goose bumps spread along my skin, my nipples hardening at his suggestive tone, at the hunger in his eyes.

"But business school," he says, blinking back up to my face. "It doesn't hold your interest the same way."

I laugh. "Uh, no."

"Then why will you do it? Spend so much of your life on something that makes you clearly unhappy?"

A spark of panic flares in my chest, but I manage to quickly tamp it down. This is my safe place—this strange space that Ansel and I have found—where I can say or do or *be* anyone I want.

And so I choose to avoid answering at all, directing the

focus back onto him. "Lots of people are unhappy with their jobs. Do you love yours?"

"Not this particular one," he says. "No."

"But you continue to do it."

"Yes . . ." he says thoughtfully. "But mine is temporary. I *know* what I want to do with my life; this job is simply one door that will lead to another. This job will let me have my pick of positions anywhere in the world. Two more years of school is a long time, and I saw the way you reacted when I brought it up." He laughs softly. "Like your life had just flashed in front of your eyes. If the prospect of school makes you unhappy . . ." His voice trails off and he watches me, waiting for me to finish the sentence myself.

"I can't dance anymore," I remind him. "Screws through my leg and three centimeters of metallic alloy artificial bone aren't something I can overcome if I just *try* hard enough. It's not mind over matter."

He spins his glass, widening the dark ring of condensation that's formed on the coaster beneath it. The ice clinks against the walls of the empty tumbler, and he seems to be considering something carefully before he says it. "Not professionally," he adds with a shrug.

I shake my head but don't offer more. He doesn't understand.

"Your career as a stripper, extinguished before it ever began."

A laugh bursts from my throat. "Which sucks because I

had a name picked out, monogrammed pasties ordered and everything."

Ansel leans against the bar and turns toward me. His eyes scan my face before slipping to my mouth and down . . . down again. It's such an obvious, silly attempt at seduction that I can't hold in my laugh. *This* is the guy I couldn't take my eyes off in Vegas, the one who drew my attention no matter where he was in the room. The one I told my entire life story to in the span of a few hours, the one I *married*, the one I've had sex with many times.

"I'm really glad you got stood up," I say, hoping the way I'm looking at him makes him feel half as wanted as the way he's looking at me.

He brushes a single finger over my knee. "So am I."

I'm not sure where to go from here and so I decide to try out brave. "Would you like to leave?" I ask. "Maybe go for a walk?"

He doesn't hesitate, just stands and motions to the bartender to pay our bill.

"I'm going to run to the bathroom," I say.

He watches me with hungry eyes. "I'll be here waiting for you."

But when I step out of the large, art deco bathroom, he's right *there* in front of me—head down, face obscured by the lack of light. Dangerous. He looks up at the sound of the door and his features look stronger here in the shadows, hard, thrown into sharp relief under the neon glow. In this dimly lit corner his cheekbones resemble carved stone, his eyes shadowed, his lips lush and exaggerated.

He doesn't give me time to hesitate, just crosses the tiny space to back me against the wall.

"I couldn't wait," he says, gripping my neck, his palm cool and steady while his thumb presses to the pulse beating wildly in my throat. It's a possessive hold, and so different from the Ansel I know that it sends a silent thrill of fear up my spine. In this game we're playing, he's a stranger again. He doesn't know me and beyond what he's told me in the last hour; I'm not supposed to know anything about him, either.

A smart girl would walk away, I tell myself. A smart, quiet girl would pretend she has friends waiting and head right out the door. She wouldn't stand in a darkened hallway with a man she doesn't know, liking the way he's manhandling her so much it never occurs to her to leave.

"I can hear you thinking," he whispers, tightening his hold. "Let go. Play with me."

And it's exactly what I need. I relax my shoulders as my head clears. The tension melts from my body as I lean into him.

Even though I'm in heels and he's inches above me, I only have to lift my chin and he's there, the tip of his nose brushing over mine.

"I don't usually do this," I say, lost in the idea of a one-night stand. Of letting this sexy stranger do whatever he wants to me. "I hardly kiss on the first date, I never—" I close my eyes and swallow, opening them again to find him smiling down at me.

"I know." His grin says, *Except that time you married me in Las Vegas.*

Except *that.*

He presses a thigh between my legs and I can feel how hard he is already. I relish the small shifts of his hips as he rocks against me.

"Want you," he mumbles, kissing me, chaste and soft. He pulls back, licks his lips, and moves forward again, moaning softly into my mouth. "Can I?"

"Now?" My heart takes off, pounding so hard beneath my breastbone that I swear I can feel my chest move from the force of it.

He nods into the kiss. "Here. It's getting busy," he says, motioning back toward the restaurant. "We'd have to be quick."

It feels like someone lights a match inside my chest and I wrap my fingers into the fabric of his shirt, pulling us both back into the empty bathroom. He follows without a word, kissing me until the door shuts behind us and the lock clicks into place.

I'm suddenly overheated, oversensitive. I can feel every inch of clothing that separates us. His hands grip my face, tongue slipping against mine, and he tastes so good, I'm almost light-headed.

The room is dark, lit overhead by another strip of neon pink. It's so easy to pretend in here, lost in light that makes everything look like make-believe, surrounded by sounds on the other side of the door. I feel the beat of the music push up through the floor and into my feet, and it's only this that reminds me there are other people on this planet beyond our kisses, our frantic hands as we try to get closer, push clothes out of the way.

My dress comes up, his shirt pulled from the waist of his pants so I can scratch my nails over his stomach. I gasp as cool air finds my skin, where my panties are damp between my legs. He moves a palm down over my navel, fingers slipping just beneath the skimpy lace waistband until he's cupping me, dragging his fingers between and over, everywhere but the place I want him.

"Want to taste this," he says.

I rock against his hand, crying out at the way the tip of his fingers tease in and out of me, gathering wetness, moving back and forth over my clit.

Picking me up, he walks us to the counter, setting me down before he kneels between my parted legs. I watch as he leans forward, looking up at me through his lashes while he reaches out, pulls my panties to the side, and flicks the tip of his tongue over me.

"Oh," I cry out, too loud and breathing so heavy I fear I might actually pass out. On instinct my hand moves to the back of his head, holding him to me and *God* it's so dirty to see him like this, head down and washed in neon while he licks me out, moans against me.

I try to stay still, not to rock my hips or be demanding, but every nerve in my body is focused on his tongue as it drags over my clit.

"Fingers," I gasp.

He swears, two fingers sliding deep, his tongue moving in practiced movements, tiny flicks alternated with long, slow licks.

"Oh God . . ." I say, on the edge of something that starts in my stomach, slips up along my spine. I twist my hands in his hair, hips rocking against him as it grows stronger. I look down and watch, nearly losing my breath when I see his hand down the front of his pants, his arm jerking in a blur of movement.

"Come up here," I say, breathless. "Please." I'm so close—*so* close—but I want us to come together.

"God yes," he says, and stands, pushing his pants down his hips.

His hair is a mess and color blooms across his cheekbones and down his neck. I feel the head of his cock as he slides it over me and I'm so wet that with just the smallest step forward he starts to slip inside.

With a gasp, he tucks his head into my neck, takes deep, steadying breaths. "I need a second," he says, and holds my hips still. *"S'il te plaît."*

When he straightens again, he reaches a hand over my shoulder, bracing himself against the mirror.

"You feel too good," he explains, pulling out slowly before pushing in again. "So fucking good."

He builds a rhythm, hips rocking against mine, the sound of his belt clanking against the counter as he fucks me. I wrap my legs around his waist and he reaches up, holds my face in one hand before pushing his thumb between my lips. I can taste myself on his fingers, on his mouth, but he can't seem to focus long enough to kiss me.

"I want to watch you come," he whispers, eyes moving across my face. He pulls his thumb back and paints a wet line across my lower lip. "I want to feel you squeezing me and I want to eat your greedy little noises."

I gasp, wrapping my fists around the hem of his shirt, pulling him harder into me.

"Say what *you* want," he growls.

"I want it rougher."

"Make it dirty," he says, licking my mouth. "You can pretend you never have to see me again. What is your most shameful thought?"

My gaze drops to his mouth as I tell him, "I want someone to hear us fucking."

His pupils dilate, reflecting the neon back to me, and he grips my thighs tightly before he begins slamming hard and slick into me, grunting roughly every time his hips press to my inner thighs.

Someone knocks on the door and the timing is perfect. It's locked, but if they walked inside they would hear the slapping of his skin on mine, see my legs on either side of Ansel's hips, my dress pushed up my body while he fucks me.

"Hurry," I cry—louder than I probably should—reaching back and gripping the faucet. My fingers feel slick around the cool metal, my skin flushed and damp with sweat.

I feel so full, stretched, with limbs loose. His body fits perfectly inside and against me, the jut of his pelvis rubbing against my clit with every thrust. The tight feeling in my stomach grows, warmer and hotter until I throw my head back, crying out as I come, lost to everything but the way my body tries to pull him in as I fall apart around him.

He follows only a moment later, movements becoming jagged and frantic, stilling against me with a muffled groan into my skin.

THE EVENING BREEZE ruffles the back of my hair and the ends tickle my chin as the scent of bread and cigarettes drifts from a café we pass on our way to the métro.

I glance over my shoulder to where rows of motorcycles are parked at the curb. "Where's your bike?" I ask.

"Home," he says simply. "I dropped it off earlier so that I could walk with you."

He doesn't say this to earn a reaction, so he misses the way my eyes turn up to him. We didn't really talk about the accident tonight, though it feels like a constant companion anytime the subject of school and life ahead is broached. But he's shown me that he's always aware of what happened and won't ever push, unlike my father, who got me a bike for my first birthday out of the hospital and repeatedly suggested I *get back on the horse*. Ansel's frankness is still something that takes me by surprise. Where I tend to agonize over everything I say—worrying whether I'll be able to say it at all—Ansel never filters. Words seem to tumble from his candy-colored mouth without even a second thought. I wonder if he's always been this unguarded, if he's this way with everyone.

The busiest part of the day has come and gone but we're still lucky to find seats together. We sit side by side on the crowded train, and I watch our reflection in the window opposite us. Even in the grimy glass and beneath the harsh, often flickering fluorescent lights, it's impossible to miss how beautiful he is. It's not an adjective I've ever used to describe a guy before, but as I look at him, taking in the angles of his jaw, the prominence of his cheekbones offset by his soft, nearly feminine mouth, it's the only one that seems to fit.

He's loosened his tie, unbuttoning the top of his dress shirt to offer up a triangle of smooth, tan skin. The open shirt frames his long neck, the tempting hint of collarbone peeking out just enough to make me wonder why I never thought of collarbones as sexy before.

As if sensing my gaze, Ansel's eyes shift from the passing blur of track on the other side of the window, and meet mine in the glass. Our reflections rock with the movement of the train and Ansel watches me too, a small, knowing smile pulling at the corners of his mouth. How is it possible to sit here like this in calm, companionable silence, when only an hour ago I had him inside me, my hands slick with sweat as my fingers fought for purchase on the faucet?

More passengers board at the next stop and Ansel moves, giving his seat to an older gentleman with heavy bags in each hand. They share a few words in French I obviously don't understand, and he takes the spot in front of me, his right arm raised to grip the handrail suspended from the ceiling.

It gives me an exceptional view of his torso and the front of his dress pants. *Yum.*

The sound of laughter draws my attention and I see a group of girls seated only a few rows away. They're probably in university, I think, and just a few years younger than me. Too old for high school but clearly still students. They sit with their heads pressed together and if their hushed giggles and wide-eyed stares are any indication, I know exactly what they're looking at. Or, rather, whom.

I blink up to find him looking down at the older man, listening and oblivious to the leering glances being cast in his direction.

I don't blame them, of course. If I saw Ansel on a train I'm positive I'd practically break my neck in an attempt to get a better look, and now the night I saw him across the bar in Vegas feels like a lifetime ago. It's in these moments I find myself wanting to congratulate past-me for doing or saying whatever it was that caught Ansel's attention in the first place and—by some act of God or alcohol I still don't understand—held it. Sometimes, I think, past-me is a genius.

He laughs a deep, masculine laugh at something the man has said, and heaven help me, the dimple is out in full force again. I immediately glance over like the jealous girlfriend—*wife*—I've become and sure enough, every head in that gaggle of girls is turned, eyes wide, mouths wider, swooning over him.

And although I've said absolutely nothing, I'm beginning to wonder if every thought I have is somehow projected onto a screen above my head. Because it's this moment Ansel chooses to glance down at me, eyes soft and warm as he reaches to brush a single finger along my bottom lip. Possessiveness sparks like a flare in my chest and I turn into his hand, pressing my mouth to his palm.

Ansel is beaming when the train comes to a stop at our station. He takes my hand as I stand and pulls me out the door, fitting his arm around my waist as soon as we're on the platform.

"You left work early," I say.

He laughs. "Are you only now realizing this?"

"No. Well . . . yes. I didn't think about it before." What he told me about his boss and his job replays itself like an echo inside my head. "You won't be in trouble, will you?"

He shrugs in that way he does, easy and loose. "I can work from home," he says. "I went in before everyone else, and even leaving as early as I did, I still worked a full day. It just wasn't a fourteen-hour one. They're going to have to adjust."

But clearly they won't have to adjust *yet*. Ansel kisses me sweetly when we walk into the flat, and then moves to his desk, booting up his laptop. As if on cue, his phone rings and he shrugs at me apologetically before answering it with a clipped *"Állo?"*

I hear a deep male voice on the other end, and then, instead of his weary work expression, see a happy smile spread over my husband's face. "Hey, Olls," he says. "Yeah, we're home."

I wave, tell him to say hi to Oliver for me, and then turn to the bedroom, grabbing my book from the couch before closing the door behind me to give them some privacy.

The bed is wide and perfect, and I lie the wrong way across it, spreading out like a starfish. I can hear sounds from the street filtering up, and let the smell of bread and roasting garlic filter through my senses while I stare at my book, idly thinking about what we might do for dinner. But of course I can't focus on a single word on the page.

Partly it's the way Ansel's smile into the phone lingers in my vision, or the way his voice sounded—so deep, relieved, relaxed—so different from how I've heard him the past few weeks. Even though he's never awkward, and we just spent the most amazing evening out together, he's still the tiniest bit formal with me, and I only see it now with the intimacy of a best friend on the other end of the line. It's exactly how I am with Lola or Harlow: unguarded, unfiltered.

I listen to his voice through the door, wanting to absorb the velvet smoothness of it, his deep belly laugh. But then I hear him clear his throat and his voice drops. "She's good. I mean, of course she's amazing." He pauses, and then laughs quietly. "I know you think that. You'll think that even when we've been married for thirty years."

My stomach does a delicious pirouette but it dips uncomfortably when he says, "No, I haven't talked to her about it."

Another pause, and then, quieter, "Of course Perry hasn't been over. I don't want any of that mess to threaten Mia." I stop, leaning closer to hear better. Why didn't he tell Oliver that Perry was here banging on the door just last night?

I hear the unfamiliar edge of frustration in his voice when he says, "I will. I *will*, Oliver, shut the fuck up." But then he laughs again, removing any tension from the conversation I'm hearing through the door, and I blink, completely confused. What is the story with Perry? What is this unknown mess of him, the unanswered questions surrounding why he wasn't in the States, and how could he possibly threaten me?

Shaking my head to clear it, I realize I either need to walk out there and let him know I can hear him, or leave. Or both. We already have enough unintentional secrets . . . at least he does.

I open the bedroom door, stepping into the living room and putting a hand on his shoulder. He jumps slightly at the contact, turning to me and then lifting my hand to kiss it.

"I can hear you," I tell him, wincing a little in apology as if it's my fault. "I'm going to go to the corner and pick up some dinner."

He nods, eyes grateful for the privacy, and then points to his wallet on the entryway table. I ignore it and slip out the door, finding I'm able to really exhale for the first time once I'm closed inside the tiny elevator.

Chapter *Chapter* FOURTEEN

ANSEL WORKS, DOING his best to carve out whatever time for me he can, while I pretend my days with him and this novelty I've only just discovered, called "leisure time," won't soon be a thing of the past. Denial is my friend.

Whatever was bothering him seems to have righted itself; he's happier, less anxious, our sex life has become decidedly more hot and less bumbling, and neither Perry nor his late night visit is mentioned again.

One morning he's up before the sun, crashing around the tiny kitchen. But instead of kissing me goodbye and heading out the door, he pulls me out of bed and shoves an apple in one hand, a tiny cup of espresso in another, and tells me that we have a shared, free day; an entire Sunday stretching clear ahead of us. Thrill warms my blood and jolts me awake faster even than the pungent smell of coffee filling the small flat.

I bite into the fruit, smile as he packs us a picnic, and follow him back into the bedroom to watch him dress. I'm mesmerized by the way he so comfortably handles his own body as he pulls on boxers and then jeans, by the way his fingers slide each button through his shirt. I'm tempted to pull off his clothes just to watch him put them on all over again.

He looks up at me, catches me watching, and instead of owning it the way I want to, I blink away, look out the window, and swallow my espresso in one hot, perfect gulp.

"Why are you ever shy with me?" he asks, coming up behind me. "After what we did last night?"

Last night we had a lot of wine after not enough dinner and I was wild, pretending to be a movie star in town for only one night. He was my security guard, ushering me into his flat to protect . . . and then seduce me. It's strange how such a simple question can be impossible to answer. *I'm* shy. It's not a quality that comes out of me in certain situations, it's my *baseline*. The magic isn't why it appears with him; it's how it so easily goes away.

But I know what he's saying; I'm unpredictable in his presence. There are nights like the one earlier this week, where it's easy to talk for hours—as if even as strangers we've known each other for years. And then there are moments like this when it should be easier than anything, and I turn away, letting the energy between us flounder.

I wonder if he thinks he married a girl with two personalities: vixen and wallflower. But before I can let the thoughts consume me, I feel the warm press of his lips to the back of my neck. "Today we pretend we're on our first date, shy girl. I'm going to try to impress you, and maybe later you'll let me kiss you good night."

If he keeps sliding his hands up my sides the way he's

doing, and keeps sucking at the sensitive spot just below my ear, I might let him go all the way before we even get out of the apartment.

But he's tired of being indoors, steering me to the dresser. He takes his turn watching me get dressed but doesn't hide his open admiration as I pull on underwear, a bra, a white tank top, and a long, lapis jersey skirt. Once I'm dressed, he whistles softly and stands, moving close and cupping my face in his hands. With two fingertips he sweeps my dark bangs to the side so he can stare more clearly into my eyes. Back and forth, he searches.

"You're truly the most beautiful woman I've ever seen." Kissing the corner of my mouth, he adds, "It still doesn't feel real, does it?"

But then he smiles as if this truth—that I have only a few weeks left here—doesn't bother him at all.

How do you do it? I want to ask him. *How does the looming, dangling end of this amuse rather than weigh on you?*

———

I FEEL ADORED and cocooned in the half circle of his arm around me as we drift past his motorcycle parked on the sidewalk and head toward the métro. His free hand carries the bag with our lunch and he swings it as he walks. He hums a song, saying hello to neighbors, bending to pet a dog on a leash. The puppy looks up at him with wide brown eyes, turning as if it wants to follow him home. *You and me both,* I think. It boggles enough that he chose the profession he did—law—but then didn't do something wild and free with it like helping old ladies or being the fun law instructor who shouts and jumps on tabletops.

"Where are we going?" I ask, as we get on the train toward Châtillon.

"My favorite place."

I bump his shoulder with mine, a playful reprimand for not telling me anything, but inside I love it. I love that he's planned this, even if he only planned it as the sun rose this morning. We change trains at Invalides and the whole process feels so familiar—dodging other bodies through the tunnels, following signs, boarding another train without thinking anymore—that I'm struck with the painful thought that no matter how much it's starting to feel that way, this place isn't really my home.

For the first time since I arrived nearly a month ago, I know with absolute certainty that I don't want to leave.

Ansel's voice pulls my attention to the door. "*Ici,*" he murmurs, taking my hand and pulling me through when the double doors part with a blustery whoosh.

We rise out of the métro and walk a couple of blocks until the view appears and I stop without realizing it, my feet planted on the sidewalk.

I'd read of the Jardin des Plantes in the guidebooks Ansel would leave for me, or the tiny maps of Paris I would find tucked into my messenger bag. But in all my days exploring I still haven't been and he must know that because here we are, standing in front of what must be the most beautiful garden I've ever seen.

It seems to stretch for miles, with lawns so green they seem nearly fluorescent, and flowers of colors I don't think I've ever seen in nature before.

We walk along the winding paths, taking in all of it. Every flower that grows on French soil is represented in this garden, he tells me proudly, and in the distance I see the museums housed on the grounds: one each for evolution, mineralogy, paleontology, entomology. Such honest and pure sciences but couched in arches of marble and walls of glass, they remind everyone how noble they are.

Everything in my vision is earth and soil but so colorful my eyes never stop moving. Even as I stare at a thick bed of violet and lavender pansies, my attention is pulled farther down the path to a blinding patch of marigolds and zinnias.

"You should see the . . ." Ansel stops walking and hums, pressing two fingers to his lips as he thinks of the word in English. Although he rarely struggles to translate something, I can't help lovingly obsessing over it when he does. It could be the little cluck of his tongue, or the way he usually gives up and says the word in soft, purring French anyway. *"Coqueli-cots?"* he says. "A delicate flower in the spring. Red, but also sometimes orange or yellow?"

I shake my head, uncertain.

"Before it blooms, the buds look like testicles."

Laughing, I guess, "Poppy?"

He nods, snapping his finger and looking so pleased with me I may as well have planted all of these flowers here myself. "Poppy. You should see the poppies here in the spring."

But the idea dissolves in the air between us and without our acknowledging it; he takes my hand again to keep walking.

He points out everything in front of us: flowers, trees, sidewalk, water, building, stone—and gives me the words in French, making me repeat them in a way that seems to grow more urgent, as if by weighing me down with knowledge I won't be able to simply climb on a plane and lift off in a few weeks.

Inside the canvas bag, Ansel has packed bread and cheese, apples, and tiny chocolate cookies and we find a bench in the shade—we can't picnic on the grass here—and devour the food as if we haven't eaten in days. Being near him makes me hungry in so many aching, delicious ways, and when I watch him lift the bread from the bag, tear a bit off, and the muscles in his arm tense and pull with the movement, I wonder how he'll touch me first when we get back to his apartment.

Will he use his hands? Or his lips and teeth in that teasing, nibbling way he has? Or will he be as impatient as I feel, pushing fabric aside just fast enough for him to be over me, inside me, moving urgently?

I close my eyes, savoring the sunshine and the feel of his fingers sliding across my back, curling around my shoulder. He talks for a while about what he loves about the park—the architecture, the history—and finally he lets words fall away as the birds take over for us, flapping and chattering in the trees overhead. For a perfect minute, I can imagine this endless life:

sunny Sundays in the park with Ansel and the promise of his body all over mine when the sun goes down.

IT'S THE FIRST time we've been together for an entire day and we're unable to undress, touch, have sex—which really is all we've known. After nearly eleven hours of walking and seeing everything we can fit into daylight, I've watched his lips pout his perfect words and his broad, skilled hands point to important buildings and his mischievous green eyes fixate on my lips and my body enough times that all I want now is to feel the weight of him moving on top of me.

I cling to the thought and the easy familiarity we've cultivated today as just *us*—Mia and Ansel—but as soon as we're back in the apartment, he kisses the top of my head and pours me a glass of wine before powering up his laptop to check his work email, promising to be quick. While he sits at the small desk with his back to me, I tuck my legs beneath me on the couch, sipping my wine as I watch the tension gradually return to his shoulders. He fires off an email that must be heated because his fingers hammer on the keyboard and he clicks send, before leaning back in his chair and running a frustrated hand through his hair.

"*Putain,*" he curses on a tight exhale.

"Ansel?"

"Mmm?" He leans forward to rub his hands over his face.

"Come here, okay?"

He takes another deep breath before he stands, then walks over to me, but as soon as I look up at his face—his eyes are flat, his mouth pulled in a straight, exhausted line—I know the spell is broken and I'll be going to bed alone. We're back to real life, where his life is his mysterious, grueling job and I'm only temporary.

We're back to playing house.

"It made more work for you, didn't it," I ask, "by taking today off?"

He shrugs, and reaches down to carefully pull my bottom lip between his thumb and index finger. "I don't care." He bends down, kisses my mouth, sucking on my lip before he pulls away. "But yes. I'll need to go into the office quite early tomorrow."

Tomorrow is Monday, and he's behind on his week already.

"Why do you do it?" The words feel awkward on my tongue; our conversations about his job have mostly been his apologizing for working so much and me telling him I understand. But I absolutely don't, and in this moment I'm mortified that I've never really asked him about it. Other than knowing he has a dragon-lady boss, and that this job will give him his pick of positions someday, I really have no idea what he does there.

"Because I won't be able to find another good position if I leave this one so soon. This is very prestigious, you see. I need to see this lawsuit through." He only needs to tell me a tiny bit about it—vague details about the corporations at war and the matter of intellectual property and sales tactics at the heart of the case—before I pull back to look at him in surprise.

I've *heard* of this lawsuit. I know the names of the two businesses going head-to-head. It's such a big case it's constantly on the news, in the papers. No wonder he's working the hours he is.

"I had no idea," I tell him. "How did you manage to go to Vegas?"

His fingers dig through his hair and he shrugs. "It was the only three weeks I wasn't needed. They were gathering depositions, and I finally had a small break. It is much more normal to take a long vacation here in Europe than it is in the States, maybe."

I pull him down on the couch next to me and he complies, but his posture tells me he's only here for a minute. He'll get up and return to his computer instead of following me into bed.

I run my hand down the front of his T-shirt and find myself looking forward to seeing him dressed for work tomorrow, and then immediately feel a tight knot of guilt form in my stomach. "Do you wear a suit and tie in the courtroom?"

Laughing, he bends and says into the skin of my neck, "I don't go to court, but no, in court they wear a traditional robe. I'm the equivalent of a junior associate here. Corporate law in France is maybe a bit different from the States, though both are different from criminal law. Here, maybe more proceedings happen across a table."

"If it's different from the States, and you're licensed to practice there, too . . . why did you come back here after law school?"

He hums, shaking his head a little as he kisses my jaw, and it's the first time he hasn't answered a question. I can't tell if I'm disappointed or fascinated.

"I hope you'll be done soon," I tell him, pressing my hand to his face and, unable to resist, stroking his bottom lip with the pad of my thumb in his signature, soothing move. "I hope it won't always be like this. I like it when you're here with me."

He closes his eyes, exhaling slowly as he smiles. "You sound like a real wife when you say that."

Chapter FIFTEEN

I'M ALMOST RELIEVED that he goes into the office Monday so I can go back to the tiny shop in the alley, holding my breath in the hope that it will be open. I think the role play is fun for Ansel; at least I hope it's as fun for him as it is for me. We get to know each other in these tiny glimpses, revealing ourselves while we pretend not to.

And tonight, I want to get him talking.

The store is open, and the same saleswoman is there, greeting me with the warmth of her smile and the familiar scent of iris. She takes me by the hand, drawing me toward the lingerie, the props.

"What are you today?" she asks.

It takes me several long seconds before I find my words, and even then, I don't really answer her question. "I need to find a way to rescue him."

She studies me for a beat before selecting a sexy soldier uniform but it isn't at all what I mean. Instead, my eyes trip on a negligee so vibrantly red, it looks like it could burn my fingers.

Her laugh is throaty and loud. "Yes, today you rescue in *that*. This time when you come in, your chin is higher, your eyes a little wicked, I think." Reaching for the wall, she hands me a single accessory and when I look down at what she's given me, it seems to vibrate in my hands. I would never have picked this on my own, but it's perfect.

"Have fun, *chérie*."

I'VE DONE MY makeup for the stage enough that I can really layer it on, making my eyes smoky and dark, my lips even fuller and siren red. I put just enough blush on my cheeks to look like I might be up to no good.

Stepping back, I examine myself in the slim mirror mounted on the bedroom door. My hair falls straight to my chin, black and sleek. My hazel eyes have more yellow than green lately. My bangs need to be trimmed; they graze my eyelashes when I blink. But the woman staring back at me likes the shadow they give. She knows how to look up from beneath her lashes and flirt, especially with the red horns barely poking out from a slim, black headband hiding in her hair.

The negligee is made of lace and layered, soft macramé tulle. The layering gives the illusion of coverage, but even in the dim candlelight I've set up throughout the apartment, my nipples are clearly visible beneath. The only other thing I'm wearing is a small, matching red thong.

This time I'm not nervous when I hear the elevator doors open down the hall, and the steady pace of Ansel's feet walking to our door.

He enters, dropping his keys in the bowl and sliding his helmet beneath the table before turning to where I sit in one of the dining room chairs I've placed about ten feet in front of the entryway.

"Christ, *Cerise*." Slowly, he slides his messenger bag over his head, carefully setting it on the floor. A heated smile starts at the corner of his mouth and lazily stretches across to the other side as he notices the horns. "Am I in trouble?"

I shake my head, shivering at the way his accent scratches *trouble* into my new favorite word, and stand, walking over to him. Letting him take in the entire outfit.

"No," I say, "but I hear you're in a situation you'd like to see changed."

He stills, brows slowly lifting. "A *situation*?"

"Yes," I say. "A *work* situation."

His eyes turn playful. "I see."

"I can help." I step closer and run my hand up his chest to his tie. Loosening it, I tell him, "I've been sent here to negotiate a deal."

"Sent by whom?"

"My boss," I say with a little wink.

He looks me over one more time and reaches up to drag the pad of his thumb across my bottom lip. It's a familiar touch now, but instead of opening my mouth and licking him, I bite.

He pulls back with a little gasp, and then laughs. "You're irresistible."

"I'm *powerful*," I correct him. "If everything goes well

tonight, with just a snap of my fingers I can finish this horrible, time-sucking lawsuit."

I pull his tie loose and blink up to see his amused expression straighten into something more earnest, more pleading. "You can?"

"You give me your soul, and I make your problems go away."

His smile returns and his hands slide forward, framing my hips. "When you look the way you do, I don't think I have much use for a soul." He leans in, runs his nose along my neck, and inhales. "It's yours. How do we negotiate this transaction?"

I push his hands away, and slide his tie off, draping it around my neck instead. "I'm glad you asked." Unbuttoning his shirt, I explain: "I'll ask a few questions so I can determine the value of your soul. If you're pristine, I'll end this tonight and make you look like a hero who broke down the other side. If you're sullied, well . . ." I shrug. "It may be messy but the lawsuit will be gone. And then I take my payment."

His dimple makes a cameo. "And what kind of questions do I need to answer?"

"I need to see how bad you've been." Lowering my voice, I add, "I hope you've been *very* bad. My boss doesn't like to pay very much, and making you look like a hero is pretty expensive in this business."

He looks genuinely confused. "But isn't my soul more valuable to you the more corrupt I am?"

Shaking my head, I tell him, "I'm only bargaining to lure

you away from the angels. I get you for a better price if they'd be unlikely to want you anyway."

"I see," he says, wearing an amused smile.

Silence slides between us and the threat of tension looms just outside the little circle our bodies form, standing so close together. For once, the rules are all mine, the game all mine, and still I feel power in this, too. My fingers shake against his chest with the reality of this full circle, closed. I'm his equal. I'm his wife, wanting to save him.

"I suppose I'm at your mercy, then," he says quietly. "If you can do what you say, I'm game."

Tilting my head, I say, "Get undressed."

"Completely naked?" Amusement returns to his expression.

"Completely."

He pushes his fancy checked blue shirt off his shoulders. I struggle to keep my attention on his face, knowing that the skin he's slowly revealing is quite possibly my favorite thing about France.

"How did you get into this line of work?" he asks, unfastening his belt.

"My boss found me, alone and wandering the streets," I tell him, unable to resist reaching forward, running my hands lightly down his chest. I love the way his breath hitches, his skin seems to tighten beneath my fingers. "He thought I'd make a good negotiator. When I found out I'd get to play with pretty boys like you, how could I resist?"

His hand pulls at his belt, sliding the smooth leather free

so fast it makes a sharp cracking sound against the stretch of leather still looped through his dress pants. It drops to the floor, and his pants follow not far behind.

When his thumbs hover in the waistband of his boxers, I can tell he's teasing me, waiting for me to look up at his face.

But I don't.

"Off," I tell him. "I need to see what I'm working with."

He lowers the shorts from his body and slowly—confidently—steps out of them. I'll never get used to the sight of Ansel completely naked. He's bronze, and strong, and *looks* like he would taste good. And God, I *know* how good it is. It's all I can do to not slide down onto my knees and lick a wet line from his balls to the tight crown of his cock.

But somehow, I manage to resist, even as he reaches down, circles his base with his thumb and middle finger, and holds it out as if offering it to me. I pull his tie from my neck and reach for his hands instead, guiding his arms behind his back and turning him to tie them together at the wrist. It's tight, but not so tight he couldn't get out if he wanted.

Turning him back around, I push lightly on his chest. "Go sit on the couch. It's time for questions."

"I'm a little nervous," he admits with a tiny wink, but walks confidently over and carefully lowers himself to the seat, hands trapped behind him.

"Men are always nervous about this part," I say, following him and straddling his thighs. I reach forward and draw a circle around the head of his cock with my index finger. "No one likes to admit all of the terrible things they've done."

"And how many men have you done this with?" This time, his voice catches on something—jealousy, maybe. Or maybe the dark thrill that comes from imagining me doing this to someone else.

These are the things I need to learn about the man I've married.

"Thousands," I whisper, relishing the way his eyes grow hard. Jealousy, then. "I'm the best negotiator out there. If you want me to remember tonight, you should probably impress me later."

I rest my ass on his thighs and then slide forward, giving his cock the briefest bit of friction against me before I slide away again. Beneath my palms, his shoulders bunch as he pulls against the bind around his wrists.

"Does it make you wet to take control, *Cerise?*" he whispers, looking torn. He's broken role, but it seems like he can't help himself. "I wish I could tell you what seeing you like this does to me."

He doesn't need to tell me; I can *see* what it does to him. But in the length of a heartbeat, I know what he's asking for. It's the same as our first night playing maid and master: *feed it to me.*

He's just doing it differently.

I reach between my legs, slip my fingers under the satin, and decide to give him a little show: I close my eyes, moan quietly as I stroke myself, rolling my hips. But when I pull my hand back, instead of putting my fingers in his mouth, I capture his chin with my free hand and paint a wet line on his upper lip, just below his nose.

He groans, and it's an amazing, gravelly, *pained* sound I want to record and play on a loop while I slide down over him and ride him. He's so hard, his cock arches up to his navel, the thick ridge nearly pressing to his belly button. A slick bead of moisture forms at the opening and slides, glistening, down his length.

My mouth waters, my chest tightens. I don't imagine my game is going to be fast. I never know if it's true, but he looks hard enough for it to be uncomfortable. "Do you want me to put my mouth on you before the questions?" I whisper, briefly breaking role. The corded tension in his neck and the vulnerable expression on his face make me want to take care of him.

"*Non,*" he says quickly, more quickly than I expected. His eyes are wide, lips wet where he's just licked them, trying to clean his skin of my taste. "Tease me."

Pushing off his lap, I stand, giving a crisp "Very well then," and bend over the coffee table to retrieve the clipboard and pen. I give him a long view of my backside, my thighs, and the red silk thong. Behind me, he exhales a deep, shaking breath.

I return to him, looking over my short list. I've written a few things just to remind myself what I want to ask him because in the heat of the moment, over his lap with him naked and looking at me like he's barely keeping his hands tied up, I'm prone to forget.

Settling back down, I run my pen down the smooth skin of his chest and rock slightly over the tight bunching muscles of his thighs. "We can start with an easy one."

He nods, staring openly at my breasts. *"D'accord."* Okay.

"If you've ever killed anyone, you're really not worth very much to me because we'll be getting your soul eventually anyway."

He smiles, relaxing a little as the game reveals itself. "I've never killed anyone."

"Tortured?"

He laughs. "I fear I'm on the receiving end at the moment, but no."

Blinking back down to my list, I say, "We can reel through the cardinal sins pretty quickly." I look up at him and lick my lips. "This is where men usually lose the most value."

He nods, staring intently at me, as if I really do hold the power to change his fate tonight.

"Greed?" I ask.

Ansel lets out a quiet laugh. "I'm an *attorney.*"

Nodding, I pretend to make note of this. "For a firm you hate, but who pays you ridiculous sums of money to represent one huge corporation suing another. I suppose that means I can also put you down for a bit of gluttony, too?"

His dimple flashes suggestively as he laughs. "I suppose you're right."

"Pride?"

"Me?" he says with a winning smile. "I'm as humble as they come."

"Right." Fighting my own smile, I look back down at my list. "Lust?"

He pushes his hips up, his cock a heavy presence between us as I gaze at his face, waiting for him to speak. But he doesn't answer aloud.

Heat ripples along my skin and his gaze is so penetrating, I finally have to look away from his face. "Envy?"

It takes him long enough to answer that I look back up at him, searching his expression. He's grown oddly contemplative, as if this is a serious exercise. And for the first time I realize maybe it *is*. I couldn't simply ask him these things as Mia, sitting across the dining room table from Ansel, though I'd want to. No one can be as perfect as he seems, and part of me needs to understand where he's damaged, where he's ugliest. Somehow it's easier to dress up as a servant of Satan to find out.

"I feel envy, yes," he says quietly.

"I need you to give me more than that." I lean forward, kiss his jaw. "Envious of *what*."

"I never used to. If anything, I tend to see the positive everywhere. Finn and Oliver . . . they will grow exasperated with me sometimes, telling me I'm impulsive, or I'm fickle." He tears his eyes from mine, looking past my shoulder at the room behind me. "But now I look at my best friends and see a certain freedom they have . . . I *want* that. I think that must be envy."

This one stings. The sting turns into a burn and it crawls up my throat, coating my windpipe. I swallow a few times before I'm able to manage, "I see."

Immediately, Ansel realizes what he's said, and ducks his head so I'll look at him. "Not because I'm married and they aren't," he says quickly. His eyes move back and forth, searching mine for understanding. "This isn't about the annulment; I didn't want it, either. It wasn't just that I promised you."

"Okay."

"I envy their situation in a different way from what you're thinking." Pausing, he seems to wait for my expression to soften before he quietly admits, "I didn't want to move back to Paris. Not for this job."

My eyes narrow. "You didn't?"

"I love the city—it's the center of my heart—but I didn't want to return the way I did. Finn loves his hometown; he never wants to leave. Oliver is opening a store in San Diego. I envy how happy they are being exactly where they want to be."

Too many questions perch on my tongue, fighting to come out. Finally, I ask the same one I asked last night: "Then why did you come back here?"

He watches me, eyes assessing. Finally he says only, "I suppose I felt obligated."

I assume he's talking about the obligation of the job he would have been insane to turn down. I can tell even if he hates it that it was a once-in-a-lifetime opportunity. "Where would you rather be?"

His tongue slips out, wets his lips. "I would at least like to have the *option* to follow my wife when she leaves."

My heart stutters. I decide to skip over *sloth* and *wrath*, far more interested in pursuing this subject. "You're married?"

He nods, but his expression isn't playful. Not even a little. "Yes, I'm married."

"And where is your wife right now while I'm sitting on your naked lap, wearing this tiny scrap of lingerie?"

"She's not here," he whispers conspiratorially.

"Do you make a habit of this?" I ask, wearing a teasing smile. I want to lift the serious cloud that's descending. "Letting in women while your wife is gone? It's good you brought her up, since infidelity is next on my list."

His face drops and *oh shit*. I've hit a nerve. I close my eyes, remembering what he told me about his father, how he was never faithful to Ansel's mother, how the parade of women through the house was finally enough to drive his mother to the States when Ansel was only a teenager.

I start to apologize but his words come out faster than mine. "I *have* been unfaithful."

An enormous black hole opens up inside me, swallowing my organs in the most painful order: lungs, then heart, and then, when I'm sure I'm suffocating, my stomach drops out.

"Never to my wife," he says slowly and after a long pause, apparently oblivious to my panic. I close my eyes, dizzy with relief. Still, my heart feels like it returns to my body slightly withered, beating weakly at the realization that he's more like his father than his mother when it comes to cheating. "I'm trying to do better this time."

It's several long seconds before I can speak, but when I do, my words come out reedy, a little breathless. "Well, this certainly tilts the negotiation in my favor."

"I'm sure it does," he whispers.

My voice wobbles a little. "I'll need the details, of course."

Finally, a tiny, unsure smile pulls at one corner of his mouth. "Of course." He leans his head back against the couch, watching me with wary eyes. "I met a woman from here," he says, adding, "or, rather, near here. From Orléans." He takes a small break, closing his eyes. I can see the way his pulse is fluttering in his throat. Even though his explanation is so factual, so detached, *he* seems amped up.

Is it just that I'm wearing lingerie and he's completely naked? Or is he worried about my reaction?

I press a hand to his chest. "Tell me," I whisper, anxiety sending a tight thrill through my veins. "I want to know everything." *I do, and I don't.*

Beneath my palm, he relaxes. "I was in law school, and we stayed together even at a distance; she studied fashion here." He pulls back and watches me before saying, "I can be impulsive with my emotions, I know. After the first couple of months . . . I knew we were more friends than lovers. But I was convinced it would be passionate again when I moved back here. I assumed it was the distance that made it not so exciting for me." Each sentence is carefully composed. "I was lonely and . . . two times I shared my bed. Minuit still does not know."

Minuit . . . I search my limited vocabulary, remembering after a beat that it means "midnight." I imagine a raved-haired beauty, her hands sliding over his chest the way mine do now, her ass pressed to his thighs the way mine is now. I imagine his cock, hard for her the way it is for me now.

I wonder whether I only temporarily have the luxury of his passion before it cools. I want to stab my jealousy with a sharp tool.

"I felt obligated," he repeats, and finally he looks at me again. "She waited for me, so I returned. I took this job I hate, but I was wrong. We weren't happy, even when I was back here."

"How long were you with her?"

He sighs. "Too long."

He's been back here nearly a year, and finished law school just before he came back. *Too long* doesn't tell me very much.

But it's time to return to something better than this. The subject is heavy, a weighted lure in my mind, pulling my thoughts under the clear surface of our game to something dreary and somber. It's not who we are.

We're married for the summer. Summer marriages don't get dragged down in heavy stuff. Besides, I'm wearing a devil costume and he's naked, for crying out loud. How seriously can we really take ourselves right now?

I pretend to make a note of something on the clipboard and then look back up at him. "I think I have all the information I need."

He relaxes in pieces: his legs beneath me first, then abdomen, shoulders, and finally his expression. I feel something unknot in me when he grins. "So it's all taken care of, then?"

I snap my fingers, and nod. "I can't make you come out

of it with a promotion, but I don't think you wanted that anyway."

"Not if it means I have to stay on much longer," he agrees with a laugh.

"Tomorrow Capitaux will drop the case and everyone will know it's because you found the document that clears Régal Biologiques of all wrongdoing."

He exhales dramatically, wiping his brow. "You've saved me."

"So it's my turn, then," I remind him. "And time to claim my payment." I lean in to suck on his neck. "Hmm, would you like to feel my hand or—"

"Your mouth," he interrupts.

With an evil smile, I move back, shaking my head. "That wasn't going to be one of the options."

He huffs out an impatient breath. Every muscle grows tight and urgent beneath my roaming hands once more and I tease him more by scratching my short nails down his chest.

"Then tell me what my choices are," he growls.

"My hand, or *your* hand," I say and press my fingers to his lips to keep him from answering too quickly again. "If you choose my hand, that's all you'll get, and you'll remain tied up. If you choose your hand, of course I'll untie you . . . but you can also watch me use my hand on myself."

His eyes widen as if he's not entirely sure who I am all of a sudden. And, to be honest, I'm not sure, either. I've never done this in front of someone before, but the words just bubbled up and out of me.

And I'm positive I know what he's going to choose.

He leans forward, kisses me once sweetly before answering. "I use my hand, you use yours."

I'm not sure whether I'm relieved or nervous as I reach behind him and pull his hands free of the tie around his wrists. Faster than I expected, he grabs me by the hips and jerks me forward, sliding the wet fabric of my underwear over his cock, grinding up into me with a low groan. Without thinking, I move with him, rocking on top and feeling the delicious press of the hard line of him to my clit. I hadn't realized how turned on I'd been being so close to him for so long, just listening to him, playing with him, but I can tell I'm soaked.

And I *want* him. I want the thick slide of him into me, the way my body is so full of his it's the only thing I can imagine ever feeling again. I want to hear his voice, encouraging and urgent in my ear, falling away into a broken mix of English and French, and—finally—the hoarse, unintelligible sounds of his pleasure.

But I'm in charge tonight for better or worse, and no direct report of Satan's would ever let a man change her plan, no matter how warm his skin, no matter how filthy he sounds when he says, "I can feel your need for me soaked through the silk."

Pushing off his lap, I pull the red fabric down my legs, kicking it onto his lap. He pulls it to his face, watching me with hooded eyes as I sit on the low coffee table. I watch as he circles his cock with his fist, and strokes up once, slowly.

It feels so depraved doing this, but I'm surprised that it

doesn't feel *weird*. I've never seen anything as sexy as watching Ansel touch himself. I pretend he's alone, thinking of me. I pretend *I'm* alone, thinking of *him*. And, like this, my fingers slide over my skin and he begins to pull himself harder, faster, his breath coming out in tiny grunts.

"Show me," he whispers. "How do you fuck yourself when I'm at work, thinking of you?"

I lie back, turning my head so I can still watch him and start to use both hands. He wants to see me let go. It's what this is about, after all: the costumes, the pretend. It's letting ourselves do anything we want. I slide two fingers inside, and use the other hand to circle outside . . . my pulse trips and races when he groans, speeding up and hoarsely telling me he wants to see me come.

It's a poor approximation of his fingers, and an even worse approximation of his cock, but with his eyes on me and the brushing rhythm of his fist tugging at his length, I feel the rush of blood to my thighs and the heavy ache between my legs build, and build until I'm arching off the table and coming with a sharp cry. With a relieved moan, he lets go after me. I push up on an elbow, watching as he spills onto his hand and stomach.

In a blur, Ansel is on his feet and pulls me down onto the floor, falling on top of me and still hard enough that he can push inside with a steady, hard thrust. He looms above, blocking out even the tiny bit of light from the few candles still burning, and reaches up to pull the strap of my negligee off my shoulder, baring one of my breasts.

"Did you come just now?" he whispers into my skin.

I nod. My pulse was barely slipping back to normal, but the feel of him stretching me even now brings all of my sensation back to the surface. I can feel his orgasm still wet on his stomach pressed to mine, on the hand he has curled around my hip. But feeling him begin to harden in me again so soon gives me a dizzying sense of power.

"If *I* had been Satan tonight . . ." he begins and then stops, his breath choppy so close to my ear.

The air between us seems to grow completely still.

"What, Ansel?"

His lips find my ear, my neck, and suck gently before he asks, "Have you ever been unfaithful?"

"No." Sliding my hands up his back, I whisper, "But I did once shoot a man in Reno just to watch him die."

He laughs and I feel my body squeezing his as he lengthens slightly, getting even harder.

I pull back slightly to look up at him. "The idea of marrying a killer turns you on? Something is wrong with you."

"I love that you make me laugh," he corrects. "*That* turns me on. Also, your body, and what you did tonight."

He cups my other breast through the negligee, thumb passing back and forth over the peak. He is strong enough to break me in half, but the way he caresses my skin, it's as if I'm too valuable to risk hurting.

I thought I might be the only one who noticed the new, fascinating sway to my hips, the heaviness of my breasts, but I'm not. Ansel lingers at my breasts, playing and pushing at them. French cuisine has been good for my body . . . though maybe I'm indulging a little more than I should. It doesn't matter; I love the feel of my curves. Now I just need to find the Frenchwoman's secret for enjoying it and still looking like she could fit inside a straw.

"You're taking care of your body." He hums into my chest, tongue sliding over my collarbone. "You know your husband wants more flesh on you. I like your hips fuller. I like to be able to squeeze your ass in my hands, feel your breasts move over my face when you're fucking me."

How does he do this? His hair falls over one eye and he looks almost boyish, but his words are coarse on my skin. His breath, his fingertips, they brush across my ribs, the bottom swell of my breast, my nipple.

He begins to rock inside me, slowly, lips moving across my neck and up to my ear. My body responds, tensing and thrilled, waiting for the pleasure I know will make me explode. Like I'm made of a thousand tiny beating wings.

"Tonight, *Cerise* . . . thank you for wanting to save *me*." He puts a tiny inflection on the last word.

It takes a beat for my brain to process the inflection but then adrenaline courses through me so fast my fingertips flush, my pulse thunders.

Come to France for the summer.

He knew his life didn't have space for this but it didn't matter. He was trying to save me first.

Chapter SIXTEEN

SOMEWHERE IN MY subconscious I sense Ansel crawling on the bed and hovering over me beneath a sun-warmed blanket cave. He wakes me up with the pressure of his stare.

I stretch, frowning up at his neatly pressed dress shirt, white with small purple geometric shapes.

"You're going in to work?" I ask, my voice still thick with sleep. "Wait," I add, once consciousness forces its way to the surface. "It's Tuesday. Of course you're going in to work."

He kisses my nose, running a warm palm from my shoulder, down over my breast, to my waist. "I only have a few weeks left of this craziness," he says.

"Me, too," I say, laughing. And then my smile drops like a hammer out of the sky and I pout. "Ugh. Why did I even say that? Now I want to eat my feelings in the form of an enormous chocolate croissant."

"Croissant," he repeats, kissing me before whispering, "Better this time, *Cerise*. But we call it *pain au chocolat*."

He touches my lip with his index finger. I smile and bite his fingertip. I don't want him to be frustrated with my impending departure, either. We're both so much happier when we're pretending it doesn't exist.

He pulls his hand back and runs it over my breast again. "I'm pretty sure Capitaux will settle eventually."

"I wish you didn't have to go."

"Me, too." He kisses me, so softly, so earnestly that something swells painfully inside my chest. It can't just be my heart because it sucks the air from my body, too. It can't be only my lungs because it causes my pulse to race. It's as if Ansel has taken up residence inside my rib cage, making everything go haywire.

"Do you have very important plans for an adventure today?" he asks.

I shake my head.

"Then today you practice speaking French," he says, resolute.

"With who?"

"With Madame Allard downstairs. She loves you and thinks we're going to have a baby soon."

My eyes go wide and I press both hands to my stomach. "I have *not* gained that much weight." I look down at my hands and ask, "Have I?"

He laughs, and bends to kiss me. "You don't look very different from when you arrived. Tell me how you say 'I'm not pregnant' *en français*. You can go downstairs and tell her yourself."

I close my eyes, thinking. "*Je ne . . . suis pas . . .* uh"—I look up at him—"pregnant."

"*Enceinte,*" he says. His eyes move over my body, and I stretch under his gaze, wondering what the chances are that he will take off his clothes and make love to me before he goes to work.

He pushes away, but I can see the tight bunching of his dress pants where he's hard beneath his zipper.

I palm him, arching my back. "Ten minutes."

I mean it to sound playful, but his eyes grow a little pained. "I can't."

"I know."

"I'm so sorry, Mia." His eyes search mine. "I knew I would be busy, what was I thinking? But you're here and I'm *wild* for you. How can I regret it?"

"Stop," I tell him, curling my hand around the shape of him. "It's the best decision I made in a long time." His eyes flutter closed when I say this, and he pushes into my palm before lowering himself over my naked body.

"It is strange, isn't it?" he asks quietly, pressing his face to my neck. "But it isn't fake. It's never really been pretend."

In a wild burst of color, images from the past several weeks pop through my vision, each one bringing such a surge of nostalgia, so much *emotion*. The disorienting first two weeks with him gone nearly every waking minute. The awkwardness of the first time we made love after we arrived. The renewed heat between us the night I dressed up as his maid. I would no more be able to serve Ansel with an annulment than I would be able to swim all the way home in a few weeks.

"What are we going to do?" I ask, my voice disappearing on the last word.

My sunshine Ansel returns as he pulls back with a smile, as if he knows only one of us at a time is allowed to consider the darker side to our impulsive—and wonderful—adventure.

"We're going to have a lot of sex when I get home from work." This time, when he pushes away, I can tell he's determined to get moving. "Let me see the naughty side again."

The comforter flaps over me with a burst of air, and when it settles, he's gone, and all I hear is the heavy click of the front door.

IT TAKES A while for Madame Allard to get around to asking me whether we're having a baby—she's determined to cycle through her thoughts on the new puppy in the building and the fresh grapes at the corner market—and then even longer for me to convince her that we are not. Her joy over my simple sentence, *"Madame, je ne suis pas enceinte,"* is enough to make me want to try to order lunch in French.

But the far less approachable grouchy waiter with the wild eyebrows at the corner brasserie makes me reconsider, and instead I order my favorite—*soupe à l'oignon*—in my standard apology-glazed English.

I wonder how many of the people in Ansel's life assume that I came back here with him because I got pregnant. Even though he was gone for only three weeks, who knows what the people in his life assume? And then I wonder: Has he told his mother? His father?

Why does the idea of being pregnant right now make me

laugh, and then make me feel a tiny bit tingly inside? *Enceinte* is such a gorgeous word. Even more gorgeous is the idea of being *full*—full of him, and the future, and this thing building between us. Even if a baby isn't growing inside me, genuine emotion is.

So is a glowing hope. Immediately, my stomach drops.

Impulsively, I pull out my phone, texting him, Do your parents know you're married?

How has it never occurred to me to ask him this yet?

He doesn't answer while I eat, and it isn't until nearly an hour has passed and I'm a mile away from the apartment, wandering aimlessly through curving alleys, when my phone buzzes in my bag.

My mother knows, not my father. And then: Does this bother you?

Knowing he's at work and I may only have his attention for a second, I type quickly: No. My parents don't know. I just realized how little we've really talked about it.

We'll talk about it later, but not tonight.

I stare at my phone for a beat. That's certainly cryptic. Why not tonight?

Because tonight you are naughty, not nice.

I'm typing my reply—basically *hell yes* and *get home as soon as you can*—when my phone buzzes with another incoming message . . . from Harlow.

I'm in Canada.

My eyes widen as I search for any other explanation than the one my brain immediately latches on to. Harlow has no family in Canada, no business in Canada. I type my question so fast I have to correct typos seven times in five words: Are you there banging Finn???

She doesn't answer immediately, and without thinking, I text Ansel for confirmation.

Not Lola.

In fact, it feels natural to text Ansel first . . . *holy crap* we have mutual people, a shared community now. My fingers shake as I type: Did Harlow fly up to Canada to visit Finn this weekend?!

Ansel replies a few minutes later, They must have texted us at the same time. Apparently she arrived wearing nothing but her trench coat.

I nod as I type my reply: That sounds like Harlow. How did she get through security without having to take that off?

No idea, he says. But they'd better not be trying to steal our costume game.

My blood simmers deliciously in anticipation. What time will you be home?

I'm here with the dragon until around 21:00.

Nine o'clock? Immediately I deflate, typing OK before slipping my phone back into my bag. But then, a thought occurs to me: He wanted me to be naughty? I'll give him naughty.

———————

LATELY, ANSEL HAS been texting me around dinnertime—when he's working and I'm home. The routine has only been going on maybe the past four days when our schedules land like this, but somehow I know to expect it around seven, when he takes his evening break.

I'm ready, in the bedroom, when my phone buzzes on the comforter beside me.

Don't forget what I want tonight. Eat dinner. I will keep you up.

With shaking hands, I press his name to call him, and wait while it rings once . . . twice . . .

"Âllo?" he answers, and then corrects to English. "Mia? Is everything all right?"

"Professor Guillaume?" I ask in a high, hesitant voice. "Is it an okay time to call? I know it isn't your office hour . . ."

Silence greets me across the line and after several long beats, he clears his throat, quietly. "Actually, Mia," he says, voice different now—not him, but someone stern and irritated at the interruption, "I was in the middle of something. What is it?"

My hand slides down my torso, over my navel and lower, between my spread legs. "I had some questions about what you were teaching me, but I can call back if there is a better time."

I need to hear his voice, to get lost in it to find the bravery to do this when he's not expecting it. When he may be sitting across the table from someone.

I can almost imagine the way he leans in, pressing the phone flush to his ear and listening carefully for every sound on the other end of the line. "No, I'm here now. Out with it."

My hand slides up and back, fingers pressing to my skin. I pretend it's his hand, and he's hovering over me, watching every expression as it passes over my face. "Earlier today in class," I start, my breath catching when I hear him exhale forcefully. I search my memory for some rudimentary law terms from my poli sci class two years ago. "When you were talking about judicial politics?"

"Yes?" he whispers, and now I know he must be alone in his office. His voice has gone hoarse, goading, deep enough that if he were here I can just imagine the way the sunshine would melt from his eyes and he would pretend to be hard and calculating.

"I don't think I'd ever been more wrapped up in a lecture before." I hold my phone between my ear and hunched shoulder, sliding my other hand up and over my breast. My breasts . . . Ansel loves them in a way no one ever has before. I always loved being able to move around them easily. But under his touch, I realize just how sensitive they are, how responsive. "I've never enjoyed a class as much as yours."

"No?"

"And I couldn't stop thinking . . ." I say, pausing for effect but also because I can hear him breathing and I want to dive into the slow, deep cadence. I feel something inside me ignite with *want*. "I was thinking what it would be like if you would meet with me outside of school."

It's several tight, pounding heartbeats before he answers. "You know I can't do that, Miss Holland."

"Can't because of the rules? Or because you don't want to?" My fingers are moving faster now, sliding easily over skin that has grown slick with the sound of his voice, the sound of his breath through the line. I can imagine him sitting behind a desk, his hand clutching himself through his zipper. Even the thought makes me gasp.

"Because of the rules." His voice drops to barely a whisper. "Also, I *can't* want to. You're my student."

Without meaning to, I moan quietly, because he *does* want it. He wants *me*, even when he's drowning at work and miles away.

How would it feel to really be his student, or to be one of the girls on the métro, watching him, *wanting* him? What if he really were my teacher, and every day I had to sit, and listen to his quiet, deep voice, unable to move forward, catch his eye, run my hands up his chest and into his thick hair?

"Mia, you're not doing anything . . . inappropriate right now, are you?" he asks, stern voice back in place. It's the first time I can't see his face when we're playing like this, but already I know him well enough to know he's pretending. His voice is never stern with me, even when he's upset. He's always even, always steady.

My back arches off the mattress, sensation pooling and warming in my thighs, low in my belly. "You want to hear me?" I ask. "Do you like to imagine me doing this here in your bed?"

"You're *in my bed*?" he hisses, sounding irate. "Mia! *Are you touching yourself?*"

The thrill of the game spins through me, making me dizzy and nearly high. I remember the way he looked over me this morning, conflicted, wanting to take me before he left for work. I remember how his mouth felt on my neck when he climbed into bed last night, how he pulls me against his chest, spooning me every night. And then, when I barely whisper, "Oh, oh, *God*," I hear his rumbling groan on the other end and completely fall to pieces under my own hand, pretending it's his, knowing how much better it will feel when it really *is* his, later.

And he can imagine me now, because he's seen me do this.

My legs are shaking and I'm crying out into the phone, riding through the wave of heat, of slick pleasure sliding across my skin. I say his name, some other things I'm not sure are even coherent but just knowing he's listening, and it's *all* he can do—he can't touch or see or feel—prolongs my release until I'm spent and gasping, my hand sliding to my hip and then down to the mattress beside me.

I smile into the phone, drowsy and satisfied . . . for now.

"Mia."

Blinking, I swallow and whisper, "Oh, God. I can't believe I did that. I'm so sor—"

"Don't go *anywhere*," he growls. "I'll be there soon to take care of this . . . this *indiscretion*."

———————

I'VE DRIFTED OFF waiting for him when the door slams open, the knob hitting the plaster of the wall just on the other side of the bedroom. Startled, I sit up, pushing my little skirt down my legs, rubbing my eyes as Ansel storms into the bedroom.

"What the fuck do you think you're doing?" he roars.

I scoot back to the headboard, disoriented and heart pounding as my brain slowly catches up to the adrenaline racing through my bloodstream. "I . . . you told me not to go anywhere."

He stalks toward me, stopping at the side of the bed and tugging his tie loose with an impatient jerk. "You broke into my *house*—"

"The door was open—"

"—and got onto my *bed*."

"I . . ." I look up at him, eyes widening. He looks genuinely upset, but then reaches forward, reminding me it's all a game by gently sweeping his thumb across my bottom lip.

"Mia, you broke about a hundred university rules and several laws tonight. I could have you arrested."

I push up onto my knees, sliding my hands up his chest. "I didn't know how else to get your attention."

He closes his eyes, moving his fingers to my jaw, down my neck to my bare shoulders. I'm wearing nothing but a short skirt and underwear beneath, and his palms slide over my breasts before he pulls his hands back, forming tight fists.

"You don't think I notice you in class?" he growls. "Up front, your eyes on me the entire hour, lips so full and red all I can think about is how they would feel on my tongue, my neck, my cock?"

I lick my lips, bite the lower one. "I can show you."

He hesitates, eyes narrowing. "I'd be fired."

"I promise I won't tell anyone."

His conflict feels so genuine: he closes his eyes, jaw tight. When they open again, he leans in and says, "If you think of this as rewarding you for breaking into my house . . ."

"I don't . . ." But he sees the lie in my face. I'm getting everything I want and my dark smile makes him growl, cup my breasts again with rougher hands.

My skin rises to meet his touch, and inside, my muscles and vital organs twist as if being wrung out, pushing heat down my chest, into my belly where it pools low, down between my legs. I want him so much I feel restless and urgent, this elemental need clawing in my throat. I dig my hands into his hair, holding him to me and barely letting him move a breath away from my skin.

But it's all a ruse. He pulls free of my grip easily, leaning back to look at me with convincing fire in his eyes.

"I had a lot of work on my desk when you called with your little show earlier."

"I'm sorry," I whisper. Being near him makes me liquid, my insides slithering and molten.

His eyes flutter closed, nostrils flaring. "What do you think it did to my concentration, knowing you're here thinking of me, touching skin that could be mine to touch?"

With his eyes anchoring mine, and to make his point, he slides a rough hand into my underwear, two fingers searching, dipping inside and finding me soaked. "Who made you this wet?"

I don't answer. I close my eyes, pushing into his hand before reaching to grip his wrist and fuck his fingers if he won't move. I'm on fire, everywhere and especially here, drowning with a clawing need to come, for him to make me come.

With a jerk of his arm he pulls his fingers from me and reaches to push them into my mouth, pressing my taste onto my tongue. His hand grips my jaw, fingers curled into the hollow of my cheeks to hold my mouth open.

"Who. Made you. Wet."

"You," I manage around his intrusive fingers and he pulls back, plucking at my bottom lip with an index finger, a thumb. "I thought about you all day. Not just when I called." I stare into his eyes, so full of anger and lust it takes my breath away. They soften as I continue to hold his gaze, and I can feel both of us stutter in our roles. I want to melt into him, feel his warm weight over me. "I think about you all day long."

He can see the truth in my expression and his eyes drop to my lips, his hands spread gently across my sides. "You do?"

"And I don't care about the rules," I tell him. "Or that you have a lot of work. I want you to ignore it."

His jaw tenses.

I say, "I want *you*. The semester will be over soon."

"Mia . . ." I can see the conflict in his eyes, and does he feel it, too? This longing so enormous it shoves everything else inside my chest into a tight corner? *Our* time together is almost over, too. How can I possibly be away from him in only a couple of weeks?

What are we going to do?

My heart turns, pounding so hard it's no longer a safe rhythm. It's cymbals crashing and the deep heavy pulse of the bass drum. It is thrashing beneath my ribs. I know what this feeling is. He needs to know.

But is it too soon? I've been here barely a month. "Ansel . . . I—"

His lips crash over mine, tongue pushing my mouth open, tasting, rolling up against my teeth. I press up, hungry for the flavor of him, of man and ocean and heat.

"Don't say it," he says into my mouth, somehow knowing I was going to put something sincere and intense out there. Pulling back, he searches my eyes frantically, pleading. "I can't play rough if you say that tonight. *D'accord?*"

I nod urgently and his pupils dilate, a drop of ink into the green and I can actually see his pulse pick up.

He's mine. He is.

But for how long? The intruding question makes me desperate, reaching for him and needing him deep in every part of me, knowing he can't really take my breath away but offering it up anyway in tiny, constant bursts.

He steps closer, and although his grip on my hair doesn't lessen, I greedily reach for his shirt, tugging it free of his pants. With shaking fingers, I work each button free and once his smooth, warm torso is exposed, I hear my fevered moan and my hands slide up across his skin, frantic. How would it feel, I imagine, to want him as much as I do and not have access? And then just tonight—a single, dangerous night—he lets me touch him, taste him, fuck him?

I would be *wild*. I would be insatiable.

He growls when I spend too long running my hands up and over his chest, fingernails scratching across his small, flat nipples, stroking the teasing line of hair leading down below his belly button and into his pants. Impatiently, he tugs at my hair, pushing his hips forward, and grunts his approval when I quickly unfasten his belt, his zipper, and shove his pants down his thighs so I can free his cock.

Oh.

It juts in front of me thick and warm; when I reach for him, he's steel in my palm. I use both hands, gripping and sliding down his length, wanting him to let go of my hair so I can bend and suck on him with as much hunger as I feel.

He exhales a tight groan as I pump him in my fist and then curls down, capturing my mouth in a brutal, commanding kiss. His mouth sucks at mine, pushing my lips apart as his fist tightens in my hair. He slides his tongue inside, pushing deep, fucking me with an unmistakable rhythm.

I won't be gentle, he's telling me. *I won't even try.*

Thrill ripples through me and I twist free of his grip, intending to lick him until he comes, but with a growled curse he pushes me back on the bed, bending to retrieve his tie so he can wrap it around my wrists and secure it to the head-board.

"Your body is for my pleasure," he tells me, eyes dark. "You're in my house, little thing. I'll take whatever I want."

He kicks off his pants and climbs over me, yanking my underwear down my legs and shoving my skirt up my hips.

With his hands flat on my thighs, he spreads my legs, leans forward, and roughly thrusts into me.

It's a relief so enormous it makes me scream; I've never before felt so full of him. I'm starving and satisfied, wanting him to stay just like this forever. But he doesn't stay deep inside me for long. He pulls back and then slams forward, gripping the headboard for leverage and taking me so roughly each thrust makes my teeth clatter, forces air from my lungs.

It's wild, and frantic, his body over mine, my legs clamped around his waist so tight I wonder if it hurts him. I *want* to hurt him, in a sick dark way I want to pull every sensation to the surface, make him feel everything all at once: the lust and pain and need and relief and, yes, even the love I'm feeling.

"I wanted to get things done tonight," he hisses, hands clamping around my thighs. He pumps hard and fast, fucking me so roughly, sweat trickles off his temple and lands on my chest. His anger is terrifying, thrilling, perfect. "Instead I need to come home and deal with a naughty student." His hips are pounding and pounding into me and he groans, eyes growing heavy. His large, rough hands reach for my breasts, and he slides his thumb across my nipple.

"Please make me come," I whisper, honestly.

I want to stop playing.

I want to play forever.

I want his approval, I want his anger. I want the sharp smack of his hand across my breast only seconds before he delivers it. *He knew.*

"Please," I beg. "I'll be good."

"Bad pupils don't get pleasure. I'll take and take and you can watch me instead."

He's moving so hard the bed is shaking, groaning beneath us. We've never been so rough. The neighbors must hear, and I close my eyes, relishing the knowledge that my husband is so completely cared for in bed. I'll give him anything.

"Watch me come," he whispers, jerking from me and gripping his cock. His hand flies down and up his length and he curses, eyes on me.

The first pulse of his release lashes me across my cheek, and then my neck, my breasts. I'll never be able to imagine a sexier sound than the deep groan he makes when he comes, the way he growls my name, the way he stares at me. He bends, sweaty and out of breath; his eyes move over my face and down, inspecting how he's decorated me. Climbing up my body so his hips are level with my face, he presses his cock to my lips, quietly ordering, "Lick it clean."

I open my mouth and lick around the tip, and then suck down, along the velvet-soft skin.

"Ansel," I whisper when I pull away, wanting to be us now. Wanting him.

Relief fills his eyes and he runs his finger across my lower lip. "You like this," he murmurs. "Pleasing me."

"Yes."

He pulls away, bending to kiss my forehead as he carefully unties my hands. *"Attends,"* he whispers. *Wait.*

Ansel comes back with a damp cloth, wiping my cheek, my neck, my breasts. He tosses it into the bin in the corner before kissing me gently.

"Was that nice, *Cerise?*" he whispers, sucking on my lower lip, tongue probing gently into my mouth. He moans quietly, fingers dancing over the curve of my breast. "You were perfect. I love being with you that way." His mouth moves over my cheek, to my ear, and he asks, "But can I be gentle now?"

I nod, cupping his face. He wrecks me with his play, with his command that so easily melts into adoration. I close my eyes, sinking my hands into his hair as he kisses down my neck, sucking my breasts, my navel, parting my legs with his hands.

I'm sore from his rough treatment only minutes ago, but he's careful now, blowing a soft stream of air across me, whispering, "Let me see you."

Ducking, he kisses my clit, licks slowly around. "I love to taste you, do you notice?"

I curl my hands into fists around the pillowcase.

"I think this sweetness is just for me. I pretend your desire has never been like this." He dips a finger inside and brings it up to my lips. "For everyone else it was never so silky and sweet. Tell me it's true."

I let him slide his finger inside and suck, wanting to make this night last for days. I'm wild for him, hoping he stays here with me. Hoping he doesn't retreat to the office and work until dawn.

"Isn't it perfect?" he asks, watching me suck. "I've never loved a woman's flavor as much as I love yours." He climbs up my body, sucking at my lips, my tongue. He's hard again, or maybe he's hard still, and he grinds into my thigh. "I crave it. I crave you. I'm too wild for you. I want you too much, I think."

I shake my head, wanting to tell him he could want me more and wilder but the words get stuck in my throat when he returns his lips to my pussy, licking and sucking so expertly now that I arch off the bed, crying out.

"Like this?" he purrs.

"*Yes.*" My hips press up from the mattress, greedy for his fingers, too.

"I'd be your slave," he whispers, sliding two fingers into me. "Give me nothing but this and your mouth and your quiet words and I'd be your slave, *Cerise.*"

I don't know how it happened, or when exactly, but he knows how to read my body, knows my tells. He teases me, pulling each sensation longer and tighter, making me wait for the orgasm I've wanted for what begins to feel like days. With his tongue, and his lips, his fingers, and his words he brings me to the edge over and over until I'm writhing beneath him, sweating, begging for it.

And just when I think he'll finally let me come, he pulls away instead, wiping his mouth with his forearm as he climbs over me.

I push up onto my elbows, eyes wild. "*Ansel—*"

"Shh, I need to be inside when you come." With quick

hands, he rolls me onto my stomach, spreads my legs, and slides in so deep I gasp, bunching the pillowcase in my fists. His groan vibrates through my bones, along my skin, and I feel the continued buzz of it as he begins to move, his chest pressed to my back, breath hot on my ear.

"I'm lost in you."

I gasp, nodding frantically. "Me, too."

His hand slides underneath me and presses, circling against my clit. I'm right there

right there

right there

and I go off like a bomb the second he presses his lips to my ear and whispers, "What you feel, *Cerise*? I feel it, too. Fuck, Mia, I feel *every*thing for you."

Chapter SEVENTEEN

*I*T'S NOT THAT I don't already think about Ansel a hefty proportion of the time, but after last night I haven't been able to *stop* thinking about him. While I sit outside at the café the next evening with Simone, I'm tempted to see if I can get him to play hooky with me tomorrow, or maybe drop in and see him tonight for a change. Being an eternal tourist alone is growing dull, but keeping busy is the far preferable alternative to being home with my thoughts all day, with the increasingly loud countdown clock ticking away in the back of my mind.

"Today was so *fucking* long," she groans, depositing the keys into her purse before rifling through it. Searching for her ever-present vapor cigarette, I suppose. Being around Gruesimone is a paradoxical comfort: she's so unpleasant, but it makes me love Harlow and Lola even more, and seeing them is the one thing I'm looking forward to when I return home. Simone pauses, eyes lighting up when she finds the familiar black cylinder in one of the inner compartments.

"Fucking finally," she says, and holds it to her mouth before frowning. "Dammit. Dead. Fuck this shit, where are my Marlboros?"

I've never felt like more of a bum in my life, but I don't

even care. Every time I consider getting organized to move home, my mind bends away, distracted by the pretty, shiny life right in front of me. The far preferable one where I can pretend money is endless, I don't really need to go to school, and it's easy to silence the gnawing voice in the back of my thoughts telling me I need to be a contributing member of society. *Just a few more days,* I keep telling myself. I'll worry about it in a few more days.

Gruesimone produces a crumpled pack of cigarettes and a silver Zippo from her bag. She lights up beside me, moaning as she inhales like that cigarette must be better than chocolate cake and all the orgasms combined. For a moment, I seriously consider taking up smoking.

She takes another long drag, the tip burning orange in the dim light. "So when do you leave again? Like three weeks? I swear to God I want your life. Living in Paris just for shits and giggles for an entire summer."

I smile and look past her as I lean back, barely able to see her face through the plume of acrid smoke. I try the words out for size, to see if they still ring with the same feeling of panic: "I start business school in the fall." I close my eyes for a moment and breathe. Yep, they do.

Lampposts pop to life up and down the street, halos of light dropping to the sidewalks below. Over Simone's shoulder, I see a familiar shape emerge: long and lean, slim hips belied by strong, wide shoulders. For a moment I'm reminded of last night, my hands gripping his narrow waist as he moved over me, his sweet expression when he asked if he could be gentle. I actually wrap my fingers around the table to steady myself.

Ansel looks up when he nears the corner, doubling his steps when he sees me.

"Hi," he says, leaning in and placing a lingering kiss on each of my cheeks. Damn I love France. Oblivious to Simone's wide eyes or gaping expression, he pulls back just long enough to grin before kissing me again, this time on the mouth.

"You're off early," I murmur into another kiss.

"I find it harder to work late these days," he says with a little smile. "I wonder why?"

I shrug, grinning.

"Can I take you to dinner?" he asks, pulling me to stand and linking his fingers with mine.

"Hi," Simone says, accompanied by the sound of her spiked heels shuffling on the sidewalk, and finally, he looks over to her.

"I'm Ansel." He gives her the customary kiss on each cheek, and I'm more than a little pleased to see her crestfallen expression when he pulls quickly away.

"Ansel is my husband," I add, rewarded by a smile on Ansel's face that could power each and every streetlight up and down Rue St.-Honoré. "This is Simone."

"Husband," she repeats, and blinks quickly as if she's seeing me for the first time. Her eyes move from me back to Ansel, almost blatantly looking him up and down. She's clearly impressed. With a shake of her head she hoists her large bag over her shoulder, before saying something about a party she's going to be late for and tossing a "well done" in my direction.

"She was pleasant," Ansel says, watching her go.

"She's not, really," I say with a laugh. "But something tells me she might be now."

AFTER ONLY A few blocks of walking in companionable silence, we turn down a street that is cramped even by Paris standards. Like most restaurants in this neighborhood, the storefront is narrow and unassuming, barely wide enough to accommodate a nest of four wooden tables out front and sheltered by a large brown and orange awning above, the word *Ripaille* written across it. It's all cream-colored panels and chalkboards scribbled with the day's specials, and long, thin windows that throw flickering shadows onto the cobbled streets just outside.

Ansel holds the door open and I follow him in, quickly greeted by a tall, rail-thin man with a welcoming smile. The restaurant is small but cozy, and smelling of mint and garlic and something dark and delicious I can't immediately identify. A handful of small tables and chairs fill the single room.

"Bonsoir. Une table pour deux?" the man says, reaching for a stack of menus.

"Oui," I say, and catch Ansel's proud smile, deep dimple present and accounted for. We're led to a table near the back and Ansel waits for me to sit before taking his own. *"Merci."*

Apparently my grasp of two of the most basic words in

French is awesome because, assuming I'm fluent, the waiter launches into the specials of the day. Ansel catches my eye and I give a small, barely perceptible shake of my head, more than happy to listen while he explains it to me later. Ansel asks him a few questions, and I watch in silence, wondering if listening to him speak, watching him gesture with his hands, or, hell, do just about anything will ever stop being ranked up there with some of the sexiest things I've ever seen.

Jesus, I am in deep.

When the waiter leaves, Ansel leans across the table, pointing at the different items with his long, graceful hands, and I have to blink several times and remind myself to pay attention.

Menus have always been the most difficult for me to navigate. There are a few helpful things: *boeuf*/beef, *poulet*/chicken, *veau*/veal, *canard*/duck, and *poisson* is fish (I'm completely unashamed to say I knew that one from countless viewings of *The Little Mermaid*), but how things are prepared or the names for various sauces or vegetables are still things I need help with at most restaurants.

"The special is langoustine bisque, which is . . ." He pauses, furrows his brow, and looks up to the ceiling. "Uhh . . . it's a shellfish?"

I grin. Lord only knows why I find his confused face so endearing. "Lobster?"

"Yes. Lobster," he says with a satisfied nod. "Lobster bisque with mint, served with a small pizza on the side. Very crunchy with lobster and sundried tomatoes. Also there is *le boeuf*—"

"The bisque," I decide.

"You don't want to hear the others?"

"You think there's something better there than soup and pizza with *lobster*?" I stop, realization dawning. "Unless it means you can't kiss me?"

"It's fine," he says, waving his hand. "I can still kiss you senseless."

"Then that's it. Bisque."

"Perfect. I think I'll get the fish," he says.

The waiter returns and both he and Ansel listen patiently while I insist on ordering my own dinner, along with a simple plate of greens tossed in vinaigrette. With a smile he can't manage to hide, Ansel orders his food and each of us a glass of wine and sits back, draping an arm over the back of the empty chair beside him.

"Look, you don't even need me," he says.

"As if. How else would I know how to ask for the large dildo? I mean, that's a really important distinction."

Ansel barks out a laugh, his eyes wide in surprise, his hands flying to his mouth to stifle the sound. A few of the other diners turn in our direction, but nobody seems to have minded his outburst.

"You're a bad influence," he says once composed, and reaches for his wine.

"Me? I'm not the one who left the translation for dildo on a note one morning, so . . . glass houses, Dimples."

"But you did find the costume shop," he says to me over his glass. "And I must say I owe you endlessly for that."

I feel my face warm under his gaze, under the implied meaning of his words. "True," I admit in a whisper.

Our food comes and beyond the occasional satisfied groan or voicing my intent to bear the chef's children, we're mostly silent while we eat.

The empty plates are cleared away and Ansel orders dessert for us to share: *fondant au chocolat*—which looks a lot like a fancy version of the chocolate lava cake we have at home—served warm with a pepper-vanilla ice cream. Ansel moans around his spoon.

"It's a little obscene watching you eat that," I say. Across the table he's closed his eyes, humming around the spoon in his mouth.

"It's my favorite," he says. "Though not as good as the one my mother makes for me when I visit."

"I always forget you said she went to culinary school. I can't actually think of a dessert my mom didn't buy from the store. She's what I like to refer to as domestic-lite."

"One day when I'm visiting you in Boston we'll drive to her bakery in Bridgeport and she'll make you anything you want."

I can practically hear the proverbial brake noises squealing in both of our thoughts. A distinct roadblock has just risen in the conversation, and it sits there, flashing obnoxiously and unable to be ignored.

"You have two more weeks here?" he asks. "Three?"

The phrase *you could ask me to stay* pops into my head before I can stop it because no, that's—*no*—really the *worst* idea, *ever.*

I keep my head down, eyes on the plate between us, swirling chocolate sauce into a puddle of melting vanilla ice cream. "I think I should probably leave in two. I need to find an apartment, register for classes . . ." *Call my father,* I think. *Find a job. Build a life. Make friends. Decide what I want to do with my degree. Try to find a way to be happy with this decision. Count the seconds until you come see me.*

"Even though you don't want to."

"No," I say blankly. "I don't want to spend the next two years of my life in school so I can go to an office I hate with people who'd rather be anywhere but where they are and stare at four walls of a boardroom one day."

"That was a very in-depth description," he notes. "But I think your impression of business school is maybe a little . . . misinformed. You don't have to end up in that life if you don't choose it."

I set my spoon down and lean back into my chair. "I lived with the world's most dedicated businessman my entire life, and I've met all of his colleagues and most of their colleagues. I'm terrified of becoming what they are."

The bill comes and Ansel reaches for it, all but slapping my hand away. I frown at him—I can take my . . . husband out to dinner—but he ignores me, continuing where he left off.

"Not every businessman or -woman is like your father. I just think that maybe you should . . . consider other uses for your degree. You don't have to follow his path."

THE WALK HOME is quiet, and I know it's because I haven't responded to what he's said and he doesn't want to push. He's not wrong; people use business degrees for all kinds of interesting things. The problem is I don't know yet what my interesting thing *is*.

"Can I ask you something?" I ask.

He hums, looking down at me.

"You took the job at the firm even though it's not really what you want to do."

Nodding, he waits for me to finish.

"You don't really like your job."

"No."

"So what *is* your dream job?"

"To teach," he says, shrugging. "I think corporate law is fascinating. I think law in general is fascinating. How we organize morals and the vague cloud of ethics into rules, and especially how we build these things when new technology comes up. But I won't be a very good teacher unless I've practiced, and after this position, I'll be able to find a faculty spot nearly anywhere."

Ansel holds my hand the few blocks to our apartment, pausing once or twice to bring my fingers to his lips and kiss them. The headlight from a passing scooter glints off the gold of his wedding band, and I feel my stomach contract in on itself, a feeling of dread settling heavily there. It's not that I don't want to stay in Paris—I love it here—but I can't deny I miss the familiarity of home, speaking to people in a language I understand, my friends, the ocean. Yet I'm beginning to realize I don't want to leave him, either.

He insists we tuck into the little bistro on the corner for a coffee. I've grown used to what Europeans refer to as coffee—intense, small pours of the most delicious espresso—and other than Ansel, I'm sure this is the one thing I will miss most about the city.

We sit at a tiny table outside and under the stars. Ansel slides his chair so close to mine his arm has nowhere to rest but around my shoulders.

"Do you want to meet some of my friends this week?" he asks.

I look at him in surprise. "What?"

"Christophe and Marie, two of my oldest friends, are having a dinner party to celebrate her new promotion. She works for one of the larger firms in my building, and I thought maybe you'd like to come. They'd love to meet my wife."

"That sounds good." I nod, smiling. "I've been hoping to meet some of your friends."

"I realize I should have done this earlier but . . . I admit that I was being selfish. We have so little time together and I didn't want to share that with anyone."

"You've been working," I say on an exhale as he basically repeats my conversation with Harlow back to me.

He reaches for my hand, kisses the back of my knuckles, my ring, before twisting his fingers with mine. "I want to show you off."

Okay. Meeting friends. Being introduced as his wife. This is real life. This is what married couples do. "Okay," I say lamely. "That sounds fun."

He grins and leans forward, placing a kiss against my lips. "Thank you, Mrs. Guillaume." And wow, the dimple, too. I am toast.

The waitress stops at our table and I sit back in my seat while Ansel orders our coffee. There's a group of young girls—around eight or nine years old—dancing to a man playing the guitar just outside. Their laughter bounces off the cramped buildings, above the sound of occasional cars or the fountain splashing just across the street.

One of them is spinning and tips over, landing just below the small deck we're sitting on.

"Are you okay?" I ask, stepping down to help her.

"*Oui,*" she says, brushing the dirt from the front of her checkered dress. Her friend crosses to us, and though I'm not sure what she says, the way she stretches her arms to the side, and speaks to her in a scolding tone, I think she's telling her she did her turn wrong.

"Are you trying to turn?" I ask, but she doesn't respond, merely watches me with a confused expression. "*Pirouette?*"

At this she lights up. "*Oui,*" she says excitedly. "*Pirouette. Tourner.*"

"Spin," Ansel offers.

She straightens her arms to the side, points her toe, and spins, so quickly she almost falls down again.

"Whoa," I say, both of us laughing as I catch her. "Maybe if you . . . um." Straightening, I pat my stomach. "Tighten."

I turn to Ansel, who translates, *"Contracte tes abdominaux."* The little girl makes a face of concentration, one I can only imagine means she's clenching her stomach muscles.

More of the girls have gathered to listen and so I take a second, moving them so they'll have enough room. "Fourth position," I say, holding up four fingers. I point my left foot out, my right foot next to and behind. "Arms up, one to the side, one out front. Good. Now *plié*? Bend?" They each bend at the knees and I nod, subtly guiding their posture. "Yes! Good!" I point to my eyes and then to a spot off in the distance, partially aware of Ansel translating behind me.

"You have to spot. Find one place and don't look away. So when you turn"—I straighten, bend at the knees, and then push up off the ball of my foot before spinning, landing on *plié*—"you're back where you started." It's such a familiar movement, one I haven't felt my body do for so long that I almost miss the sound of cheering, the loudest of them coming from Ansel. The girls are practically giddy and taking turns, encouraging each other and asking me for help.

It's getting late and eventually, the girls have to leave. Ansel takes my hand, smiling, and I glance over my shoulder as we walk away. I feel like I could have watched them all night.

"That was fun," he says.

I look over at him, still smiling. "What part?"

"Seeing you dancing like that."

"That was one turn, Ansel."

"It might be the single sexiest thing I've ever seen. *That* is what you should be doing."

I sigh. "Ansel—"

"Some people go to business school and run movie theaters or restaurants. Some own their own bakery, or dance studio."

"Not you, too." I've heard this before, from Lorelei, from Harlow's entire family. "I wouldn't know the first thing about that."

He makes a point of looking over his shoulder, back in the direction we just came. "I respectfully disagree."

"Those things take money. I hate taking money from my father."

"Then why do you take money from him if you hate it?" he asks.

I throw the question back at him. "You don't take money from *your* father?"

"I do," he admits. "But I decided long ago it's the only thing he's good for. And a few years ago, when I was your age, I didn't want my mother to feel like she needed to support me."

"I don't have enough money to live in Boston without his help," I tell him. "And I guess in a way . . . I feel like he owes me this, since in the end I'm doing what he wants."

"But if you're doing what *you* want—"

"It's *not* what I want."

He pulls us to a stop and holds up a hand, not even a little fazed by the weight of this conversation. "I know. And I'm not really thrilled at the idea that you will leave me soon. But putting that aside, if you went to school, did something *you* wanted to do with it, you would make the decision yours, not his."

I sigh, looking back down the street.

"Just because you can't dance professionally doesn't mean you have to stop dancing for a living. Find the spot in the distance and don't look away, isn't that what you told those girls? What is your 'spot'? Finding a way to keep dance in your life?"

I blink away, back down the block to where the girls are still twirling and laughing. His spot is teaching law. He hasn't taken his eyes off that point since he started.

"Okay, then." He appears to take my silence as passive agreement. "Do you train to be a teacher? Or do you learn to run your own business? Those are two different paths."

The idea of having a dance studio makes a warring reaction explode in my belly: elation, and dread. I can barely imagine anything more fun, but nothing would cut off my relationship with my family more thoroughly than that.

"Ansel," I say, shaking my head. "Even if I *want* my own studio, it's still about getting *started*. He was going to pay for my apartment for two years while I got my degree. Now he's not speaking to me and there is no way he'd get on board with that plan. There's something about dance for him . . . it's as if he doesn't like it on a visceral level. I'm realizing now that, whatever I do, I'll have to make it work without his help." I close my eyes and swallow thickly. I've taken such a profound mental vacation from the reality of my future that I'm already exhausted after only this tiny discussion. "I'm glad I came here. In some ways it's the best decision I ever made. But it's made things more complicated in some ways, too."

He leans back, studies me. I adore playful Ansel, the one who winks at me across the room for no reason, or talks lovingly to my thighs and breasts. But I think I might *love* this Ansel, the one who seems to really want what's best for me, the one who is clearly brave enough for both of us. "You're married, no?" he asks. "You have a husband?"

"Yes."

"A husband who makes a good living now."

I shrug and look away. Money talk is exceedingly awkward.

As playful and goofy as he can be sometimes, there is nothing but sincerity in his voice when he asks, "Then why would you need to depend on your father to do what *you* want?"

———————

UPSTAIRS IN OUR apartment I follow him into the kitchen and lean against the counter as he reaches into the cabinet for a bottle. Ansel turns, shakes two ibuprofen tablets into my palm, and hands me a glass of water. I stare at my hands and then up at him.

"It's what you do," he says, offering a tiny shrug. "After two glasses of wine you always take ibuprofen with a big glass of water. You're a lightweight."

I'm reminded again how observant he is, and how he manages to catch things when I don't even think he's paying attention. He stands, watching as I swallow the pills and put the empty glass on the counter by my hip.

With each second that ticks by when we aren't kissing or touching, I'm terrified the easy comfort we have tonight will evaporate and he'll turn to his desk and I'll turn to the bedroom alone.

But tonight, while we stare at each other in the muted light provided by the single bulb above the stove, the energy between us seems to only grow more electric. This feels real.

He scratches his jaw and then tilts his chin to me. "You're the most beautiful woman I've ever seen."

My stomach flips. "I'm not sure I believe that I'm—"

"*Stay,*" he interrupts in a tight whisper. "I'm dreading the day you leave. I'm losing my mind thinking about it."

I close my eyes. This is half what I've wanted him to say, and half what I was most afraid to hear. I pull my lip between my teeth, biting down my smile when I look back at him. "I thought you just told me to go to school to open my own business someday."

"Maybe I think you should wait until I'm done with this case. Then we can go together. Live together. I work, you study."

"How could I stay here until the spring? What would I

do?" It's been wonderful, but I can't imagine another nine months living idly as a tourist.

"You can find work, or you can just research what's involved in opening a studio. We'll leave together, and you can defer school for one year."

If possible, this is even more insane than my coming here in the first place. Staying means there is no end to *us*—no annulment, no fake marriage—and there is an entirely new trail blazed ahead.

"I don't think I can stay here and be alone so much of the time . . ."

He winces, dragging a hand through his hair. "If you want to start now, go and I'll come next spring. I just . . . *Is* that what you want?"

I shake my head, but I can see in his eyes he correctly reads my gesture to be *I don't know.*

My first few weeks here I felt both like I was completely free, and also a bit of a leech. But Ansel didn't invite me here only to be generous or save me from a summer at home or spent psyching myself up to start school. He did it for those reasons and because he *wanted* me.

"Mia?"

"Mmm?"

"I like you," he says in a whisper, and from the slight shake of his voice, I think I know what he's really saying. I feel the words like a warm breath across my neck, but he hasn't stepped any closer. He's not even touching me. His hands are braced on the counter behind him, at his hips. This bare admission is somehow more intimate from a few feet away, without the safety of kisses or faces pressed into necks. "I don't want you to leave without me. A wife belongs with her husband, and he belongs with her. I'm always selfish with you, asking you to move here, asking you to wait until it's good for my career before you leave, but there it is."

There it is.

I tear my eyes from his and look down at my bare feet on the floor, letting the heavy drumming of my heart take over my senses for a beat. I'm relieved, terrified . . . but mostly I'm euphoric. He told me he couldn't play the other night if I said it out loud, and maybe it's the same fear again, that we can't keep it light, can't let it go in a few weeks if one of us says *love*.

"Do you think you could ever," he starts after a few beats of silence, his lips pulled up to one side in a smile, "like *me*?"

My chest squeezes at the earnest vulnerability in his expression. I nod, swallowing what feels like a bowling ball in my throat before saying, "I'm already in like with you."

His eyes flame with relief, and the words tumble out in a long, jumbled string. "I'll get you a new ring. We'll do it all over again. We can find a new flat with memories that are only ours . . ."

I laugh through an unexpected sob. "I *like* this flat. I like my gold band. I like my fractured memories of our wedding. I don't need anything new."

He tilts his head and smiles at me, dimple flirting shamelessly, and it's all I can take. Reaching out, I hook a finger through a belt loop on his pants and tug. "Come here."

Ansel takes the two steps to me, pressing the length of his body so closely to mine I need to tilt my chin to look up at him.

"Done talking, then?" he asks, hands slipping around my waist, bracketing me.

"Yeah."

"What do you feel like doing now?" His eyes manage to look both amused and ravenous.

I slip a hand between us and palm him through his jeans, wanting to feel him come to life under my touch.

But he's already hard, and grunts when I press into him, his eyes falling closed. His hands slide up my over my chest, around my shoulders and higher, cupping my neck.

The sweep of his thumb across my bottom lip is like a trigger: a warmth spreads through me and it turns nearly immediately to a hunger so hot, my legs grow weak. I open my mouth, lick the pad of his thumb until he slides it inside and, with dark eyes, watches me suck. In my palm, he lengthens further, twitching.

He steers me to my right, walking me backward out of the kitchen, but stops after only a few steps, cupping my face to kiss me. "Say it again?"

I search his eyes for his meaning before I understand. "That I like you?"

He nods and smiles, eyes closing as he bends to lick the tip of his tongue across my lips. "That you *like* me." Ansel looks down at me from under the heavy fall of his hair over his brow, tilting my head back with his hand on my jaw. "Let me see your neck. Show me all of that gorgeous skin."

I arch my neck and his fingertips skim along my collarbone, strong but gentle.

He undresses me first, in no particular hurry. But once my skin is exposed to the cool air in the flat and the heat of his attention, I pull at his shirt, fumble with his belt. I want my hands on every inch of him at once, but they always gravitate to the smooth expanse of his chest. Everything in the world I find sexy, I find there: The firm, warm skin. The heavy drum of his heart. The sharp spasms of his abdomen when I scratch my short nails over his ribs. The line of soft hair that always tempts my hands lower.

Even in the small flat, the bedroom feels too far away. His fingers drift down my chest, breezing past my breasts as if it isn't where they intend to be. Over my stomach and lower, past where I expect him to slide two fingers and play with me. Instead, his hand smooths down my thigh, his eyes watching my face as his fingertips linger on my scar, on skin that's not quite sensitive, not quite numb.

"It's weird, maybe, that I love your scar as much as I do."

I have to remind myself to breathe.

"You thought it was the first thing I noticed, but it wasn't. I didn't even pay attention to it until the middle of the night, when you finally lay down on the bed and I kissed from your toe to your hip. Maybe you hate it, but I don't. You *earned* it. I'm in awe of you."

He pushes away from me slightly so he can kneel down and his fingers are replaced by his lips and tongue, hot and wet against my skin. I let my mouth fall open and my eyes flutter closed. Without this scar, I'd never be here. Maybe I'd never have met Ansel.

His voice is raspy against my thigh. "To me, you're perfect."

He pulls me with him to the floor, my back to his front, my legs straddling his. Across the living room, I can see our reflections in the dark window, can see the way I look spread around his thighs.

He pets me, fingers sliding up and down the crease of my sex, teasing at penetrating me. On my neck, his mouth sucks and licks until he's at my jaw and I turn my head so he can kiss my lips, his tongue slipping inside and curling over mine. Ansel pushes his middle finger inside me and I cry out, but he continues stroking slowly as if he's feeling every inch of me.

Releasing my lip from between his teeth, he asks, "*Est-ce bon?*"

Is it good? Such diluted words for something I'm sure I *need*. The word *good* feels so empty, so plain, like color bleached from paper.

Before I even know I've answered, my voice fills the room. "More. *Please.*"

He slides his other hand up my body to my mouth, pushing two fingers inside against my tongue and pulling them out, wet. Ansel glides them across my nipple, circling in the same rhythm as his other hand between my legs. The world narrows to these two points of sensation—on the peak of my breast and his fingers on my clit—and then shrinks further until all I feel is circles and wet and warm and the vibration of his words on my skin. *"Oh, Mia."*

I've been helpless before: trapped beneath a car, under the sharp command of an instructor, burned by my father's heated disdain. But never like this. *This* kind of helpless is liberating; it's what it feels like to have every nerve ending rise to the surface and drink in sensation. It's what it feels like to be touched by someone I trust with my body, trust with my heart.

But I want to feel him inside me when I fall to pieces, and my release is too close to the surface. I lift my hips, take hold of him, and lower myself down his length as we both let out shuddering groans.

We stay motionless for a few seconds, as my body adjusts to him.

I slide forward and up. Back and down. Again, and again, closing my eyes only when his shaking voice—*Just . . . please . . . faster . . . faster Mia*—breaks away and he slides his hands up the front of my body, to my neck. His thumb strokes the delicate skin at the hollow of my throat.

It shouldn't be so easy to bring me back to this point again, and again, but when Ansel drops one hand to my thigh, and moves it between my legs, his broad fingertips circling, his quiet, hoarse sex voice telling me how good it feels . . . I can't stop my body from giving in.

"C'est ça, c'est ça." I don't need him to translate. *That's it,*

he said. That's him touching me perfectly, and my body responding just as he knew it would.

I don't know what sensation to focus on; it's impossible to feel each thing at once. His fingers digging into my hips, the heavy length of him stroking inside me, the feel of his mouth on my neck sucking sucking sucking so perfectly until that tiny flash of pain where he pulls a mark to the surface.

I feel like he's taking over every part of me: filling my vision with the things he's doing, reaching into my chest and making my heart beat so hard and fast it's terrifying and thrilling in equal measure.

He pushes up beneath me, moving so I'm spilled onto my hands and knees and we both moan at the new depth, and the new visual in the window of him braced behind me. His hands curl around my hips, head falls back, and eyes close as he begins to move. He's the portrait of bliss, the picture of relief. Each muscle in his torso is flexed and beaded with sweat but he manages to look more relaxed than I've ever seen him, lazily thrusting into me.

"Harder," I tell him, my voice thick and quiet with need.

His eyes open and a dark smile spreads over his face. Digging his fingers tighter into the flesh around my hips, he drives brutally into me once, pausing, and then picks up a perfectly punishing rhythm.

"Harder."

He grips my hips, tilting them, and grunts with effort as he pushes deep, hitting me in a place I've never known existed and making me cry out, clutched by an orgasm so sudden and overwhelming I seem to lose the use of my arms. I fall to my elbows as Ansel holds me by my hips, rutting rhythmically, his voice coming out in sharp, deep grunts.

"Mia," he rasps, stilling behind me and shaking as he comes.

I collapse, boneless, and he catches me, cradling my head to his chest. With my ear pressed against him, I can hear the heavy, vital pounding of his heart.

Ansel rolls me to my back, carefully sliding back into me as he always seems to, even when we're done, and watching my face with clear, serious eyes.

"It felt good?" he asks quietly.

I nod.

"You like me?"

"I do."

Our hips rock together slowly, trying to hold on.

Chapter EIGHTEEN

"SO WHAT TIME is this party?" I mumble into my pillow. Ansel rests heavily on top of me, his front to my back, the fabric of his suit pressed against my bare skin, his hair tickling the side of my face. I start to laugh, struggling to get away, but this only encourages him. "*Mmpf.* You're so heavy. Do you have bricks in your pocket? Get off me."

"But you're so warm," he whines. "And soft. And you smell so good. Like woman and sex and me." His fingers find my sides and curl, tickling me relentlessly until he rolls me to my back and then he's there, hovering above me, his thumb tracing my mouth. "The party's at seven," he says, eyes mossy green and filled with a weight that tells me he'd much rather take off the suit than get out of this bed. "I'll meet you here and we'll go together. I promise not to be late."

He leans down and kisses me, making a sound that's somewhere between contentment and longing, and I know he's telling himself not to get carried away, that as good as this is, there will be time for more later. *After* work.

I push my hand beneath his jacket and tug his shirt free

from where it's tucked into the waistband of his pants, as I unapologetically search for skin.

"I can hear you thinking," I say, repeating the line he's used on me at least a dozen times. "Wondering how much time you have?"

He groans and lets his head fall to my neck. "I can't believe there was a time when I used to be up and practically out the door before my alarm even went off. Now I don't want to leave."

I push my hands through his hair, scratching lightly against his scalp. He works to keep the majority of his weight off me, but I can feel him relax more every second.

"Je ne veux pas partir," he repeats, voice a little rough now. *"Et je ne veux pas que tu partes."*

And I don't want you to leave.

I blink up to the ceiling, wanting to commit every detail of this moment to memory.

"I can't wait to show you off tonight," he says, brighter now, pushing up onto his elbow and looking down at me. "I can't wait to tell everyone how I tricked you into proposing to me. We'll ignore the pesky detail that you're leaving me soon."

"Hide my passport and I'm here for good."

"You think I haven't already thought of that? Don't be surprised if you come home one day and it's gone." He leans in, kisses me before pulling back. "Okay, that's creepy; it's in the top of the dresser where it belongs."

I laugh, swatting him away. "Go to work."

He groans and rolls off me, lying on his back on the bed. "If I didn't have a meeting today with a client I've been waiting months to talk to, I'd call and say I'm feeling sick."

I prop my chin on his chest, looking up at him. "It's a big one?"

"Very big. What happens today could mean the difference between this case ending in the next six weeks, and dragging on for months and months."

"Then you should get started."

"I know," he says on an exhale.

"And I'll be here, waiting for you at seven." I haven't even finished the sentence and he's turned to me, smiling again. "And you won't be late."

He sits up, takes my face in his hands before kissing me deeply, tongues and teeth, fingers that slip down my body to brush over my nipple.

Standing abruptly, he does the world's most hilarious version of the robot beside the bed. He bleats out the words in an automaton voice: "I won't be late."

"Did you just do that so I'd think you're adorable even if you're late tonight?"

"I *won't* be late!" But he robots again anyway, sandy hair falling over his forehead, and then moonwalks out of the room.

"Worst dancer ever!" I yell after him. But it's a total lie. He has rhythm and an ease in his skin that can't be taught. A true dancer is fun to watch, whether or not they're dancing, and I could watch Ansel for hours.

He laughs, calling out, "Be good, Wife!" and then the door clicks behind him.

––––––

BUT OF COURSE he's late.

At seven thirty Ansel bursts into the flat, and becomes a whirlwind of activity: tossing off his work clothes, pulling on jeans and a casual button-down shirt. He kisses me quickly as he sprints to the kitchen to grab a bottle of wine and then pulls my hand, guiding me out of the apartment and into the elevator.

"Hi," he says breathlessly, pressing me against the wall as he reaches to push the button for the ground floor.

"Hi." I barely get the sound out before he's kissing me, lips hungry and searching, sucking at my bottom lip, my jaw, my neck.

"Tell me you really, really want to meet my friends, or else I'm taking you back there to undress and fuck until you're hoarse."

I laugh, pushing him away slightly and kissing him one more time squarely on the lips before saying, "I want to meet your friends. You can undress me later."

"Then tell me a story about Madame Allard, because that's the only way I'm going to quickly lose this erection."

––––––

MARIE AND CHRISTOPHE'S building is only a few blocks away from where we emerge from the métro and when it comes into view I stop and stare. Ansel's apartment manages to be both small and airy. There's nothing over-the-top or pretentious about any of it: it's an older building, and as easygoing and comfortable as he is. *This* place . . . is not.

The façade is stone, and while it has an aged look about it—easily blending with the surrounding construction—it's clearly been renovated, and at no small cost. The apartments on the bottom floor are each anchored by a set of wide steps, capped with red doors and gleaming brass knockers. The second and third floor apartments boast arched windows leading to individual balconies with ornate ironwork of tiny metal blossoms erupting from intricate molded vines.

Trees line the busy street, and beneath the welcome shadow they provide I take a moment to gather myself and prepare for a room of strangers and conversations I probably won't understand. Ansel presses his palm to my lower back, whispering, "Ready?"

Weeks ago the very idea of doing this—without Lola or Harlow to carry the conversation if I lost Ansel in the crowd and went mute—would have made me shudder in horror. I don't know what it will be like upstairs, but if the roaring laughter coming from the window is any indication, the party is already in full swing, even this early in the evening. I just hope everyone up there is as nice as Ansel promises me they will be. I catch a glimpse of our reflection and startle slightly. I look at myself every morning, but it's different in the windows of this place somehow. My hair is longer, bangs swept to the side instead of cutting a straight line across my forehead. I've gained a little weight and feel less boyish, more like a woman. My skirt is from a small shop near Montmartre, my face is bare of all but the slightest hint of makeup, but still glowing. It's fitting that I look different; I *feel* different. And beside me, Ansel towers above, his arm protectively curled around my waist, and I see in the reflection when he bends to catch my attention. "Hey."

"I was looking at that cute couple." I nod to the window.

After studying us for a long, quiet beat, he plants a sweet kiss on my lips. "Come on, *Cerise*."

Marie answers the door with a happy yelp, and pulls us into the melee, kissing my cheeks before passing me off to Christophe's open arms.

"It is Ansel's Mia!" he yells in English to everyone, and a roomful of people turn and look at me with wide, curious eyes as Ansel hands the bottle of wine to Marie.

"Hi." I raise my hand, waving lamely, sinking into Ansel as his arm finds my waist again.

"We are so glad to finally meet you!" she says, kissing each of my cheeks again. "You are even more beautiful than your photo." My eyes widen and Marie laughs, curling her arm through mine and pulling me farther into the apartment, away from my husband, who is nearly immediately swallowed by a circle of his friends. He lifts his chin, watching as Marie leads me down the hall.

"I'll be fine," I yell over my shoulder, even if it's only half true. I really didn't expect to be separated from him only seconds after walking in the door.

Inside, it's every bit as elaborate as I had guessed it would be from the street. The walls are papered in muted gold damask and from where I stand I can see two marble fireplaces, each framed with delicate molding. Bookcases bursting with books and small, beautiful vases border one wall; the opposite is lined with floor-to-ceiling windows, all overlooking a lush courtyard. Despite the amount of *stuff* inside, the apartment is charming and large enough that even with the number of people currently milling about, there's plenty of space to mingle with some degree of privacy.

We pass a small library, wander down a hall lined with people drinking and talking, who all seem to quiet as I pass— maybe I'm being paranoid but I really don't think so—and into a wide, brilliant white kitchen.

"I will take you back out there, but they are like wolves. Excited to see him, excited to meet you. Let them accost him first." Marie pours me a generous glass of wine before curling my hand around it, laughing. "How do you say . . . 'strength in a glass'?"

"Liquid courage?" I offer.

"Yes!" She snaps her fingers and kisses my cheek again. "There are many nice people here and they all love your husband so they will love you. Look around, I will introduce you to everyone in just a minute!"

She jogs off when the doorbell rings again and, after waiting a beat to see if it's Ansel who has walked into the kitchen—it isn't—I turn to look out the tall, narrow kitchen windows with a stunning view of Montmartre.

"I bet that view never gets old."

I turn to find a beautiful, redheaded woman looking out the adjoining set of French doors. She's maybe a few years older than I am, and her accent is heavy, so thick it takes me several beats to translate what she's said.

"It's gorgeous," I agree.

"You're American?" When I nod, she asks, "You live here? Or are visiting?"

"I live here," I answer, and then pause. "Well . . . for now. It's sort of complicated."

"And married," she says, pointing to my ring.

"I am." Absently, I twist the gold band around my finger. If she didn't hear Christophe's boisterous announcement when we entered only five minutes ago, it strikes me as a little weird that this is one of the first things she says.

"What is his name?"

"Ansel," I say. "Ansel Guillaume."

"I know him!" she exclaims, smiling widely. "I have known him for many years." Leaning in conspiratorially, she adds, "Very handsome and the most charming man."

Pride mingles with unease in my chest. The woman seems nice enough, but a little pushy. It feels as though we've skipped a smoother entrée into conversation. "He is."

"So you are here as a student? Or for work?" she asks, sipping from her glass of red wine.

"I'm just here visiting this summer," I explain, relaxing a little. My shyness can come off as aloof, I reason. Maybe people often misinterpret her intensity as aggression. "I start school in the fall."

"Then you are leaving soon," she says, frowning.

"Yes . . . still trying to figure out the timing."

"And what about your husband? His job is very import-ant, no? He cannot just leave Paris and go with you?" Her ex-pression shows nothing but polite interest, but her stream of questions has me back on edge. When I don't answer for a long beat, she presses. "Haven't you talked about any of this?"

"Um . . ." I begin, but I have no idea how to respond. Her blue eyes are wide and penetrating, and behind them I see something larger there. Hurt. Restrained anger. I look past her and see that there are a few people in the kitchen now, and they are all watching us: fascinated, eyes wide in sympathy, as if observing a car crash in slow motion.

I turn back to her, growing anxiously suspicious. "Sorry . . . I don't think I got your name."

"I didn't give it to you," she says, with a small tilt of her head. "Maybe I am misleading you by pretending I'm not fa-miliar with your situation. You see, I know Ansel very, *very* well."

Understanding clicks like a lock in my mind.

"Are you Minuit?"

Her smile is elated, in an eerily wicked way. "Minuit! Yes, perfect, I'm Minuit."

"I assumed you had black hair. I don't know why," I mumble, more to myself than anything. I have the sense of being balanced on a teeter-totter: I'm still not sure whether I'll land on my feet in this conversation. I want to turn and look desperately around for Ansel, or Marie, but Minuit is watching me like a hawk, seeming to feed on my discomfort.

Somewhere behind me, I hear Ansel's deep laugh coming toward us down the hall, hear him sing a few lines of the crazy French rap song he's played the past couple of weeks as he shaves in the morning.

"I sh-should go," I say, placing my drink on a table next to me. I want to find Ansel. I want to pull him aside and tell him about this conversation. I want him to take me home and erase her thunderous expression from my memory.

Minuit reaches for my arm, stopping me. "But tell me, how are you enjoying my apartment, Mia? My bed? My fiancé?"

My heart literally stops, my vision blurs. "Your *fiancé*?"

"We were going to be married before you came along. Imagine my surprise when he came back from a silly American vacation with a wife."

"I don't . . ." I whisper, looking around the room as if anyone there would help me. A few people look on with sympathy, but no one seems brave enough to interrupt.

"He only *called* me Minuit, you see," she explains, her red hair sliding over her shoulder as she leans forward, "because I could never fall asleep. We got a new bed for our beautiful flat. We tried *everything* to wear me out." Tilting her head, she asks, "How do *you* like sleeping in our fancy new bed in our beautiful flat?"

I open my mouth, and then close it again, shaking my head. My pulse is racing, my skin clammy and flushed.

I'll get you a new ring. We'll do it all over again. We can find a new flat with memories that are only ours . . .

I need to get out of here.

"We were together for six years. Can you even grasp how long that is? Six years ago you were only a child."

Her accent is so thick and I'm continually falling behind, grasping on to individual words to cobble together my comprehension. But I understand *six years.* Ansel called it "too long," but I never in my wildest dreams imagined it would be such a significant fraction of their lives. Or that they were going to be married. I don't even know when they broke up—I'd assumed they broke up when he moved back here almost a year ago—but from the circles under her eyes and the way her hand is shaking around her glass, I know I'm wrong.

My heart seems to tear apart, piece by piece.

I hear Ansel enter the kitchen, hear him yell, *"J'ai acheté du vin!"* as he holds up two open bottles of wine to the small crowd gathered.

But his expression falls as his eyes catch mine across the room and then drift to the woman at my side.

She leans closer, whispering directly in my ear, "Six years ago you had not yet been run over by a truck, huh?"

My head whips around, back to her, and I stare up at blue eyes so full of anger it takes my breath away. *"What?"*

"He tells me *everything*. You're a tiny spot of time," she hisses, pinching her thumb and forefinger together. "Do you have any idea how many times he does crazy things? You're his most ridiculous impulse, and he has no idea how to fix this mistake. My taste was still fresh on his mouth when he saw you in your trashy hotel."

I want to vomit. The only thing I know is that I need to *move,* but before I can manage to put one foot in front of the other, Ansel is at my side, his hand curling tightly around my arm.

"Perry," he hisses to the woman. *"Arrête. C'est ma femme. C'est Mia. Qu'est-ce que tu fous là?"*

Perry?

Wait. *Perry?*

I blink down to the floor as it all makes sense. His best friends in the world, the four of them. Ansel, Oliver, Finn, and Perry. Not another man . . . a woman.

A woman he was with for *six years.*

Four of us, together all day long . . . I don't know that I'll ever know anyone in the way I know those three . . . Those relationships are some of the best and . . . complicated of my life . . . We missed our families together, we comforted each other, we celebrated some of the proudest moments of our lives.

I feel my face heat, my lips part in a gasp. How many times did Ansel let me assume Perry was another man, a *friend*? I told him everything about myself, about my life and fears and relationships, and he spoke only in vague generalities about Minuit and their "too-long" relationship.

She looks thrilled, like a lioness that caught a gazelle. She wraps her arm around his bicep, but he shakes it off, reaching for me again.

"Mia."

I pull out of his grasp. "I think I'll probably leave now."

There are a million other things I could say—a million other biting things someone like Harlow or Lola would say right now—but for once I'm glad I won't give voice to any of them.

He calls after me but I'm already running to the stairs, tripping down the tight spiral. Behind me, his feet pound on the wood; my name echoes down along the banister.

"Mia!"

My mind bends away from understanding what just happened back at the party. Two magnets pushing apart.

The sidewalk is bare, cracked, and crooked as I turn on Rue La Bruyère, sprinting into the small curve at St.-Georges. It's funny that I know where I'm going now, so I can properly run away.

I catch my breath between two buildings. I think he went looking for me the other way; I don't hear him anymore.

There are too many things I have to figure out now: how fast I can pack, when I can leave, and why Ansel left me to be blindsided tonight by a woman he was planning to marry before I came along. I have no idea why he kept this from me, but I feel the shards of panic pushing deep into my lungs, making it hard to breathe.

How old this city is. The plaque on the building I'm up against states it was built in 1742. This structure alone is older than any love affair alive in this country. Ours might be the youngest, even though it always felt as though we were picking up where our souls left off on a thread much further up the line.

I know now that I love him, that what we have is real, and that I probably loved him that first second I saw him from across the room, enjoying my happiness as much as I did. For whatever Lola and Harlow say about it, I'm a true believer.

It is possible to fall that fast.

Chapter NINETEEN

ABOUT TWO BLOCKS from our apartment I know he's behind me again, far enough back to give me some space, close enough that he knows where I am. Upstairs in the narrow hallway, I fumble with my keys as he bursts through the door to the stairwell, out of breath. At least he was smart enough to let me take the elevator alone.

The flat is dark now, the sun no longer lingering in the sky, and I don't bother to turn on any lights. Instead, I lean against the doorway to the bedroom and stare at the floor. He stops in front of the kitchen, directly across from me but leaving about four feet in between. Slowly, his breathing returns to normal. I don't even have to look directly at him to know he feels miserable. From the corner of my eye I can see his slumped posture, the way he's staring at me.

"Talk to me," he whispers, finally. "This is a horrible feeling, Mia. Our first fight, and I don't know how to make it okay between us."

I shake my head, looking down at my feet. I don't even know where to start. This is so much more than a first fight. A first fight is what happens when he keeps leaving the toilet seat up or washes my new silk dress in hot water. He kept me in the dark about Perry, about a fiancée he had, for *two months*—and I don't even know why.

I'm drowning in humiliation and we both seem so unbelievably naïve for thinking this was anything but a joke. This entire thing is such an epic rebound for him. Six years with her and then he jumps into a marriage with a stranger? It's almost comical. "I just want to go home. Tomorrow, I think," I say, numbly. "I was planning on leaving soon anyway."

I thought he was leaning against the wall but realize he wasn't only when he seems to collapse back against it. "Don't," he breathes. "Mia, no. You can't leave early because of *this*. *Talk* to me."

My anger flares, renewed at the slight measure of disbelief in his voice. "I *can* leave because of this! How could you let me walk into that? I was completely blindsided!"

"I didn't know she would be there!" he insists. "Marie and Christophe are my friends from before; she doesn't really know them. I don't know why she was there!"

"Maybe because you were *engaged*? I don't even know where to start. You've been lying to me, Ansel. How long were you going to let me believe Perry was a guy? How many times did we talk about *him*? Why didn't you just tell me from that first moment in Vegas when I asked where 'he' was?"

He takes a careful step forward, hands held out in front of him like he's approaching a wounded animal. "When you first called Perry 'he,' none of us thought to correct you, because we were in a *bar*. I had no idea we would be drunk and married a few hours later—"

"I've been here for *weeks*. You could have told me as soon as we got here that your fiancée lives nearby and oh, by the way, she's Perry, the fourth member of your super-close gang—*who is not a guy!*" I press a shaking hand to my forehead, remembering the night someone came to the door while we slept, remembering how distracted Ansel was when he came back to bed—and how almost *naked*—how I asked him who it was and he said it was Perry, but again didn't correct me when I called Perry *he*.

"Oh my God, that night someone came to the door? And when I came home you were talking to *her* on the phone, weren't you? You left the room to go talk to the girl you were going to marry but—*oops!*—you married me instead! No wonder she's so fucking pissed!"

He's been speaking over me in tiny, pleading bursts, saying, "No," and "Mia," and "Wait," and finally he gets a word in: "It's not like that at all. After Vegas, I didn't know how to tell you! Did I even need to make a big thing of it so soon? She wasn't my girlfriend anymore! But then she called, and she came over . . ."

"Fiancée," I correct, "*not* girlfriend."

"Mia, no. We broke u—"

"Have you seen her? Besides that night?"

He regards me anxiously. "We had lunch twice."

I want to punch him for that. Especially since I *never* got a lunch with him during a workday.

"I know, Mia," he says, reading my expression. "I know.

I'm sorry. I was hoping if we spoke face-to-face, she would stop calling and—"

"And did she?"

He hesitates. "No." Ansel pulls his phone from his pocket. "You can read her texts, if you want. Or listen to her voicemails. You can see I never encouraged her. *Please,* Mia."

I push my hands into my hair, wanting to scream at him but not sure I can open my mouth again without bursting into tears. The last thing I want is to hear her voice again.

"I wanted to tell you everything the night we played sinner and devil," he says. "But I didn't know how, and then we moved past it. After that, it seemed to become impossible."

"It's *not* impossible; it's simple. You just correct me any one of the hundreds of times I got it wrong and say, 'No, Mia, Perry is a *chick* and I was with her for *six fucking years* and oh, by the way? I was going to marry her.' Instead you tell me about *Minuit* and deliberately mislead me."

"I didn't want to make you worry! I never expected you would have to meet her!"

I gape at him, my stomach plummeting. Finally, the truth. He simply hoped he wouldn't have to *deal.* "You think that makes it okay? That you lied about her by omission? That because I would never meet her it would be *okay?*"

He's already shaking his head. "That isn't what I mean! We needed better roots," he says, motioning between us frantically and closing his eyes as he struggles to find words. Even now my heart twists for him and how he seems to lose his ability to speak English fluently when he's upset. He takes a deep breath, and when he opens his eyes and speaks again, his voice comes out steadier: "You and I were in a precarious place when you first came here. It was impulsive for both of us to do this. Work is a nightmare for me right now, but I wanted to make time for you. And then it became something more than fun and adventure with us. It was"—he pauses and his voice catches the tiniest bit—"it was *real*. We needed more time, just us. I didn't want anything coming into this flat with us, especially not her."

As soon as he says it, the words seem to echo back to him and his face falls a little.

"She *lived* here," I remind him. "Even when you told me about Minuit, you didn't say you lived together, that you were engaged, that you'd been together for so many years. That you had sex in *that* bed. If you had told me about her when I first got here—the full story—it wouldn't even have been a problem. But tonight, the only person in that apartment who didn't know what was going on was me, your *wife*."

I turn, walking into the bedroom, planning to crawl into bed before remembering it's the bed they got *together*, hoping maybe Perry would sleep better on it. I groan, turning around and walking right into Ansel's broad chest.

When I try to push past him, he stops me, gripping my shoulders with shaking hands. "Please don't walk away."

I feel like a tornado is crashing around in my mind, but as usual, even though I'm so mad at him I could scream, the feel of his body so close and his hands sliding up my arms is so comforting, it starts to make order out of the chaos. His eyes soften and he blinks down to my mouth. "We need to keep talking about this."

But when I try to speak, the words come out choked, stunted. "Y-y-y-y—" I close my eyes, trying again. "Y-y-y-y-you—"

Fuck!

I open my eyes, not sure what reaction I'll see in his face because he's really never heard me stutter and it hardly ever happens anymore.

His eyes are wide and his face contorted in pain as if he's broken me. "Shit, Mia."

"D-d-don't."

"Mia . . ." He groans, pressing his face to my neck.

I push him away, wanting pretty much anything other than his sympathy right now. The anger makes my words come out sharper, and with each one I deliver, my tongue relaxes. "Y-you were w-with her so long. I just . . . tonight *I* felt like the other woman, you know? For the first time yesterday, I felt like your wife. But tonight I felt like I'd stolen you from *her*."

"*No,*" he says, relief washing over his expression as he pushes my hair off my face so he can kiss my cheek. "Of course we broke up before I met you."

Fuck. I have to ask. "But how long before you left?"

His face falls and I feel like I can hear every second tick past as he hesitates to answer.

"Ansel."

"A few days."

My heart sinks and I close my eyes, unable to look at him. "She moved out while you were gone, didn't she?"

Another hesitation. "Yes."

"You broke up with your girlfriend of six years only a few days before you married me."

"Well, technically we broke up three weeks before I met you. I'd been biking across the States before Vegas," he reminds me. "But it felt like it ended a long time before that. We both knew it was over. She is clinging to something that doesn't exist anymore." He cups my cheek and waits until I look up at him. "I wasn't looking for anything, Mia, but that's why I trust what I feel for you. I've never wanted anyone the way I want you. It's unlike anything I've ever known."

When I don't say anything to this, he asks, "Can I tell you now? Everything?"

I don't bother answering out loud. On the one hand, it seems a little late for a full disclosure. On the other, a sick part of me wants to know everything.

"Bike and Build started in May, and went through September," he begins. "Finn, Olls, Perry, and I all became close within days of orientation. It was that kind of experience, okay, where everyone is thrown together and some friendships solidify, and others don't? But ours, it did."

He pauses, trailing his fingers down my arm.

"But it wasn't an immediate affair with Perry and me, not

sexual. She wanted it. At least, Oliver and Finn always insist that she wanted something with me from the first few days. I think I started to notice what they meant, maybe in July? And by August, I felt so much fondness and friendship for all of them that I would give her anything." Pulling back so he can look at me in the dim light from the moon, he says, "Even sex. We only were lovers twice on that trip. A random night in August, when we were very drunk. And then, a few weeks later—after it had been so awkward and loaded with us—we were together on the last night before the excursion ended."

My stomach twists in a strange combination of relief and pain and I close my eyes, forcing away the image of his hands on her body, his mouth full of hers.

"After that, Perry came back here, and I moved to Nashville for school. We were together without ever really discussing it. She assumed we were, and I wanted to give her that. We saw each other maybe two times a year, and everything else I told you was true. She got to know me well on the trip, sure. But I was *twenty-two*. I was not the same man then that I am now and we grew apart very quickly."

He lowers his voice, sounding pained. "And as a love affair, it wasn't ever passionate, Mia. It was . . ." He curses, wiping a hand across his face. "Like in . . . how do you say it?" He looks at me and I look away, unable to resist the adorable way his lips push forward as he searches for words. "*Cendrillon?* The fairy tale with the stepmother?"

"Cinderella?" I guess.

He snaps, nodding, and continues, "Like in Cinderella. I

think we both wanted the glass shoe to fit. Do you understand?"

"Yes."

"She was the one I cheated on, two times. It is my most guilty thing, Mia. I realized I couldn't do it anymore, that I'd done exactly what I always said I wouldn't do, like my father, okay? I called to do the right thing for once and end things with her, and"—he pauses, taking a deep breath—"Perry couldn't wait to tell me she turned down a design job in Nice so we could finally be together in Paris."

I blink away, refusing to feel bad for him.

"So I . . ." He trails off, looking for the right word, and I'm more than happy to help him out here.

"You chickened out."

He nods. "Okay, yes. And that really wasn't fair to her. I should have ended things."

"We both know I came here to escape my problems. But all this time you're acting like some sort of benefactor, when *you're* escaping, too. You used me to escape having to deal with her. You're impulsive and do things without thinking, and, look, you married me. You convinced yourself you were being responsible, or doing the right thing by bringing me back, but you were really just making up for your past mistakes with Perry. *I'm* your way to make up for that. *I'm* your proof that you're not your father."

"Non," he insists, voice as sharp as a blade. "I escaped into you, yes. But not because I was using you to prove something to myself, or make up for some mistake. I didn't have to

get your ticket; I didn't have to track you down at the zoo. I *know* I'm not my father; it's why I was disappointed with myself and how I treated Perry. I escaped into you because I *fell in love* with you."

I let his words echo around the room until they're drowned out by the sounds of horns and motorcycles and delivery trucks rumbling down narrow cobblestone streets late at night. I don't even know what to think. My heart tells me to trust him, that he wasn't intentionally keeping things from me for nefarious reasons, and that it really was just awkward and difficult to find the right time.

But my mind tells me it's bullshit, and that if he wanted to develop real trust between us, he wouldn't have used her nickname with me, he would have just told me who she was to him, that they lived together *here*, and how one of his closest friends is now his ex-fiancée. I want to shove him away for withholding information in our safest place: during role play, and the honesty it gave us.

It really isn't that he has a past that bothers me. It's the way he's been keeping me in the dark, keeping me separate from the rest of his life, lying until he thinks we've reached some imagined milestone where he can be honest. And really, whether it's intentional or not doesn't matter. Maybe he didn't think we would last past the summer, either.

"Have you felt real passion for me?" he asks quietly. "I'm suddenly very worried I've ruined this."

After barely a breath, I nod, but in a way I worry I'm answering both questions: actual, and implied. The passion I feel for him is so intense it's pulled me into his arms right now, even feeling as mad as I do. My skin seems to hum with warmth when I'm this close to him; his scent is overwhelming. But I'm also worried that he has ruined this.

"I've never felt this before," he says into my hair. "Love like this."

But my mind keeps looping back to the same question, the same dark betrayal. "Ansel?"

"Hmm?" His lips brush over my temple.

"How could you tell her about my accident? What made you think it was okay to share that with her?"

Ansel freezes beside me. "I did *not*."

"She knew," I say, growing angry again. "Ansel, she knew I'd been hit. She knew about my leg."

"Not from me," he insists. "Mia, I swear. If she heard anything about you—other than your name, and that you're my wife—it would be from Oliver or Finn. They're all still friends. This has been so weird for everyone." He searches my eyes, lowering his voice when he says, "I don't know why she talked to you. I don't know why she went up to you tonight; she knows I would never be okay with her doing that."

"You talked to her on the phone," I remind him. "She came here in the middle of the night. You met her for lunch when you were even too busy to stay for breakfast with me. Maybe she doesn't think the two of you are really done."

He takes a few seconds to respond, but his hand spreads possessively across my breastbone, thumb sweeping up to the hollow of my throat. "She knows we're done. But I'm not going to pretend like it was an easy breakup. It hasn't been easy for her to know you're here with me."

There's a softness in his voice I can't handle right now, some sympathy for her and what she's going through that makes me feel insane. Somewhere in my rational brain I'm glad he cares how this is for her; it means he's not a complete asshole. It means he's a good guy. But really, he fucked up so enormously, I don't have the bandwidth to admire him while I'm still this angry.

"Yeah, I wouldn't worry too much, I'm pretty sure she came out with the upper hand tonight." I push him away when he reaches for me.

"Mia, that's not—"

"Just stop."

He grabs my arm when I begin to walk away and spins me, pressing my back to the wall and staring me down with a look so intense it causes goose bumps to rise along my skin. "I don't want this to be hard on either of you," he says in a deliberately patient voice, "and I know the way I've handled it was all wrong."

I close my eyes, pressing my lips together to quell the vibrating hum I feel at his firm touch. I want to shove him, pull his hair, feel the weight of him pinning me down.

"I followed *you* out of the apartment," he reminds me, bending to kiss my jaw. "I *know* it isn't my job to make sure she's okay anymore. But if what she feels for me is even a fraction of what I feel for you, I want to be careful with her heart, because I can't imagine what I would do if you left me."

It seems impossible that words alone could make me feel like my chest is caving in.

He licks my earlobe, murmuring, "It would wreck me. I need to know that you're okay right now."

His hands grow busy on my body in a tight, desperate sort of way. Maybe to distract me, maybe to reassure himself. He works his way down my front, over my thighs, bunching my skirt in his fist as he pulls it up over my hips.

"Ansel . . ." I warn, but even as I turn my head away from his lips, I tilt my pelvis into his touch. My hands form fists at my sides, wanting more, and rougher. Needing reassurance.

"*Are* you okay?" he asks, kissing my ear.

I don't turn away when he kisses my chin again, and not even when he moves higher, eyes wide and careful as he kisses my mouth. But when his hand moves between my legs, and he growls, "I'm going to make you so wet," as his fingers slip beneath my underwear, I find the resolve to push his arm away.

"You can't fix this with sex."

He pulls back, eyes wide in confusion. "What?"

I'm incredulous. "You think you can just calm me down by making me *come*?"

He looks baffled, nearly angry for the first time. "If it calms you down, if it makes you feel better, then who the hell cares *how it happens*?" His cheeks bloom with a heated blush. "Isn't that what we've been doing all this time? Finding a way to be married, to be *intimate* even when things are scary or new or just too fucking surreal to process?"

I'm thrown, because he's right. It's exactly what we've been doing, and I *do* want to be pulled out of this moment. Distraction, coping, muddling through—whatever it is, I want it. I want to stop talking about all of this. I want him to push away all the doubts in my head and give me the part of him that only I get to see now.

"Fine. Distract me," I dare him, teeth clenched. "Let's see if you can make me forget how mad I am."

It takes him a moment to process what I've said before he leans in again, teeth grazing my jaw. I exhale through my nose before my head falls back against the wall and I give in. His hands return to my waist, rougher now, yanking my shirt up and over my head before he works my skirt down my hips and into a puddle on the floor.

But even as he cups me in his hand, sucking in a jagged breath through his teeth and whispering, *"Tu es parfaite,"* I can't touch him back with any sort of tenderness. I feel punitive and selfish and still so angry. The combination pulls a tight choking sound from my mouth and his hand stills where he'd been pushing my underwear aside.

"Be angry," he rasps. "*Show* me what angry looks like."

It's a beat before the words bubble up, but when they come growling out, it doesn't sound like me: "Your mouth."

I unleash the girl who lets herself feel anger, who can punish. I shove his chest hard, both palms flat to pectorals, and he stumbles back, lips parted and eyes wide with thrill. I push him again, and his knees meet the edge of the bed and he crumples backward, scooting up to the headboard and watching me stalk him, climb on him until my hips are level with his face and I can reach down and grab a fistful of his hair.

"I'm *not* okay," I tell him, holding him back as he tries to push forward, to kiss me, lick me, maybe even bite me.

"I know," he says, eyes dark and urgent. "I *know*."

I lower my hips and hear a primitive cry tear from my throat as his open mouth makes contact with my clit and he sucks, lifting his arms and wrapping them in tight bands around my hips. He's wild and hungry, letting out perfect pleading growls and satisfied moans when I begin to rock and ride him, my fist in his hair.

His mouth is both soft and strong, but he's letting me control everything—the speed and pressure and it's so good but God, *I want you in me so deep I feel you in my throat.*

Ansel laughs against my skin and I realize I've said this out loud. Irritation washes over me like a heated blush and I pull away, humiliated. Vulnerable.

"No," he whispers. "No, no. *Viens par ici.*" *Come here.*

I make him work for it, fingers coaxing and his soft pleading noises until finally he pulls my hips back down and urges me with fingers pressed into my flesh to chase my pleasure again, to give him this in this twisted game of me giving him what he needs by riding his face.

I'm prickling everywhere—along my neck and down my arms, feeling hypersensitive and overheated. But the sensitivity is nearly unbearable where he's licking me, because it's too good, it's nearly impossible that I can be this close, so soon so soon

so fucking soon

but I am.

The top half of my body falls forward, fingers white-knuckling the headboard, and I'm coming, screaming, pressing so hard into his mouth I don't know how he can breathe but he's savage beneath me—*still*—hands gripping my hips and not letting me budge for a second until my muscles go lax and he can feel my orgasm subside against his lips.

I feel ravaged and worshipped as I slip, boneless, to the bed. I feel his fear and his love and his panic and finally, I let loose the sob that's been held back in my throat for what feels like hours. In a quiet rush, I know we're both sure of one thing: I'm leaving.

He moves to my ear, and his voice is so jagged it's barely recognizable when he asks, "Do you ever feel like your heart is twisted inside your chest, and somebody has their fist wrapped around it, squeezing?"

"Yes," I whisper, closing my eyes. I can't see him like this, the sadness I'm sure I'll see on his face.

"Mia? Mia, I'm so sorry."

"I know."

"Tell me you still . . . like me."

But I can't. My anger doesn't work that way. So instead of waiting for me to answer, he bends to kiss my ear, my shoulder, whispering into my neck words I don't understand.

Slowly, we catch our breath and his mouth finds its way to mine. He kisses me forever like this—and I let him—it's the only way I can tell him I love him even as I'm also saying goodbye.

IT SEEMS TO go against every instinct I have to be the one getting out of bed first, and dressing in the dark while he sleeps. As quietly as I can, I pull my clothes from the dresser and dump them into my suitcase. My passport is just where he said it would be—in the top drawer of the dresser—and something about this tears at the thin lining still holding me together. I leave most of my toiletries behind; packing them would be loud and I don't want to wake him. I'm going to seriously miss my fancy new face cream but I don't think I would be able to walk away from him if he was awake, watching me silently, and especially if he was trying to talk me out of this.

It's a trickle of hesitation I should listen to—maybe a message that I'm not sure this is the best idea I've ever had—but I don't. I barely even look over at him—still mostly clothed and sprawled out on top of the covers—while I'm packing and dressing and searching the desk in the living room for a piece of paper and a pen.

Because once I step back into the bedroom and I do see him, I can't imagine looking away. Only now do I realize I hadn't taken the time to appreciate how ridiculously hot he looked last night. The deep blue button-down shirt—slim-cut to fit the wide stretch of his chest, the narrow dip of his waist—is unbuttoned just beneath the hollow of his throat, and my tongue feels thick with the need to bend down, suck on those favorite transitions of mine: neck to chest, chest to shoulder. His jeans are worn and perfect, faded over time in all the best, familiar places. At the thigh, over the button fly. He didn't even take off his favorite brown belt before falling asleep—it's just hanging open, his pants unbuttoned and slung low on his hips—and suddenly my fingers itch to pull the leather free of the loops, to see and touch and taste his skin just one more time.

I probably can't, but it *feels* like I can see the trip of his pulse in his throat, imagine the warm taste of his neck on my tongue. I know how his sleepy hands would weave into my hair as I worked his boxers down his hips. I even know the desperate relief I would see in his eyes if I woke him up right now—not to tell him goodbye, but to make love one last time. To forgive him with words. No doubt true makeup sex with Ansel would be so good I'd forget, while he was touching me, that there was ever any distance between us at all.

And now that I'm here, struggling to be quiet and leave without waking him, it fully registers that I can't touch him again before I go. I swallow back a tight, heavy lump in my throat, a sob I think would escape in a sharp gasp, like steam under pressure, pushed from a teapot. The pain is like a fist to my stomach, punching me over and over until I want to punch it back.

I'm an idiot.

But damn. So is he.

It takes so many long, painful seconds for me to pull my

eyes away from where he lies and down to the pen and paper in my hands.

What the hell am I supposed to write here? It's not good-bye, most likely. If I know him at all—and I do, no matter how small a drop that knowledge felt last night—he won't leave the rest of this to phone calls and emails. I'll see him again. But I'm leaving while he sleeps, and given the reality of his job, I may not see him for months. This isn't exactly the right moment for a see-you-soon note, anyway.

So I opt for the easiest, and the most honest, even if my heart seems to twist into a knot in my chest as I write it.

> This isn't never. It's just not now.
>
>   All my like,
>
>   Mia

I really need to figure out my own messes before I blame him for shoving his in the proverbial box, and keeping them under his proverbial bed.

But fuck, did I want this to be *now, yes, forever*.

Chapter TWENTY

*I*T'S STILL DARK when I step out onto the sidewalk, and the lobby door swings closed behind me. A taxi waits, headlamps extinguished while it idles at the curb, its shape swathed in a circle of artificial yellow light from the streetlamp above. The driver glances at me from over the top of his magazine, expression sour, face lined in what appears to be a permanent look of distaste.

I'm suddenly aware of how I must look—hair a mess and last night's makeup still smudged around my eyes, dark jeans, dark sweater—like some sort of criminal slinking off into the shadows. The phrase "fleeing the scene of the crime" rings through my head and I sort of hate how accurate it feels.

He steps from the cab and meets me at the back of the car, trunk already open and smoldering cigarette suspended from his frowning mouth.

"American?" he asks, his accent as thick as the puffs of smoke that escape with every syllable.

Irritation grates at my nerves but I only nod, not bothering to ask how he knew or *why* because I already know: I stick out like a sore thumb.

Either he doesn't notice my lack of response or he doesn't care because he takes my suitcase, lifts it without effort, and deposits it in the trunk of the car.

It's the same bag I arrived with, the same one I hid after only a few days because it looked too new and out of place in the middle of Ansel's warm and comfortable flat. At least that's what I'd told myself at the time, tucking it away inside the closet near his bedroom door where it wouldn't serve as a daily reminder of my impermanence here, or that my place in his life would end as soon as the summer did.

I open my own door and climb inside; closing it with the least amount of sound I can manage. I know how well noises travel through the open windows and I absolutely don't let myself look up or imagine him lying there in bed, waking to an empty flat or hearing the closing of a taxi door on the street below.

The driver drops into the seat in front of me and meets my eyes in the rearview mirror expectantly. "Airport," I tell him, before looking quickly away.

I'm not even sure what I'm feeling as he puts the car into gear and slips into the street. Is it sadness? Yes. *Worry, anger, panic, betrayal, guilt?* All of those. Have I made a mistake? Has this entire *thing* been one colossal bad choice after another? I had to leave anyway, I tell myself; this was just a little ahead of schedule. And even if I didn't, it was right to get some space, some perspective, some clarity . . . right?

I almost laugh. I feel anything but clarity.

I vacillate so wildly between *last night was no big deal* and *last night was a deal breaker,* between *leaving is the right thing to do* and *turn around you're making a huge mistake!* that I begin to doubt every thought I have. Being alone and stuck in my own head on a thirteen-hour flight is going to be torture.

The taxi moves too fast through the empty streets, and my stomach lurches much in the same way it did that first morning here, but for an entirely different reason this time. There's a part of me that would almost welcome throwing up right now, would find it preferable to the constant, pressing ache I've had since last night. At least I know vomiting would pass and I could close my eyes, pretend the world isn't spinning, that there isn't really a hole in my chest, the edges raw and jagged.

The city whips by in a blur of stone and concrete, industrial silhouettes dotting the same horizon as buildings that have stood for hundreds of years. I press my forehead to the glass and try to block out every moment of that first morning with Ansel. How sweet and attentive he was, and how I worried I was ruining it all and it would be over before it ever really began.

The sun isn't up yet but I can make out trees and grassy fields, muddied blurs of green that border the freeway and bridge the distance between stretches of urban sprawl. I have the eeriest sensation of moving backward through time, and erasing everything.

I pull out my phone and bring up the airline app, log in,

and search through the available flights. My decision to leave looks even more glaring in the too-bright light of the screen as it cuts through the darkness, reflecting back to me in the windows at my side.

I hover over the arrival city and nearly laugh at my imagined dilemma over choices, because I know I've already decided what I'm going to do.

The first flight of the day leaves in just over an hour, and it seems too easy to make the necessary selections and book my return trip with barely a hiccup.

Finished, I shut off my phone and tuck it away, watching out at the bleary city as it begins to wake on the other side of the glass.

There were no messages so I can assume Ansel is still asleep, and if I close my eyes I can still see him, body stretched over the mattress, jeans barely clinging to his hips. I can remember the way his skin looked in the low light while I gathered my things, the way the shadows drew him like canvas covered in charcoal. I can't bring myself to imagine him waking up and realizing I'm gone.

The taxi stops at the curb and I see the price on the meter. My fingers tremble as I find my wallet and count out the fare. The broad, colorful bills still look so foreign in my hand that on impulse I fold the entire stack, pressing them into the driver's waiting palm.

On the plane there are no phones, no emails. I haven't bothered to pay for internet and so there's nothing to distract me from the loop of images and words echoed back to me in dramatic—and maddening—slow motion: Perry's expression slowly morphing from amiable to calculating, then from calculating to irate. Her voice as she asked how I was enjoying her bed, her *fiancé*. The sound of footsteps, of Ansel, of our shouted words and the sensation of rushing blood filling my head, my pulse hijacking every sound.

Aside from the few hours of sleep I manage to snag, this is the soundtrack throughout my entire flight and if possible, I feel even worse when we finally touch down.

I move in a fog from the plane to customs to baggage claim, where my single enormous suitcase waits for me on the spinning carousel. It no longer looks as new, marred in a few places as if it's been thrown around and dropped, caught against the moving conveyer belt; it looks pretty close to how I feel.

At a coffee shop nearby, I open my laptop and find the file I've neglected all summer, labeled only "Boston."

Inside is all the information I need for school, the emails about schedules and orientation that have arrived in the last few weeks, ignored but tucked safely away where I promised myself I'd deal with them later.

Apparently, later is today.

With the energy provided by a pot of coffee and the growing buzz over finally making the right decision, I log in to the Boston University MBA student portal.

I decline my financial aid.

I decline my spot in the program.

I finally make the decision I should have made ages ago.

And then I call my former academic advisor, and prepare to grovel.

I STARE AT the FOR RENT section in the local newspaper. Part of the deal in my agreeing to attend graduate school was that my dad would pay for my apartment. But after what I've just done, I don't think he'll support me, even if from where I stand it feels like the best compromise. I know he'll be more likely to break something with his bare hands than give me a penny. I can't bring myself to live under his thumb anymore anyway. Living in Paris has pretty much shot my budget to hell, but after a quick glance at the paper, there are a few places I can afford . . . especially if I can find a job relatively soon.

I'm still not ready to turn on my phone and face what I'm sure is a mountain of missed calls and texts from Ansel— or even worse, nothing at all—and so I use a payphone in front of a 7-Eleven just down the street from the coffee shop.

My first call is to Harlow.

"Hello?" she says, clearly distrustful of the unknown number. I've missed her so much that I feel tears sting at the corners of my eyes.

"Hey," I say, that single word thick and coated in homesickness.

"Oh my God, Mia! Where the fuck are you?" There's a moment of pause where I imagine she pulls the phone from her ear and glances at the number again. "Holy shit, are you *here*?"

I swallow back a sob. "I landed a couple of hours ago."

"You're home?" she shouts.

"I'm in San Diego, yeah."

"Why aren't you at my house right now?"

"I have to get a few things organized." *Like my life.* In France, I found my spot in the distance. Now I just need to keep my eyes pinned to it.

"Organized? Mia, what happened to Boston?"

"Listen, I'll explain later but I'm wondering if you can talk to your dad for me?" I take a shaky breath. "About my annulment." And there it is, the word that has been tickling in the back of my thoughts. Saying it out loud sucks.

"Oh. So it went downhill."

"It's complicated. Just, talk to your dad for me, okay? I need to take care of some stuff but I'll call you."

"Please come over."

Pressing the heel of my hand to my temple, I manage, "I'll come over tomorrow. Today I just need to get my head on straight."

After a long beat, she says, "I'll have Dad call his lawyer tonight, and let you know what he says."

"Thanks."

"Do you need anything else?"

Swallowing, I manage, "I don't think so. Going to look at apartments. After I check into a motel and catch a nap."

"Apartments? *Motel?* Mia, just come stay here with *me.* I have an enormous place and can definitely work on my sex-volume issue if it means I get you as a roomie."

Her apartment would be ideal, in La Jolla and perfectly

situated between the beach and campus, but now that my plan has formed, it's unbreakable. "I know I sound like a psychopath, Harlow, but I promise, I'll explain why I want to do it this way."

After a long beat I can sense her acquiescence, and for Harlow, that was remarkably easy. I must sound as determined as I feel. "Okay. Love you, Sugarcube."

"Love you back."

Harlow emails me a short list of places to check out, with her thoughts and comments on each one. I'm sure she called her parents' Realtor and had her find things that were fit to exact specifications of safety, space, and price, but even though she doesn't know where I want to live, I'm so grateful for Harlow's busybody tendencies that I nearly want to weep.

The first apartment I see is nice and definitely in my price range, but way too far from UCSD. The second is close enough that I could walk but it's directly over a Chinese restaurant. I debate with myself for an entire hour before deciding there's no way I could stand smelling like kung pao twenty-four hours a day.

The third is listed as "cozy," furnished, above a garage, in a quiet residential neighborhood, and two blocks from a bus stop that's a direct line to the college. And thank God, because after paying the long-term airport parking bill I had upon returning, there's no way I'll be able to afford a campus parking permit. I'm relieved the apartment was listed only this morning, because I'm sure it will be snatched up quickly. Harlow is a goddess.

The street is lined with trees and I stop in front of the wide yellow house. A wide lawn spreads out on both sides of the stone walkway, and the front door is painted a deep green. Whoever lives here has a way with plants, because the yard is impeccable, the flower beds thriving.

It reminds me of the Jardin des Plantes, and the day I spent there with Ansel, learning—and promptly forgetting— the name for everything in French, walking for hours with my hand in his, and the promise of a future where I could do that with him whenever I wanted.

The woman who owns the house, Julianne, leads me inside, and it's as close to perfect as I can imagine. It's tiny, but warm and nice with tan walls and clean white trim. A cream-colored sofa sits in the center of the single main room. One corner opens to a small kitchen with a window that looks down into the shared backyard. The open floor plan reminds me so much of Ansel's flat that for a painful heartbeat, I have to close my eyes and take a deep breath.

"One bedroom," she says, and crosses the room to flip on a light.

I follow and peek in. A queen bed fills almost the entire space, a set of white bookcases suspended above.

"Bathroom in there. I'm usually gone before the sun is up so you can park back here."

"Thanks," I tell her.

"The closets are small, there's horrible water pressure, and I guarantee the teenage boys who take care of the lawn will be absolute piglets when they see you, but it's cute and quiet and there's a washer and dryer in the garage you can use whenever," she says.

"It's perfect," I say, looking around. "A washer and dryer sound like absolute heaven and I can definitely handle piglet teenage boys."

"Yay!" she says, smiling wide, and for a tiny, desperate heartbeat I can imagine living here, taking the bus to school, starting to figure out my life in the sweet studio above her garage. I want to tell her, *Please, let me move in right now.*

But of course she's rational, and with a tiny apology in her eyes asks me to fill out the background check form. "I'm sure it will be fine," she says with a wink.

———————

I'VE ONLY BEEN gone a few weeks, but checking into a motel in my hometown makes me feel like I'm returning to a city that has long since evolved without me. As I drive to the motel, I find a hidden pocket of San Diego I've never explored before, and although the corner of my dark city feels oddly foreign, the idea that there's a different future for me here from any I had imagined before is powerfully reassuring.

My mother would kill me for not staying at home. Harlow wants to kill me for not staying with her. But even in the dim light and the cacophony of the I-5 freeway just outside my window, it's exactly what I need. I check my bank balance for about the fiftieth time since landing. If I'm careful, I could make it to the start of school, and by then—thanks to my former advisor and the man who has gained me entrance to the MBA program that once heavily courted me at UCSD—I'll have a small, rare stipend to help make ends meet. But even though the rent is reasonable in the studio, it would still be tight and my stomach flips imagining having to ask my father for money. I haven't talked to him in over a month.

You are married? You have a husband, no? Ansel said, and *God,* that night feels so long ago. Curling into sheets that smell like bleach and cigarette smoke instead of summer grass and spice, I struggle to breathe and not completely lose my shit at eight at night in a dark motel room.

My neglected phone suddenly feels heavy in my pocket and I pull it out, let my finger hover over the button before I finally power it on.

It takes a few moments to load, but when it does, I see I have twelve missed calls from Ansel, six voicemails, and even more texts.

Where are you? the first one says.

You've left, haven't you. Your suitcase is gone.

You didn't take everything. I imagine him waking, finding me gone, and then walking from room to room, seeing the things I must have chosen to bring with me and the things I left behind.

Your ring isn't here, did you take it? Please call me.

I delete the rest of the messages but not the voicemails, a secret part of me knowing I'll want to listen to them later when I'm alone and missing him. Well, missing him *more.*

I'm not even sure how to reply.

I realize now that Ansel can't be the answer to my problems. He fucked up by not telling me the truth about Perry and their past, but I'm fairly sure it had more to do with him being a stupid boy than wanting to keep me in the dark. This is why you get to know someone *before* you marry them. And the truth is that his lie was convenient for me, too. I'd been hiding in Paris, using him and the thousands of miles between France and the States to avoid the things that are wrong with my life: my dad, my leg, my inability to create a new future for myself beyond the one I lost. Perry might have been a total bitch but she was right about one thing: the only one moving forward in this relationship was Ansel. I was content to sit there, waiting, while he went out and conquered the world.

I roll onto my back and instead of replying to Ansel, I write a group text to my girls.

I think I found a place to live. Thanks for sending the list, H. I'm really trying not to lose my calm right now.

Let us come to your motel, Harlow answers. We're going nuts not knowing what the hell is happening.

Tomorrow, I promise them.

Hang in there, Lola says. Life is built of these little horrible moments and the giant expanses of awesome in between.

I love you, I reply. Because she's right. This summer was the most perfect stretch of awesome I've ever had.

Chapter TWENTY-ONE

JULIANNE REALLY IS a goddess because she calls before eight in the morning. With the time change, I was awake before five, and have been pacing the tiny motel room like a mad-woman, praying it would all work out and I wouldn't have to spend another day apartment hunting.

"Hello?" I answer, phone trembling in my shaking hand.

I can hear the smile in her voice. "Ready to move in?"

I give her my most grateful—and enthusiastic—yes and then I look around the dingy room after I hang up, and laugh. I'm ready to move into an apartment ten minutes away from my parents' house, and I hardly have anything to take with me.

But before I can go, there's one more call I need to make. As much as my dad refused to acknowledge my passion for dance, or even be kind about it, there is one person who *was* at every dance recital, who drove me to every rehearsal and performance, and hand-sewed my costumes. She did my makeup when I was tiny and watched me do it myself when I grew older, and stubbornly independent. She cried during my solos, and stood up to cheer. I'm horrified to realize *only now* that Mom weathered my father's disapproval for years while I was dancing, and she weathered it because it was what I wanted to be doing. She was there when I moved into the hospital room for a month and quietly drove me, when I was depressed and deadened, to the dorms at UCSD.

I wasn't the only one who lost a dream after my accident. Of anyone in my life, my mother will understand the choice I'm making.

I can hear the shock in her voice when she answers. "Mia?"

"Hi, Mom." I squeeze my eyes closed, overcome with an emotion I'm not sure I'll be very good at articulating. My family doesn't discuss feelings, and the only way I learned was through threat of torture by Harlow. But my awareness of Mom's strength during my childhood and what she did to help me chase my dream is probably one I should have had a long time ago. "I'm home." I pause, adding, "I'm not going to Boston."

My mom is a quiet crier; she's a quiet *everything*. But I know the cadence of her tiny gasping breaths as well as I know the smell of her perfume.

I give her the address to my apartment, tell her I'm moving in today and that I'll tell her everything if she comes to see me. I don't need my things, I don't need her money. I just sort of need my *mom*.

––––––

TO SAY I resemble my mother is an understatement. When we're together, I always feel like people think I'm the Marty

McFly version of her that has traveled from the eighties to present day. We have the same build, identical hazel eyes, olive skin, and dark, straight hair. But when she steps out of her enormous Lexus at the curb and I see her for the first time in over a month, I have the sense that I'm looking at my reflection in some sort of fun-house mirror. She looks the same as she always does—which is to say not exactly thriving. Her resignation, her *life settling,* could have been me. Dad never wanted her to work outside the home. Dad never took much interest in her hobbies: gardening, ceramics, living greener. She loves my father, but she's resigned herself to a relationship that doesn't give her much at all.

She feels tiny in my arms when I hug her, but when I pull back and expect to see worry or hesitation—*she shouldn't be cavorting with the enemy, David will be furious!*—I see only an enormous grin.

"You look amazing," she says, pulling my arms to the side to take me in.

This . . . okay, this surprises me a little. I showered under the dull dribble of a motel shower, have no makeup on, and would probably perform crude sexual acts for access to a washing machine. The mental picture I have of myself falls somewhere between homeless shelter and zombie. "Thanks?"

"Thank God you're not going to Boston."

And with that, she turns and opens the back of her SUV and pulls out a giant box with surprising ease. "I brought your books, the rest of your clothes. When your dad calms down you can come pick up anything I've missed." She stares at my surprised expression for a beat before nodding to the car. "Grab a box and show me your place."

With every step we climb to my little apartment above the garage, an epiphany hits me directly in the gut.

My mom needs a purpose as much as any of us do.

That purpose used to be me.

Ansel was as scared to face his past as I was to face my future.

I push open the front door, giant box nearly tumbling out of my arms onto the floor, and I somehow manage to make it to the table in the living-dining room. Mom puts the box of my clothes down on the couch and looks around. "It's small, but really sweet, Lollipop."

I don't think she's called me that since I was fifteen. "I kind of love it, actually."

"I can bring you some of the photographs from Lana's studio, if you want some art?"

My blood buzzes in my veins. This is why I came home. My family. My friends. A life here that I want to make. "Okay."

Without much more preamble she sits down and looks directly at me. "So."

"So."

Her attention moves to my left hand, hanging motionless at my side, and it's only now that I realize I'm still wearing my wedding band. She doesn't even look a little bit surprised. "How was Paris?"

With a deep breath, I move to sit beside her on the couch and unload everything in a tumble of words. I tell her about the suite in Vegas, about how I felt it was my last hurrah of sorts, the last fun I would have until some undetermined point when I would snap out of it and magically realize I wanted to be just like my father. I tell her about meeting Ansel, the sunshine of *him,* and how I nearly felt like I was confessing to him that night. Unloading. Unburdening.

I tell her about the marriage. I skip one hundred percent of the sex part.

I tell her about escaping my life to go to Paris, about the perfection of the city, and how it felt initially to wake up and realize I was married to a complete stranger. But also, that it went away and what came instead was a relationship I'm not sure I want to give up.

Again, I skip every detail of the sex part.

It's hard to explain the Perry story, because even as I begin, she has to sense that it's the reason I left. So when I get to the part about the party, and being cornered by the Beast, I almost feel like an idiot for not having seen it coming a mile away.

But Mom doesn't. She still gasps, and it's that tiny reaction that unleashes the flood of tears, because this entire time I've wondered how huge an idiot I am. Am I a minor idiot, who should have stayed to hash it out with the hottest man alive? Or am I an enormous idiot for leaving over something anyone else would consider minuscule?

The problem with being in the eye of the storm is you have no sense of how big it really is.

"Honey," Mom says, and nothing else follows. It doesn't matter. The single word holds a million others that communicate sympathy and a sort of fierce mama-bear protectiveness. But also: concern for Ansel, since I've painted him accurately, I think. He's good, and he's loving. And he *likes* me.

"Honey," she repeats quietly.

Another epiphany hits me: I'm not quiet because I stutter. I'm quiet because I'm like my mother.

"Okay, so." I pull my knees to my chest. "There's more. And this is why I'm here, instead of Boston." I tell her about walking the city with Ansel, and our conversations about school, and my life, and what I want to *do*. I tell her that he's the one who convinced me—even if he doesn't know it—to move home and go back to my old dance studio at night to teach, and to attend school here during the day so that I'm as prepared as I can be to run my own business someday. To teach kids how to move and dance however their bodies want. I assure her that Professor Chatterjee has agreed to admit me to the MBA program at UCSD, in my old department.

After taking this all in, Mom leans back and studies me for a beat. "When did you grow up, Lollipop?"

"When I met *him*." Ugh. Stab to the gut. And Mom can see it, too. She puts her hand on my hand, over my knee.

"He sounds . . . good."

"He *is* good," I whisper. "Other than the secrecy over the Beast, he's amazing." I pause and then add, "Is Dad going to shun me forever?"

"Your father is difficult, I know, but he's also smart. He wanted you to get your MBA so you have *options,* not so you'd be exactly like him. The thing is, sweetheart, you never had to use it to do what he wanted. Even he knows that, no matter how much pressure he puts on you to follow his path." Standing, my mom makes her way to the door and pauses for a beat as I let it fully sink in that I really don't know my dad very well. "Help me bring in the last couple of boxes and then I'm heading home. Come over for dinner next week. Right now you have other things to fix."

———

I'D PROMISED LOLA and Harlow that they could come over as soon as I was moved in, but after unpacking, I'm exhausted and want nothing other than sleep.

In bed, I hold my phone so hard in my hand I can feel my palm grow slippery and I struggle to not reread every one of Ansel's steady messages for the hundredth time. The one that arrived since I unpacked says: If I came to you, would you see me?

I laugh, because despite everything, it's not like I can just decide to stop loving him; I wouldn't ever refuse to see him. I can't even bring myself to take off my wedding ring.

Looking down at my phone, I open the text window and reply for the first time since I left him sleeping in the apartment. I'm in San Diego, safe and sound. Of course I'd see you, but don't come until it works for the case. You've worked too hard. I reread what I've written and then add, I'm not going anywhere.

Except back to the States while you lie sleeping, I think.

He replies immediately. Finally! Mia why did you leave without waking me? I've been going crazy over here.

And then another: I can't sleep. I miss you.

I close my eyes, not realizing until now how much I needed to hear that. The sensation pulls tight in my chest, a rope wrapped around my lungs, smashing them together. My careful mind tells me to just say *thank you*, but instead I quickly type Me too, and toss my phone away, onto the bed before I can say more.

I miss him so much I feel like I'm tied in a corset, unable to suck enough air into my lungs.

By the time I pick it up again, it's the next morning and I've missed his next three texts: I love you. And then: Please tell me I haven't ruined this.

And then, Please Mia. Say something.

This is when I break down for the second time, because from the time stamp I know he wrote it in his office, at *work*. I can imagine him staring at his phone, unable to concentrate or get anything done until I replied. But I didn't. I curled up into a ball and fell asleep, needing to shut down as if I'd unplugged.

I pick up my phone again, and even though it's seven in the morning, Lola answers on the first ring.

———

ONLY A LITTLE over an hour later I throw open the door and rush into a mass of arms and wild hair.

"Quit hogging her," a voice says over Harlow's shoulder and I feel another set of arms.

You'd never know it hasn't even been two months from the way I start sobbing onto Lola's shoulder, holding on to both of them as if they might float away.

"I missed you so much," I say. "You're never leaving. It'll be small but we can make it work. I was in Europe. I can totally get with this now."

We stumble into my tiny living room, a mess of laughter and tears, and I shut the door behind us.

I turn to find Harlow watching me, sizing me up.

"What?" I ask, looking down at my yoga capris and T-shirt. I realize I don't look red-carpet ready, but her inspection feels a little unnecessary. "Ease up, Clinton Kelly. I've been *unpacking* and then *sleeping*."

"You look different," she says.

"Different?"

"Yeah. Sexier. Married life was good for you."

I roll my eyes. "I assume you're referring to my little muffin top. I have a new unhealthy relationship with *pain au chocolat*."

"*No,*" she says, moving closer to examine my face. "You

look . . . softer? But in a good way. Feminine. And I like the hair a little longer."

"And the tan," Lola adds, dropping onto the couch. "You *do* look good. Your rack, too."

I laugh, squeezing into the seat next to her. "This is what France with no job and a patisserie around the corner will get you."

We all fall silent and after what feels like an eternity of silence, I realize I'm the one who has to address the fact that I *was* in France, and now I'm *here*.

"I feel like a horrible human being for how I left."

Lola pins me with her glare. "You are *not*."

"You might disagree when I explain."

Harlow's hand is already raised in the air. "No need. We know what happened, no thanks to you, you withholding asshole."

Of course they've heard the entire story. More accurately, Lola heard it from Oliver who heard it from Finn who had the good luck of calling Ansel only an hour after he woke to find his wife and all her belongings gone. For a bunch of dudes, they're awfully gossipy.

We catch each other up in the easy shorthand we've developed over the past nearly twenty years, and it's so much easier to spill everything for the second time since I've been back.

"He fucked up," Harlow assures me once I get to the part where we're headed together to the party. "Everyone knows it. Apparently Finn and Oliver have been telling him to fill you in about the situation for weeks now. Perry calls him all the time, texts him constantly, and calls Finn and Oliver to talk about it nonstop. Their breakup didn't seem to surprise anyone but her, and even that seems to be up for debate. I guess Ansel was worried it would spook you and is counting the days until he can move back here. From everything I've heard, he's completely head over heels in love with you."

"But we all agree he should have told you," Lola says. "It sounds like you were blindsided."

"Yeah," I say. "The first time he takes me to a party this nice girl started talking to me and then her face melted and she turned into a vengeance demon." I lean my head on Lola's shoulder. "And I knew he had a long-term girlfriend so I don't know why it was such a leap to tell me it was Perry, and that he lived with her, and even that they were engaged. Maybe it would have been weird but it made it weirder that it was this big secret. Plus, six years with someone you don't love that way? That seems insane."

Lola falls quiet, and then hums. "I know."

I hate the small twinge of disloyalty I feel when I criticize him this way. Ansel was shaped by his experience growing up in the strange, possessive, and betrayal-filled relationship his parents had. I'm sure loyalty and fidelity mean more to him than romantic love, or at least he thought they did. I wonder, too, how much of his time with Perry was about proving he's not as fickle as his father. I'm sure staying married to me is at least *somewhat* about that—no matter how much it was my insistence in the first place. I need to decide if I'm okay with it being both about proving something to himself *and* loving me.

"How is he doing?" Harlow asks.

I shrug and distract myself by playing with the blunt ends of Lola's hair. "Good," I say. "Working."

"That's not what I'm asking."

"Well, from the whole game of telephone, you guys probably know more than I do." Deflecting, I ask, "How is Finn?"

Harlow shrugs. "I don't know. Good, I guess."

"What do you mean you don't know? Didn't you just see him?"

She laughs and makes tiny air quotes as she repeats the words *see him* under her breath. "I can assure you I did not go to Canada for Finn's sparkling personality *or* conversation skills."

"So you went up there for sex."

"Yep."

"And was it good enough to go back?"

"I don't know. If I'm honest, I don't particularly *like* him that much. He's definitely prettier when he doesn't speak."

"You really *are* a troll."

"I love that you act like you're surprised. Finn and me? Not a thing."

"Okay, Mia, enough avoidance," Lola says quietly. "What happens next?"

Sighing, I tell her honestly, "I don't know. I mean this is what I'm supposed to be doing, right? School? Figuring out what I want to do with my life? The irresponsible thing was going to France in the first place. The grown-up thing was coming home. So why do I feel like it's all backwards?"

"Oh, I don't know." Harlow hums. "Maybe because it sounds like you guys were figuring out a new plan together?"

I nod. It's true. "I felt so safe with him. Like, my brain didn't always know but my body did? I didn't know his favorite color or what he wanted to be when he was ten, but none of that mattered. And the silly things I knew about Luke, the giant list of stuff in my head I thought made us compatible . . . it seems so laughable when I compare it to my feelings for Ansel."

"If you could erase this one thing from your time with him, would you still be with him?"

I don't even have to think about it. "Absolutely."

"Look, I watched you lose the most important thing in your life and there was nothing I or anyone else could do to make it better. We couldn't turn back time. We couldn't fix your leg. We couldn't make it so you could dance again," Harlow says, voice uncharacteristically shaky. "But I can tell you not to be an idiot. Love is fucking hard to find, Mia. Don't waste it because of some stupid lines on a map."

"Please stop making sense," I say. "My life is confusing enough right now without you making it worse."

"And if I know anything about you, I'm pretty sure you'd already reached the same conclusion. You just needed someone smarter to say it first. I mean, I'm not downplaying what he did, it was a dick move. I'm just playing devil's advocate here."

I close my eyes and shrug.

"So we're talking the big L-word, aren't we?"

"Lesbians?" I deadpan.

She levels me with a glare. Serious-getting-in-touch-with-her-feelings Harlow is not someone you want to mess around with. "What I *mean*," she says, ignoring me, "is that this wasn't just about banging the sweet, filthy French boy."

"It never really was just about banging the French boy," I tell her. "I think that's what freaked you out."

"Because it's *big*," she says, and then high-fives me as we all yell, "That's what she said!"

But then her expression sobers again. "Even when Luke left," she continues, "I knew you'd be okay, you know? I told Lola, 'It's hard now but give her a few weeks. She'll bounce back.' This is . . . different."

"It's almost laughable how different it is."

"So you're . . . what?" When I still don't have any idea what she's asking, she goes on. "You asked me to talk to my dad about the annulment but is that really what you want? Are you two talking at all? And don't shrug again or I'll jump across this couch and punch you."

I wince and shrug. "We text."

"Are you in high school?" Harlow asks, swatting my hand. "Why don't you *call* him?"

Laughing, I tell them, "I'm not ready to hear his voice yet. I'm just getting settled. I'd probably get on the next plane to Paris if I heard him say my name." Sitting up and turning so I can look at both of them, I add, "Besides, Ansel is out there climbing the ladder and I was like a hamster running in a wheel. I need to get my act together so if he does ever get here, he doesn't feel like he has to take care of me." I stop talking and look up to see them watching me still, expressions completely neutral. "I needed to grow up, and Ansel being an idiot pushed me out of the nest in a way. He's the one who got me excited to come back here to school. I just wish I hadn't left mad."

"Don't be too hard on yourself," Lola says. "I'm just so happy you're here."

"God, so am I," Harlow says. "I was losing serious sleep with all your middle of o'dark-thirty phone calls."

I throw a pillow at her. "Ha, ha."

"And what about a job? You know my dad would hire you to come sit and look pretty in one of his offices. Want to confuse the hell out of some middle-aged executives for the summer?"

"Actually, I got a job."

"That's great!" Lola grabs my hand.

Always the more skeptical one, Harlow continues to watch me. "Where?"

"My old studio," I say. And that's all I have to say, really, because barely a moment has passed before both Lola and Harlow are practically in my lap.

"So proud of you," Lola whispers, arms wrapped tight around my shoulders.

"We've missed seeing you dance. Fuck, I think I might cry," Harlow adds.

I laugh, halfheartedly trying to push them away. "It won't be the same, guys. I'll—"

"For us it will," Lola says, pulling back just enough to meet my eyes.

"Okay, okay," Harlow says, and stands to look at each of us. "Enough of this sentimental business. We're going to get something to eat and then we're going shopping."

"You guys go. I'm headed to the studio in a little bit to talk to Tina. I need to shower."

Lola and Harlow exchange a look. "Fine, but after you're done we're going *out* out. Drinks on me," Lola says. "A little welcome home for our Sugarcube."

My phone vibrates along the table and Harlow reaches for it, pushing me away with her long, glamazon arms. "Oh, and Mia?"

"Yeah?" I say, trying to get around her.

"Pick up the damn phone when he calls or call him yourself. You have ten voice messages and let's not even talk about your texts. It doesn't have to be today, doesn't even have to be tomorrow, but stop being a wimp. You can go to school and work and pretend you're not married, but you can't fool us into thinking you're not completely in love with this guy."

———

THE DRIVE TO the studio that afternoon is definitely weird. I expected to feel nervous and nostalgic, but realize almost as soon as I'm on the road that although I've made this drive hundreds and hundreds of times, Mom accompanied me on every single trip. I've never actually been behind the wheel for this particular journey.

It unwinds something in me, to take control of a course I'd moved along so passively for so long. The unassuming strip mall appears just past the busy intersection at Linda Vista and Morena, and after I park, it takes a few minutes for me to process how different it looks. There's a glossy new frozen yogurt place, a Subway. The big space that used to be a Chinese restaurant is now a karate studio. But tucked in the direct center of the row, and updated with a new sign, new smooth brick exterior, is Tina's studio. I struggle to press down the tight swell in my throat, the nervous lurching of my stomach. I'm so happy to see this place—no matter how different it looks—and also a little heartbroken that it won't ever be what it used to be for me.

I'm light-headed with emotions and relief and sadness and just *so much of everything,* but I don't want Mom or Harlow or Lola right now. I want Ansel.

I fumble for my phone inside my bag. The hot air outside seems to press against me like a wall but I ignore it, hands shaking as I type my passcode and find Ansel's picture in my favorites list.

With breaths so heavy I'm actually worried I might have some sort of asthma attack, I type the words I know he's been hoping for, the words I should have typed the day I left—I like you—and press send. I'm sorry I left the way I did, I add in a rush. I want us to be together. I know it's late there but can I call? I'm calling.

God, my heart is pounding so hard I can hear the whoosh of blood in my ears. My hands are shaking and I have to take a moment, lean back against my car to get myself together. When I'm finally ready, I open my contacts again and press his name. It takes a second to connect, before the sound of ringing moves through the line.

It rings, and rings, and finally goes to voicemail. I hang up without leaving a message. I know it's the middle of the night there, but if his phone is on—which it clearly is—and he wanted to talk to me he would answer. I push down the thread of unease and close my eyes, trying to find comfort in how good it feels to even admit to myself and him that I'm not ready for this to be over.

Pulling open the door to the studio, I see Tina standing just inside, and I know from her expression—jaw tight, tears pooled on her lower lids—that she's been watching me since I got out of my car.

She looks older, as expected, but also just as poised and delicate as ever, with her graying hair pulled back tight in a bun, her face bare of any makeup except her trademark cherry-red lip balm. Her uniform is the same: tight black tank top, black yoga pants, ballet slippers. A million memories are wrapped up in this woman. Tina pulls me into a hug and trembles against me.

"You okay?" she asks.

"Getting there."

Pulling back, she looks me over, blue eyes wide. "So tell me."

I haven't seen Tina in four years, so I can only assume she means *tell me everything*. Initially, after I was discharged from the hospital, she came to the house to visit at least once a week. But I began making excuses why I needed to be out of the house, or upstairs with my door closed. Eventually she stopped coming by.

Still, I know I don't need to apologize for the distance. Instead, I give her the highly abbreviated version of the past four years, ending with Vegas, and Ansel, and my new plan. The story gets easier every time, I swear.

I want this job so bad. I need her to know that I'm okay—I'm *really* okay—and so I make sure to sound strong, and calm. I'm proud that my voice doesn't waver once.

She smiles when I'm done and admits, "Having you join me here is a dream."

"Same."

"Let's do a little observation before we dive right in. I want to make sure you remember our philosophy, and that your feet remember what to do."

She's mentioned an informal interview on the phone, but not an actual instruction session, so my heart immediately takes off, rapid-fire beats slamming against my breastbone.

You can do this, Mia. You lived and breathed this.

We move down the short hall, past the larger studio reserved for her teen class and to the small studio at the end, used for private lessons and her beginner's class. I smile to myself, expecting to see a line of little girls waiting for me in black leotards, pink tights, and tiny slippers.

Every head turns to us as the door opens and my breath is pulled from my body in a sharp exhale.

Six girls are lined up in the classroom, three on either side of the tall man in the middle, bright green eyes full of hope and mischief as they meet mine.

Ansel.

Ansel?

What the . . . ?

If he's here, then he was in this building only a half hour ago when I called. Did he see that I called? Has he seen my texts?

He's wearing a fitted black undershirt that clings to the muscles of his chest, and charcoal-gray dress pants. His feet are bare, his shoulders squared just like the girls beside him, many of whom are stealing peeks and barely suppressing giggles.

Lola and Harlow sent him here, I'm sure of it.

I open my mouth to speak but am immediately cut off by Tina, who, with a knowing smile, sweeps past me, chin in the air as she announces to the class, "Class, this is Mademoiselle Holland, and—"

"It's actually Madame Guillaume," I correct quietly and turn sharply to Ansel when I hear him make an involuntary sound of surprise.

Tina's smile is radiant. "Pardon me. Madame Guillaume is a new instructor here, and will be leading you through your stretches and your first routine. Class, will you please welcome our new teacher?"

Six little girls and one deep voice chant in unison, "Hello, Madame Guillaume."

I bite my lip, holding back a laugh. I meet his eyes again and in an instant I know he's read my texts and is holding back his own excitement over being here, over hearing me refer to myself as his wife. He looks tired, but relieved, and we have an entire conversation with just that look. It takes everything in me to not go to him and let myself be wrapped up in those long, strong arms.

But as if she's read my mind, Tina clears her throat meaningfully, and I blink, straightening as I respond, "Hello, girls. And Monsieur Guillaume."

A few giggles erupt but are quickly squelched with a sweeping look from Tina. "We also have a guest today, as you have clearly noticed. Monsieur Guillaume is deciding if he would like to enroll in the academy. Please do your best to model good behavior, and show him how we conduct ourselves onstage."

To my absolute amusement, Ansel looks ready to dive right into the world of being a little ballerina. Tina steps back against the wall, and I know her well enough to know this isn't any test at all; it's only a surprise for me. I could laugh it all off, and tell them to start their stretches while I talk to Ansel. But he seems ready for action and I want her to see that I can do this, even with the biggest, most gorgeous distraction in the world right in front of me.

"Let's start with some stretching." I turn on some quiet music and indicate the girls should do what I do: sit on the floor with my legs stretched in front of me. I curl down, reaching my arms out until my hands are on my toes, telling them, "If this hurts then bend your legs a little. Who can count to fifteen for me?"

Everyone is shy. Everyone, that is, except Ansel. And of course he quietly counts in French, "Un . . . deux . . . trois . . ." as the girls stare at him and wiggle on the floor.

We continue with the stretches: the bar stretch at the lowest ballet barre, the jazz splits that make the girls squeal and wobble. We practice a few pirouettes—if I live to one hundred, I will never stop laughing at the image of Ansel doing a pirouette—and I show them a straddle stretch, with my leg pressed flat against a wall. (It's possible I do this purely for Ansel's benefit, but I'll never admit it.) The girls try, giggle some more, and a few of them become brave enough to start showing Ansel what to do: how to hold his arms, and then some of their made-up leaps and spins.

When the class takes a loud, chaotic turn, Tina steps in, clapping and hugging me. "I'll take over from here. I think you've got something else to take care of. I'll see you here Monday evening at five."

"I love you so much," I say, throwing my arms around her.

"I love you, too, sweetheart," she says. "Now go tell *him* that."

———

ANSEL AND I slip out of the room and pad wordlessly back down the hall. My heart is pounding so hard, it seems to blur my vision with every heavy pulse. I can feel the heat of him moving behind me, but we're both silent. Out of the studio and past my initial surprise, I'm so overwhelmed that at first, I don't even know how to start.

A hot breeze curls around us as we push open the door to the outside, and Ansel watches me carefully, waiting for my cue.

"*Cerise* . . ." he starts, and then takes a shuddering breath. When he meets my eyes again, I feel the weight of every ticking moment of silence. His jaw flexes as we stare at each other, and when he swallows, the dimple flickers on his cheek.

"Hi," I say, my voice tight and breathless.

He takes a step up off the curb but still seems to loom above me. "You called me just before you arrived."

"I called from the parking lot. It was a lot to process, being here . . . You didn't answer."

"No phones allowed in the studio," he answers with a cute smile. "But I saw the call light up my screen."

"Did you come straight from work?" I ask, lifting my chin to indicate his dress pants.

He nods. There's at least a day's worth of stubble shadowing his jaw. The image of him leaving work and heading straight for the airport—*to me*—barely taking enough time to throw a few things into a small bag is enough to leave my knees week.

"Please don't be mad," he says. "Lola called to tell me you were here. I was on my way to meet you three for dinner.

Also, Harlow mentioned that she would break both my legs along with any other protruding appendages if I didn't treat you the way you deserved."

"I'm not mad." I shake my head trying to clear it. "I just . . . I can't believe you're actually here."

"You thought I would just stay there and fix it at some random point in the future? I couldn't be so far from you."

"Well . . . I'm glad."

I can tell he wants to ask, *So why did you leave like that? Why didn't you at least tell me goodbye?* But he doesn't. And I give him serious points for it, too. Because although my entrance into and departure from France were both impulsive, he was the reason both times: one blissful, the other heartbroken. At least he seems to know it. Instead, he looks me over, eyes lingering on my legs visible beneath my nude tights, below my short dance skirt.

"You look beautiful," he says. "In fact, you look so beautiful I'm a little at a loss for words."

I'm so relieved I burst forward. He curls into me and his face is in my neck. His arms seem long enough to wrap several times around my waist. I can feel his breath on my skin and the way he shakes against me, and when I say, "This feels so good," he just nods, and our embrace seems to go on forever.

His lips find my neck, my jaw, and he's sucking and nibbling. His breath is warm and minty and he's whispering in French, some words I can't translate but don't need to. I hear *love* and *life* and *mine* and *sorry* and then his hands are cupping my face and his mouth is on mine, eyes wide and fingers shaking on my jaw. It's a single, chaste kiss—no tongue, nothing deeper—but the way I'm trembling against him seems to promise him that there's so much more, because he pulls back and looks victorious.

"Let's go, then," he says, dimple deepening. "Let me thank your girls."

I'm starving for him, for us to be alone, but somehow even more excited just to have him here, with my friends, like this. Taking his arm, I pull him to my car.

ANSEL PUTS HIS dress shirt back on as he talks about his flight, the odd feeling of leaving just after work and arriving here at dawn and then having to wait all day to see me . . . all kinds of little details that skirt the edges of the bigger What Now? I steal glances at him as I drive. With the darkening sky behind him, he looks undeniably polished and gorgeous in his lavender button-down and slim charcoal pants. Even though I'm clearly just coming from a dance class, I'm not going to bother changing. If we went back to my place, no doubt we would stay there, and I need to see my girls, to thank them. And maybe more important, to let *him* thank them.

I slip on some more functional flats and take him directly to meet Harlow and Lola at Bar Dynamite, pulling him through the crowd, smiling so huge that my *person* is with me, my husband, my Ansel. They're sitting in a curved booth, sipping drinks, and Lola sees me before Harlow does. Dammit if her eyes don't immediately well up with tears.

"No." I point at her, laughing. For all her tough exterior she is *such* a sap. "We aren't doing that."

She laughs, shaking her head and sweeping them away, and it's a strange blur of greetings, of my favorite people and husband hugging each other as if they're the best of friends and merely haven't seen each other for a while.

But in a way, it's true. I love him, so they do, too. I love them, so he does, too. He pulls two chocolate bars from the inside pocket of the jacket he has slung over his arm and hands one to Lola and the other to Harlow. "For helping me. I got them at the airport, so don't look too excited."

They both take them, and Harlow looks down at hers and then back at him. "If she doesn't bang you tonight, I will."

His blush, his dimple, a quiet laugh, and the teeth pressing into his lip again and I'm done for. Fucking kill me now.

"Not a problem," I tell her as I toss his jacket onto the seat and drag him, wide-eyed and grinning, after me onto the dance floor. I honestly don't care what song is playing—he's not leaving my side the entire night. I step into his arms and press into him.

"We're dancing again?"

"There's going to be a lot more dancing," I tell him. "You may have noticed I'm taking your advice."

"I'm so proud of you," he whispers. He rests his forehead against mine before pulling back, meeting my eyes. "You just implied you're banging me tonight." His grin gets bigger as his hands snake around my waist.

"Play your cards right."

"I forgot my cards." His smile wilts dramatically. "But I did bring my penis."

"I'll try not to break it this time."

"In fact, I think you should try your hardest."

The bass shakes up through the floor and we've been semi-yelling this playful banter, but the mood slides away, cooling between us, and the moment grows a little heavy. We've always been best at flirting, best at fucking, but we've had to pretend to be someone else for us to open up sincerely.

"Talk to me," he says, bending to whisper the words into my ear. "Tell me what happened that morning you left."

"I sort of felt like I had to step up and face what comes next," I say quietly, but he's still bent close, and I know he's heard me. "It was shitty of you not to tell me about Perry, but really it just gave me the shove I needed."

"I'm sorry, *Cerise*."

My chest tightens when he calls me this pet name and I run my hands up and down his chest. "If we're going to try to do this, I need to know you'll talk to me about things."

"I promise. I will."

"I'm sorry I left the way I did."

His dimple flashes for the tiniest second. "Show me you're still wearing my ring and you're forgiven."

I hold up my left hand and he stares for a beat before bending to kiss the thin gold band.

We sway a little, not moving much, while all around us people bounce and shake and dance on the floor. I lean my head into his chest and close my eyes, breathing in every part of him. "Anyway, we're done with all of that. It's your turn to babble tonight."

With a little smile, he bends close, kissing first my right cheek, and then my left. And then he touches his lips to mine for several long, perfect seconds. "My favorite color is green," he says against my mouth, and I giggle. His hands slide down my sides, arms wrap together around my waist as he bends close, kissing his way up my neck. "I broke my arm when I was seven, trying to ride a skateboard. I love spring, hate winter. My childhood best friend's name was Auguste and his older sister was Catherine. She was my first kiss, when I was eleven and she was twelve, in the pantry at my father's house."

My fingers glide over his chest, up his throat, and link at the back of his neck.

"My greatest trauma was my mother leaving for the States, but otherwise—and even though my father is a tyrant—my childhood was quite nice. I was terrible at math in school. I lost my virginity to a girl named Noémi when I was fourteen." He kisses my cheek. "The last woman I had sex with was my wife, Mia Rose Guillaume." He kisses the tip of my nose. "My favorite food is bread—I know it sounds horribly boring. And I don't like dried fruit."

I laugh, pulling him in for a real kiss—finally—and *Oh. My. God.* His mouth is warm, already accustomed to mine. His lips are both soft and commanding. I feel his need to touch, to taste and fuck barely restrained, and his hands slide down over my ass, pulling my hips into him. His tongue barely touches mine and we both groan, pulling apart and breathing heavily.

"I'm not sure I ever made a woman come with my mouth before I met you," he admits. "I love kissing you there. And I love your ass, it's perfect." With this, I feel his length stir against my stomach as his hands squeeze me. "I like any kind of sex with you, but I prefer being on top of you . . . You make missionary feel dirty the way you grab and move under me."

Holy shit. I squirm in his arms. "Ansel."

"I know the exact sound you make when you come; you could never fake it with me." He smiles, adding, "Again."

"Tell me everyday things," I beg him. "This is killing me."

"I hate killing spiders, because I think they're amazing, but I'll do it for you if you're afraid of them. I hate being a passenger in a car because I prefer to drive." He kisses his way to my ear, whispering, "We can live in San Diego, but I want to at least spend summers in France. And maybe we will move my mother here when she is older."

My chest almost aches with the force of each heartbeat. "Okay."

He smiles and I touch his dimple with the tip of my finger. "And you really are moving here?"

"I think in February," he says with a little shrug. As if it's so easy. As if it's a done deal.

I'm relieved, and I'm torn. It makes me giddy to have it so easily settled, but it's only July. February is so far away. "That seems really far away."

"I'll visit in September. October. November. December. January . . ."

"How long are you staying?" Why haven't I asked this yet? I'm suddenly dreading his answer.

"Only until tomorrow." My stomach drops and I feel suddenly hollow. "I can miss Monday," he says, "but need to be in to work on Tuesday for the first phase of the hearing."

There's not enough time. I'm already pulling him through the crowd, back to the table.

"You guys—"

"I know, Sugarcube," Harlow says, already nodding. "You have twelve hours. I have no idea what you're doing in this place. Go."

So not only did they know he was coming, they knew when he was leaving. They've talked through all of it. Holy hell I love my friends.

I kiss Harlow, I kiss Lola, and shove our way to the front exit.

SOMEHOW WE MANAGE to make it back to my apartment with our clothes still on. I pray we don't wake Julianne as we trip, kissing, up the driveway, and then bang into the side of the garage, where Ansel slides his hands up under my dress and beneath my underwear, begging me to let him feel me. His fingers are warm and demanding, pushing aside the flimsy lace and sliding back and forth over my skin.

"You feel unreal," he whispers. "I need you bare. I need to see you."

"Then get me upstairs."

We trip and crash our way up the wooden stairs to my apartment, slamming against the door as he kisses down my neck, his hungry hands grabbing my ass, pulling me into him.

"Ansel," I laugh, weakly pushing at his chest so I can dig my keys from my bag.

Once inside, I don't bother to reach for the lights, unwilling to drag my hands away from his body even long enough to find the switch. I hear my keys drop, followed by my bag and his coat, and then it's just the two of us in the dark. He has to bend to me, wrapping his arms around my waist to lift me to his mouth.

"I like your place," Ansel says, smiling into the kiss.

I nod against him, tugging his shirt from the waist of his pants. "Would you like the tour?"

He laughs when I grow frustrated as my fingers fumble with his dress shirt in the dark. Why are there so many damn buttons?

"This tour includes the bed, yes?" he says, and swats my hands away, making quick work of the last few and finally shrugging out of his shirt.

"And the table. And the couch," I say, distracted by the miles of smooth, perfect skin suddenly in front of me. "Maybe the floor. And the shower."

It's only been a few days since I touched him but it feels like a year, and my palms slip down his chest, nails curving along the toned lines of his stomach. The sound he makes when I lean forward and kiss his breastbone is something between a growl and a needful moan.

He slips my leotard from my shoulders, pushing it down my arms until my hands are trapped at my sides. "Let's start with the bedroom. We can make the circuit later."

"We do have twelve hours to kill," I say. He takes my bottom lip between his teeth and I whimper, having missed him so much it's like the band around my chest has been broken and I can breathe, deep and full.

The bed is the biggest thing in the apartment and even in the dark, he finds it easily.

He backs to the mattress, kissing me the entire way, and sits down, moving to pull me between his open legs. His hands smooth along the skin at the back of my thighs, up and down until his fingers reach the hem of my underwear. The streetlight down the driveway cuts a dim cone of light across one wall, and I can just make out his face, his shoulders. His pants are open and his cock is already hard, the tip peeking above the waistband of his boxers, the length pressed flat to his stomach.

He pulls me forward and I feel the heat of his mouth on my neck. "Twelve hours isn't nearly enough," he says, pushing the words into my skin. He licks a line between my breasts, sucks on my nipple through the lace of my bra. I struggle to free my hands and he takes pity on me, pushing my clothes the rest of the way down my body and letting them pool at my feet.

Finally able to move, I push my fingers into his hair and it's just like I remembered—his sounds, his smell, the way my skin flashes hot when he sucks the skin below my collarbone—how did I think I could live a day without this?

"Want this off," Ansel says, reaching behind me to unfasten the tiny clasps of my bra. His hands pass the straps, moving the opposite direction as they fall down my arms and his hands slide up over my shoulders and then down my chest, cupping my breasts. Leaning forward, he palms one, kissing the other.

He makes a small sound of approval and moves one hand down over my ass. "And these. Take them off." His mouth closes over one nipple, tongue flicking against the peak.

This is the point where I would have needed to disappear inside of someone else, to quiet my mind with costumes and make-believe. But right now, the only person I want to be is me.

"You, too," I say. "Pants off." I watch with unrestrained hunger as he stands, and pushes the rest of his clothes to the ground.

Ansel doesn't prompt me further, just inches his long frame to the head of the bed, lies down, and waits until I slip my fingers beneath the lace and push my panties down my hips. Wordlessly he reaches for himself, gripping his cock at the base and stroking up slowly.

I climb up the bed, hovering over him with my thighs bracketed on either side of his hips. He releases his cock, and it juts up, hard against his stomach, his eyes wide and focused on the diminishing space between our bodies. With impatient hands, he grips my hips, pulling me higher, positioning me over him.

His jaw is flexed, neck arched back into the pillow, and he growls out a *Touch me.*

I run my hands up his chest and lower, sliding my fingers down his length and cupping his balls, his hip. There's something so dirty about being above him this way. I'm bare for him to see, exposed. I can't hide my face in his neck and disappear beneath the weight and comfort of his body.

This is new for us, seeing him here in *my* apartment and *my* bed, his messy head of hair in the center of my pillow. His eyes are glassy, his punch-colored lips red from my kisses, and it makes me possessive in a way I've never known before.

"You're so warm," he says, reaching between my legs. "So ready." His fingers slip easily along my skin, exploring, before he grips his cock and moves it against me. I can't look away from his face, from his focused concentration where our bodies are touching, and it's like the air has been sucked from the room, incinerated with a single gasp.

He pushes forward with every small flex of his hips upward, closer, closer, until he's there, finally, pressing barely inside. I sink down on him slowly, breathing so hard and fast and unable to close my eyes because his expression is unreal: eyes squeezed shut, lips parted, cheeks splotchy and red as he gasps beneath me, overcome.

It's too full, too much, and I give my body a second to get used to the feel of him so deep. But it isn't what I want; I don't *want* to be still; I want to feel the thick slide of him and his rough hands growing hungrier. I want to feel him all night.

I start with just gentle rocking over him, lost in his reactions as much as he seems lost in the feel of me. His hands grip my hips, anchoring but letting me drive, and finally he opens his eyes, looks up at my face, and smiles, showing the pure essence of Ansel: bright eyes, playful dimple, and his sweet, filthy mouth.

"Give me a little show, *Cerise*. Break me."

With a grin, I lift my body and slide down, and then a little faster, and a little faster, mesmerized by the tiny wrinkle between his brows as he watches my face, concentrating. He angles his hips, satisfied when I gasp, and reaches between us to touch me, pet me, stroke me, and quietly whispers to ride him faster and rougher.

"Let me *hear* the fucking," he growls, pushing up into me. "Let my little wild one out."

He watches with rapt attention as I start to come—and he whispers, "Oh, *Mia*, that's it"—my hands planted on his chest, my eyes focused on his parted lips and I beg him, "Please, oh, please." I feel my head begin to fall back as the pleasure climbs. "I'm there, I'm *there*."

He gives me a tiny nod, a tiny smile, and presses his fingers harder against me, watching as I shatter into pure sensation, bucking on him and finally closing my eyes against the intensity of it, the silvery, blinding release as I collapse against his chest.

The world tips, the soft sheets are at my back, and I feel

his hand between my legs, touching me before guiding himself back inside and then he's moving on top of me—long, sure strokes—his chest pressed to mine. He's warm and his mouth moves over my neck, to my mouth, where he sucks and tastes, growling low curses and words like *wet* and *come* and *sweet wet skin* and *deeper, so deep, so deep.*

I slide my hands down his back, gripping his ass and relishing the bunching of the muscle in my hands as he moves, curling into me and moving hard when I spread my legs wider, dig my nails into his skin, and buck up beneath him, feeling another orgasm take shape at the edges.

I gasp his name and he speeds up as he glances at my face, grunting out a quiet *Yes. Fuck.*

His brow is sweaty, his eyes on my breasts, my lips, and then he pushes his body away just enough that he can watch where he's moving in me. He's wet from me, so hard everywhere—muscles tense and ready to snap, ready to explode. The position has always been our best, the friction, the fit of him against me, and he circles his hips, looking between our bodies and then at my face, back down and up again, finally exhaling a tight burst of air as I whisper, *"Oh."*

He groans in relief when I push my head into the pillow, wild beneath him and coming with a sharp cry.

"I'm close," he growls, arching his head back and closing his eyes. "Oh, God, Mia."

He collapses on me, hips pivoting so wild and deep in me that we're nearly pressed to the headboard, his hands curling into fists around the pillow beside my head. He cries out as he comes; the sound echoes off the ceiling and the quiet, still-blank walls.

My senses come back to me one at a time: first the feel of him still inside me, the weight of his body, warm and slick with sweat. My own body is tender, leaden with pleasure.

I hear the sound of his labored breath in my ear, the quiet *I love you.*

After that I can taste and smell the salt of his skin when I kiss his neck, and I begin to make out the shape of his shoulders above me, the slow rocking as he begins moving again, just feeling.

He brushes the hair from my face and looks down at me. "I want to pretend," he says.

"Pretend?"

"Yes."

He pushes up to hover above me and I run my hands down his sweaty chest, touching where he disappears inside. A tremor moves up my spine and I feel the heat of his gaze, the pressing weight of his attention as he scans my face, dissects my expression.

"Pretend what?" I ask.

"That it's six months from now." His fingers comb through my hair, smoothing the damp strands from my forehead. "And I'm living here. I want to pretend that I'm through with the case and we're together. Permanently."

"Okay." I reach up and pull his face to mine.

"And maybe you have a showgirl costume and have finally learned how to juggle." He kisses me and then pulls back, brows drawn in an expression of mock seriousness. "You're not afraid of heights, are you?"

"*That's* your fantasy?"

He tilts his head, his smile a little mischievous. "It's certainly one of them."

"And the others?" I ask. I'd wear anything for him, but I know I could be myself for him, just as easily. I want to spend every night loving as much as I love right now.

For the hundredth time I wonder if the words I haven't said are written above my head, because his smile widens, reaching his eyes in that way that sucks the breath straight from my lungs.

"I suppose you'll have to wait and see."

Acknowledgments

FINISHING A BOOK is a weird feeling . . . since we've done this a few times now, we recognize it: we're happy to be done with something we're proud to put our names on . . . and never really ready for it to be over.

As always, thanks to our agent, Holly Root, who is one of our most favorite people. You just *get* us. You laugh at our dirty jokes, roll your eyes in all the appropriate places, and every once in a while surprise us with your own closet pigletry. Becoming part of #TeamRoot is still one of our best days ever, and we are so amazed at the balance you have found in the past year. *You inspire.* Thank you, ninja.

We say it in every book, and we'll say it again: our editor, Adam Wilson, is captain of this crazy ship, and the laughing we get from reading his comments is probably the only abdominal workout we get all year. (Don't worry, it's not that sad a state—he's really funny.) Don't forget what you gave us permission to do. *We* certainly haven't.

So much love to Jen Bergstrom, Louise Burke, and Carolyn Reidy for rocking the XX chromosome and showing the world how it's done. You listen to our ideas, push when you need to, and support us tirelessly. We can't imagine anywhere better than Gallery Books and are so proud to be part of the Simon & Schuster family.

Thank you to our publicists Kristin Dwyer and Mary McCue. When do we get to do it again? (We won't write too much here because otherwise we'll get sappy. *You did so good, girl.*)

Cupcakes for Liz Psaltis, Lisa Litwack, John Vairo, Jean Anne Rose, Ellen Chan, Lauren McKenna, Stephanie DeLuca, Ed Schlesinger (for just being Ed), Abby Zidle, and everyone we got to hug when we took over the thirteenth floor of the Simon & Schuster Building. Sup, Trey. LOL Y U SO AWSUM?

Writing a book is hard, but writing a good book would be impossible without our amazing pre-readers: Tonya and Erin, we basically owe you each a shirtless cabana boy and a lifetime subscription to Harry and David's Fruit of the Month Club (aka Lo's dream gift). Thank you for your honesty, always. Thank you, Monica Murphy and Katy Evans, for reading, loving, and pointing out what worked, and what didn't. Margaux Guyon-Veuillet is the mastermind behind the French translations of the Beautiful series, and she made sure we not only got the language right here, but the details of the city as well. That said, any remaining errors are ours entirely.

Lauren Suero, you rock our world. Thanks for everything you do, Drew.

Thank you, Nina and Alice, for December and every day after.

Thank you to every blogger for your love and enthusiasm. Writing a book is only one step; helping it find its way into the world is another. We're so grateful for every one of you.

To those of you who read our books, come to see us at signings, show us your tattoos, hug us, tell their friends to read our books, tweet us, flail with us, yell at us, post on Facebook, share your TMI, leave reviews, send us dirty jokes/pics/videos, and just let us be a part of your lives—the biggest, warmest, most sincere thank-you ever.

Kiddos, you give us a reason to do what we do and pulling ourselves away from these books at the end of the day is easy because we get to see your faces. Dr. Mr. Shoes and Blondie, thanks for a hundred, million things every day that are way too personal for public consumption.

Christina, there could be only one you for me. "← quote powers activate.

Lo, remember that day in Paris when we came up with this idea? As tired as I was, I wish we could do it all over again. And I promise not to flip you off this time. I love you more than words can say. Thanks for being the other half of my "←

About THE AUTHORS

CHRISTINA LAUREN IS the combined pen name of longtime writing partners/besties/soulmates and brain-twins, Christina Hobbs and Lauren Billings, *New York Times, USA Today*, and #1 International Bestselling authors of the Beautiful Bastard series. Some of their books have kissing. Some of their books have A *LOT* of kissing. You can find them online at christinalaurenbooks.com, or at @seeCwrite and @lolashoes on Twitter.

Turn the page for a sneak peek of

ROWDY THING

**Book Two in
Wild Seasons
from Christina Lauren
Coming November 2014**

Chapter ONE

Harlow

*H*AVING ESCAPED THE bedroom of the second-worst lay of my life, my usual morning coffee-and-croissant routine is further thrown off by this random Starbucks in this random neighborhood. Toby Amsler: Fantastically flirty, hot, and with the added bonus of being on the UCSD water polo team—he had all the makings for a night of world-class, toe-curling fun.

False advertising at its finest.

You see, when it comes to potential love interests, guys typically fall into three basic categories: the manwhore, the misunderstood, and the mama's boy. The *manwhore*, in my experience, comes in any number of shapes and sizes: dirty rock star, muscled quarterback, even the occasional irresistible hot nerd. Their skill in bed? Generally dirty talk and endurance. Both of which I'm a fan.

The *misunderstood* often take the shape of an artist, a quiet surfer, or a soulful musician. These boys rarely know what the hell to do, but at least they're willing to try for hours.

The *mama's boy* is easiest to spot. Here in La Jolla, he usually drives his mom's hand-me-down Lexus and keeps it in pristine condition. This type takes his shoes off as soon as he walks indoors and always maintains eye contact while speaking. In bed, the mama's boy offers few benefits, but at least they tend to be tidy.

Toby Amsler turned out to be the rare combination of mama's boy *and* manwhore, which somehow made him inexplicably worse in bed. The only thing worse than his vacuum-suction oral skills was being woken up by his mother bringing him tea and Cheerios—without knocking—at six in the morning. Not my finest wake-up call.

I'm not sure why I'm surprised. Despite what film and music would have women believe, they're *all* hopeless when it comes to the female orgasm. Guys learn sex from watching porn, where giving the camera a good view is the goal and no one really cares if it works for the girl, because she'll pretend it's awesome regardless. Sex happens up close, and *inside*, not at camera's length. Guys seem to forget that.

The couple in front of me is ordering at a snail's pace. He wants to know, "What's good for someone who doesn't like coffee?"

Probably not a coffee shop, I want to snap. But I don't, and remind myself that it's not this particular man's fault that all men are clueless, that I'm frustrated and cranky. I'm not usually prone to dramatics, I'm just having a bad morning and I need to breathe.

Closing my eyes, I take a deep breath. There. Better.

I step away, scowling at the pastry case while contemplating my choices, immediately worked up again.

And then I blink, narrowing my eyes as I peer closer at the case. Or rather, at the reflection in its glass.

Is that . . . no . . . Finn Roberts . . . standing behind me?

Leaning forward, I can see that visible beside my own reflection, and in line just behind me is . . . Finn. My brain does the immediate mental patdown. Why isn't he in Vancouver? Where am *I*? Am I awake? Am I having a Finn Roberts Nightmare in Toby Amsler's twin-sized waterbed?

I'm convinced it's a trick of the light. Maybe my brain has finally shorted out on the one morning I'd give my left arm for an orgasm—*of course that would make me think of Finn, right?* Finn Roberts, the *only* guy who ever managed to dodge my convenient guy-category strategy—Finn Roberts, the notorious ex-husband-of-twelve-drunken-hours-in-Vegas, who was good with hands, lips, *and* body, and who made me come so many times he told me he thought I passed out.

Finn Roberts, who turned out to be an asshole, too.

Trick of the light. It can't be him.

But when I chance a tiny glimpse over my shoulder, I realize it really *is* him. On his head is a faded blue Mariners cap pulled low over hazel eyes lined with the longest, thickest lashes I've ever seen. He's wearing the same hunter green T-shirt with his family's company's white fishing logo that he had on when I surprised him in his hometown only a little over a month ago. His arms are tanned, muscled, and crossed over his wide chest.

Finn is *here*. Fuck. Finn is *here*.

I close my eyes and groan. My body gives in to a horrifying reflex: immediately, I feel soft and warm, my spine arches as if he's pressing up behind me. I remember the first moment I knew we would hook up, in Vegas. Drunk, I'd pointed to him and dropped out loud to everyone, *Probably gonna fuck him tonight.*

To which he'd leaned over and said directly into my ear, *That's sweet. But I like to be the one doing the fucking.*

And I know if I heard his voice right now—deep, calm as still water, and a little hoarse by nature—as keyed up as I am, I'd probably have an orgasm in the middle of this coffee shop.

I *knew* I should have just driven to Pannikin for my usual morning fix. I stay silent, counting to ten. One of my best friends, Mia, jokes that I'm only quiet if I'm surprised or pissed. Right now, I'm both.

The skinny barista kid catches my eye by leaning forward. "Would you like to try our pumpkin spice mocha?"

I nod, blankly.

Wait, what? No, that sounds disgusting! A tiny, still-functioning corner of my brain yells at my mouth to order my usual: large coffee, black, no room. But I'm frozen in my stunned silence, while the Starbucks barista squeaks out my order with a black Sharpie. In a daze, I hand over the money and shove my wallet back into my purse.

I steady myself and when I turn to go wait for my coffee, Finn catches sight of me and smiles. "Hey, Ginger Snap."

Without turning to face him, I study him over my shoulder. He hasn't shaved this morning, and his dark stubble cuts a dangerous shadow on his jaw. His neck is deeply tanned from working on the wide-open ocean all summer. I let my eyes travel lower, because—let's be real—I'd be a fool to not drink in the sight of him before telling him to go fuck himself.

Finn is built like one of Lola's comic book superheroes— all broad chest and narrow waist, thick forearms, muscled legs. He gives the feeling of impenetrability, as if that golden skin of his covers titanium. I mean, sweet Jesus, the man works with his hands, sweats when he works, fucks like it's his vocation, and was raised by a father who expects, above anything else, that his sons are capable fishermen. I can't imagine any of the guys I know standing next to him and looking anything other than snack-sized.

His smile slowly straightens and he tilts his head a little, repeating, "Harlow?"

Although the shadow of his hat partially hides his eyes, I can tell they widen slightly when I lift my attention from his neck, and now I remember how his gaze feels like a hook. I close my eyes and shake my head once, trying to clear it. I don't mind swooning if the situation calls for it, but I hate the feeling when it tries to shove aside my very well-deserved, righteous indignation.

"Hold. I'm contemplating my response."

His brows pull together in confusion . . . at least I *think* it's confusion. I suspect on Finn confusion looks the same as impatience, frustration, and concentration. He's not exactly an open book. "Okay. . . ?"

Here's the problem: After our matrimonial adventures in Vegas, I flew up to see him. I showed up in Vancouver, of all places, wearing nothing but a coat. *Surprise!* We had sex for nearly twelve hours straight—rowdy sex, loud, on-every-flat-surface sex—and when I told him I had to head to the airport he just smiled, leaned over to slide his phone off the nightstand, and called me a cab. He'd just come all over my tits, and he called a *cab* to drive me to the airport. In fact, it pulled up at the curb behind Finn's brand-new cherry red Ford F-150.

I'd calmly, actually, concluded that we aren't a good fit, even for the occasional border-crossing booty call, and called it a day.

So why am I so angry he's *here*?

The barista offers the same drink special to Finn, but he makes a mildly disgusted face before declining and ordering two large, black coffees.

This makes me even more irritated. His reasonable reaction should have been *mine*. "What the hell are you doing at my coffee shop?"

His eyes go wide, mouth forming a few different words before one comes out. "You *own* this place?"

"Are you high, Finn? It's a *Starbucks*. I just mean it's my neighborhood," I lie.

His eyes fall closed and he laughs, and the way the light catches the angle of his jaw, and the way I know exactly how that stubble would feel on my skin . . . *argh*.

I tilt my head, staring at him. "What's funny?"

"It was a real possibility in my mind that you *could* own this Starbucks."

With a little eye roll, I reach for my drink and march out of the store.

Walking to my car, I stretch my neck, roll my shoulders. *Why am I so annoyed?*

It isn't like I expected a carriage to be at my disposal when I showed up unannounced at his little seaside house. I'd already slept with him in Vegas, so I knew the no-strings-attached arrangement. Clearly I was there because I wanted good sex. Actually, I wanted—no, I *needed*—confirmation that the sex was as good as I'd remembered.

It was *so* much better.

So obviously it's the bad-Toby-Amsler-sex hangover that's killing my calm. This chance meeting with Finn would have gone very differently if I hadn't *just* left the bed of the first guy I slept with after him—the first guy I'd been with in two months—and if that experience hadn't been so unsatisfying.

Footsteps slap the asphalt behind me and I start to turn just before a powerful hand curls around my bicep. Finn grabs me harder than I think he's intended, and the result is that my pumpkin monstrosity tilts and spills onto the ground, barely missing my shoes.

I give him an exasperated look, tossing my empty cup into a trashcan near the curb.

"Oh, come on," he says with a little smile. He hands me the cup he had balancing on top of the other. "It's not as if you were going to drink that. You wouldn't touch the instant vanilla spice stuff I had at my place."

Taking the coffee he's offering, I mumble my thanks and

look to the side. I'm acting exactly like the kind of woman I never want to be: jilted, martyred, put out.

"Why are you pissed?" he asks quietly.

"I'm just preoccupied."

Ignoring this, he says, "Is it because you came all the way up to Vancouver Island, showed up at my house wearing only a trench coat in the middle of July, and I banged you hoarse?" The smirk in his voice tells me he thinks I couldn't possibly be pissed about *that*.

He'd be right.

I pause, looking up to study him for a beat. "You mean the day you couldn't even be bothered to put on some clothes to take me to the *airport*?"

He blinks, his head jerking back slightly. "I skipped an entire shift when you showed up. I *never* do that. I left for work about a minute after the cab left."

This . . . is new information. I shift on my feet, unable to maintain eye contact anymore, instead looking past him to the busy street in the distance. "You didn't tell me you had to work."

"I did."

I feel my jaw tighten with irritation when I blink back up to his face. "Did not."

He sighs, pulling his cap off, scratching his crazy bedhead and then putting the cap back on. "All right, Harlow."

"What are you doing here, anyway?" I ask him.

And then I remember: Ansel is in town visiting Mia, and we're all headed to the grand opening of Oliver's comic store,

Downtown Graffick, tomorrow. Canadian Finn, Parisian Ansel, and the dry-witted Aussie Oliver: the bridegrooms of Vegas. Although four of us got quick annulments after our wedding shenanigans, Mia and Ansel decided to make a real go at this marriage thing. Lola and Oliver have become friends, bonding over their shared comic and graphic novel love. So, whether we like it or not, Finn and I are expected to be a part of this band of misfit buddies.

"Right," I mumble. "The opening is this weekend. You're here for that."

"I know they won't be stocking *Seventeen* and *Cosmo*, but you should come by and check it out anyway," he says. "The store looks good."

I lift the coffee cup to my nose and sniff. Black, unadulterated coffee. Perfect. "Of course I'll be there. I like *Oliver.*"

He swipes a palm over his mouth, smiling a little. "So. You're pissed about the cab?"

"I'm not *pissed*. This isn't a lovers' spat and we aren't having a *quarrel*. I'm just having a bad morning."

Narrowing his eyes, he looks me over, from head to toe. He's so damn observant, it makes me blush, and I know as soon as his smile reappears that he's deduced that I didn't come from home. "Your hair is all crazy, but what's interesting is you look a little hard up. Like maybe you didn't quite get what you needed somewhere."

"Bite me."

Finn steps closer, head tilted slightly to the side with that infuriating half-smile. "Say please, and I will."

With a laugh, I push him away with my palm flat to his very nice, very hard chest. "Go away."

"Because now you want it?"

"Because you need a shower."

"Listen," he says, laughing. "I won't chase you down again if you go running away, but we're going to see each other from time to time. Let's try to be grown-ups."

He turns without waiting for my reply and I hear his truck alarm chirp as he unlocks the door. I make a bratty little *fuck-you* face and display my middle finger to his retreating form, but then I pause, my heart tripping over itself with an abrupt rush of adrenaline. Finn is climbing in the same cherry red truck that was parked at the curb in front of his house. Only now it's covered in the dust and grime accumulated from miles and miles of driving.

Which begs the question, if he's only visiting for the weekend, then why did he bring his truck all the way here from Vancouver?

See how Chloe and Bennett got together in the book that started it all...
More Than 2 Million Reads Online—FIRST TIME IN PRINT!
PICK UP OR DOWNLOAD YOUR COPY TODAY!
"The perfect blend of sex, sass, and heart!" —S. C. Stephens, bestselling author of Thoughtless
Beautiful BASTARD
A Novel
CHRISTINA LAUREN